THE VANISHING KIND

A NOVEL OF SUSPENSE

ALICE HENDERSON

WM
WILLIAM MORROW
An Imprint of HarperCollinsPublishers

THE VANISHING KIND. Copyright © 2025 by Alice Henderson. All rights reserved. Printed in the United States of America. No part of this book may be used or reproduced in any manner whatsoever without written permission except in the case of brief quotations embodied in critical articles and reviews. For information, address HarperCollins Publishers, 195 Broadway, New York, NY 10007.

HarperCollins books may be purchased for educational, business, or sales promotional use. For information, please email the Special Markets Department at SPsales@harpercollins.com.

FIRST EDITION

Designed by Nancy Singer
Jaguar art © @jenesesimre/stock.adobe.com
Map by Jason C. Patnode

Library of Congress Cataloging-in-Publication Data has been applied for.

ISBN 978-0-06-322305-9

24 25 26 27 28 LBC 5 4 3 2 1

For my parents, who took us on epic camping trips
and encouraged my love of nature

For all the activists and nonprofits out there working to save the jaguar
and myriad other species who need our help

And for Jason, kindred spirit and fellow adventurer

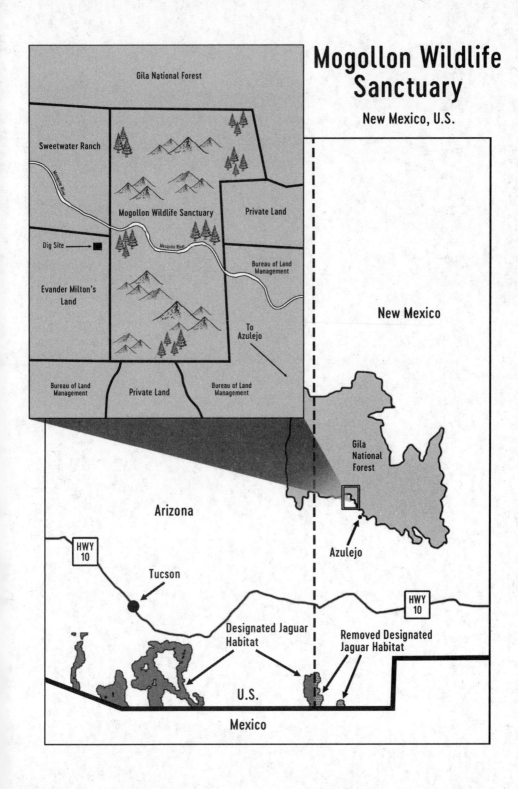

Mogollon Wildlife Sanctuary

New Mexico, U.S.

PROLOGUE

Berkshire University, New Hampshire
Eight years ago

After the recent rash of campus burglaries, the last thing Dane Fisher wanted was to be alone in this building late at night. But he was behind on his work, so he had little choice.

He hated working into the night. The university got spooky then. Its usual clamor of students in the halls rushing to class, trucks making deliveries to the cafeteria, all vanished in the evening. The only sounds left now were the hissing of the HVAC system blowing through the vents and the occasional weird creaks from the place settling. The building had been standing since 1879, and though Dane had worked here for two years cleaning artifacts, the place endlessly surprised him with its repertoire of eerie groans and strange middle-of-the-night noises. Sometimes he felt like it was alive, breathing around him.

His colleague Nora loved to work in the building at night. She swore that the quiet solitude helped her concentrate. But Dane felt the opposite, that the freaky sounds and stillness just made him hyperaware and alert, distracting him.

He listened to the AC kick on, felt the stirring from the vent above him, and returned his focus to his work. Before him lay an assortment of artifacts from a recent dig in the Scottish Highlands that Berkshire University had done in tandem with the University of Edinburgh. All manner of Celtic jewelry had been found, a treasure trove in a two-thousand-year-old grave. So far he'd cataloged and cleaned rings, cloak pins, and a chalice. But the stunning masterpiece was an intricate gold torque inlaid with garnet, amber, red coral, and other semiprecious stones, all accented by elaborate zoomorphic designs, whirls, and spirals the Celts were so famous for. The piece was stunning.

He shifted in his uncomfortable chair and pulled the work light closer to him, peering through its magnifying lens. It flickered, then went out. He reached over and jiggled its cord where it was plugged in, bringing it back to life. His department had next to no funding. Much of their equipment didn't even work without some degree of jury-rigging.

He eyed the torque. If the university sold just this one piece to a private collector, his department would be able to upgrade all its equipment—its aging computers, its ancient spectrometer—and still have funding left over. He turned it in his gloved hands, admiring his handiwork, the removal of dust and grime of the ages, restoring the torque to its original glory.

He thought of his old 1990 Ford Bronco, the one that had broken down just two days ago, leaving him stranded halfway between the campus and his tiny apartment. Late for work, he'd had to leave the vehicle on the side of the road and order an Uber, something he couldn't afford. But the professor he worked for brooked no tardiness or slacking, and his car's breaking down would have definitely slotted him into the professor's "slacker" category. Dane should have had it checked every 20,000 miles, the professor would have admonished him. Should have psychically known that it would break down and had the Uber waiting.

Hell, even Dane could use the money from the torque. He watched it gleaming in the light, the stones flashing.

Suddenly, before he'd even made the conscious decision to do it, he slipped it onto his neck. The gold felt heavy against his collar-bones. He placed his fingers over it, temptation sweeping over him. He closed the collar of his button-down shirt, covering the torque completely. He could just walk out of here. Tonight. With the torque. There'd been that rash of burglaries on the campus lately. Computers had been stolen, a stereo microscope taken from the zoology lab. Hell, they'd even made off with a 3-D printer. If a few artifacts disappeared, who would suspect he was the culprit? He'd worked in the lab for two years. Been a student in the department for six. He was well-liked. Trusted. He could jimmy the lock on the safe where they kept the most valuable pieces. Make people think that thieves had broken in. And of course they'd steal the torque. It was worth more than anything else.

He stood up. His heart hammering. Was he really going to do this? Could he get away with it? Where would he sell the torque? What did they always call those people in the crime shows he watched? Fences? Yes. He'd have to find a fence. Did he know any shady characters who might know a fence? He frowned. Maybe Donny from his undergrad days. That guy was always stealing little stuff and selling it to pawnshops. Sure, Donny might know a guy, but it would be someone who sold the occasional guitar or diamond ring—certainly no one who would be able to sell a priceless antiquity like this torque.

His nervous hands pulled his shirt tighter, fingers fastening the top button, making sure no one would be able to see the artifact. The lab had no cameras. He paused, his heart thumping. He hadn't stolen anything since he was six and had pocketed some penny candy at the neighborhood market.

A shuffling noise in the hallway made him jump. It wasn't the HVAC. Footsteps echoed down the hallway. He froze. They stopped outside the lab door. He debated ripping off the torque and replacing it. What if it was his boss? Maybe he'd forgotten something and had come back to pick it up. He glanced at the wall clock: 8:30 P.M.

The door handle moved. The person was coming in. No time to take off the torque. The door flew wide, and Dane's mouth fell open. Framed there stood a man entirely in black, wearing a ski mask to hide his face. And gripped in his hand, unbelievably, was a small crossbow, aimed right at Dane.

The man pointed to the artifacts on the table and made a *give them to me* gesture.

Dane froze. His mouth went dry. Sweat beaded on the back of his neck. "Take 'em, man," he finally said, his voice cracking. He raised both hands in a placating manner and backed away from the lab table. "No problem. Just take them."

He continued to back up, moving toward the door on the other side of the lab.

The figure advanced, eyes fixed on the gold artifacts. Dane turned and ran, bracing himself for the feeling of a bolt tearing through his back. But none came. He reached the door. Wrenched it open. Ran into the hallway.

His mind flew to the campus police. He could call them. But damn it, he'd left his phone on the lab table.

All the offices in the building were locked at this hour. Everyone had gone home for the weekend. No access to any phones.

Next door. The planetarium. His friend Jack ran the night show there. It would have gotten out at eight P.M. He might still be there. The building would be unlocked, and a phone sat on the admission desk.

He raced out of the archaeology building to the planetarium next door. Just as he reached it, Jack appeared, jingling a ring of keys and readying to lock up the building for the night.

"Jack!" Dane cried. "Wait!"

But even then he heard the door to the archaeology wing bang open behind him. Dane glanced over his shoulder, seeing the masked man dash through the door, fast in pursuit, the crossbow raised.

"Call the campus police!" Dane shouted to his friend. Jack

ripped open the planetarium door, holding it for Dane, who ducked inside. They started to pull it closed behind them, but the thing was on hydraulics and hissed closed slowly, not fast enough. The masked man reached them and Jack dashed to the desk as the thief snaked his arm in through the door and forced himself inside the planetarium.

Jack had just lifted the receiver off the phone when the man fired the crossbow. A bolt shot out and pierced Jack through the neck. Dane watched in horror as his friend pitched backward and crashed to the floor, blood spurting from his neck wound. Dane reached him and clamped a hand on the gushing artery, then stripped off his shirt and wadded it up, pressing it to the wound. But in just a few seconds, his friend's eyes glassed over and he breathed one final gasp.

The masked man advanced. Dane reluctantly let go of his dead friend and raced for the set of double doors on the other side of the room. He slammed into the exit bars and tore outside, the masked man close behind.

While most of the buildings were deserted for the night and no one milled around the walkways, at the edge of campus, a football game was in full swing. Crowds. Campus police. He just had to reach it.

Up ahead, he could see the stadium lights, nighthawks circling in the glare, catching bugs attracted by the glow. The crowd cheered and he heard an airhorn go off. He was close to safety now.

Something hissed in the air and pinged off a metal lamppost beside him, and Dane watched as a bolt ricocheted and clattered to the ground. He dared a glance back over his shoulder, saw the man pausing to load another bolt into the weapon.

Dane ran on. He was only a thousand yards or so from the stadium. From here he could see the distant security guards at the gate. "Hey!" he yelled, but they couldn't hear him over the chanting crowd.

The killer was close now, running again at full speed, closing in. "Where is the torque?" he heard the man shout. "That's all I want."

The torque! In his terror, he'd completely forgotten he was wearing it. Of course that's what the man wanted. It was probably worth tens of thousands of dollars. And he knew now that this man would kill to take it. But maybe he'd spare Dane. He hadn't seen the man's face. He'd probably just killed Jack because he'd been about to alert the cops.

Still running, Dane tugged at the torque, unclasping it from his neck. Then he tossed it behind him.

He heard the man stumble and glanced back to see him catch it before it hit the cement of the sidewalk.

Dane raced on. He was much closer to the security guards now, saw them chatting and shifting their weight by the admission gate of the stadium. "Hey!" he yelled again, but just as the word blended in with the shouting of the football attendees, he felt something sharp slam into his back. A stabbing pain erupted in his chest. He brought his hand up to his rib cage, feeling something sharp poking through there. A bolt. It had gone all the way through him. Warm stickiness flowed over his fingers. He gasped for a breath and went down on one knee. His vision tunneled as he struggled to breathe; then a wave of dizziness swept over him. He slumped down on the walkway, just two hundred yards from the stadium gates, and darkness overtook him.

ONE

Los Angeles, California
Present day

Alex Carter swayed to the music, feeling the rhythm through her body. Beside her, her best friend, Zoe Lindquist, moved effortlessly, gracefully flowing with the pulse of the song. The dark purple and blue lights of the dance club flashed, a white beam strobing with the throb of the electronic dance beat. Alex felt the tension go out of her body and Zoe met her gaze and grinned.

"This place is great!" her friend shouted above the music.

Alex nodded. She had to admit it was pretty fun. She hadn't been dancing like this since her grad school days when she lived in San Francisco. It felt good just to move, to simply hear the rhythm and melody and become one with the music without a million thoughts racing through her head.

They danced to a few more songs and Alex could feel the crush of more people packing in by the minute. She gestured over to the bar and Zoe left the dance floor with her. They sidled up to the counter, and immediately the burly bartender shot over to Zoe and took their drink order. Alex wasn't surprised. Zoe was a successful A-lister, an actor who'd been starring in films for years. She was extremely attractive, and on top of that, exceedingly nice and tipped well. It was a dynamite combination, and wherever they went, they always got excellent service.

"Are you having fun?" Zoe shouted above the music. Her long blond hair fell in artful waves around her face, her makeup perfectly applied to accentuate her green eyes. Alex felt a little out of place. She never styled her wavy brown hair, and she wore only a hint of eye shadow and a slinky purple shirt and slim black jeans that Zoe had picked out for her on Rodeo Drive. She couldn't remember the last time she'd worn a dress.

Alex nodded. "I am!"

The bass thumped through the club, and for a moment Alex peered out at the crowd, people there to see and be seen, to hook up, to flirt, to schmooze. Zoe wasn't the only A-lister Alex spotted while glancing around. It was a well-known and exclusive club, a place Alex wouldn't have a chance of getting into if she hadn't been with Zoe. Her friend thrived on this kind of scene, and Alex loved seeing her happy.

Zoe had insisted Alex come down for a couple of months for a visit after her last field study in Washington State. She'd put Alex up in a lavish guest bedroom in her nineteen-room mansion, and for weeks now they'd been clubbing, eating in three-star Michelin restaurants, shopping, attending lavish parties and concerts. They hadn't spent a single night in. After months and months of being in the wilderness, mostly alone, it was like getting all her urban activity in at one time.

She felt her phone vibrate in her back pocket and pulled it out. She grinned. It was Ben Hathaway, the regional director of the Land Trust for Wildlife Conservation, a nonprofit organization she'd done a couple of jobs for in the past.

She swiped to answer the call, but soon found she couldn't hear him at all. "Just a sec," she said into the phone. Then she turned to Zoe. "It's Ben. I have to take this."

"Cute Ben?"

Alex shook her head amusedly, though she had to admit she agreed with Zoe. He was cute.

"Take your time," Zoe said suggestively.

Alex ducked outside, dodging people as they jockeyed for position at the velvet rope that held them off from the club. The implacable bouncer eyed her as she left, and Alex said, "I'll be right back."

He answered with pursed lips and a stern look that said, *We'll see if I let you in then.*

Halfway down the street, it grew a little quieter and she could finally hear Ben.

"Sorry about that," she told him.

"Am I imagining things or were you in a club?" he asked.

"I was."

"What? Alex Carter in a dance club?" He laughed.

"I'm in L.A. visiting my college friend."

"Sounds like fun!"

"It really has been."

"It's good to hear your voice," Ben told her.

She felt a flush of pleasure. "And good to hear yours."

"Listen, I've got a job for you if you're interested."

"I'm all ears."

"We've got a large sanctuary in New Mexico, near the Gila National Forest. We think it's got some prime jaguar habitat."

"Jaguars . . . wow." She knew they were incredibly endangered in the United States.

"Recently the U.S. Fish and Wildlife Service designated critical habitat for them, but it's not a lot of land, and we think if we can show that they're using our sanctuary, we can petition the government to expand that critical habitat."

"And didn't the Center for Biological Diversity just submit a petition to Fish and Wildlife to reintroduce the jaguar into its former habitat in that area of New Mexico?"

"Yes, they did."

She pressed the phone to her ear, wincing as a car raced by and honked. A drunk patron from the club stumbled out into the street, almost getting hit.

"We'd like you to do a species presence survey," Ben continued. "Put out cameras and hair snares, and if possible, collar a jaguar if you find one. We've already secured all the necessary permits."

"When would I start?"

"As soon as possible. I can meet you there in three days, if you like. Take you around, show you your digs, bring up the equipment you'd need. We can get you a flight to Albuquerque. It's the nearest big airport to the preserve. Are you interested?"

A huge grin spread across her face. "Absolutely."

"Think you could make that time frame?"

"Sure thing."

"This is great!" he said, and she could hear the happiness in his voice. "And this time I'll actually have some time to show you around. It won't be like before."

"Fantastic." She could already imagine them out there together, exploring the terrain.

For the other two gigs she'd done for the LTWC, one in Montana locating wolverines and one in Washington state looking for a lone mountain caribou, Ben had been able to spend only a few hours at the sanctuaries with her. Based in D.C., he was incredibly busy and had to travel extensively for the organization. She knew that he loved being in the field more than handling the administrative work, and imagined he was excited to spend some time out in the wild.

"I've got to warn you, though," he added. "The digs are pretty minimal."

Alex had spent many field seasons in a small backcountry tent, so the lavishness or sparsity of lodgings didn't affect her much. "No problem."

"Great! I'll have our travel planner contact you and work out the details of your flight. We'll arrange for you to rent a four-wheel-drive car. You'll need it up there. A lot of bumpy dirt roads."

"Thanks for the opportunity," she told him.

"My pleasure. And it'll be great to see you again."

Alex felt a warm sensation in her stomach at his words. She didn't want to complicate her working relationship with the LTWC, but she had to admit that she enjoyed spending time with Ben, a kindred spirit. Not a lot of people shared her love of remote places.

"See you soon, Alex," he told her.

She smiled. "Looking forward to it."

She hung up and returned to the bouncer, who narrowed his eyes as she approached. But he relented and unclipped the velvet rope so she could go inside.

"Hey!" cried a man who'd been waiting beside the rope. "How come she gets to go in?"

"Connections," the bouncer said, towering over the man.

Inside, she spotted Zoe still at the bar. "So what's up?" her friend asked her.

"Got a gig."

"Let me guess. Finding a lost Sumatran rhino in the jungles of Peru."

"That rhino's a long way from home."

"That's why he's lost."

Alex laughed. "He wants me to see if jaguars are using a preserve the land trust has in New Mexico."

"Jaguars?" Zoe raised her eyebrows. "I thought they only lived in the jungles of South America."

"They do live there. But they also live in Central America, and we've got a few here in the U.S. There used to be a lot more of them, but now they're critically endangered."

"Let me guess," Zoe said, frowning. "The fur industry decimated them."

"It certainly didn't help."

"And you think you can find them?"

"I hope to."

Zoe screwed up her face. "But aren't you afraid one might attack you while you're out there?"

"No. Jaguar attacks are ridiculously rare. They'd rather get the hell out of there if they see a human. In fact, the only fatal attacks I'm aware of happened at zoos. Jaguars have an unfair reputation, just like grizzlies and wolves."

"So when would you leave?"

"He wants to meet there in three days." Alex saw Zoe's face fall a little and instantly felt bad. "But I've had so much fun with you here," she assured her friend.

"I thought maybe you'd fall in love with the urban life and move closer to me. You know, get some cool place in L.A. where we would hang out." Zoe gazed around the dance floor. "You'd be amazed at how hard it is to find genuine people you can trust here."

Alex *could* imagine it and had seen it in action, with people cozying up to Zoe, hoping to get something out of her—an introduction to a director or an in to an exclusive Hollywood party—without any real interest in knowing her.

"I'd love to come back," Alex said. "If you'll have me."

Zoe brightened. "Absolutely. And you're right. This has been so much fun. It's just my own rotten luck that my closest friend would rather be out in the middle of the sticks gathering samples of reindeer poop than hanging out here in all this luxury with me."

"And let's not forget that *my* closest friend would rather go to fancy clubs and dance and eat gourmet food than be out in the sticks helping me collect said poop."

Zoe grinned and they hugged. "Well, we still have a little bit of time to live it up." She lifted her drink and handed another to Alex.

Alex clinked her glass. "Cheers to that."

"To our friendship," Zoe added. They drank a few sips, and then

Zoe put down her glass. "Let's dance!" And she pulled Alex back out onto the dance floor.

Alex moved to the music, but already her mind was a thousand miles away, imagining a return to the wild, where she felt the most at home.

TWO

Three days later, Zoe took Alex to the airport in her car service. The driver waited patiently while Zoe and Alex said their good-byes. Alex hefted her backcountry pack onto her shoulders, grabbed her laptop case, then hugged her friend. "This has been great," she told Zoe.

"It really has been. So good to see you."

Walking toward the terminal, Alex turned one last time to wave to her friend, knowing they'd get together again soon, as they always did. They'd met as undergraduates, when Alex was an oboist in the pit orchestra for *Man of La Mancha* and Zoe had played Dulcinea. They'd instantly hit it off. Zoe had gone on to L.A., to a series of successful roles in high-budget features, while Alex had covered a lot of ground in search of endangered species, but their friendship had remained strong, and for that Alex was grateful.

After checking her backpack at the baggage counter, she made her way through security, then purchased a mystery novel from a bookstore near the gate. Finally they began boarding the plane. She needed to work during the flight, to brush up on the latest jaguar research, and Alex braced herself in expectation of her seatmate.

She somehow always managed to be seated next to people who loved to talk *at* her instead of *with* her. Maybe she had a kind face. Maybe she was too polite. Whatever the reason, whenever she flew anywhere, her seatmate was often unable to pick up on the usual leave-me-alone cues. She didn't mind a pleasant greeting or even conversation springing from "What brings you to Albuquerque / Washington, D.C. / San Francisco?" or wherever she was headed. But inevitably, when those pleasantries were over and Alex would open her laptop to work, the person would not pick up on that hint and would continue to talk, usually about something tedious.

Read the room, would be how Zoe would put it to these people.

Alex sat down in her row by the window, and as the plane started to fill up, a balding man in his sixties with a white comb-over and beet-red face plunked down in the middle seat. He stashed a laptop under the seat in front of him, then immediately reclined and stretched out, his legs spilling over into her space.

He eyed her and struck up a conversation about the weather and where they were headed. Then as the plane took off, he decided that Alex had to hear about a boat he'd bought and was fixing up.

"It's a 1940 Chris-Craft."

Alex nodded politely and opened her laptop as the plane leveled off. "That's great."

"It's in pretty rough shape. Taking a lot of work to get her up to snuff."

"I'm sure you'll do a great job."

He readjusted his bulk in the seat, his knee pressing suddenly against her leg. She shifted away from him. "Had to refinish the deck and rails, and then about two months in . . . or was it three months in? No, wait, I remember it was two months in, because my nephew had his birthday party and we were thinking the boat would be ready so I could host it on there . . ."

Alex started to wilt, nodding politely.

". . . but it turned out that it wasn't ready, so we ended up having it at Aunt Doreen's house. She's a real peach, Aunt Doreen. She's not really my aunt. She's sort of a friend of the family, you know, and . . ."

As he droned on, Alex started to check out, nod, and look away. Finally, though she hated to be rude, she said, "I've got to do some work," and turned her attention to her computer. Thankfully, he just grunted and pulled the in-flight magazine out of the pocket in front of him.

Alex dove into the latest jaguar research. At one time, jaguars roamed throughout the Western Hemisphere, occupying territories ranging throughout South America, Central America, and the United States. There were records of them in California, Texas, New Mexico, Arizona, and Colorado. British colonists reported seeing large spotted cats in Appalachia. Early reports from European naturalists in the 1700s placed them in North Carolina, Kentucky, Ohio, and even the Lake Erie region of New York. But now jaguars lived only in disconnected patches of habitat in the American Southwest and down to Argentina. This meant that young jaguars had to brave unfriendly terrain to cross into new territories. Ranches, roads, clear-cut land, private property, poachers, and more—all posed dangerous threats to these traveling jaguars.

Jaguars had been driven out of 50 percent of their historical range. They were missing completely from countries where they once roamed, such as El Salvador and Uruguay, and were nearly gone from the U.S.

Alex hoped she'd capture images of a jaguar on the remote cameras she'd place out. As they passed over the Rockies, her gaze drifted to the window, and she peered down on myriad snowy peaks and sunlit rivers that cut through steep valleys like shiny ribbons.

The plane landed in Albuquerque, and her seatmate jumped up, forcing his way into the throng of deboarding passengers. Because she had a window seat, Alex was compelled to wait while people rushed past her, eager to get off the plane. As usual, no one would let her into the flowing mass of passengers, instead just rushing by or standing there blocking her row.

Finally she was able to shinny out and grab her laptop case from the overhead bin, stowing her computer back inside. She made her way off the plane, thanking the crew as she did so. She exited the jetway, walking down long corridors of restaurants, bars, and shops selling clothes, magazines, books, snacks, and New Mexico trinkets like cactus-shaped salt and pepper shakers and T-shirts that read "The Land of Enchantment."

As she headed toward the baggage claim area, she spotted Ben Hathaway standing amid a swarm of people awaiting arriving passengers. He spotted her and waved, and she waved back. A smile broke out on her face. It was good to see him.

He looked just as great as ever—tousled brown hair, a worn flannel shirt over a Zion National Park T-shirt, faded jeans, and hiking boots. She reached him, maneuvering through the crowd. She wasn't sure if she should shake his hand or hug him, but he pulled her into a welcoming embrace.

"How was your flight?" he asked, stepping back.

"Great. I had the window seat, so I got to watch the Rockies pass by far below. All those snowy mountains and river valleys. Gorgeous."

"Nice. Can I take your bag?" he offered, gesturing at her laptop case.

"Oh, no thanks. I've got it."

Together they continued to baggage claim, where they waited for some movement at the carousel. "How was your flight?" she asked him.

"Great! Got in this morning. Already got you a rental car, ate some lunch here at the airport." A klaxon sounded and a red light spiraled on top of the carousel. It began to disgorge bags as the belt groaned into motion.

People hurriedly grabbed their luggage, still talking excitedly with relatives and friends. She saw a woman, probably in her early twenties, spot her parents as they hurried up to the baggage carousel. They hugged like they hadn't seen each other in years, and Alex felt a little pang. She missed her parents. Her mom had passed away when Alex was only twelve, and she hadn't seen her dad in months.

She guessed from the young woman's University of Oregon sweatshirt that she'd been away at college.

"Is that your bag?" Ben asked, pulling her out of her reverie. He pointed to a large backcountry pack as it was spat out onto the belt.

"That's it."

He stepped into the cluster of passengers and hefted it off the belt, then lifted it onto his own back.

Alex felt a little shy about that. She hadn't had an actual permanent place to live since she'd given up the lease on her place in Boston. That meant that the pack was heavier than usual, full of not just her backcountry supplies like her tent and her sleeping bag, but also all her clothes, her hiking boots, some books. But Ben didn't look like he struggled under the weight at all.

"You hungry?" he asked as he rejoined her.

"I had an interesting boxed lunch on the plane."

He chuckled. "I see."

It actually hadn't been that bad, a vegetarian meal the travel planner had arranged for her. Usually places got lazy with vegetarian options, offering a simple salad, but this one had been pasta in a pesto sauce along with a delicious cookie.

"Is there anything you need to pick up in town? This is the closest big city to the preserve, which is still about three and a half hours away. There's a really small town called Azulejo where you can get groceries when you need to, but anything else we should pick up here."

Alex thought a minute. "Well, there is one thing I need to get."

"What's that?"

"A bottle of Calvin Klein's Obsession."

"Excuse me?"

Alex laughed. "Jaguars and other cats are attracted to it. In fact, they've used it to capture and relocate human-eating tigers in India. I can sprinkle it on the hair snares to up my chances."

"Wow. Okay, then."

"I would have picked some up in L.A., but I didn't want to pack it in with my checked bag. Can you imagine if the bottle broke in there with all my clothes?"

He gave a low whistle. "Well, you'd certainly attract jaguars while you were hiking around then."

She grinned, shaking her head.

They took an escalator down to an underground tunnel and passed through into the parking garage. Ben headed toward a red Jeep. He unlocked it and placed her backpack in the back seat, then handed her the keys.

"Here you go. This one's yours." Then he gestured to a Ford Expedition parked next to it. "And this one's mine." She could see that he'd already stowed away his carry-on in it, a small black suitcase that would fit in an overhead bin, along with two massive suitcases with checked baggage tags. She wondered if they held all the field equipment she'd need. "My flight out tomorrow is really early, and I didn't want you to have to drive out to the preserve, then take me back here and have to do the drive again. So is it okay if you follow me out to the sanctuary?"

Alex felt a twinge of disappointment. She'd been looking forward to talking on the drive. "Of course." She smiled.

"Oh, and here." He dug through his carry-on and produced a couple of two-way radios. He handed her one. "There won't be much cell reception out there. This way we can talk as we go."

"Great!"

They climbed into the cars and headed out of the garage, Alex following Ben. They took a freeway to a large box store, where Alex purchased the bottle of cologne, some tools and wire for the hair snares, and enough food to last for her first few days. Ben visited the produce section and got them some fresh food for dinner that night.

They took the freeway out to a smaller state road, then to a less well-maintained county road.

Along the way they chatted over the radios, talking more this time than on previous visits. They had grown more comfortable with each other, and the talk came easily. Ben told her about an anti-poaching project they'd been working on in South Africa and a new sanctuary they'd just acquired in Borneo, an area that had been decimated by palm oil plantations. Their preserve there served as a refuge for orangutans, Sumatran rhinos, and other critically endangered species.

She told him about her visit to L.A., the culture shock of dancing in clubs and going to parties and being around so many people, but the joy of seeing her old friend Zoe.

Having caught up, they just drove comfortably together, a small caravan of two, commenting on the scenery and the sky, enjoying being in each other's company.

After a little over three hours, they passed through the town of Azulejo, just a speck on the map in the vastness of that part of New Mexico. While the town was indeed tiny, it appeared vibrant. They passed a couple of art galleries, then a few restaurants serving Mexican, Guatemalan, Chinese, and Thai food. The town even had an old cinema that had been converted into a playhouse. Delightful turn-of-the-last-century buildings lined the main street.

"I was here a few months ago," Ben told her, "checking on the preserve. A biologist came to town and gave a presentation on the petition to reintroduce jaguars in this area. It was pretty packed."

"How did it go?"

"Most people were excited. But then during the Q&A, things got dicey. A few ranchers were up in arms that their cattle would get predated on, even though the biologist had explained how rare that was. Then these two other guys almost came to blows with the biologist, saying that if we built the border wall in such a way that jaguars could pass through it, we'd get swamped with illegal immigrants. It got pretty ugly. We almost had to call the police, but the guys ended up storming out."

"That sounds scary."

"It was pretty intense. But I think most people were happy about the thought of restoring the jaguar to its historical range."

They left the town, passing houses dotted along the road. They turned down another small county route, its pavement cracked and full of potholes.

Ben pulled off onto a dirt lane and she followed, bouncing along the worn track until they came to an intersection. He clicked on his radio. "This is where everything splits off. There's national forest to the north, bits and pieces of Bureau of Land Management scattered all around, and then the Sweetwater Ranch to the northwest. We've been talking with them for a few years, actually, helping them make their cattle ranch more environmentally and wildlife friendly. And then to the southwest you've got Evander Milton's place. He's a pretty eccentric gazillionaire. He isn't there much. He has houses all over the world. He's got a sizable house on his land, but that's it. No cattle or other buildings." He pointed out of the window to the left. "And up this road is our sanctuary." He pulled onto that dirt road, and Alex found it narrow, steep, and bumpy. They rose from the desert floor up through scrub, and then into a high-elevation pine forest.

She lowered the windows, and a welcome breeze fluttered through her hair. She could smell the sweet scent of juniper trees.

They climbed up and up, Ben slowing his Expedition at times to maneuver it over large potholes and sharp rocks that jutted from the roadbed. Alex gripped her steering wheel as her Jeep juddered and jolted forward.

At last, amid a cluster of massive ponderosa pines, a tiny cabin came into view and the road ended.

Ben pulled up in front of it and stepped out. "Here we are!"

Alex parked and climbed out.

Ben gestured toward the cabin. "This was built in the 1890s by a prospector looking for silver in the hills of New Mexico." He moved to a padlock on the front door and unlocked it. "I'm afraid it has only one room." He swung the door wide.

They stepped inside and Alex cast her gaze around. It contained a wooden table and chair where she could work, a small propane stove, and a deep sink with a pump handle.

"The water is piped in from a well. It drains into a gray water tank that we empty out every few months."

A woodstove stood in one corner, but she didn't think it had been used in years. A woodrat had made a nest inside it. Beside it sat a portable propane heater. An old Coleman gas lantern rested on the table, but Alex had brought along several solar-powered lamps that she intended to use. Two cots were stacked against one wall, presumably so those same packrats wouldn't nest on them.

Beside the cots stood a Bluetti AC200MAX power generator. Measuring a couple of feet high by a couple of feet wide, it would be capable of recharging her laptop, phone, and other devices. Next to it rested a slim black case. Ben moved to it. He picked it up and unzipped it, pulling out several folding solar panels. "Let's get these set up outside and recharge the Bluetti."

They made quick work of it, propping up the panels in a sunny patch in front of the cabin and plugging in the power station. He gestured for her to follow him around the side of the house. "There's an outdoor shower over here. Cold water only, I'm sorry to say. But you'll have an amazing view of the forest while you're in it." He chuckled.

"I've brought along my sun shower," she told him. She'd stowed it in her pack, a large sack that she could fill with water and then hang from the existing showerhead. All day the water would heat up in the sunlight, so that when she got home at night, she could take a warm shower, especially if she was feeling sweaty from hiking.

"That'll help! The water drains into the gray water tank, too. And hey, check this out!" He walked her over to a small outhouse on one side of the cabin. "It's got a brand-new composting toilet! We just had it installed a few months ago."

"Luxurious!"

They returned to the cabin and Ben grabbed each cot, shook it off, and then laid them out against one wall by the table. Then he went out to his rental car and hauled the two massive bags inside. He laid them on the floor and unzipped them. Inside he'd packed at least a dozen remote cameras, batteries, memory cards, a tranquilizer gun, and several GPS collar cameras.

"That's a lot of gear!" she told him. "Thanks for hauling all that out here."

"Thank *you* for doing the study!" He shifted his small suitcase over to one of the cots. "Are you tired? Want to rest a bit, or do you want to see the sanctuary?"

"I definitely want to see it." Now that she was out here, hearing birdsong, smelling the scent of pine on the wind, she wanted nothing more than to get out there, to delve into the preserve's habitat.

This was always her favorite part of visiting anywhere new: acquainting herself with the different tree and flower species, figuring out what new species of birds she was listening to, learning about the geology. It was her dad who had inspired her to be so curious. She'd moved around a lot as a kid because her mom was a pilot with the Air Force. Every time they settled somewhere new, her father would get a bunch of nature guides for the area and he and Alex would explore together, learning all about the new place. He was a professional landscape painter, and she loved to watch him sketch while they were out together.

"Give me a sec," she said, and toted her backcountry pack over to the other cot. She dug through it, finding her daypack, her water bottle and filter, a lightweight fleece jacket, and her crushable sun hat. She transferred all this to the daypack except the hat, which she put on. It was a wide-brimmed black fedora she'd had for years, and she loved it.

"Very fetching," Ben said as she turned, ready to leave. He pulled an old canvas daypack, binoculars, and water bottle out of his suitcase, followed by a worn Glacier National Park baseball cap. Then they set off into the wilds of the preserve.

THREE

For the rest of the day, Alex and Ben hiked and talked, passing through a wide range of habitats. Up high, where the cabin stood, grew ponderosa pines. As they hiked to lower elevations, they passed through juniper and aspen woodlands and then wide-open spaces with ocotillo and numerous cactus species. Alex had read on the plane that much of the area had been formed by volcanic eruptions over the last twenty-five to fifty million years or so. Towering reddish columns of petrified ash rose up from the desert floor around them, the spires of rock brilliant in the afternoon sunlight. Springs trickled from crevices in rocks, creating their own little ecosystems of delicate green maidenhair ferns and mosses.

Brilliant orange and yellow lichen grew on cliff faces. Clusters of volcanic rock cropped up at regular intervals, creating a whimsical landscape of rocks, windblown sand, cacti, and green patches of juniper.

They hiked out to a good-size river. "This is the Mesquite River," Ben told her. "It passes through the preserve. It's one of the reasons we were so happy to acquire this land a few years ago. It's an excellent refuge for wildlife."

The river was about twenty feet wide, the water four feet deep in the middle, its rushing waters vibrantly clear, showing off colorful stones on the creek bed. She spotted a few fish darting along the bottom. Willows clustered along the bank.

Ben sat down on the sandy river's edge and Alex joined him, perching on a lichen-covered boulder beside him. Above them stretched the sapphire-blue sky, small white clouds drifting near the western horizon. The wind sighed through the willows.

She closed her eyes, feeling the sun on her face, hearing the lyrical notes of a nearby cactus wren.

They sat together companionably, reveling in the grandeur of their surroundings.

"Hey, look at this," he said, pointing to a wet spot of mud beside him. Pressed there perfectly was the track of a large cat.

Alex stood up and bent over it.

"Think it's a jaguar?" he asked.

She dug into her pack and pulled out a tool she'd gotten recently for measuring tracks and scat. It was a flat piece of plastic with rulers on two sides. Usually she used the multitool her father had given her for scale, but she'd decided to get something with incremental measurements on the side to make things a little easier. She laid it down beside the print and snapped a couple of photos. It measured 3.1 inches wide and 3.5 inches long, with no visible claw impressions. She bent down to examine it closer. "It's a mountain lion, I think," she said. "Jaguar prints are much bigger. But that's still really exciting."

Ben leaned in to peer closer. "I'll say." He glanced around. "I love this place. I'm so glad you're going to be out here. And I don't even have to rush off today. I just hope this is a peaceful assignment for you this time. I can't tell you how bad I feel about what happened in Montana and Washington."

Alex thought back to those previous LTWC jobs and all that had happened there. She was lucky to be alive. She shook her head ruefully. "Those were pretty crazy."

"Are you doing okay after all that?"

She gazed up at the sky, thinking. "Yes," she said finally. "I think it's all made me stronger."

They hiked around the preserve some more, refilling their water bottles at little springs. In some places, hot springs trickled through the rocks, evidence of the area's volcanic origin. As the sun dipped behind the distant mountains, they started back for the cabin. Despite having hiked for quite a while, Alex knew she'd still seen only a small portion of the preserve. It was massive.

Ben took off his cap, running a hand through his wavy brown hair. "So how are you going to decide where to place out your cameras and hair snares?"

"I'm going to build a habitat suitability model."

He turned to her. "How do you build one of those? We use them all the time, but you know, I've never known exactly what goes into creating one. I'm not much of a computer guy."

"I can show you tonight, if you like."

He smiled. "I like. And I'll cook us dinner."

"That would be great!"

They reached the cabin just as it grew dark. Alex powered on a couple of her solar-powered lamps and placed them around the room. The Bluetti power station had completely charged, so she folded up its solar panels and stowed them. She hefted the unit back inside the cabin, staggering a bit under its weight.

While Ben boiled a pot of spaghetti on the propane-powered range, Alex sat down at the table and booted up her laptop. She opened up a program called ArcGIS Pro, which she'd use to build the habitat suitability model.

As the heat of the day faded, the cabin grew cold. Ben fired up the propane heater and soon warmth filled the cabin.

He started mixing up a sauce from fresh tomatoes, basil, and a little garlic and oregano he'd picked up that day at the store in Albuquerque. It smelled amazing as it simmered.

He moved to peer over her shoulder. "So explain to me what you're doing."

She brought up a satellite image of the preserve that she'd

downloaded when she was still in L.A. "You start with an image like
this. Every pixel in this image represents a small portion of the land.
It might have trees or desert floor or a stream on it. So the next step
is to download other layers of data that are pertinent to the species'
needs, like water sources, temperature and precipitation, types of
tree cover, availability of food, human population density, distance
from roads, and so on. You layer it all together and assign a value to
each of the pixels. A rating of five is ideal habitat, and one is habitat
the jaguar likely won't use. Then once you get the model's results,
you go out into the field and ground-truth it, see if the model accu-
rately predicted suitable habitat."

"Fascinating." They heard a pop from the stove as the sauce
spattered on the counter. "Oops! Be right back."

He shut off the propane range and brought steaming plates of
spaghetti to the table. Alex closed her laptop and dug in, hungry
after their long hike. "This is fabulous," she told him. She knew she
wouldn't eat this well for the rest of her stay here. She was a min-
imalist when it came to food—it was just something she ate to fuel
her body. She'd be living off simple dishes, nuts, fruits, and energy
bars—all things that wouldn't require complicated preparation.

"I don't usually cook," he admitted. "If it were just me, I'd probably have just scarfed down an energy bar or something."

She laughed. "We really are two peas in a pod."

When they finished eating, she retrieved her laptop and finished
the habitat suitability model. It determined which spots would be
most likely to support jaguars and Alex made note of them.

"Tomorrow I'll start going out to these places. If the model
checks out, then I'll start putting out cameras and hair snares."

When they finished dinner, Ben washed the dishes at the little
sink. He'd brought a pack of cards and they played a few hands of
gin rummy. He was easy company, and Alex felt very comfortable
around him, which was pretty rare for her. As he dealt out another
hand, they heard the call of a Mexican spotted owl just outside.

Faces lighting up in unison, they moved as one to the door and opened it to listen. It called out again, and they heard another owl answering it some distance away. Alex knew that the species was threatened, and it thrilled her to know they were making the sanctuary home.

"Magical," Ben breathed.

She suddenly became aware of his closeness, their shoulders touching in the doorway. She felt a tinge of electricity pass through her. She liked him. A lot. But she didn't want to complicate her working relationship with the LTWC.

If he even likes me like that, she thought. She was terrible at telling when a man was romantically interested.

The owls exchanged a few more calls and Alex breathed in the night air. Then Ben turned to her in the doorway, standing close. His intense green eyes met hers, his handsome face lit by the inviting soft glow from the solar lights.

"Alex," he said, then paused.

"Yes?" She braced herself.

"I . . ." He continued to gaze at her, and her stomach did a little flip-flop. "I . . ." He looked away. "I guess I should turn in. My flight is at an ungodly hour tomorrow, and there's that three-and-a-half-hour drive back to the airport."

She blinked. "Of course. You should get some rest."

He moved to his daypack and Alex turned away politely as he shucked out of his clothes and changed into a pair of long johns. Then he crawled into his mummy bag.

Alex turned off one solar light and dimmed the other, bringing it over by her cot. She changed into thermal underwear, doused the light, and climbed into her own sleeping bag. She lay there in the darkness, listening to Ben breathing, wondering if he was asleep, feeling torn. Finally she closed her eyes and tried to sleep, lulled by the sound of the wind outside.

She awoke hours later to the sound of Ben moving around. She opened her eyes, finding the room barely lit by a light on its lowest setting. Through one of the windows, she could see just a glimmer of predawn glow.

"Sorry," he said. "I was trying not to wake you."

"No problem." She propped herself up on one elbow.

He had already packed everything up.

"You're off?" she asked.

"Unfortunately. I'd much rather stay here with you and put out cameras."

She unzipped her bag and climbed out, stretching.

"It's been great to see you again," he told her.

"You too, Ben." She felt that pang of disappointment return. She didn't want him to leave.

"Take care, and keep me posted," he told her.

They hugged again, and she breathed in the scent of him. "I will."

Then he pulled away and moved to the door. He turned back with a smile. "See you soon, Alex."

"See you, Ben."

He passed through the door, closing it behind him. Outside, she waited for the sound of his car engine to start up. But it didn't. She imagined him stowing his bag, climbing into the driver's seat. But she still didn't hear the ignition. Her heart thumping, she wondered if he was debating coming back to say something. She tensed, listening on the other side of the door. But then, a few minutes later, the engine did start up, and she heard him slowly turn around in the drive and make his way down the dirt road.

She turned back around, feeling an unexpected surge of loneliness. This was the first time she'd been alone since she left Washington State. But this was what she did. This was what she loved to do. She returned to the warmth of her mummy bag, closing her eyes again, her mind playing over what an amazing time she'd had yesterday. A tangle of thoughts crowded in, about Ben, about how to find any jaguars that might be there.

Finally, unable to go back to sleep, she got up and started to make some hot tea. Adventure lay before her, and she couldn't wait to start out.

FOUR

On her fifth day in New Mexico, Alex drove to the nearest town, Azulejo, to stock up on groceries. She'd spent the last few days hiking around the preserve, ground-truthing her habitat suitability model.

As she pulled onto the main street, she found the town's plaza full of people, little tents set up to offer food, crafts, and art. A banner strung over the main street declared it was the Twelfth Annual Azulejo Art Festival.

She found a welcoming shady spot in a nearby parking lot and pulled over in her rental Jeep.

Because Ben had warned her that the cabin had no landline and no cell service, she'd purchased a DeLorme InReach satellite communicator in L.A. She couldn't afford a sat phone, nor could the LTWC, but she could text on the satellite communicator if she got into a bad situation. It had an SOS mode that would summon search and rescue, even a medevac helicopter if she needed it. But it could also be used to communicate with people in less dire situations, like if she just needed her emergency contact to summon AAA if she got stuck in a ditch somewhere.

But here in town, she hoped she'd have cell reception. Retrieving her phone, she powered it up. When two bars appeared on the screen, she smiled. She'd been wanting to talk to her dad, not just to catch up, but to set him up as her emergency contact on her satellite communicator. She climbed out and walked to the shade of a large piñon pine.

He answered on the second ring. "Pumpkin!"

"Hi, Dad!"

"How are you? How was the rest of your visit with Zoe?"

"It was fabulous. I ate too much rich food and drank too many cocktails and danced at clubs."

"That sounds like a bit of all right. Culture shock?" he asked.

She chuckled. He knew her too well. "Definitely. But it was so good to see Zoe, and being in a city like that, surrounded by people, as much as I liked it, really brings home that I made the right choice when I left Boston." A couple of years ago, Alex had made the tough decision to leave behind the urban life she'd been trying to build with her boyfriend of many years and take on the LTWC gig studying wolverines in remote northwestern Montana. They'd broken up a few months before her leaving, and she'd moved to Boston just to be with him. It had been the right choice.

"You already in New Mexico?" he asked.

"Yep. And it's gorgeous. Can't wait to see if I find a jaguar." She'd phoned her dad the day after the job offer had come in. "How are you doing?"

"Good, good. Working on a series of seascapes. I'm going to apply for a residency at Point Reyes National Seashore." A successful landscape painter, Alex's dad loved nothing more than painting in the national parks.

"That would be fabulous! When's the deadline?"

"In about three weeks."

"Let me know what happens." She shifted gears. "So, Dad, it's pretty remote here. I won't have a landline like I've had before, and no cell service once again. So I have this satellite communicator. Would you be my emergency contact?"

"Of course! You're not worried about something bad happening, are you?"

"No, not at all. I just wanted to program you into the unit in case I need a tow or something like that and have no cell signal to call AAA. There's some pretty rough terrain out there."

"I'd be happy to."

They talked more about what books they were reading, mostly thrillers and golden age detective fiction, and he told her about an interesting article he'd read in the *New York Times* about a wolverine spotted in Yellowstone National Park.

Then they hung up and Alex decided to call Zoe, too, since she had reception.

Zoe answered, her familiar voice making Alex grin. They had indeed had fun in L.A. "Hi, Zoe!"

"Alex! How was your flight out to New Mexico?"

"Had a chatterbox again," Alex lamented.

"Oh no! The curse continues," said Zoe, and laughed. "I always get some quiet woman who's crocheting or something."

"Maybe they don't want to disturb you, thinking you are in hiding or something, since you always wear a big floppy hat and sunglasses that cover half your face." Zoe had to fly incognito, as, being an A-lister, she'd get swarmed by people.

"You may have a point there. So what are your digs like?"

Alex cracked a smile. "You'd love them! No indoor bathroom, no electricity, no AC."

Zoe laughed sarcastically. "Sounds like heaven!" Zoe could not be without her creature comforts. She'd once dated a photographer for *National Geographic,* and he'd taken her on a backcountry trip in the Sierra Nevada along the John Muir Trail. They had spent two nights out, and Zoe had survived, secretly gritting her teeth the whole time, grossed out by pretty much everything—like having to spit her toothpaste into a ziplock bag and then "bring it back with her to civilization." And she didn't even want to mention "having to dig a hole for . . . you know." As sweet as the photographer was, she broke up with him as soon as she got back, worried he'd ask her to camp somewhere again, even if he was "the dreamiest photographer *ever* with the prettiest smile you've ever seen." As far as Alex knew, they were still friends, but it was the last time Zoe had been camping.

"You could always come back here," Zoe offered. "I have more than one indoor bathroom, you know. I even have internet!"

"Tempting," Alex mused, although in truth she loved every minute of being out in the sticks. "There's no landline this time, so I won't be in much regular contact. But I'll call you next time I'm in town resupplying and we can catch up!"

"So what are you planning for this first week?" Zoe asked her.

"Loading up on groceries, then back to the cabin. Tomorrow I'll start placing out hair snares and remote cameras."

"How do you get them to touch the hair snares?"

"You'll love this. Calvin Klein's Obsession."

Zoe snorted out a laugh, the real, genuine, unabashed guffaw she was embarrassed about and resisted doing in public. "What?"

"It attracts cats. It contains a synthetic version of the musk from civet glands. So I'll string up some wire and spritz it, and hopefully if any jaguars are around, they'll come check it out. Maybe rub against it. Then I can send the hair along to a geneticist who volunteers with the land trust, and we can determine if it's more than one jaguar and if they're related."

Zoe was still chuckling. "Obsession for science. Wow."

"So how are things going with you?" Alex asked.

"Incredible. We're about to start shooting on my next project." Alex could hear her friend's excitement through the phone.

"The spy movie you've been so excited about?"

"Yes!"

"So explosions and gunfights?"

"Hell, yes! Plus political machinations and cool gadgets."

"Sounds like a lot of fun!"

"Tell me about it." Zoe paused, then laughed. "Is there something wrong with us? I mean, I'm all excited about explosions and gunfights, and you're all excited to be looking for an endangered cat in the middle of nowhere."

Alex laughed. "There is definitely something wrong with both of us. And I'm glad for it. It's no fun being boring."

"Agreed."

"So how does the rest of your week look?" she asked Zoe.

"Tomorrow we start fight choreography. I really love the combat trainer on this project. I've worked with him before, and he always cracks me up. He's got a really dry wit. Then I'll run some lines with my costars. An informal read-through."

"What's the shooting schedule like?"

"Three weeks of principal photography in locations around New York City. The whole shoot has been moved forward because of difficulties with permits, so we're rushing to be ready."

"Tight!"

"Yep. And shooting in a city can have a lot of unknowns you have to accommodate for on the spot, like people accidentally walking into shots, loud city streets, and let's not underestimate crazy bicycle guy."

"Who?"

"Every time I shoot a movie in a big city like that, we have to do it really early in the morning and shut down a few roads. And last time there was this crazy bicycle guy who rode through the scene during a take. We told him it was a live set and he started yelling that it was a public street and he has every right to be there and that it's rich people like us and big corporations who are ruining the world, thinking we can just buy anything."

"Sounds delightful."

"Well, at least he wasn't a jaguar or anything. A crazy bicycle man isn't going to eat your face off." She paused. "Or maybe he would, depending on how crazy he is."

Alex laughed. "Well, break a leg. I hope it all goes well!"

"You, too! Only definitely don't break a leg out there. Keep in touch. Let me know how it's going. Otherwise I'm going to imagine you out there dying of thirst or falling in some canyon or something and languishing there with a broken pelvis, unable to crawl out."

"Have you been watching *I Shouldn't Be Alive* again?"

"I can't help it! Not when my best friend goes out to these remote places. I want to know what to expect."

Alex thought of another show they'd watched just before Alex left. It had been about a father and son who went out hunting on ATVs and got pinned beneath them.

"I'll try not to fall into any ravines."

"Or get your face eaten off," Zoe added.

"Or get my face eaten off. And good luck with crazy bicycle man."

"Thanks."

They hung up and Alex felt a little bittersweet. The loneliness of the coming weeks stretched before her, and though she relished this time in the wilds, she also admitted that she did enjoy interacting with another human being she clicked with.

She returned to the car to retrieve her wallet, readying to walk down to the town's little grocery store. She climbed in the Jeep, rooting around in the back seat for her reusable bags. She had to stock up on food for the next few days. All of it had to be nonperishable, too, because she had no way to refrigerate it. Looked like she'd be surviving off coffee, pasta, peanut butter, nuts, energy bars, and fruit over the next few weeks.

At the little grocery store, she purchased enough food to last her for a week, then returned to her car. She stashed the groceries amid the heap of gear in her back seat. Then music drew her gaze down the street toward the plaza. She listened, smiling, and finished packing away the food. She had time to check out the art show, so she strolled in the direction of the festival. She passed a sidewalk drawing contest in full swing, participants chalking amazingly detailed depictions of street scenes, animals, and landscapes along the walkways.

She reached the center plaza, finding numerous artists selling their wares from shaded tents: oil paintings, watercolor sketches, elaborate wood carvings. Many had come from neighboring New Mexico counties, and the festive atmosphere was contagious. Alex smiled as the band struck up another lively number, trumpets, bass, and an accordion filling the air. A few people danced. She meandered by the tents, impressed at the artists' talents.

On the main street, she passed an art gallery that was hosting a show. A sandwich board out front touted that Pilar Jacinto, world-renowned sculptor and owner of the gallery, would be unveiling her latest masterpiece.

Attendees milled in and out of the gallery, sipping wine and laughing and talking. Alex loved seeing what different people's creative visions inspired, and decided to stop in there, too. She walked into the invitingly cool interior, her eyes adjusting to the lack of dazzling sunlight.

In the center of the room stood a huge metal sculpture of a butterfly. The metal had been tinted in different vivid shades of blue, purple, and gold. The sculpture was striking, all gleaming metal. A woman Alex guessed to be in her early eighties stood next to it, beaming proudly. Ardent admirers clustered around her, commenting on the butterfly as she answered questions. Beside her stood a demonstration table with scraps of metal, and a torch with adjustable heat that was able to oxidize the steel to produce different hues.

Alex approached, feeling a little shy and awkward as she often did around strangers, and eavesdropped for a few minutes as Pilar described her method. Then the artist walked over to the demonstration table, put on her welding goggles and gloves, and fired up the torch, welding a seam along one scrap of metal at varying temperatures. She grinned as she did it, and Alex smiled, gratified to see someone who so obviously loved her art. Then she set the torch down, removed her protective gear, and returned to speak with the crowd.

As people moved on, Alex approached her. "That's an incredible sculpture. Such vivid colors!"

Pilar nodded her head graciously. "Gracias. It's a new technique I've been trying."

Behind Pilar hung a massive oil painting of the New Mexico desert, sweeping terrain painted in beige, tan, vivid red, and gold. Alex was impressed to see the signature in the corner read "Pilar Jacinto." "You painted that, too?" she asked.

Pilar looked over her shoulder. "Sí. You like it?"

"It's stunning!"

"Thank you. I used to paint more than sculpt." She curled her arm, making a muscle with her biceps. "But I like the workout of hefting around those big metal pieces." She laughed.

"Buff!" Alex exclaimed, admiring the sinewy muscle.

"Are you visiting our town?" Pilar asked. "A fellow artist?"

Alex shook her head. "If only. My father is an incredible painter, and I always wanted to be able to draw like him. But I'm a wildlife biologist. Just got hired to see if any jaguars are on the nearby Mogollon Wildlife Sanctuary. Are you familiar with it?"

She nodded. "Sí, sí. My grandson Arturo is a big wildlife enthusiast. He was happy to see that land get protected." She lifted her eyebrows. "Do you really think you might find a jaguar there?"

"I hope to. Have you ever seen one in this area?"

Pilar shook her head. "But my family has been in this area for generations. We have a big spread south of here, closer to the border, and my grandfather told me that he used to see jaguars."

Alex's heart lifted. "That's wonderful. Did he say where exactly?"

Pilar thought for a moment. "All over the place, he said. Here, near the old Gila Cliff Dwellings, way down near the Animas Mountains, all the way to the border. But I haven't heard of any being seen since his time."

Alex's heart sank back down. "The sanctuary has some great jaguar habitat. They're very adaptable animals."

"I hope you find one," Pilar told her. "I hope you find a whole family of them."

Alex grinned. "Me, too."

A couple approached the table, and Alex stepped aside so they could chat with Pilar. "Nice meeting you," she told the sculptor.

"Mucho gusto," Pilar returned.

Alex was just about to take a tour of the gallery and look at the paintings on the wall when the sound of a gunning engine pulled her attention to the street.

A white pickup truck wheeled around the corner at the nearest intersection. Two huge white flags streamed behind it, and as they flapped in the wind, Alex was able to make out the insignia of a clenched fist beneath a star on one of them. The other sported the well-known insignia of a white supremacist group.

The truck raced down the street, four men riding in the back and two up front, all wearing skull masks. The truck veered for the plaza. Alex tensed, staring out in alarm.

A patron beside her, an old man with a wizened, tanned face, noticed her nervousness. "They just like to give people a scare now and then and ride through town," he told her, as if it was something that happened every day. But he, too, remained vigilant beside her.

Then a second beat-up white truck hove into view, roaring down the street. This one, too, held men with skull masks. Three men in the back of the truck hunched over something. Alex noticed that neither truck sported a license plate.

The second truck screeched to a halt in front of the gallery. Then Alex saw a flash of fire and realized too late that the men were lighting Molotov cocktails. One stood up in the back of the truck and hurled the incendiary device straight through the window of the art gallery. Glass smashed, shattering over the artwork.

"Everyone get back!" Alex yelled, running for cover. The fiery alcohol spattered everything around her. Immediately a box of sketches caught on fire, then a tablecloth.

Another Molotov soared through a second window, shattering it on impact and lighting fire to a demonstration station where a man was painting in oils. His jar of turpentine erupted into flames and he leapt back.

Two people grabbed fire extinguishers and tried to put out the advancing blaze, while others used large drop cloths in an attempt to smother it. But as more fiery bottles crashed through the windows, their attempts proved futile and the fire advanced.

FIVE

Alex could hear the men in the truck outside jeering and yelling but couldn't make out what they were saying. Some of it just sounded like unintelligible primal roars. Then she heard, "Go back to your own country!" and "You're not wanted here!" followed by a hateful deluge of racial slurs that made her jaw drop.

All around Alex, people screamed as Molotov after Molotov crashed through windows and sailed through the main door.

She could see the men hurling explosives in other directions, too, toward the bandstand and sidewalk art competition, people screaming and fleeing down the street.

Alex faced the fiery inferno before her with dismay. There was no way anyone was escaping through the front of the art gallery now. The entire area roared with fire.

Everyone had pressed toward the back as confused shouts filled the room.

"It's locked!"

"Maria has the key!"

"¿Dónde está Maria?"

When Alex reached the rear of the building, she found it blocked with a metal grated door, apparently a security measure that had been installed. People rattled the gate, but the thick steel was firmly locked.

"Maria's not here! She's at home, sick!"

"Does anyone have the key?"

Alex pushed through the crowd and then spotted Pilar, who was pulling at a shelf that had toppled in the chaos. Alex saw that it was blocking a door. Alex ran to her. "Is that another way out?" she asked, gesturing at the door.

Pilar shook her head. "No. It's the supply room." She banged on the door. "Arturo!" she shouted through the door. "Arturo!" She turned to Alex. "My grandson! I had sent him into the supply room to get some more scrap metal, and I think he's trapped in there!" She faced the blocked door with horror.

Alex reached through the open back of the shelving and placed a hand on the door's surface, then withdrew it immediately. The surface was blisteringly hot.

"Pilar," Alex gasped, her throat burning from the acrid fumes and smoke. "Can you cut through the lock on that back door with a torch?"

Pilar's eyes went wide, and she stared over her shoulder where everyone clustered, pulling on the locked gate. "What? Is it locked? My assistant's not here. She has the gate key, and she was sick today."

"If you can go cut through that lock, I'll get this shelf free and get him out if he's in there," she told Pilar.

Pilar bit her lip, clearly reluctant, then turned toward where everyone pressed against the back wall, unable to get out. "Okay," she agreed, and hurried off.

Alex took in the problem. The door opened outward, toward her. Alex eyed the shelving unit. It was well used and rickety, probably toppled when someone slammed into it. She braced her back against one end of the leaning shelf and pushed upward. When it gave a little, she shoved it to one side, and it fell with a jarring smash onto the floor. But its base still blocked the door. Unable to budge it farther, she sat down on the floor, pressed her legs against the bottom of the shelf, and managed to inch it away from the door.

Wrapping her hand in her sleeve, she gripped the door handle and wrenched open the door. Dense black smoke spiraled out and she could barely see anything. Her eyes and lungs burned, and she pulled her T-shirt up over her nose and mouth in an attempt to filter out some of the smoke.

She could barely make out anything but utter darkness and billowing black smoke. A small window high up in the room had been broken, letting in a square of diluted light. But the smoke was so thick that the light was quickly blocked as black tendrils spilled out of the room, sweeping past her as she stood with the door open. "Arturo?" she called out.

She coughed and sputtered, unable to breathe. Tentatively she took a step into the room. A blast of heat hit her. But now as the smoke cleared a little, she could see that just one corner of the room was on fire. A man lay sprawled a couple of feet from the door, his face covered in a towel.

She rushed to him and grabbed his arms. He groaned as she tugged him toward the door. They reached the toppled bookcase and he coughed and sputtered. "What happened?" he gasped.

He leaned on her shoulder as they stepped over the overturned shelving. She could see Pilar at work at the door, people pressed close. In just the few minutes she'd spent opening the storage room, the fire had completely consumed the front of the gallery and was now roaring in the center of the room.

A cheer erupted as Pilar severed the lock with a cutting torch and the gate swung open. Patrons poured out into the alley behind the gallery. Pilar spotted Alex with Arturo and rushed over to him.

He coughed, then relieved, gave her a wry smile. "You're supposed to be going *away* from the fire, abuelita," he said before erupting into a coughing fit.

They helped him outside, following the others down a narrow alley to the main street beyond.

As they emerged from the alley, Alex gasped when she took in the scene before her. The trucks were gone now. Several businesses belched fire and smoke, completely burned. Pilar stared around at them in horror. She gripped Arturo's arm.

He shook in anger. For several long minutes, they gaped at the chaos. Then he muttered, "They only hit businesses owned by Latina families."

Alex scanned the street for any sign of the trucks, but they had vanished, the destruction complete. She saw that the town plaza lay in ruins, tents burned, paintings scattered, people looking on in dismay as flames consumed their art.

"What can we do?" Alex asked helplessly, seeing one family clutching one another outside their ruined bakery. "Do you know who those men were?"

Pilar shook her head. "I'm familiar with that group, but not their individual members. They always hide their faces."

Arturo wiped soot off his face with one sleeve as a coughing fit overtook him. He gasped. "I didn't even see what happened. Just suddenly the window broke and everything caught on fire." He leaned over, hands on his knees, his body racked from smoke inhalation.

Alex thought of the missing license plates, the covered faces, the anonymity of the old white pickups. There must be dozens of trucks just like them within a hundred-mile range.

She helped Pilar over to the little park, where she could sit down in the shade. Then she and Arturo moved down the street, helping people where they could. Ambulances and fire trucks finally arrived, and firefighters doused the flames while EMTs treated bruises and minor burns. Several people were rushed to the hospital with severe burns and smoke inhalation. They administered oxygen to Arturo, who refused to leave, insisting he had to stay to help.

In the aftermath, as the police arrived and started taking statements, Alex just stared out at the destruction. She told a deputy everything she'd noticed—the flags, the beat-up pickups, the masks. But she didn't know how much it would help. The deputy told her they were aware of the group but hadn't yet determined the identities of the men.

She felt helpless as she walked away, seeing the suffering the men had left behind. She hoped the cops would catch them, and soon.

Back at the cabin, she took a shower, the water washing away black from smoke and soot. She rinsed out her clothes and hung them outside on a clothesline. After changing into fresh clothes, she sat down inside at the small wooden table.

Starting up her computer, she pulled up her habitat suitability model, but she couldn't concentrate. She felt distracted and upset, flashing on the day's trauma. Those poor business owners and their families.

She stared at the satellite image of the preserve and forced herself to double-check the places where she thought the cameras should go. She had to do a little more ground-truthing in a few areas, confirming that the places in her computer model did indeed reflect good jaguar habitat when viewed in person.

But her mind kept drifting back to the chaos in Azulejo, wondering if the men would be back.

SIX

The next day, Alex slept in later than she had intended, exhausted from the day before. She sat up on her narrow cot, running her fingers through her tangled hair. After the chaos and violence of what had occurred in town, she relished the thought of a long stint of being alone in the wild.

She loaded up her daypack with a remote camera, some fresh batteries and memory cards, her mirrorless camera, her water bottle and filter, and a few energy bars.

The air outside was hot and dry, and she chose a lightweight, wicking hiking shirt and pants, tied her long, wavy brown hair back in a ponytail, and donned her favorite worn SPF 50 wide-brimmed black hat.

She'd already selected the target site for this camera on a previous outing. She set off, climbing down from the high plateau where the cabin sat, out of the shade from the ponderosa pines and into a drier stretch where juniper trees grew. As she descended, ocotillo overtook the desert floor, brilliant green stalks with tiny leaves. In a few places their brown, porous skeletons lay sun-bleached on the sandy soil. Here and there prickly pears grew, their large green paddle leaves bristling with spines. She delighted at a brilliantly red-blooming claret cup hedgehog cactus, its chubby stem segments looking like a cluster of fat little hedgehogs.

Huge gray-brown rock formations jutted dramatically around

her, deep cool shadows clustering on their northwest sides at this time of day. She gravitated toward those shady sections whenever she got the chance, crossing the desert floor and preparing to climb to higher ground. As she gained elevation, the air cooled noticeably as she moved into clusters of juniper and piñon pine. A small mountain stream trickled between rocks and trunks, and she followed it upward, stopping occasionally to drink from her water bottle. She followed the creek to its source, a spring burbling out cold water. Using her special purifying filter, she refilled her water bottle and took another long, welcome drink, gazing around her.

A buzzing sound drew her attention to a patch of deep blue larkspur, where she spotted a broad-tailed hummingbird hovering among the blooms, its iridescent ruby-magenta throat flashing in the sunlight.

Her whole body gave a deep, grateful sigh. *This was the life.* Out here, all she could hear was the trickling water and the sigh of wind in the trees. A covey of Gambel's quail scooted by, emitting their distinctive high-pitched cry. No traffic, no one shouting, no smell of exhaust. The air was redolent with juniper and she breathed it in, grateful she'd lucked out with these gigs from the LTWC. They allowed her to be in wild places like this and do helpful work for endangered species.

Since she was six years old and first learned about extinction, Alex had worried about wildlife. As a kid she'd done odd jobs for neighbors to earn cash to send to nonprofit organizations like Greenpeace and the Center for Biological Diversity. She'd wanted to join an anti-whaling ship, convinced her six-year-old self would have no problem swabbing decks, towing lines, and hoisting jibs. Her parents had finally managed to convince her to stay home and volunteer at the local wildlife rescue and rehabilitation center, so instead of spotting whaling ships, she mucked out raccoon cages and fed specialized formula to baby opossums and rabbits.

As she grew older, she took up activism for wildlife causes, distributed petitions, wrote letters, and eventually got her PhD in wildlife biology, focusing on detection methods for endangered species and the restoration of their habitat.

She reached the place where she wanted to hang the first remote camera and slung off her pack. Two trees stood the perfect distance apart. She pulled out a length of barbed wire for a hair snare and wrapped it gently around one of the trunks, then spritzed the wire with the Obsession perfume. As wildlife passed by the wire, a bit of their hair would snag.

Then she strapped the remote camera on the opposite tree, facing the hair snare. She put in new batteries and a memory card. Whenever an animal crossed the camera's infrared beam, the device would snap a picture or record a video. She took a few test shots to be sure the camera was working, then secured the housing with a padlock.

She stepped back, admiring her handiwork. Jaguars would love this area with its water source and shadowed trees.

People often thought of jaguars as an exotic tropical species that wouldn't be found in the U.S., but jaguars were actually quite adaptable. They could live in coniferous forests, deserts, grasslands, swamps, even beaches. Unlike many other felines, they loved to swim. And they were incredibly smart. Of all the big cats, they had the largest body-to-brain ratio.

She imagined one now, moving stealthily through the trees. They were the third largest of the big cats, smaller only than lions and tigers, and were exceedingly agile and lithe, with almost no stored fat. Jaguars in South America, where prey was more abundant, could weigh in at a whopping 350 pounds, while jaguars here in the borderlands of the Southwest weighed in at closer to 120 pounds. And they were long; their tails made up a third of their length, for a total body length of nine feet.

She wondered what the carrying capacity of the preserve was for jaguars, the number of individuals a piece of land could support, taking into account water, food availability, and the presence of potential mates. Because every jaguar had its own unique pattern of rosettes in its coat, she would be able to tell from the remote camera images if more than one individual was present, and DNA from the hair snares could determine sex and any familial relationships.

She hiked back down, taking a different route to explore more of the preserve. As she changed elevation, a variety of habitats revealed themselves: juniper and Mexican piñon pine forests; towering ponderosa trees with their sunlit alligator skin bark; conical blue Engelmann spruce trees silhouetted against the azure desert sky, lending a rich pine scent to the air; copses of white-trunked aspen with quavering green leaves; the desert floor bristling with spiny cane cholla growing in clumps beside blooming red ocotillo.

She stopped to eat a late lunch atop a plateau, able to see the terrain around her for what she guessed was at least a hundred miles. As she ate an energy bar, in the far distance, she could make out a vast stretch of Chihuahuan Desert, with its brown and blond sands and heat waves shimmering along the ground. She could see a few irrigated circular fields, dirt roads, and scattered houses. She was on a finger of the preserve that cut between the land belonging to Evander Milton, the man Ben had described as an eccentric gazillionaire, and the Gila National Forest, where ranchers grazed their cattle on public land. She'd done an internet search on Milton, but still wasn't sure how exactly he'd made his money. He traveled the world, and she noticed with chagrin that he was a big-game trophy hunter.

She headed down the mountain, veering in the direction of Milton's property. She hadn't seen that side of the preserve yet and hoped more optimal jaguar habitat was there.

As she descended, the sound of voices filtering through the trees made her stop. She could hear the clinking of metal and music playing from a radio.

She came through the tree line and peered down a steep embankment. The preserve ended where she stood, with Milton's property beyond. A hive of activity bustled below. Three people perched over various gridded-off areas, two digging with small spades, the other using brushes. The grids had been demarcated using wooden pegs and string. Two dusty SUVs and a truck waited in a small flat area off to one side. Some distance away from the gridded area stood a sleeping tent, a beat-up camper van, and two almost new-looking RVs. A work tent stood nearer to Alex, and through one open flap, Alex could see a man with short black hair seated at a laptop. A table held lanterns, shovels, spades, and other tools. Outside this larger tent, a solar panel caught sunrays. The man emerged from the tent, clad in khakis, and consulted an iPad. He gestured for one of the diggers to move to a particular grid.

She smiled. An archaeological dig. She'd always been fascinated with unearthing ancient artifacts and the discovery of how and when long-vanished peoples lived their lives.

She accidentally loosened a small rock under her boot and it bounced down the steep embankment. The movement drew the attention of the man at the tent.

He turned toward her, shielding his eyes from the sun with one hand. "Hello!" he called.

"Hello!" she answered.

"Are you the biologist?"

"I am!"

"Come on down!"

She had no idea how he knew about her, but wanting to check out the dig, she scrambled down the steep embankment.

He strode forward, a beautiful white smile in a face the color of terra-cotta. Sweat glistened in his short black hair, and he held out a hand. "Dr. Enrique Espinoza," he said by way of greeting. "Director of the chaos you see before you."

She shook his hand, finding his grip warm and firm. "Dr. Alex Carter," she told him, deciding to use her title, too. When in Rome and all that.

"Milton mentioned that a wildlife biologist was staying at the Mogollon Wildlife Sanctuary next door."

She had no idea how Milton knew that. Maybe he'd talked to Ben. Or just heard local scuttlebutt.

"What are you digging for?" she asked.

Espinoza's face lit up. "The grave of a sixteenth-century Spanish conquistador, Simón de Aguirre. And the best part," he started, then suddenly looked chastened, "or I guess you could say the *worst* part, is that he had looted a bunch of Aztec artifacts and they're buried here with him."

She looked at the sheer scale of the dig. "That's a big grave site." It looked far too expansive to be a single grave.

"That's the interesting part. He was pretty paranoid, apparently, and stashed his stuff all over the place. We still haven't even found his body yet, just a few small gold Aztec pieces."

"How did you even know to dig here?"

"Local lore, if you can believe it. Evander Milton is an avid armchair archaeologist. He pored over old primary sources and listened to the locals' oral histories. We dug in a few spots before we hit gold, literally." He flashed that brilliant white grin again, and his enthusiasm was infectious. He gestured around at the others hard at work in the dust. "These are my grad students. We've been at this location for about a week." One woman with long black hair had joined a freckled, redheaded male colleague at the edge of a grid. Both looked to be in their twenties, while the man Espinoza had directed earlier must have been in his late seventies.

"Jesus Christ!" yelled the younger male student, springing to his feet and stumbling backward out of his grid. He landed hard on his butt, cradling one hand against his chest. The woman rushed to his side and knelt down by him.

Even from where she stood some distance away, Alex could see blood streaming down his wrist, dripping onto his jeans.

"Damn it!" Espinoza cursed and ran over to the cluster of students. "That's the other thing about this dig," he yelled over his shoulder to Alex. "Simón booby-trapped it."

SEVEN

Alex hurried behind Espinoza, who immediately assessed his student. A long slice ran the length of his palm. Alex peered down to where he'd been digging, seeing a partially uncovered stone slab. A long slit ran the length of it, with a spring-loaded blade jutting out. The student's blood still dripped off the blade.

"Let's get you to the tent," Espinoza said, placing a hand on the man's shoulder, "and fix you up."

He helped the student stand and ushered him toward the work tent. "I'm beginning to think I need to employ a medic for this site," he said to Alex as they stepped into the shade of the tent.

Espinoza broke out a med kit and quickly cleaned and dressed the wound. "I'd say you're done for the day, my friend," he told his student, who looked on forlornly. The female student hovered nearby. Then she met Alex's gaze and said, "Hi, I'm Ming Lin."

Alex smiled. "Alex Carter. Nice to meet you. Though not the best circumstances. Your poor colleague."

Ming shook her head. "Third injury this week. Guy was gonzo for his booby traps. We found a stone sarcophagus. It was empty except for a series of blades triggered when we removed the lid. That was the first one to get us."

"And they still work? After all this time?" Alex asked, amazed.

"Some of them," grumbled the injured student. "Others not so much. Over the centuries things like crossbow strings tend to decay." Alex raised her eyebrows at the mention of a crossbow. "But the dude was a genius for traps," he went on, watching as Espinoza neatly packed away the medical supplies into their box.

"That's Desmond Oliver," Ming explained. "He's just bitter because the last two traps got him."

"It's like they're after me in particular," he muttered, then turned to Alex and nodded. "Sup."

"Hi," Alex said back.

Just then the older man lifted the door flap to the tent. His thinning grizzled hair was shorn close to his scalp, his umber face beaded with sweat. "We found something," he said excitedly to Espinoza.

"What is it?" the archaeologist asked, stashing the med kit on a shelf.

"You'd better come look for yourself."

Espinoza straightened up, then grinned at Alex. "Shall we?"

As they all left the tent, Espinoza gestured toward the older man. "Gordon there is one of my best students. Working on his PhD. He almost didn't do it. He was a stockbroker before this. Can you believe it? That man there, all happily covered in dirt right now? He almost didn't go back to school. Told his wife he'd be eighty-two by the time he got his degree. Apparently she told him, 'You're going to turn eighty-two anyway. You may as well be eighty-two and an archaeologist.' And he applied to UNM that same day."

Alex grinned. "Wise woman."

They followed Gordon over to the grid he'd been working, and everyone gazed transfixed at the dirt.

Gordon climbed down a short ladder into the pit and finished brushing off a stone carving about the size of a loaf of bread. As he uncovered more of its features, Espinoza gasped. "You're kidding me," he breathed.

A moment later, Espinoza was down the ladder himself, stooping over the find. Gordon brushed dirt away from a carved stone face, then chubby arms, finally revealing a statue of a fat baby. But its face wasn't that of a cherubic infant. It sported fangs and a flattened skull.

"It's a werejaguar." Espinoza squatted next to it. He took the brush from Gordon and continued to sweep off the surface. "I don't believe it. This isn't Aztec. This isn't even Mayan." He rocked back on his heels, peering up at his students. "It's Olmec. Could be more than three thousand years old." He shook his head in disbelief. "This must have been passed down over generations, from the Olmec era to the Mayan to the Aztec. Incredible!"

Though just a visitor to the dig and not wanting to intrude, Alex couldn't help herself. "Werejaguar?" she asked.

Espinoza peered in wonder at the object, grabbing one of his student's cameras and snapping a series of photos of the artifact in situ. Then he looked up at her. "The Olmecs were fascinated with jaguars. Believed they were symbols of power and royalty."

"A few Mesoamerican murals show women having sex with jaguars," Desmond added, cradling his injured hand. "And from that came baby werejaguars."

"Sometimes they'd show the babies crawling out from the underworld in these eerie poses," Ming said, "emerging from the world of darkness. They typically are snarling, fat little babies with flattened skulls, sometimes sporting fangs and claws."

"They even found one Olmec man who had his teeth ground down to the nubs so he could wear a set of jaguar dentures," Espinoza added.

Alex raised her eyebrows. "Wow. That's dedication."

Espinoza nodded. "This tradition of venerating jaguars was also popular with other cultures. Aztec and Mayan rulers wore jaguar skins and sat on thrones carved to look like jaguars. Then there's the Temple of the Jaguar in Chichén Itzá. And let's not forget the two rampant stone jaguars that flank the staircase in the Mayan city of Copán."

"Or all of the Mayan jaguar gods and goddesses," Ming put in, "like God L and Ixchel."

Espinoza stared down at the statuette, a huge grin on his face. "Yes, jaguars were incredibly important to the Maya. They symbolized the divine right of rulers."

Desmond peered down into the pit, still gripping his hand. "Traditional Mayan belief held that a jaguar god ruled the night. His spots were said to be the stars. And the Aztecs didn't see a great bear when they looked at Ursa Major. They saw a jaguar."

Espinoza peered up at Alex. "Desmond specializes in archaeo-astronomy."

The student nodded. "It's fascinating."

"Aztecs had a military order called the Jaguar Knights," Ming added. "They wore the pelts of jaguars into battle, and shamans could shapeshift into jaguars. In the Aztec creation myths, there were five suns, or eras of creation, each ending in the destruction of humanity. In the first sun, jaguars devoured all the people."

Espinoza stood up, brushing off his pants. He turned to Gordon. "Excellent work! Finish cleaning it off and photographing it, and then bring it up to the main tent."

Gordon nodded. "You got it."

Espinoza climbed up out of the pit and joined Alex at the top. "Come see what we've found so far," he offered.

"I'd love to."

Together they walked back to the work tent. He held open the flap for her and she stepped through. Inside stood a long table with dozens of artifacts laid out on it, all being carefully labeled. To one side towered shelving with artifacts that still needed to be sorted through. Several laptops lay open on the table, along with work lamps and stacks of papers.

He gestured at the table and shelves, and Alex walked slowly past all the objects. Most of it was sixteenth-century European: fire steels, medieval horseshoe nails, copper and iron crossbow bolts, sword points, links from chain mail.

Espinoza pointed to a cylindrical bronze object about three feet long. "We even found this. He was definitely not traveling light."

Alex stared at it, puzzled. "What is it?"

"The wood has rotted away. It's a wall gun. Basically a supersize musket. They are so heavy that to fire one, you had to rest it on a wall."

"How heavy is it?"

"About forty pounds."

She raised her eyebrows. "Yeah, definitely something you couldn't run into battle with."

Then she saw several small gold statuettes, clearly Aztec in design, just pocket-size. Two depicted men, and one seemed to be of a big cat, a jaguar. She grinned at the sight of it.

"This is most of what we've found so far. We have more back at the university." He crossed his arms. "So what are you studying out here?"

Alex smiled. "Believe it or not, I'm looking for jaguars."

"Seriously? Now that's a coincidence," he said, gazing down at the small gold jaguar statue. "You think they're here in New Mexico?"

"They've been here in the past. One was even killed farther north of here, in the Datil Mountains. They've been crossing back and forth across the border with Mexico. I'm here to see if they're using this wildlife sanctuary and if there's anything we can do to restore habitat for them here."

Alex knew that the number of confirmed, recorded jaguars in the United States between 1848 and 2008 was eighty-four, though very likely far more went undetected. Both males and females had been present, and until the 1960s, this very likely represented a breeding population.

"Have you seen any yet?"

"I haven't been that lucky. But I'm putting out remote cameras and hair snares, hoping one might be here."

"I actually don't know a lot about them," he confessed.

"It'll be great if I can get photos of them on the cameras. And I can send any snagged hair to a lab for DNA. The cameras record sound, too, in case I get any vocalizations."

"Like roaring?"

"Exactly." Alex gave a small laugh. "They kind of sound like an old man clearing his throat when they roar, actually."

"Do they purr?"

Alex shook her head. "Sadly, they can't purr. With felines, species can either purr or roar. They can't do both."

"Why is that?"

Alex touched her throat. "It's the hyoid bone. In small cats, like house cats, pumas, ocelots, and lynxes, the hyoid bone is ossified, which allows them to purr. But in big cats like lions and jaguars, it's flexible, which lets them roar."

"I didn't know that." Espinoza mused for a moment. "That's really interesting that it's jaguars you're studying, considering what we found here today and what we're still looking for."

Alex lifted an eyebrow. "What else are you looking for?"

"Certainly not a werejaguar statuette. I wasn't expecting that. That's just a total bonus." Espinoza grinned. "Rumor has it that Simón made off with quite a few other priceless artifacts. One of them is a ceremonial jadeite jaguar dagger that's more than seventeen hundred years old."

Alex raised her eyebrows. "Wow!"

"And jaguars aside, perhaps most valuable of all, he claimed to have made off with over a dozen scrolls, tales inscribed by the Maya. We could learn so much. They might be astronomical records or religious documents or histories. We just don't know. And that's the part that excites me the most. So much was destroyed during the Spanish conquest. Manuscripts, knowledge, murals. Any artifacts we find now can shed light on those ancient cultures."

He gestured toward the dig site outside. "Of course, we don't *know* if he had those scrolls or artifacts. We're just piecing things together from his own papers and from other primary sources left by Spanish friars at the time. But apparently Simón was one greedy bastard and had an eye for treasure."

He stepped over to the shelves where the artifacts were waiting to be cataloged. "I spent a year in Spain going over sixteenth-century manuscripts that had been brought back to Europe. Several of them had been written by Simón de Aguirre himself, relating his plunders and battles in Central America. He had originally planned to return to Spain and live a life of wealth and power with his spoils. But he got paranoid and was convinced any men he sailed with would steal his treasure and throw him overboard. So he decided to remain here and send only the records of his conquests back with other Spaniards so that the king would be proud of him. He himself stayed here and started burying his loot, devising booby traps to catch thieves. He'd intended to build his own empire here, but before he could start, something happened to him."

"What?"

Espinoza scrunched his face. "We don't know. It's only through tales handed down by oral tradition that we even know he's probably buried around here somewhere. But given how much of his loot we've recovered already, we suspect he's nearby, the old so-and-so."

She examined the shelves and all the artifacts they'd found so far. "You've got some fascinating work ahead of you. I hope you find some scrolls."

He grinned, nodding, following her gaze. "So do I."

"I appreciate your showing me around."

"My pleasure. Come back anytime."

They shook hands and Alex ducked out of the tent, squinting

in the bright light. She scrambled back up the steep embankment, crossing over into the preserve again.

There she stood for a few minutes, watching gold, red, and scarlet start to color the western sky. She hoped jaguars were out here, seeing this same vista, safe on the preserve. She watched a red-tailed hawk wheeling high above, riding the thermals.

Then she set off for the cabin, wanting to beat the darkness. But as she hiked back, her mind drifted to the violence in the town. She wondered what those men were planning next. People often asked her if she was afraid of wolves or bears or mountain lions when she was hiking alone in remote places. But it wasn't wildlife that made her uneasy. It was humans.

EIGHT

Over the next couple of days, Alex checked one of her cameras and hung out two more. Wondering how Espinoza and his students were getting along, she took a short side trip to look down on the dig site before continuing on to her next camera placement. She loved to see them at work, feeling the contagious excitement of the discovery. She wondered if they'd yet found the scrolls or the jadeite jaguar dagger that Espinoza had described.

She reached the steep embankment leading to the site and peered down, finding the students hard at work, perched over their individual grids. Espinoza stood in front of the work tent, one hand on his hip, staring intently at his tablet.

Alex let her gaze wander off into the distance. The air was so clear today that she could see for what she guessed was at least a hundred miles. She breathed in the fresh air, feeling a welcome breeze. She loved this.

Then movement drew her eyes down to the valley floor far below. A dust trail plumed up from a narrow dirt road there. She couldn't see it from this distance, but a vehicle was clearly driving fast in her direction. It seemed to idle for a time where the forest service land met Milton's, and after a moment, turned up the small dirt track that led to the dig site. It wove between trees, climbing higher and higher, going so fast that the plume of dust took on massive proportions, throwing up a cyclone of dirt behind it.

She fished her binoculars out of her pack and adjusted the focus wheel to see who it was. Someone was in a hurry.

Espinoza looked up from his tablet, seeing the dust cloud, which now billowed up over the trees, carried on the wind toward the dig site. "Cover the pits!" he cried to his students as the wall of dirt approached.

Students leapt up, grabbing tarps and dragging them hastily over the grids.

The truck tore onto the dig site, and instantly her stomach sank. It was a white truck with a flag streaming behind. She fixed her binoculars on it, squinting at the spiraling dirt and flapping fabric. It was the same symbol the men had carried through the town, a fist beneath a star, and the three men in the cab wore the same skull masks. No one crouched in the back of the truck this time, and she spotted no flash of flame from Molotov cocktails. But just as before, the truck had no plates.

It did two complete donuts, tearing over the vegetation by the students' vehicles, spraying the site with dust, then screeched to a halt. The driver gunned his engine as the dirt cloud settled.

Alex watched Espinoza cough, vainly trying to wave away the dust in the air. She wondered if he'd charge up to the truck, shouting in anger. But he stayed where he was at the mouth of the tent, looking uncertain. She trained her binoculars back on the truck. The three men piled out of the cab. The masks didn't cover their necks, and she could see that they were all white and sunburned, wearing dirty jeans and white undershirts.

All three carried handguns strapped to their hips, and Alex's gut turned over.

"What's all this?" the driver boomed. He took in the tent, the camper van and RVs, the dusty vehicles. "An illegal immigrant camp?" Even from up on the ridge, she could hear what he was saying. Voices carried in the wilderness.

Desmond and Ming crouched over the tarps, trying to keep them pinned down as the dust settled.

Finally Espinoza stepped away from the tent. "Who are you, and what are you doing up here?"

The driver marched up to Espinoza, too close, looking him up and down with a sneer. "Who are you supposed to be?" he asked the archaeologist. The two men followed.

"I'm in charge here," Espinoza told him.

The driver gave a low chuckle, then nudged one of the other men from the truck. "Listen to this guy. 'I'm in charge here.' So you're in charge are you, Paco? In charge of what?" The driver eyed the students, who hung back, looking nervous.

Espinoza waved at the tarps. "This is a delicate archaeological dig you've disturbed. All the dust you kicked up is damaging the site. You're trespassing and you need to leave."

The driver chuckled again. "Oh, *I* need to leave, do I? Is that how it is? I think I've got way more of a right to be here than you do, *Paco*." He said the name in an increasingly sneering voice. "You got documentation on you?"

Espinoza licked his lips. The sour lump churned in Alex's gut.

Gordon spoke up. "He's an esteemed professor at the University of New Mexico, you idiot, which is a hell of a lot more than I'm guessing *you* are, bucko," he yelled.

"What the fuck did you say?" roared the driver, wheeling on Gordon.

Espinoza held up a placating hand. "It's all right, Gordon." He turned to the men. "Look. We've got every right to be here. But you're trespassing. I'm afraid we'll have to call the sheriff and report you if you don't leave immediately."

But the driver didn't budge. Instead, he took a step closer to Espinoza. "I *said, Paco,* do you have documentation?"

Espinoza shook his head. "Look here. This isn't Nazi Germany, and I don't have to show you anything."

The driver laughed. "And there it is, boys," he roared to his comrades. "No proof he's a citizen. What did you do, swim the river and then get these poor people to take you in?" He looked around at the students. Then he noticed Ming.

"And where the hell did *you* wash up from?" he asked her. Ming's face burned crimson with anger.

He turned back to Espinoza. "I think it's *you all* who need to leave. This here's federal land. Owned by the citizens of the United States of America. And you don't look like no citizen to me."

"Actually, this is private property, and you're trespassing," Espinoza told him calmly.

But the man just raised his hand and pushed the archaeologist's shoulder.

Gordon rushed toward them and the driver's cronies shoved him violently to the ground. Alex cringed as he crashed down on his butt in a plume of dirt, Desmond and Ming rushing to his side to pick him up.

"Stay down, boy!" the leader sneered to Gordon.

"Now listen here!" Espinoza roared. "If you don't leave immediately—"

But the driver thrust his hands forward, landing with a solid impact on Espinoza's chest. The archaeologist staggered backward, grabbing one of the work tent poles and managing to stay standing.

Alex had seen enough. She quickly rummaged through her pack, finding her satellite communicator. She powered it up, her stomach churning as it searched the sky to get a satellite fix. She didn't have a way to directly contact 911 on it, but as soon as it locked on moments later and determined her location, she sent a text to her dad with the coordinates, instructing him to send police to her location immediately.

"I think we need to teach this old boy a lesson," the driver said, advancing on Espinoza. "String him up. Gut him for the buzzards."

Desmond and Ming started toward the men, but suddenly one of the cronies pulled his handgun from the holster on his hip. "You all just stay back. We'll get to you soon enough."

The driver grabbed Espinoza's collar and shoved him, forcing him to the ground. Espinoza scrambled back to his feet, looking terrified and flustered. Alex got the feeling he'd never been in a fight in his life.

The driver reeled a meaty fist back and then slammed it into Espinoza's nose. It erupted in blood, Espinoza spiraling backward, arms windmilling before he stumbled over a rock and landed flat on his back.

"Hey!" Alex yelled from the ridge. "I've called the cops! They're on their way."

The driver stopped in his tracks, head whipping around, trying to pinpoint her location. But between the dazzling sun and the trees on the ridge, he couldn't spot her. "You didn't call no cops," he yelled in her direction, shielding his face with one hand. "There's no signal out here."

"I have a satellite phone," she embellished, "and I've given the cops descriptions of you and your truck. They're on their way."

The driver hesitated. Alex debated whether she should slide down the embankment. The way the driver faced off against Espinoza was sloppy, a brawler. Alex had studied the martial art Jeet Kune Do since she was a kid, and if worse came to worst, she could step between him and Espinoza, do some damage to the guy.

The driver looked at his friends. "I think we better go," the crony with the gun said, doubt in his voice. He spoke so quietly that Alex almost couldn't hear him from her position.

"Oh, so *you* think we should go," sneered the driver, imitating his tone condescendingly. "Why don't you just shut the fuck up?" the driver yelled with fury. "Get in the damn truck."

The gunman continued to aim his pistol at the students but backed up to the cab of the vehicle.

"This ain't fuckin' over!" the driver yelled in her general direction, but she knew that he still couldn't pinpoint her location.

He kicked sand at Espinoza, then stormed toward the truck himself. He got in and fired up the engine, spinning the truck around violently, sending up huge sprays of dust and dirt. Then they roared off down the road, driving so fast she thought their axle might break on the pitted road.

She scrambled down the embankment, half sliding, half running, and jogged over to Espinoza. His students crowded around him, helping him to his feet.

"Who the hell were those guys?" Ming asked. She produced a bandanna and handed it to Espinoza, who held it to his bloody nose.

"I have a feeling they'll be back," the archaeologist muttered.

Gordon walked over, gingerly feeling his lower back. "Jerks just about broke my tailbone. I landed on a rock."

Desmond turned to Alex. "Did you really call the cops?"

"Not exactly," she admitted, and explained what she'd done.

"I wonder if the cops will actually send anyone out," Espinoza mused. He stared around at his students. "Does anyone know who those men were?"

"The symbol on the flag was kinda familiar," Desmond said. "I think I've seen that flag in footage of white supremacist rallies. I can check the Southern Poverty Law Center's website when we get back to an area with internet."

Alex was familiar with the SPLC, a nonprofit that tracked hate groups across the U.S. She wanted to look up the symbol, too, find out exactly what they were dealing with, if it was a known threat or some new group that had sprung up.

After helping Espinoza back inside the work tent, she told them about what had happened in town, the Molotov cocktails, the fire in the gallery.

"We heard about that," Ming breathed. "Those poor people."

"It was awful," Alex agreed. "We definitely need to give all the info we can to the cops. They might have been wearing masks and had no plates, but we could at least describe their heights, mannerisms, that kind of thing."

"When the cops show up, I'll do it," Espinoza told her, pressing the bandanna against his nose and wincing. "And I'll follow up with them later. I have to go into town to resupply, and I'll visit the police station. We need some more batteries and our food supply is running low out here." Then he turned to her. "You, dear lady, I suspect saved our collective bacon. Won't you come back for an official tour? I could show you around the grids and you could see how we work. And I could cook you up my amazing camp stove eggplant parmigiana." He turned to his students. "You all can partake in the feast."

Behind his back, Ming shook her head vigorously, while Desmond ran a hand across his throat in a gesture that communicated the concoction was downright lethal. Gordon pointed a finger at his open mouth and rolled his eyes, pretending he was gagging.

Alex stifled a smile. "You don't have to cook for me, but I'd love an official tour."

The students breathed a collective sigh of relief at her response.

"Anything you wish. Stop by anytime," Espinoza said, and reached out to grip her hand affectionately.

Alex nodded, taking his hand. "I will."

Ming offered Alex a soda and they waited for the police.

NINE

Half an hour later, a police cruiser pulled into the dig site. A rail-thin cop climbed out, standing about six-four, with a crop of blond hair and high cheekbones in a pink face. "I'm Deputy Wentworth," he told them. He had kind eyes and listened patiently, taking notes while they described what happened. Alex remembered seeing him the day the men had attacked the town, though he hadn't been the deputy who took her statement that time.

"We're aware of this group causing trouble," Wentworth told them. "If you want to come in and file a formal statement, we'd appreciate it."

As Deputy Wentworth drove away, Espinoza shook his head. "Hell of a day." Alex and he exchanged numbers in case they needed her further. Then he turned around in his chair to look at his students. "Anyone have any ibuprofen? My nose is killing me."

She said her goodbyes, left them to their administrations, and headed back up the embankment. At the top, she used the satellite communicator to let her father know all was well. He wrote back, relieved.

Then she continued on, hiking through a juniper forest and climbing up to the top of a steep plateau. A space between the trunks of Mexican piñon pines allowed her a glimpse at the dry valleys below. She pulled at the collar of her T-shirt, fanning it, inviting a breeze. The heat clung to her, pressing in on her.

She loved this work, breathing in the scent of piñon and ponderosa pines, hearing the wind sighing in the boughs. In the searingly blue sky above her, four vultures circled, riding the late afternoon thermals.

She fanned her shirt again. Here in the shade of the forest she had a brief respite from the daytime swelter. And at night, everything cooled considerably, and Alex could stare up at the stars, almost no light pollution to wash out the dazzling Milky Way. She took off her hat, running her fingers through her long brown hair, grateful for the tiniest breeze.

She replaced her hat, one hand on her hip, and gazed up into the canopy of the ponderosa pines. Jaguars would like this little section of the preserve. A small creek burbled nearby, tumbling between large rhyolite rocks, grasses and wildflowers growing along its bank. This would be an excellent spot to place a camera. She'd chosen a few more, most near water sources: another small spring, two small creeks, and a seasonal pond.

But she wasn't even sure if a jaguar could make it safely this far north into New Mexico with all the obstacles it would face today, from roads and housing developments to poachers. Even just getting into New Mexico at all across the international border would be a challenge.

In 2005, the REAL ID Act gave the Department of Homeland Security the power to ignore all existing federal, state, and local environmental laws when constructing border walls. Because of this, nearly fifty laws had been waived while building roads and obstructions along the border with Mexico, including the Endangered Species Act, the Antiquities Act, the Clean Water Act, the Clean Air Act, the National Environmental Policy Act, and the National Wildlife Refuge System Improvement Act.

During the construction of border structures, the government did no environmental assessments to reduce damage to either wildlife or ancient cultural sites. Private land was seized in some cases, and the American Indian Religious Freedom Act was ignored. Though environmental nonprofits sought to overturn this ability to disregard laws, in 2008, the U.S. Supreme Court ruled in favor of it. To date, it had been the largest and most sweeping waiving of laws in U.S. history.

Alex had followed news of sections of wall going up with considerable interest. An impenetrable wall covering the entire border with Mexico would prevent not just the jaguar from crossing, but many other wildlife species, including gray wolves, mountain lions, ocelots, jaguarundis, bears, and more. In addition to the wall, other activities along the border affected jaguar movement, including habitat destroyed and fragmented by roads, dazzling floodlights, and cacophonous noise.

Some of this construction plowed through wildlife areas once protected by the Environmental Protection Agency, including the nearby San Bernardino National Wildlife Refuge at the Arizona / New Mexico border, and Organ Pipe Cactus National Monument.

Alex had just read a study that found that ninety-seven species, several of which were endangered, were currently negatively affected by the existing wall. If a coast-to-coast wall were completed, then a whopping 1,500 species would be affected, some already in danger of extinction.

But the wall did not have to be an impenetrable obstruction. In fact, Alex had been researching how a virtual wall would be highly effective. It would use electronics such as cameras and motion detectors to monitor anyone illegally crossing the border.

And not all physical sections of the border wall were constructed in a way that prevented wildlife movement. While many areas hosted massive thirty-foot-tall steel and concrete pedestrian walls that prevented anything from crossing, other areas sported barbed wire fences or vehicle barriers, large steel beams welded together that prevented cars from crossing the border but allowed wildlife to continue to move through these obstructions. Other

steep, remote, and mountainous sections had no fencing at all because building there proved extremely difficult and expensive. It
was in these more remote sections that jaguars would be most likely
to cross. And if the border patrol wanted to monitor these areas,
they could use motion sensors and cameras, methods that didn't
prevent wildlife from moving between habitats.

She just hoped that more jaguars would be able to navigate the
myriad threats and find safety here. She took a long drink from her
water bottle. This heat was a marked change from her last few assignments. She'd spent a snowy winter in Montana searching for
wolverines, and an icy spring in the Canadian Arctic tagging polar
bears in Hudson Bay. After that, she'd spent months searching for an
elusive mountain caribou in Washington State, and while that had
been among the peaks of the Selkirk Mountains, the alpine summer
there had been brief and hot at times. But this heat was something
entirely new. At night, crickets sang in the lingering warmth of the
day, definitely something she didn't hear in her chilly stays in Montana or Manitoba.

And all of that was far different than the two months she'd just
spent with Zoe in L.A.

She thought of Zoe's massive mansion in the Hollywood Hills
and the numerous black-tie galas and spur-of-the-moment parties
celebrities had thrown on their estates. The culture shock had hit
Alex hard. Zoe had taken her shopping for "better clothes," as Alex
had only polypropylene shirts, nylon hiking pants, and boots. And
while it wasn't Alex's usual scene, they'd had a blast together, laughing, going on disastrous double dates, dancing and imbibing drinks
at exclusive clubs.

Alex paused to set up another hair snare and camera trap. She
spritzed the wire with Obsession and then stood back to take in the
scene before her: the trees, a burbling creek.

Finally, as the sun dipped down behind the mountains, Alex
hiked back to the cabin.

Being out in the wilds after L.A. wasn't the only stark transition. Moving from Zoe's posh L.A. mansion to her current digs had taken a bit of adjustment. The small cabin was also quite a change from the vast, spooky expanses of the abandoned Snowline Resort where she'd studied wolverines or the coziness of the motel room where she'd stayed while studying polar bears in the Canadian Arctic. It wasn't even like the comforts of the 1930s ranch house in Washington State where she'd searched for the elusive mountain caribou.

Feeling happy that she'd made progress over her first few days on the preserve, Alex hiked back as the shadows of twilight descended over the sanctuary. She showered and ate a quick dinner. Tomorrow she'd check the cameras she had placed out.

As she laid down on the cot in the darkness, she thought of the jaguars who had ventured north into the U.S. in the last few years.

In March of 1996, rancher and mountain lion hunter Warner Glenn had been tracking a big cat with his dogs for four days in the Peloncillo Mountains of Arizona. They cornered it on a rocky ledge, and to his astonishment, Glenn saw that it was actually a jaguar, not the mountain lion he'd expected. He could have shot it on the spot, but instead he decided to take photographs.

Six months later, another mountain lion hunter named Jack Childs was tracking a big cat with his dogs outside Tucson, Arizona. The dogs treed it, and to Childs's amazement, it was no mountain lion, but a jaguar. Like Glenn, instead of shooting it, Childs pulled out his camera and snapped photos. He then became fascinated that jaguars were in the area and the experience led him to form the Borderlands Jaguar Detection Project with his wife, Anne Childs. Together, they put up cameras all along the Arizona-Mexico border in 2001, seeking to capture images of jaguars. By 2004, they had captured photographs of the big cats, and by using the unique rosettes to identify them, determined that one of them, named Macho B, was the same one Childs had photographed in 1996.

Eight different jaguars have been sighted in the American

Southwest since 1996. Alex hoped that her research would add to that number.

For now, though, she worried about the threats they faced, and then her restless mind shifted to the violent incident at the dig site. Those men were out there even now, and she feared what they would do next.

TEN

The next day, Alex rose and prepared a quick breakfast of nuts and fruit. She'd been on a coffee kick lately but hadn't bought any because she had no way to refrigerate the oat milk. So instead she made a strong cup of English breakfast tea and added several lumps of sugar.

She brought the meal out to the small wooden bench in front of the cabin. Around her the forest woke up, birds singing their dawn chorus. She heard the throaty gurgling of a Chihuahuan raven and then the talkative chattering of a Steller's jay. A mountain chickadee rang out with its distinctive *chee dee dee* call. In the distance, she heard the drumming of a Northern flicker.

Taking a deep breath, she drank in her surroundings, then sipped her tea. The nuts tasted delicious, and she bit into a juicy apple. For a few minutes she mused on her life, of everything that had led her to be here in this moment. Her PhD. Her first offer to study wolverines with the LTWC. Her decision to leave Boston to pursue her dream of working in the wilderness. Finally saying goodbye to her most recent romantic relationship, which hadn't been working for some time.

She sighed. It had all been the right decision.

She finished her meal and sat drinking the rest of her tea. But then the sound of a car engine cut through the quiet trees. Birds stopped singing. The wind blew toward her, and she caught a hint of dust on it. The engine noise grew louder and the dust more intense. Someone was driving up the dirt road to the cabin.

Alex froze, fear suddenly thumping inside her. Maybe the men at the dig site had figured out who she was and where she was staying. She stood up and hurriedly went inside. The door sported a dead bolt and she engaged it.

She grabbed her tranquilizer gun and loaded a dart into it, then stood perched by the window, staring out.

But then the vehicle bounced around the bend and into view. It wasn't a white pickup but a shiny black Range Rover. It pulled up beside her Jeep and a well-dressed man stepped out. He wore a three-piece suit, of all things—a black vest, a jacket, and slacks. A pressed white shirt and red tie completed the ensemble. White hair lay slicked back from a prominent forehead, his skin the color of ivory. He smoothed his hair down and removed a pair of sunglasses, snapping them neatly into a case, which he placed back in the car. He was a big man, standing about six-four, with a burly build, but he moved daintily.

Shod in shiny dress shoes, he stopped to frown at the dusty path leading up to the cabin door.

Alex waited at the window, taking in his immaculate, expensive clothes.

He spotted her there and said, "Dr. Carter?"

"Yes."

"I'm Evander Milton."

Relief flooded through her. She placed the tranq rifle down on the table and unlocked the door. She stepped out. "Hello! Dr. Espinoza has mentioned you."

Milton raised his eyebrows, stopping about ten feet away from her. He didn't extend his hand. "Did he now?"

"Yes, he took me around the dig a little bit. Fascinating history behind it."

He narrowed his eyes, staring intently at her, frowning slightly. Then a small smile appeared. "It is, isn't it?"

The smile didn't reach his eyes and Alex's gut took a sour little turn. Something was off about the guy.

"What brings you all the way up here?" she asked him.

"I wanted to make you an offer." He crossed his arms over his chest. "It's a handsome one."

She waited expectantly, but he didn't continue. Instead, he stared around at the old cabin, then her Jeep.

"Yes?" she prompted.

"You know I own the property where the dig site is?"

She nodded.

"It's quite a spread. I'd like to purchase this piece of land, too." He peered at her. "Interested?"

"Well, I'm afraid I don't own this land. The land trust does."

"Oh, I know," he said impatiently. "I thought you could talk to them for me."

She pursed her lips. "I can certainly let them know you're interested, but I doubt they'd want to sell. This land was donated to them by the former owner, and they've put a conservation easement on it. It means it can never be developed."

He waved a dismissive hand. "Got no interest in developing it. Just want to buy it."

Alex wasn't sure what to say. "I can let my contact there know."

"That's it?"

"Excuse me?"

"That's all you can do?" Anger tinged his tone, and suddenly Alex just wanted to be rid of him.

"I don't hold any special sway or power with them, if that's what you're asking."

"That is what I'm asking."

"Sorry. All I can do is let them know. I could give you the regional director's number."

He stared down at her for a few long, awkward moments, arms still crossed. Then that faint smile returned. "Guess that's all I can ask for, then."

"Just a sec." She ducked inside the cabin, wanting to close and lock the door after herself, and found Ben's business card among her things. She copied the phone number onto a scrap of paper and returned.

"Here you go."

He leaned over and took the scrap from her hand gingerly. He was an odd duck, she thought. Big and ungainly, yet fastidious and fussy.

"Thanks, doc," he said, then pivoted on his heel and returned to his Range Rover. "Good luck with finding those jaguars," he told her. Apparently he'd discussed her with Espinoza.

"Thanks." She watched him drive down the steep dirt road, a beige dust cloud marking his progress, billowing in the wind.

When the last of the debris died down, Alex returned to the cabin. Ben had told her that Milton didn't raise cattle. Why would he need such a huge spread? Maybe just for the satisfaction of owning it? She frowned.

Casting aside the uncomfortable encounter, she grabbed her pack and started loading up for her outing that day. She packed more food, her water bottle and filter, two more remote cameras. Now that she had a better feel for the sanctuary and where any jaguars might be, she strapped the dart gun to the outside of the pack and also gathered up a handful of darts, vials of sedative, and its counteragent. Then she put a collar camera into the pack.

If she found a jaguar and was able to tranquilize it, then she'd affix the collar camera to it. She'd programmed it to record ten-second video clips that would be uploaded via satellite to the cloud, where she could download them. The collar would also record the animal's body temperature and location via GPS. It would allow her to not only track a jaguar's movements, but also see what it was eating and how much time it spent hunting and resting. She could also observe any obstacles it encountered, such as poachers or difficulties navigating border wall obstructions.

Normally she would have waited to take everything until she had confirmed the presence of an animal on a remote camera. The weight of the extra gear added a lot to her pack, but she didn't like the thought of actually encountering a jaguar and not being prepared. She might have only one shot to tranq one and affix the collar, and she didn't want to miss the opportunity.

Done packing, she hefted the weight onto her back and cinched down the straps. As she stepped outside and locked the door, she could already tell it was going to be another scorcher. She donned her trusty hat and set off.

As she broke from the trees around the cabin, the sun beat down on her. She thought of the task ahead, of all the unique traits that made jaguars so fascinating.

Unlike big cats like lions, who tended to be socially gregarious, jaguars were solitary. When jaguars met in the wild, they avoided fighting. Wounds could become infected, even life-threatening, and broken teeth and claws could lead to starvation. They hunted alone and sought out other company only to mate.

Female jaguars took care of the cubs alone. In the United States and Mexico, females typically had two cubs, and four in South America. Cubs weighed just two pounds at birth, sometimes even less. Their bright blue eyes turned gold as they grew older. Cubs tagged along with their mothers for at least a year and a half—sometimes as long as three years—learning how to hunt and navigate terrain. When they followed their mothers through thick vegetation, they kept track of the bouncing black tip of her tail. Mothers had to be vigilant, on the lookout for male jaguars, who, while not inclined to fight with other adults, were known to kill cubs to drive the female back into estrus in order to mate with her.

The eyesight of jaguars was incredibly good, far more sensitive than that of humans. Their eyes absorbed much more light, having more rods than cones, but this made them largely color blind. The reflective layer or tapetum lucidum (literally "bright carpet") at the backs of their eyes bounced light back, which was why their eyes glowed when hit with a source of light. The black markings around their eyes, just like the greasepaint on the faces of football players under bright stadium lights, cut down on the sun's glare. Some researchers believed that they used these same black markings to communicate with other cats by adjusting their facial movements.

She hiked out to the first remote camera she'd placed in the field. After unlocking its padlock, she swung it open and used its small screen to quickly scan through the photos. It had captured images of several mule deer, a covey of Gambel's quail, a family group of collared peccaries, a lone black bear, and even a mountain lion. This last photo had been taken at night, the mountain lion's eyes glowing in the image.

She swapped out the memory card with a fresh one and checked the battery level. Still good. She'd go over the images on the bigger screen of her laptop when she got back to the cabin, make sure she didn't miss anything.

She hiked on, wanting to place another camera in an area that her habitat suitability model had detected. She entered a small copse of Mexican piñon pines.

Movement to her right caught her eye. She paused, staring through the branches. A flash of brown and dark green clothing appeared through the trunks. Then someone emerged into a small clearing—a man, probably in his twenties, with his long blond hair pulled back in a ponytail and a beige face that betrayed a lot of time spent in the sun. He wore sunglasses, and an enormous duffel bag hung on his back, the handles strapped awkwardly around his shoulders. He labored under the weight of it. Sweating profusely, he staggered on, not seeing Alex where she stood in the neighboring copse of trees. She watched as he stopped in the clearing and hefted the prodigious sack off his shoulders. He unzipped it and pulled out a gallon-size jug of water and placed it on the ground.

Then another figure came into view, this time a woman, following behind, with a backpack so full she struggled under the weight. Her pale face, framed by blue and purple braids, was red with the effort of hiking. She paused and slung off her pack, pulled out a gallon of water, and set it beside the other one.

"Two more!" the man said, turning to smile at the woman. He lifted the duffel back on with considerable effort and she followed suit with her pack. They continued on, not spotting Alex in the trees. Alex had an instinctive sense about people, and she didn't feel like they were up to anything malicious.

"Hey," she called, stepping out from the trees.

They turned, spotting her now where she stood. "Hey there," the man called back, his brow crinkling in uncertainty.

She walked toward them. "What are you doing?"

He pointed to the jugs on the ground. "Placing out water. You know, for families who might be walking through here."

Alex nodded, understanding. Migrants.

He wiped his sweating brow. "It's thirsty country out here."

"It sure is."

The woman didn't seem too sure what to make of Alex, so she remained quiet, squinting at her in the bright sunlight.

Alex held out her hand, smiling. "Alex."

The man broke into a crooked grin and gripped her hand warmly. "Dave." He nodded toward the woman. "And this is River."

"Hey," the woman said a little shyly, but she shook Alex's hand, too.

Dave hefted the sack off his back with a relieved sigh. River did the same, exhaling with visible relief.

Dave eyed her judiciously. "I gotta say, when you called out to us, I thought we were busted. You're not gonna bust us, are you?"

She shook her head. "I think what you're doing is very compassionate."

He took off his sunglasses, revealing blue eyes and crinkled laugh lines. "Whew. Okay, cool. Some people don't have that same opinion around here."

"Tell me about it. I've met a few myself."

"Are you with the land trust?" River asked, tucking an errant braid of blue hair behind her ear.

"I am. I'm out here looking for jaguars." She regarded them with interest. "I don't suppose you've seen any?"

"Oh, man, I wish," Dave said with enthusiasm. "Seen 'em in the Pantanal. I spent a year teaching in Brazil. Loved it down there! They sure are beautiful cats." He gazed around. "You really think they're out here? Is it jungly enough for them?"

"They're actually pretty adaptable. Desert, pine forest, jungle."

He lifted his eyebrows. "Wow. I didn't know that."

"What will you do if you find them?" River asked.

"We're hoping to get more areas designated as critical habitat for them. There were two small areas in New Mexico that had been designated for them. But in 2021, a U.S. district judge ruled to remove those parcels, so now jaguars have no designated habitat in this state." She gestured toward their packs, now sprawled on the ground. "How many more jugs do you have?"

"Today? Between the two of us, fourteen gallons."

Alex did some quick calculations. At 8.3 pounds per gallon, that was more than 116 pounds. "Wow, that's a lot of weight!"

"Tell me about it," he agreed.

"Every time we put a gallon out, it's like a huge relief," River added. "We did sections of the Gila last week. We managed to put thirty jugs out there over the course of a few days." She rubbed at her lower back, stretching, obviously relishing the short break. Her skin was bright red and chafed where the shoulder straps had been.

"I did have a nice, comfortable backpack like hers," Dave

lamented, "but it was stolen out of my car. I've had to make do with this guy in a pinch," he said, gesturing at the duffel bag. "Found it in a thrift store in Azulejo. Not the most comfortable way to do it." Dave squinted into the bright sun. "The government sometimes puts out water, usually by the beacons. You seen those?"

Alex shook her head.

"Tall solar-powered towers," he explained. "If a migrant is in trouble, like sick or in danger because of a smuggler or dying of thirst, they can get help through these beacons. You press a button and they know exactly where you are. Sometimes there's water at the base of them. But you have to find the beacons first. We figured we'd help out a little." He lifted his hat, wiped again at the sweat on his brow. "I mean, can you imagine? You leave some violent war-torn place in South or Central America with your family, walk hundreds of miles north hoping to find somewhere you can live without your life being threatened all the time, only to die of thirst along the way? Awful."

Alex shook her head. She couldn't imagine. Families, children, and the elderly forced to leave their homes to survive, walking north, having to carry their belongings on their backs. It would take a hell of a lot of fortitude, determination, and stamina, that was for sure.

She didn't want to hold the pair up any more than she already had. "Well, good luck," she told them.

Dave gave a rueful grin. "Thanks, we'll need it. Between sun-stroke and avoiding anti-immigrant vigilantes, we've got our work cut out for us."

"It's a party," River answered.

Once again they hefted their heavy loads onto their shoulders. Dave gave a wave and set off with River beside him. Alex watched them go, then took off her hat and let cool air blow through her hair. She just hoped they wouldn't run into any of the men who had made threats at the dig site.

ELEVEN

Alex watched the pair until they were out of sight, moving down an embankment. She sighed. They were lucky to have each other.

Isolation was the one aspect of her work that Alex struggled with. She loved the wilderness, loved being alone in it, steeping in that quiet and solitude, the feeling of being just another animal out in a forest, part of a delicate ecosystem. She'd never felt the need to be super social, to go to a lot of parties, or to date numerous people. She'd never felt the urge to have a large circle of friends or hang out in bars or clubs.

She had her two good friends in her life—Zoe and her dad. She knew she could count on them for anything, that they were absolutely there for her and that they supported and encouraged her, even when they worried that she spent time in such remote places and had encountered her share of dangerous situations.

But sometimes, especially after Alex had been alone for days, the isolation got to her a little bit. She would have appreciated some like-minded companion who also loved the wilderness and wildlife to hike with, to share stories with of bear and wolf encounters, to share in the wonder of magical places like this.

And she had to admit, with no small degree of chagrin, that she missed romance and passion. Her last relationship hadn't ended well. She'd fallen in love with a fellow student named Brad Tilford when they were both grad students at UC Berkeley. He was studying law and was going to change the world, working for civil rights. She was studying wildlife biology and was going to save endangered species.

But as the years passed, his goals shifted. After graduation, he took a job with a corporate law firm in Boston. Alex moved there to be with him, away from the wild, doing environmental impact studies in urban environments. He'd pressured her to stop going out into the field altogether. They'd slowly fallen apart, their ideals becoming just too different, and she'd moved away from Boston and him to take the LTWC job on the remote wildlife sanctuary in Montana to search for wolverines, those elusive creatures that dwelled in the snowy mountains of the high alpine. Her spirit had soared at being out in the wilderness again, and she knew beyond a doubt that she'd made the right decision to leave, even though the breakup had been tough.

Since then she hadn't dated anyone, though she definitely felt like Ben Hathaway was a kindred spirit. And then there was Casey, the helicopter pilot she'd flown with out on the vast ice of Hudson Bay as they searched for polar bears. He'd been such a powerful ally out there on that cold terrain, a combat medic who had served with the UN peacekeeping forces. Her heart suddenly thumped and she took a deep breath. Casey. Enigmatic, unpredictable, mysterious Casey. She wondered where he was. She hadn't heard from him since she was stationed in Washington State, searching for mountain caribou. He'd told her then that there was something he had to do but had remained vague about what it was. A sudden nervous flutter moved through her stomach. He was different from anyone else she'd ever known, devoted to doing the right thing, even when the right thing was far from legal.

Did she want to see him again? Instantly her heart said yes. But her mind hesitated. There were parts of him, deep parts of him, that were troubled and possibly even broken. But she didn't think he would ever harm her. However, she also knew that very same courtesy did not apply to others. He could kill if pushed to the limit. But she knew now, after their harrowing ordeal out on the ice in Canada, that she could, too, if her life or the life of someone she cared about was threatened.

Zoe had encouraged her to start dating again. But it wasn't like her job made it easy to meet people. Most of the time she was alone, out walking transects in some remote corner of the wilderness. Zoe pushed her to set up an online dating profile, but Alex balked at that suggestion. She'd heard horror stories of having to wade through jerk after jerk. She had no interest in just hooking up with men randomly and casually. She longed for true, meaningful connection. Maybe she'd find it with someone she'd meet online. It was possible. So far she hadn't had time to set up a profile. Zoe had offered to do it for her, and maybe Alex would go for that eventually. But she admitted she dreaded the thought of having to message with who knew how many people before meeting anyone of substance. *If* she ever met someone of substance.

Shrugging off her feeling of loneliness, Alex approached a steep trail that led to the top of a plateau.

As she climbed, the cliff wall beside her streamed with little seeps, and delicate ferns and algae clustered in those areas, creating a lush green garden wall.

The seeping water meant that the trail sported patches of mud at times, and each time she crossed one, she stopped to look for tracks. At the fourth muddy section, her breath caught in her throat. A cat paw print. She bent down, studying it closer.

The toes were more spread apart than they would be on a mountain lion, and the print was much bigger, 4 inches long by 4.8 inches wide. She straightened up, breaking into a grin. This was a jaguar.

She'd found one. She snapped a series of photos using her measuring tool as a reference.

Excitedly she continued to climb, her pack suddenly feeling much lighter, her spirits lifted. The narrow trail wound steeply up the side of the mesa. A few times drop-offs of more than a hundred feet plunged away on her right, and she tread carefully and slowly past these sections.

As she neared the top of the mesa, small lone trees extruded from the crevices in the rocks, their roots exposed. From the branches of one, she heard the familiar gurgling, throaty talk of a raven.

Shielding her eyes against the sun, she peered up, spotting the black bird in the tree above her.

"Hello there," she said.

The raven clacked its beak and gurgled again.

Rosetta Stone really does need to get cracking on a raven language edition, she thought, remembering an earlier discussion with her dad.

The raven cocked its head, regarding her with interest.

"Having a good day?" she asked it.

It clacked its beak again.

She resumed her climb and at last reached the top of the mesa. She gazed across a lush little oasis. Piñon and juniper clustered around her. Springs had created little rivulets of water where bright orange globemallow, purple aster, and golden monkeyflower grew. No wonder the jaguar made the treacherous climb up here. It was the wettest area she'd encountered yet on the preserve. This section was higher elevation, just the kind of habitat her model had predicted the jaguar might like. She punched a victorious fist in the air. The preserve *was* being used by a jaguar. Now she just had to figure out where it was crossing onto the preserve and if it was leaving it, and they could improve the habitat there, talk to the neighboring landowners about doing the same. Hopefully they would be amenable.

Unable to stop grinning, she walked along one of the rivulets, finding more jaguar tracks. Slinging off her pack, she dug out one of the remote cameras and found an ideal pair of trees beside a small pool of water. She strapped the camera to it and put in batteries and a memory card, then attached the hair snare to the opposite tree and spritzed it with cologne.

Feeling lighthearted, she took a few test photos to ensure the camera was working, dancing around by the pool of water. She checked the little screen inside the camera, laughing at the photos of her striking a classic *Saturday Night Fever* disco pose. She erased the images, closed the camera, and secured the housing with a padlock.

Then she hefted her pack back onto her shoulders and walked a circuit of the plateau, searching for more tracks and other jaguar spoor. If she found some scat, she could bag it and send it to the lab tech who volunteered for the LTWC. From the sample, they could determine what the jaguar had been eating and if it had been exposed to any environmental pollutants, like persistent organic pollutants, or POPs, such as DDT, which were released into the environment by a variety of human activities, including agriculture, pesticides, manufacturing, and industrial processes.

In an apex predator such as a jaguar, these pollutants became very concentrated as they worked their way up the food chain in a process called biomagnification.

In addition, heavy metals such as mercury and lead entered the environment through the burning of fossil fuels, cement production, and smelting. The biggest cause of this kind of pollution was coal-fired power plants.

When she reached the far end of the plateau, she peered down another near-vertical cliff to the valley floor far, far below. She squinted into the distance, the sunlight bright even with her sunglasses on. Distant mountains shimmered with heat. Dirt roads crisscrossed the area below.

As she stared down the steep drop-off, something caught her eye. A black opening, not too far below the lip of the mesa. A lone tree stood beside her, clinging to the rock and soil at the very edge of the falloff. She tested it for her weight by pushing on it. It held.

She gripped the trunk and leaned out a little to get a better look at the opening below.

A cave. Curiosity bloomed inside her. She wondered if it had been occupied by humans in antiquity or visited by anyone recently. Maybe wildlife used it as a shelter, if wildlife could get down to it. Certainly birds could reach it. Maybe even condors, who were finally working their way back into New Mexico. Another tree clung precariously to the cliff beside the opening, a small, scraggly piñon pine.

She made a mental note to explore the cave later. She had her climbing ropes with her, strapped to the outside of her pack.

For now she continued her circuit of the plateau, looking for more jaguar spoor, heading back toward the trail she'd taken up.

When she reached the head of the trail, she paused and lifted her hat off her head. A welcome breeze drifted over her, cooling her instantly. She fanned herself with the brim, staring out at the vast valleys below, the tiny little circles of green that marked irrigated farms, the wide dun-colored plains crisscrossed with tiny dirt roads.

She squinted, pondering the scene. It seemed like suddenly she couldn't see as far out as she had on the other side of the mesa. At first she thought a layer of haze hung in the air, obscuring the more distant mountains. But as she watched, the haze moved toward her, becoming taller and more opaque. While at first it had appeared tan and diffuse, now it grew more solid, darker browns and reds.

A sandstorm, she realized, and moving fast. The wind hit her a moment later, a sudden gust that threatened to rip the hat right out of her hand. She held on to it, then cinched it down onto her head.

The air blew hot, whispering through the pines around her. The sandstorm obscured the distance faster than she thought possible, and she watched with surprise as it quickly reached the bottom of the mesa. Now all Alex could see down there was a vague wall of brown steadily climbing upward.

Her hat almost blew off again, so she stowed it in the side pocket of her pack. Weighing her options, she hesitated. There was no way she could take that treacherously steep trail back down in a sand-storm. Right now she was high up on the plateau, very exposed, with just the trees, which could offer little protection. She heard a hissing noise, then a roaring as the sandstorm hit the windward side of the mountain.

She felt the first few grains strike her skin, carried ahead of the main storm. She watched as a wall of sand rose up over the edge of the mesa, sweeping toward her, blocking out the sun. The light around her dimmed. Looking for shelter, she braced herself, stunned at the sheer speed the storm traveled. She took off toward the trees at the center of the plateau, not sure what to do.

Then her mind flew to the cave she'd seen. She shrugged off her pack, quickly untying the rope fastened to the side of it. Hefting her pack onto one shoulder, she raced for the cliff edge and the lone tree that stood there. She wove between trees and shrubs, sensing the storm at her back, not sure if she could outrun the wall of sand.

Her pack slapped at her back, but she didn't want to pause to sling it over both shoulders. She ran on, feeling biting sand needling the back of her neck. As she ran, a painful stitch developed in her side, and she gasped for a decent breath. Finally she reached the cliff edge and eyed the lone tree.

Years of erosion had worn away some of its roots on the steep side, and she hoped it would hold her full weight. She'd only leaned on it before. Quickly she tied the rope around the base of the tree. The full blast of the sandstorm hit the top of the mesa now, roaring toward her, the hissing of sand like something alive. Tiny particles struck her bare neck and arms, growing more and more intense, sandblasting her.

She tasted grit in her mouth, crunching against her teeth, and pulled a bandanna from her back pocket. She cinched it around her nose and mouth, then continued to struggle against the wind to affix the rope. Sand lashed at her exposed arms and hands, debris scraping her fingers as they worked. She almost had it tied. The sunlight plummeted, the world taking on an eerie red glow around her as the sandstorm roared over the top of the plateau like a grim rising specter with its arms spread wide.

She tried to stare up, to see the path of the storm, but sand rattled against her sunglasses. She felt the sting of particles entering her eyes. No time to attach a climbing harness. She wrapped the rope around her waist and swung herself over the edge of the cliff.

TWELVE

Alex braced her boots against the rocks and loose soil, lowering herself as quickly as she dared. She felt the full force of the storm reach her side of the mesa, sand hissing around her, raining down her neck, pelting her bare head. She spotted the cave below and swung into it, feet landing on the soft dirt inside. She wobbled at the lip, almost falling back out before she managed to grab a jutting rock at the cave's mouth. She steadied herself, then scrambled completely inside.

Spinning around, she stared out as the wave of sand poured down the cliff above and below her like a waterfall of stinging pellets.

She shook out her hair, finding it caked and grimy with dirt. Her eyes stung and teared, grains of sand lodged there. Groping around half-blind, she managed to find her water bottle in her pack and poured some of the contents into her eyes, washing them out. She stood and blinked, listening to the roar of the storm, like a hissing snake outside the cave.

A cool wind blew from the dank interior of the place, and she reveled in the relief from the heat, despite the circumstances that had brought her to seek shelter here.

The storm roared on and on, and Alex stood at the mouth of the cave, stunned at the size of the onslaught. Extreme drought had caused the land to dry out to a dangerous extent. One good wind moving through the area was now able to pick up an enormous bar-rage of sand and dirt and move it for miles.

She took a long pull on her water bottle, grateful for the shelter, and watched in wonder as the storm played out around her. Finally the roar turned to a susurration and then to a distant whisper. She watched the sinuous wave of tan and brown lose momentum on the lee side of the mesa, sweeping down into the valley before petering out completely.

She wondered if it had caught the archaeological team un-awares. They would have been hit by it first. It had certainly come out of nowhere for her. She hoped they were okay.

Now that the threat of the storm had passed, Alex brushed most of the loose sand from her arms and neck and turned toward the back of the cave. Deep black met her gaze. She pulled out her headlamp from her pack and switched it on, the beam piercing the inky dark. To her surprise, the cave ran deeper than she expected. A sloping floor led down around a bend, and she stepped forward. As she rounded the turn, she found another bend, the circle of light illuminating gray rock as she progressed. This final corner revealed the end of the cave, a large room that smelled of old earth and stone.

As she played the beam over the ceiling and far wall, Alex gasped.

Decorating the cave wall before her was a nearly intact ancient painting of a jaguar. The rosettes on its spotted coat still showed vividly, its long claws poised, ready to strike, its teeth bared. She walked in awe toward it, studying the brilliant pigments. In a few places, a seep had streamed down over the painting from above, streaking through parts of the tail. One foot was missing, the victim of a slab of rock sloughing off. Alex cast her light over the floor of the cave, finding the errant stone lying there, the jaguar's detached foot bright in the beam.

She almost pulled out her phone to snap a few photos, then

instantly thought better of it. The flash could damage the art. Instead, she took a few images without the flash. They turned out dim, but readable. She had to show this to Espinoza. She wondered how old the painting was. Hundreds of years? Older?

She turned in a circle, taking in the cave. Aside from a few fallen rocks, nothing else cluttered the floor. No errant cigarette butts or beer cans. No modern graffiti covered the walls. She wondered how many people knew this cave was up here. It wasn't in plain sight and certainly wasn't easy to get into. Most caves like this would have played host to various teenage parties over the years, but this one looked untouched. The jaguar was lucky.

Returning to the mouth of the cave, she took a GPS reading, sticking her arm out under the open sky to get a good signal. Then she pocketed the unit and stowed her water bottle. Staring out, she confirmed that the sandstorm had completely died down. Time for her to head back up. She still had a long hike back to her cabin that afternoon.

She slung on her pack and then tested her weight on the rope. It held. She hoped it would continue to hold as she scrambled back up. Now, though, she took the time to step into her climbing harness and secure herself more firmly.

Giving a nod toward the ancient jaguar painting, she whispered, "I hope I find some of your kin." Then she swung out from the cave opening and started to climb.

Alex reached the top of the mesa and untied the rope, thanking the tree profusely for saving her bacon. After stowing away the climbing rope, she checked that her remote camera hadn't been damaged in the sandstorm. Luckily, the lens had been facing away from the cloud of dirt, and sand hadn't forced its way inside the housing.

She returned to the top of the trail on the far side of the mesa and started down. The air had cooled a little and Alex made fast progress down the steep path. Along the way, she enjoyed the greenery around the seeps. About halfway down, she spotted another narrower path leading off in a direction she hadn't yet explored.

She checked her watch. It was late afternoon, but she still had time to do a little more hiking before she needed to head back to beat the darkness.

Taking the new branch, she headed down, finding this path even steeper. At the bottom of the mesa, a small game trail meandered off to the north, and she took it. She passed into a section of woodlands, piñon pine and juniper trees offering more welcome shade.

When she was almost at the edge of the wooded section, the sound of distant mooing made her stop. Cattle.

She wondered if she'd accidentally crossed off the preserve and was on private or national forest land. She hadn't seen any property markers, but that wasn't surprising along vast tracts of land like this.

At the edge of the woods, she spotted a fence, and farther along that fence, two people working. Both wore cowboy hats and denim shirts with jeans. One was a woman with a long silver braid down her back, the other a man with short white hair, the back of his neck burned. The woman worked a posthole digger while the man drove home large fence posts.

As Alex stepped from the cover of the trees, the woman turned, spotting her. To Alex's surprise, the woman broke into a large grin. She elbowed the man's arm and pointed at Alex. The man took off his hat, fanned his face, and peered at Alex. Then he, too, smiled.

The woman waved her over. "Hello!"

Alex stepped out. The section of fence in front of her looked brand new and hadn't been strung with wire yet, so Alex stepped through it. "Hello!" she called back.

The woman eyed her. "Are you the biologist with the land trust?"

"Yes," Alex called back.

The couple stepped forward, both extending their hands.

"I'm June Claymore," the woman said. Then she nodded at the

man. "This is my husband, George Fremont." She shook Alex's hand and then made a sweeping gesture at the land around them. "We're the owners of the Sweetwater Ranch that you see before you."

"Nice to meet you," Alex told her, then shook George's hand, too. She remembered Ben mentioning the ranch, that they'd been mitigating damage to the environment.

He fanned his face more with his hat. "We heard you were up there. Are you really hoping to tag a jaguar?"

Word sure got around out here. "I am. If we can figure out what route they're taking, we can improve that habitat. Even better if we can collar one with GPS, figure out where they're crossing the border. Then we could lobby for that section to have a virtual wall monitored with surveillance and motion sensors, rather than a physical barrier." She suddenly felt self-conscious, realizing that this was probably more than they were asking about.

"Sounds like you have your work cut out for you," June commented.

Alex eyed them hopefully. "Have you ever seen one here?"

George shook his head. "Nope. Not a one. But ever since we heard that those two mountain lion hunters spotted some over in Arizona in the nineties, we've been hoping they're out here."

"Wouldn't it be amazing to see one?" June put in.

Alex was surprised by their positive attitudes. She knew that ranchers were often in conflict with carnivores and that many viewed predators as mere vermin, threats to be eliminated.

"We've been thinking of putting out remote cameras just like Jack Childs did. You know about that? The Borderlands Jaguar Detection Project?"

Alex nodded. "I do."

"There's a whole jaguar craze there now."

Alex broke into a relieved smile. "I know. It's great!"

"So we really want to see one now," George finished. "Think they're really here?"

Alex took off her hat, letting the cool wind carry away some heat. She wanted to be sure they were truly jaguar-friendly and wasn't sure if she should let them know she'd spotted tracks. "I don't see why not. They're very adaptable."

"We talked to Ben Hathaway about it last year," June told her. "Do you know him?"

Alex grinned. "Of course! He mentioned your ranch to me."

"He came down to talk to us," June continued. "Wanted to know how we felt about a jaguar moving through our land, thought we might be concerned about predation on our herd."

George nodded. "We really dug into the whole topic after that. We don't want to have to kill native wildlife if we can help it. So we came up with a bunch of ways to protect both the herd and the jaguar."

June gestured at the fence. "Like this barrier to the woods. Jaguars prefer the trees, so if we can keep the cattle out of them, there is less chance of an encounter."

"We ended up implementing a lot of other nonlethal methods, too. Like we do all our calving near our main buildings where there's more human activity," George told her.

June nodded. "And we use guardian animals. We've got some llamas out there with our herd, as well as a few dogs."

George rested one hand on a fence post. "And we've made efforts to restore habitat for predators' natural prey, like deer and javelinas."

This was smart. Alex knew that one threat to the jaguar was the reduction of its available natural prey. As humans overhunted animals such as javelinas and deer, jaguars had less to eat. And when farming or ranching replaced natural habitat, prey animals tended to move on to more biodiverse locations, again leaving predators with reduced food sources.

June shucked off one of her gloves and rubbed her hand. "Our next step is to put out some motion-detector noisemakers and lights. Ben suggested we put out some guzzlers, too, for local wild-life."

Alex was familiar with the term, specially designed bins in-stalled in the ground and filled with water, with wildlife-friendly ramps leading down into them. That way, if a deer or other animal fell into the water source, it could easily climb back out.

"We've got four now at various places around the ranch," George went on. "They refill with rainwater and snowmelt, and a little help from us."

Alex regarded them with gratitude. "This is all wonderful! I'm so happy to hear it. These are great actions toward cohabitating with wildlife."

George nodded. "We agree, and we have talked to our friends about it. Some are taking steps."

But June shook her head, putting one hand on her hip. "Others are too stubborn or just don't care. The old adage 'The only good predator is a dead predator' is still pretty prevalent."

Alex had also heard the phrase "Shoot, shovel, and shut up," for when ranchers killed endangered wildlife. Cattle grazing leases were dispensed by the Bureau of Land Management or the U.S. For-est Service, for which ranchers were charged a fee. The leases were renewable, and the government could restrict or regulate access if it found that the grazing allotment was in an endangered species' critical habitat. So there was a lot of pushback.

"Like our neighbor over there," June went on, gesturing to the west. "He grazes his cattle in the Gila National Forest. He's in deep with this Wildlife Services guy. I don't know how many wolves, coy-otes, bears, and mountain lions they've killed over the years, but it's a lot."

George frowned. "You might meet the Wildlife Services guy while you're out here. Name's Roger Trager. Talk about a guy who loves his work for all the wrong reasons."

June harrumphed. "The man is just damn rude on top of everything else. You know he once explained to me how to ranch? My family's been doing it for generations. He's never been a rancher in his life." She shook her head. "We've heard he can be hired out on a freelance basis to kill pretty much anything you want, even if it's not exactly legal." She frowned. "We don't know much about that Milton guy who bought the land to the south of here. Do you know anything about him? Like if he's planning to graze that land?"

Alex furrowed her brow. "I don't think so. I'm not sure what he does for a living, but he does fund archaeological digs."

June nodded. "We heard about that. Digging for treasure, no less. Can't wait to hear what they find."

Alex shared her enthusiasm.

"Hey," June said, her face lighting up. "Do you want to place a few remote cameras at our guzzlers? I'll bet if a jaguar is in the area, he's getting drinks there at night."

Alex grinned. "I'd love to! Thank you!"

"We have to run into town tomorrow, but why don't you come down to our spread the day after that? I can give you a map that shows the locations of all the guzzlers," June offered.

"That's a real help. I appreciate it."

"Say eight P.M.? Then we'll cook you up a proper dinner!" she went on. "George makes some mean black bean, corn, and beef fajitas."

Alex winced. It was always awkward for her when someone was kind enough to offer to cook her dinner but didn't know she was a vegetarian. She decided to just be up front about it. "I'd really appreciate that! But . . . umm . . . I actually don't eat meat. Can I have mine without the beef?"

June laughed. "Of course. Our own son is a vegetarian. Can you believe it? George here has figured out a ton of ways to cook up beans for him."

"Where is your son now?" Alex asked, wondering if he helped them with the ranch.

"He's in grad school at the University of New Mexico."

"Botany," George noted, not without a little chagrin, Alex noticed.

"But it's what he loves," June added, placing a gentle hand on her husband's back.

Alex adjusted the weight of her backpack on her shoulders. "Well, I'll let you get back to it. I look forward to seeing you again."

"You too," they said in unison.

They exchanged phone numbers and then Alex waved and turned back to the forest.

As Alex walked away, she felt conflicted. While she very much appreciated the couple's efforts, cattle ranching was extremely detrimental to the environment and wildlife. Currently, almost a third of the land on the planet was being used to raise livestock. Forests were clear-cut to make way for cattle, including vital Brazilian rainforests. In the United States, the beef industry took up significant cropland. Cattle caused erosion and damaged soil, stream banks, and fragile wildlife habitat. When they belched, methane escaped into the atmosphere, a greenhouse gas many times more potent than carbon dioxide.

So-called predator control programs caused the deaths of tens of thousands of native animals each year, driving species like the Mexican gray wolf to near extinction. And while many Americans loved to watch wildlife and ecotourism was at an all-time high, the livestock industry threatened the very animals those Americans longed to see, including wolves and grizzly bears. The industry also sought to block legislation that would reintroduce these animals into some of their historical ranges.

On top of that, miles and miles of fencing negatively impacted migrating wildlife, proving fatal to species who collided with it, such as the sage grouse.

But at the same time, Alex knew that the cattle industry was here to stay, and that anything ranchers could do to mitigate the damage was extremely important, so she very much appreciated the couple's efforts.

She hiked back to the cabin, still brushing sand from her clothing and hair. At the outside shower, she reveled in the warm water that had heated under the day's intense sun. When she finally got all the grit and sand out, the sun had set and a chill descended. She hurried inside and cranked up the propane heater.

After preparing a quick dinner of corkscrew pasta with pine nuts and marinara sauce, she sat down with it at the little table. She wanted to read more about the history of the jaguar. What the ranching couple had told her had intrigued her.

She called up more of the academic papers she'd downloaded while she was still in L.A. and dove in while eating her dinner.

Though they have been known to climb trees and swim into water to catch prey, jaguars most often killed by ambush. They crouched, waiting, and when they spotted prey, they crept forward, inching ever closer. Then they sprang, pouncing on their prey. Their bite was the strongest of all the big cats, owing to a powerful jawbone with fewer teeth, which allowed room for more muscles. Unlike other cats, they didn't suffocate their prey by clamping down on the throat. Instead, they bit down into the skull, piercing it. Rough protuberances on their tongues then allowed them to strip flesh off carcasses.

The scientific name for jaguar, *Panthera onca,* translated as "the sharp-clawed predator of all prey." And that name fit perfectly, as Alex knew that researchers had found more than a hundred different species in their scat.

This wide variety of prey ranged from larger animals like deer, peccaries, and tapirs, to smaller mammals like raccoons and armadillos, reptiles like snakes and lizards, and even fish and insects. They hunted from dusk to dawn, preferring the dark hours of night, as their coloration helped them blend in with shadowed vegetation.

Like most big cats, a jaguar could move prey larger than itself, and jaguars often used this strength to drag their prey off to a concealed location to consume it. But they didn't usually bury their kills like mountain lions did.

She turned her attention to two of the jaguars whose Arizona sightings had gone viral.

The same jaguar that Jack Childs had photographed in 1996, Macho B, had continued to visit Arizona until 2009. Remote cameras captured his image a few times. Unfortunately, he had passed away in 2009 due to complications from being tranquilized and tagged by wildlife officials. His death resulted in a flurry of action on behalf of jaguars. Federal funds paid for a four-year study through the University of Arizona, exploring ranges in both Arizona and New Mexico. However, when only one jaguar was discovered in this survey, a male named El Jefe, USFWS decided to greenlight a disastrous copper pit mine in the jaguars' sensitive habitat of the Santa Rita Mountains. Researchers found this unfortunate, as there were very likely more jaguars out there than just the one captured on camera.

El Jefe was caught on a remote camera in 2015. To get to Arizona from his likely original home in Mexico, 125 miles to the south, El Jefe braved considerable threats. He had to cross roads, farmland, ranches, and housing developments, all while avoiding poachers. He was an instant hit, with videos of him viewed millions of times. He was celebrated with a mural in Tucson and even had a beer named after him. He was still moving between the U.S. and Mexico to this day.

Alex finished her dinner, her eyes growing tired. She washed her plate and fork and turned off the propane heater, knowing it was dangerous to leave it running while she slept. Then she crept into her warm mummy bag. She'd intended to read a mystery novel she'd picked up at LAX, but the air grew so cold in the cabin that she couldn't bear to stick her arms out of her sleeping bag. With her arms still tucked in, she tried to read awkwardly on her side using her headlamp but finally had to give it up.

She lay in the darkness, hearing the owls again. At first she didn't think she'd be able to sleep, given what she'd read about the plight of jaguars, wondering how many had been poached over the years since they'd been listed under the Endangered Species Act.

But organizations like the Northern Jaguar Project gave her hope. A nonprofit out of Tucson, they operated a series of remote cameras along the border of Arizona and Mexico. They had purchased a large ten-thousand-acre ranch to set up a preserve in Mexico. They prohibited hunting and removed the cattle from it. These two steps allowed the prey base of the jaguar to rebuild itself and enabled vegetation decimated by overgrazing to revive. Wanting to go a step further, they founded Viviendo con Felinos (Living with Cats), which reached out to neighboring ranchers about how to live peaceably with the big cats. Numerous ranchers joined in, banning hunting on their land. Then Viviendo con Felinos asked these ranchers if they would place remote cameras on their properties, and paid the landowners for every photo taken of jaguars, bobcats, mountain lions, and ocelots. The prey species rebounded, and so did the jaguars in Mexico. Although ranchers were paid for any livestock taken by a predator, the amount they were paid for photos was more lucrative.

Alex rolled onto her back, her mind then churning over the sandstorm and the amazing painting she'd discovered. The next time she visited the dig site, she looked forward to letting Espinoza know about it. Then her thoughts drifted to Ben, wondering how he was, if he'd had a good flight back. And finally her mind wandered to enigmatic Casey, wondering if she'd get a postcard from him. She hadn't had a chance yet to change her mailing address and forward all her mail from Zoe's place to here. Not with all the chaos that had roiled through town.

But she'd told Zoe all about Casey and knew that the next time she chatted with her old friend, Zoe would let her know if anything had arrived from him. She wondered where he was, if he was out there somewhere, facing the odds, trying to right some wrong. Her heart rate kicked up a little and she grew more awake. Obviously thinking about him was not going to be conducive for sleep.

So instead she closed her eyes, but still sleep did not come. Her mind churned over the presence of the jaguar and the attack at the dig site.

THIRTEEN

The next day, Alex awoke, relieved that she'd finally been able to doze off in the wee hours of the night and get some rest. Today she wanted to check several cameras that lay a considerable distance apart, so she set off early, just as the sun was peeking above the distant mountains. She crossed the Mesquite River, the glow of the yellow early morning light turning the waters into a sparkling gold as they reflected the sky.

She knew that natural corridors like this river course were vital to the survival of not only jaguars but also many other species. Such corridors would allow for much-needed genetic diversity, and Alex would love it if better corridors could be established for the borderland jaguars. These migrating jaguars were of vital importance. The fact that they ventured to the north, breaking away from the nearest stable jaguar population in Sonora, meant that they might in fact carry valuable genetic traits, making them highly adaptable and therefore of particular importance to the survival of the species.

Researchers like Alex believed that these jaguars were pushing north again, in part out of a response to climate change. As the earth warmed, the southwest United States grew hotter, its vegetation and climate more similar to that of Mexico.

She stopped at one of her cameras, reviewing its photos on the small internal screen. It had captured images of another group of peccaries, a wide-eyed ringtail with its signature white mask, and a desert cottontail. Then she grinned; the camera had picked up a video of a foraging white-nosed coati, a diurnal relative of the raccoon that ate insects, worms, fruits, berries, and tubers. This one had a handsome masked face and a long tail. But the rest of the photos yielded no jaguars. Just to be safe, though, she swapped out the memory cards so she could review the photos on the bigger screen of her laptop back at the cabin.

Alex hiked along the shadowed side of a large rock outcropping, relishing the breeze and the break from the heat. She stopped, leaning against the cool stone, and took a long drink from her water bottle. The sound of trickling water drew her attention, and she followed it to a little seep in the rock. Water streamed from a crevice, creating a magical island of life around it: delicate stems of Fendler's false cloak fern, maidenhair fern, and emerald moss.

Then the sound of crunching gravel brought her gaze up, and moments later, a tentative mule deer doe stepped around the corner, startled to see her there.

Alex stood absolutely still, and the deer stared at her. Then Alex backed up, giving the doe room. After a long, tentative moment, it stepped forward and drank from the seep. Alex loved how areas like this, spaces that at first glance would seem to have less life than a wet area in the mountains, still teemed with all manner of activity: deer, javelinas, scorpions, songbirds, kangaroo rats, and hopefully even jaguars. She smiled as she watched the doe finish her drink and then step gingerly away to graze on an alderleaf mountain mahogany shrub.

Alex had just resumed her progress when the beating sound of a helicopter's rotors drew her attention to the west. She spotted the chopper moving quickly over the terrain, keeping low. It stopped and hovered, then turned back in the direction it had come from. But moments later it returned, hovering, darting, wheeling. It looked like it was chasing something. She got out her binoculars, but the craft was too far away for her to make out any kind of markings, only that it was dark green. She didn't know if it was private or a government helo, cops chasing a fugitive or maybe border patrol.

She had just turned back to her camera when a rapid succession of loud reports rent the quiet afternoon. She started, then focused her binoculars on the helicopter again. It was closer now, skimming over some trees. Its sliding door had been slung open, and now she could see a man hanging there in the opening, leaning out, rifle at his shoulder. Two more shots rang out.

What the hell? Alex adjusted the focus wheel on her binocs, trying to make out any markings on the bird that would identify the agency. But she didn't see any, only a registration number painted in black on the tail: N5643Z.

The helicopter wheeled in the sky and then took off at a faster clip, the man still leaning out of the open doorway. More rifle shots cracked, the sound reverberating off the rock formations around her.

What the hell are they shooting at? Alex wondered. She couldn't tell from this distance if they were over private land, the preserve, or the national forest.

Then the helicopter dipped, coming in her direction, fast. The rotor chop grew in intensity, startling the deer that had been grazing nearby. It took off with a bound, black-tipped tail flicking high in the air, leaping through the low bushes and disappearing over a rise.

The helo sped in Alex's direction, moving lower and lower. She ducked out of sight into the thick branches of juniper trees, her heart suddenly fluttering, not knowing what their intentions were.

The helicopter raced overhead, so low that the rotor wash tossed the tree canopy and kicked up a massive cloud of dust that spiraled around Alex. The helo shot by, and Alex's heart jumped into her throat when the sudden pounding of paws beside her made her whirl around. She pivoted, seeing a mountain lion race by, panicked, dodging and weaving in the bushes.

Who the hell are these guys? Poachers? They certainly weren't your average run-of-the-mill subsistence hunters, not with a helicopter like that. She knew that U.S. government agents often culled wolves and mountain lions from helicopters. But she had no idea if this was the case now.

The helicopter spun its tail around and hovered, the man leaning out to take aim at the cougar, despite being over the preserve. Before she'd thought it out, she instinctively raced out into a clearing beneath the chopper and waved her arms, drawing the gunman's attention.

"This is protected land!" she shouted, though with the hard beating of the rotors, she knew there was no way he could hear her. The gunman raised his rifle barrel up into the air, away from the cougar, but the chopper didn't move away. She saw him saying something to the pilot over his headset. She could see a little of the pilot—just his profile, long greasy blond hair, and a bright orange T-shirt. Then the gunman turned back to her, waving at her to get out of the way. He pointed a finger at the mountain lion, which had briefly stopped in the shadow of the rock outcrop, its chest heaving. The man took aim again. Alex ran in that direction, waving her arms and shouting, "No! This area is a sanctuary!"

Once again the man lifted the rifle barrel away from her and the cougar, glaring down at her. Dirt spiraled in the air, momentarily blocking her view of him, and for a few heart-stopping moments she braced herself for the impact of a round. But none came. The dust cleared for a split second, whipping in torrents in the dry air, and she heard the helicopter moving off. Wiping dirt from her face, trying to get a clear view, she saw it heading off toward the national forest. The mountain lion sprinted in the opposite direction.

As the dust settled, she saw the helicopter in the distance, hovering over what she estimated was the border of the preserve. She watched the helo descend, dropping out of sight beyond a ridge of rocks. Moments later, the sound of the rotors wound down. They'd landed and shut off the motor, probably only a couple miles away from her.

She turned, trying to spot the mountain lion again, but it was well away. She waited for five minutes and then ten, listening, but didn't hear the chopper again. Maybe their crossing onto the preserve had been an honest mistake, and once they realized it, they'd called off the hunt.

She jotted down the helo's call number in her field notebook. She'd definitely report the incident the next time she was in town.

She resumed her trek, all the while keeping her eyes glued to the ground for any sign of a jaguar print or other spoor. But her mind kept pulling her back to the harrowing encounter, wondering if they were poachers and would kill not only the mountain lion, but any jaguars they spotted, too. Hunting had already taken a devasting toll on the jaguar population.

She hoped that whoever the men were in the helicopter, they wouldn't poach the jaguar.

After she'd visited another camera and checked its hair snare, she stopped to gaze out.

In the distance, dark storm clouds gathered, gray and flat, hovering over the desert terrain. She came to a dry creek bed and crossed it quickly, knowing that a deluge of rain from a storm miles away could fill the gulley with a torrent of dangerous water. But it remained dry.

As she stepped into the cool shade of a stand of piñon pine, she took off her hat, allowing the breeze to lift her hair. Then suddenly the unmistakable feeling of being watched descended over her. Her first thought was of the mountain lion. She scanned the trees and the nearby rock outcroppings but didn't see it—not that she expected to. If it was there, watching her warily, it would be a master of stealth.

Alex's uneasiness intensified and her gut tugged at her. Over the years, she'd learned to trust this gut response.

More than once in her life someone had given her a bad feeling, even if they gave her no specific reason to make her ill at ease. Then later she'd learn that they'd committed some vile act. When she was an undergrad, an economics major had asked her out. He was friendly, funny, easygoing. Everyone liked him. He had irresistible charisma and a host of friends. But for some unknown reason, she had a bad feeling about him and didn't want to be alone with him. She'd turned down the date. A month later she learned he'd tried to attack a woman at her dorm while they were on a date. Thankfully the woman had gotten away and reported him.

Alex trusted her disquiet and moved deeper into the shelter of the trees. The feeling abated a little bit.

She thought of the men in the helicopter and wondered where they were. She hadn't heard or seen the helicopter take off again.

Then suddenly a bullet whizzed by her head, striking a tree trunk behind her. She dropped, taking cover behind a cluster of New Mexico locust shrubs. She glanced up, seeing a hole in the tree bark where the bullet was embedded. It had come from the north.

Crouching, she pivoted on her heels, then stood up and took off at a sprint, racing to the cover of a large rock outcropping to the south. She ran a zigzag course, waiting for another crack of a rifle, but none came. She reached the safety of the rocks and rounded the outcropping, pressing her back against the warm rhyolite.

Her heart thumped painfully in her chest. She could hear footsteps now, crunching on the small rocks close to where she'd been before. She continued to work her way around the outcropping, keeping the massive stones between her and the shooter. She wove between locust bushes, trying to keep to patches of soft sand lest the rocks crunch beneath her boots, too.

Another shot cracked through the silence, all birdsong around her stopping. Splinters of rock flew off the stone beside her, and she realized he'd flanked her.

Ducking down, she tried to determine his current position, but the chipped rock surface didn't offer any clues. Her throat went dry, her desire just to bolt in a random direction becoming almost too much to bear.

Then a man stepped out from the trees to the east, the gunman from the helicopter. "Hey there," he called, walking closer. He shouldered his rifle. "You shouldn't creep around like that. Thought you were a mountain lion. Could have gotten yourself killed."

Alex stood up, glaring at him. With her purple tank top and black hiking pants, she could hardly have been mistaken for a mountain lion. "What the hell are you doing?" she yelled back.

"Like I said, looking for that mountain lion. It's gotten too close to the national forest where a herd is grazing."

"This isn't the national forest," she told him angrily. "It's the Mogollon Wildlife Sanctuary, and you can't kill anything on it."

"Just doing my job, ma'am," he responded, a smug smirk on his face.

"And what *is* your job?"

"Wildlife Services."

Alex clenched her jaw. This must be the guy, Roger Trager, that June and George had told her about. She was all too familiar with Wildlife Services. It was a branch of the United States Department of Agriculture responsible for killing a staggering amount of native wildlife. She'd looked at their statistics for a recent year, and saw with horror that they'd killed 421 black bears, 324 gray wolves, nearly 600 bobcats, more than 64,000 coyotes, and a devastating number of animals of other species, including more than 9,000 white-tailed deer, over 1,800 yellow-bellied marmots, more than 9,000 black-tailed prairie dogs, and over 19,000 mourning doves, as well as representatives of other species, for a whopping total of over 403,000 native animals in just that year alone.

And she remembered June and George saying that Trager

hired himself out on a freelance basis to anyone wanting to get rid of an animal, even if it wasn't entirely legal. "You should know you can't kill anything here," she told him, frowning.

"Just trying to protect the herd," he said again, as if she didn't have a valid point at all.

"You need to leave," she insisted.

"Forgive me for not introducing myself," he said, as if he hadn't heard her. "Bad manners. I'm Roger Trager. I protect the ranches around here. If your organization is going to have a wildlife sanctuary bordering on land used for grazing cattle, you're going to have to deal with predators cutting through here."

"All wildlife is safe on this sanctuary," she told him, her jaw set.

"But not all wildlife is equal. Or welcome. Some are dangerous to the herd. You setting up a *sanctuary* for them here means they can come down and kill cattle any time they want." The way he said "sanctuary" made it sound like a bad word.

Alex knew that it was actually a tiny percentage of cattle that got predated on by native carnivores. The last figure she had read, compiled by the National Agricultural Statistics Service, or NASS, was that less than a quarter of 1 percent of cattle fatalities were caused by native carnivore predation, and that was with all predators combined: mountain lions, wolves, bears, coyotes, lynxes, bobcats, and so on. Over 99 percent of pre-slaughter cattle fatalities were actually due to other causes, such as starvation, exposure, and disease.

"Do freelance work, too," he told her, droning on. "In case you ever get problem wildlife."

"I assure you we won't be needing your services." She felt her fists ball at her sides. "And you're trespassing."

He shrugged. "My mistake. You know there aren't any fences demarcating where the sanctuary starts."

She gritted her teeth. "That's because fences limit wildlife movement, which would sort of defeat the purpose of providing a space where they can shelter."

He spat a long stream of tobacco into the dirt. "Should put up some fences."

"There are signs," she informed him. "Every two hundred feet along the boundary."

"Guess I didn't see 'em."

She knew full well that he was absolutely aware he was on the sanctuary. He had the vibe of someone who'd worked in the area for years and felt entitled to trespass wherever he wanted. She also knew he was just trying to scare her off, angry that she'd ruined his kill shot on the mountain lion.

He tugged on the brim of his hat. "Guess I'll be going."

She waited while he turned and hiked back toward the national forest. Worried he might take another shot and that she'd be the victim of "an unfortunate hunting accident," she kept close to the shelter of the rocks. She'd definitely report him next time she was in town.

About twenty minutes later, she heard the helicopter engine start up, then watched as it rose into the sky, veering off over the national forest.

She let out a breath. That had been close.

FOURTEEN

Feeling rattled, Alex looked forward to continuing her trek to more of her cameras. She hiked far from the border with the national forest, up a rise, and down through a slot canyon. A cool breeze blew down the length of the canyon, and as she stepped on the soft sand, she took off her hat, grateful for the shade provided by the steep walls.

At the other end of the canyon, she pulled the memory card from one of her cameras and checked the hair snare beside it, excited to see a small tuft of gold and black hairs snagged there. Pulling out her tweezers and sterile gloves, she plucked the fur from the snare and dropped it into a small envelope. She'd send it to the DNA tech that the LTWC worked with to see if it was a jaguar. She couldn't help but grin.

As Alex was stepping away, she noticed a pile of feline scat. Given the proximity to the fur in the hair snare, it was likely from the jaguar. Donning fresh gloves, she took samples, placed them in stoppered tubes, and stowed them away in her pack. The DNA tech could also run molecular and isotopic analysis on the scat to glean information about the jaguar's diet, stress levels, reproductive status, and more.

She moved on, visiting a nearby spring to check for tracks, finding those of mule deer, raccoon, ringtail, and what looked like the small footprints of a crevice spiny lizard. She took photos and then crossed into a thicket of saltbush. The sharp branches scraped at her bare arms.

When she emerged from the thicket and stepped down, her boot went into a hole. She staggered, losing her balance, and pitched toward the ground, her pack riding up on her hips and slamming into the back of her head.

She cursed, landing on her hands. Craning her neck back, she saw that she'd stepped into a hole about six inches deep. She'd been so busy navigating the scratchy branches that she hadn't been looking down.

She pulled her foot out and stood up, readjusting her pack. Staring down at the hole, she tried to figure out what animal had dug it. It wasn't a burrow. It went straight down and was very round and precise. She cast around on the ground, seeing several more, some as deep as a foot, others shallower, no more than a couple of inches. In a few places, she could see grooves where someone had stabbed a spade or trowel into the ground, then finger marks in the soil where they had scraped some dirt out by hand.

What the hell?

She backed up, searching for more of the strange holes, and now she saw boot prints. She stooped over to study one. The dirt there was compacted and she could clearly read the brand name of the boot in the print: North Face. She wondered if it was one of the white supremacists or the archaeology students, or even one of the two activists she'd encountered. She hadn't looked at their feet. She knew it wasn't Espinoza. She'd noticed he wore a nice pair of Salomons. The prints also looked crisp and new—no worn spots in the sole. Who would have been over here, digging strange little holes? Trager? She hadn't even thought to look at his shoes. It's possible he wore these. One of the ranchers maybe, or Milton. It all seemed very odd.

Her ankle giving her a bit of grief as she gingerly stepped forward, she almost fell into another hole and stepped to the side of it just in time.

Even stranger, she now noticed, the holes were dug at even intervals along a straight line.

She followed them, finding more of the same boot print. She saw only the one brand and suspected the person had been alone.

Then she froze. Clearly preserved between two of the boots was a large feline paw print. Her breath caught in her throat. It was too big to be a mountain lion. She found another one and then another, veering off from where the human prints led.

Now she followed the feline prints instead. Jaguar.

Excitedly, she followed the prints to a seep in a rock outcropping, the water there keeping the ground moist enough to preserve prints. The tracks led right up to the trickle of water, and she imagined the jaguar had stopped there for a drink. She found three more prints leading away from it, to the west, and tracked them. But there the soil turned dry and loose again. Dirt was disturbed in a few places where something had walked, but it was too indefinite for her to determine what kind of animal it was. She followed the disturbed ground for about a quarter of a mile, then found a clear deer track. She cast around for any sign of the jaguar spoor. None. She'd lost it.

She made a U-turn, hoping to find where the jaguar had come from. She passed the strange holes again, the boot prints. For a time the jaguar and human prints seemed to walk side by side, but when she looked closer, she saw that the boot prints were slightly fresher. The jaguar prints had begun to dry more around the edges. So the human had come by later, perhaps tracking the big cat. Alex frowned. Did that mean it *was* Trager out here? But if so, why dig the strange, regular holes? Had he placed some kind of lure in them? A scent?

Alex shrugged off her pack and got down on her hands and knees. She sniffed at several of the holes, but all she could smell was damp soil. She stood up, leaving her pack there, grateful for a break from the weight and for the breeze on her sweaty back.

She followed the jaguar prints, and in a few dozen feet, they veered off from the human tracks. In this direction, too, the dirt became drier and looser, sandy in places, and soon she was unable to follow them anymore. She took off her hat, peering into the distance in the direction the tracks had come from, into a section of piñon pines. She stood there for a few minutes, scanning the horizon, hoping to see a flash of the big cat's colorful coat. But all she could see were the tree trunks swaying in the breeze and the deep azure of the high desert sky above them.

She returned her attention to the ground, finding disturbed earth here and there where the jaguar might have walked. She followed these patches for a time, but they led to another rock outcropping, and here she lost even the vaguest hints entirely. The jaguar had probably leapt from the rock there. She backed up, scanning the rock face for any sign of it, but struck out.

Now she returned to the human tracks, wondering where they had come from. But as with the jaguar, she encountered loose, sandy soil where the tracks disappeared. She headed in a straight line in that direction, hoping to pick them up again, but once again had no luck.

Reluctantly, Alex returned to her pack, wondering if even then a jaguar might be watching her, clocking her movements from a perch on the rock outcropping. She pulled out her binoculars and scanned the area, hoping to luck out. But when she didn't see anything, she pulled out her camera and snapped a number of pictures of each big print, using her plastic measuring tool for scale. She took photos of the boot prints, too. From now on, she'd be paying more attention to people's footwear. She suddenly laughed out loud, thinking of

Zoe. Her friend always paid special attention to people's shoes, but for entirely different reasons. Jimmy Choo, Louis Vuitton, or Gucci, these boots definitely weren't.

As the sun dipped low in the sky, Alex headed back to the cabin. She'd made a lot of progress that day, and she looked forward to reviewing all the images from the remote cameras.

As she hiked, she wondered if the lone jaguar would meet up with any others. Though jaguars were not social like lions, they nevertheless communicated with one another. Both males and females left secretions that communicated age and sex. They also scraped against trees, created mounds of leaves, scratched places on the ground, and dropped scat. Secretions emitted from between their toes left scented oils behind in their wake. Rubbing their faces against various surfaces recorded where they had passed. When reading these signs, jaguars pulled back their facial muscles into a particular grimace called a flehmen, allowing extra airflow for picking up on minute details. Then a special olfactory gland called Jacobsen's organ did its work, interpreting this wealth of data.

Back at the cabin, Alex made a bowl of rice and beans for dinner. Then she loaded up images from the remote cameras. She passed through photos of another ringtail, its eyes reflecting back the light, a coyote, a bobcat, a herd of mule deer, and more than a few images of waving branches. The cameras' infrared beams were a little on the sensitive side, so in addition to moving wildlife, any stirring caused by wind also set them off. She sped through dozens of photos of swaying branches and bushes.

But she didn't see any jaguars and felt a little bit low. But she also knew that it would be a miracle to get one and that she just had to persist.

The jaguar's territory could well be extending beyond the preserve's boundaries, so capturing it on-camera would be difficult. But if it had already established a territory in the sanctuary, it would be patrolling the area. When food was more abundant—for example, in a rainforest—the territories of males usually extended about ten square miles, while a female had a slightly smaller range. But in the borderlands area here, where prey wasn't as rich, Alex knew the jaguar would need a bigger territory.

Over the years, researchers learned that jaguars could occupy territories that spanned more than 525 square miles.

She went through the rest of the photos, creating a database of all the species she'd observed so far. Finally, aching, she crawled into her mummy bag. She shut her tired eyes, dreaming of exploring more of the preserve and possibly even sighting the jaguar, who even now was out there, slinking in the darkness.

FIFTEEN

The next day, after she'd finished her rounds, Alex showered and got dressed to have dinner at the Sweetwater Ranch. She didn't have any fancy clothes with her. She'd left those with Zoe. So she just put on a clean pair of hiking pants, a black thermal shirt, and a purple jacket.

She left early, with plenty of time, because she wanted to stop by the dig site and tell Espinoza about the jaguar painting she'd found in the cave.

She drove the narrow dirt road down from the preserve and turned off onto Milton's land, following the rough road to the dig site. She found it busy as usual; Gordon, Desmond, and Ming bent over grids, Espinoza checking their work.

He waved when she pulled up.

"This is a pleasant surprise," he said when she got out. "Come for your official tour? Or a beer?" His nose was bandaged from where his attacker had punched him, the skin around his eyes black and bruised.

She gestured at his nose. "That looks painful."

"It's getting better."

"Well, I'm actually on my way to the Sweetwater Ranch. They've invited me for dinner," she told him. "But I wanted to stop by on my way and show you something."

He lifted his eyebrows. "Oh?"

"Found something that you might be interested in." She brought out her phone. Pulling up an image of the jaguar painting, she handed him the device. "Check this out."

He lifted his sunglasses off his nose, resting them on top of his head, and peered at the image. After a sharp intake of breath, he asked, "Where did you see this?"

"It's in a cave, near the top of a plateau on the preserve."

He stared at it, zooming in and out on different parts of the photo. "Can you take me to it?" he asked almost breathlessly.

"Of course."

He glanced around secretively, then whispered to her, "You have enough time to see something before you have to be at your dinner?"

She nodded.

"Come with me." He ushered her inside the work tent. There he grabbed a water bottle and flashlight from a table and moved to the tent's rear entrance. Alex followed. He unzipped it and stuck his head out, staring around. Then he said, "Okay. Everyone's busy. Follow me." He exited the tent, Alex in tow, and started off across the scrubland. They climbed down a steep embankment, crossed an arroyo, and passed through several stands of piñon pine. The sun dipped behind the distant mountains, painting the sky in dramatic tones of pink, gold, and scarlet.

They entered another creek bed and he followed its path into a narrow slot canyon. Towering rock walls rose hundreds of feet on both sides, and Alex peered up in wonder. The ground grew sandy beneath her feet, and she could see depressions where wildlife had traveled. Millions of years of water erosion had smoothed the canyon walls, the rock rippled in places. Shadows overtook them, the setting sun not reaching the depths of the canyon. She stared up to the ribbon of pink and golden sky far above them.

Halfway into the canyon, Espinoza stopped. He ran his hand along one wall. His eyes fell on a wide crack in the rock a few feet ahead, masked by the presence of a seep and a rich hanging garden of vegetation. "Here," he said quietly, waving her toward it.

They approached, and when they reached it, she saw that the opening, though narrow at first, widened. Espinoza gently parted the vegetation and squeezed into the crack, disappearing. "Come on," he whispered from the other side.

Alex pressed into the cool rock, sliding along the opening, and then emerged into a huge cave. Espinoza pulled out the flashlight and shone the beam around the cavernous expanse.

Alex's jaw dropped. Hidden inside the cave was an Ancestral Puebloan cliff dwelling in incredible condition. Houses towered above the cave floor, built high along the walls, hand-hewn stone building blocks cemented with adobe mortar. The remains of time-worn ladders lay scattered on the floor. Here and there burned circles marked places where fires had been lit and tended to.

"What do you think?" Espinoza asked, his voice full of awe.

"I think it's amazing!" she breathed, her voice, even at nearly a whisper, reverberating around the space.

"Hardly anyone knows about this site. I was one of the original excavators for it, way back in grad school. I won't admit how many years ago," he added with a rueful chuckle.

Alex guessed he was only around fifty, so it couldn't have been that long ago.

She took in the wooden beams, the expert mortar jobs on the walls of the houses. To the side of the housing area lay an intact kiva, a ceremonial circular depression in the ground with a hole in the center for a fire and a chimney. Its roof had long since fallen away, but she could still see decaying fragments of it on the ground.

"This is just hidden away here?"

"It's protected by the U.S. Antiquities Act. And the state of New Mexico prosecutes anyone who vandalizes such a site."

"It's just . . ." Words failed her. She imagined this place long ago, when the sounds of human voices and laughter filled the space, the scent of a wood fire, the barking of dogs. "How old is it?"

"About a thousand years, we estimate." He looked at her and

grinned, a mischievous smile on his face. "You want to see the best part?"

"There's more?" she asked, astonished.

"Oh yes. Come on." He led her past several houses, rounding a corner at the end of the ruin. He stopped before the cave wall there. Several rock ledges jutted from the vertical surface. Above the very top ledge, high above them, a jaguar painting decorated the surface, its colors still vibrant. The jaguar was leaping, its jaws open, sharp teeth bared, red gums pulled back. It looked incredibly similar to the one she had found.

Alex took in a sharp breath. "Oh, wow."

"I think it's the same artist, don't you? Show me your pic again."

Alex pulled out her phone and brought up the photo she'd taken in the cave. The style was the same, the color choices. "I think you're right."

Espinoza stepped back, shining the beam of his flashlight over the art. "They say that the word 'jaguar' is passed down from *yaguara,* or *yaguareté,* Tupí-Guaraní words from the Amazon that roughly mean 'he who leaps' or 'the beast who kills with a single leap.' I always thought this was a perfect representation of that."

Alex marveled at the height of the painting. "How did the artist get all the way up there?"

"Must have been a ladder back then."

"Definitely."

She took in the colorful artwork, marveling at the animal's facial expression, its sense of movement. It felt like it might leap down from the wall. She could almost feel, in that deep, cavernous space, the ghosts of the people who had painted it and the reverence they'd had for the animal. "How many jaguars do you think lived up here when this was painted?"

He pursed his lips. "More than do now, I can tell you that."

She felt grim, sadness creeping up on her. So many had been hunted and killed. "Yes. More than now."

In the nineteenth and twentieth centuries, Alex knew that thou-sands of jaguars had been killed for the fur trade throughout the Americas. In 1969 alone, nearly 10,000 jaguar skins were imported into the U.S. Finally, in 1975, jaguars came under the protection of CITES, the Convention on International Trade in Endangered Spe-cies. But even then, enforcement of those protections was left up to individual countries, where the level of enthusiasm to protect the jaguar varied.

Jaguars were also killed as European immigrants moved into the West, decimating populations in California, Arizona, New Mex-ico, and Texas. Like many other native predators, the jaguar, along with bears, wolves, coyotes, and mountain lions, were considered threats to livestock. So the government paid hunters for each jaguar killed. Arizona had been the only remaining state to host a known breeding population, but a U.S. Fish and Wildlife Service agent killed the last known female in Arizona in 1963 as part of a predator control program.

The big cats were also killed for use in folk medicine as aphro-disiacs.

Espinoza's eyes met hers in the gloom. "I'm glad you're doing what you're doing."

She managed a small smile. "Thanks. I just hope it can make some kind of difference." Then she grinned wider. "I did find some tracks."

He turned and clapped her on the shoulder. "Fantastic!"

"But haven't seen one yet."

"I have a feeling you will."

She smiled. She liked Espinoza. Liked his spirit and his easy na-ture. She didn't feel too comfortable with most people, especially right off the bat, and appreciated his laid-back manner.

"Do your students know about this site?" she asked.

Still gazing up at the painting, he said, "Nope. Just me. I slink off here sometimes to think. Or feel sorry for myself. Or wonder why the heck I went into this field. It's not all caviar and limos, you know."

She laughed. "You're crushing all my illusions. There was a time I wanted to be an archaeologist."

"Was it right after the first time you saw *Raiders of the Lost Ark*?"

Alex chuckled. "How did you know?"

"That movie got me, too. Switched my major the next day."

"What was your previous major?"

"Accounting."

"Wow. That's pretty different."

"I'll say. Good practice, though. I've pinched more pennies as an archaeologist than I ever did studying accounting."

"I hear you. Wildlife biology isn't exactly a gold mine, either."

Espinoza lifted a finger. "But we're making a difference. And that's way more important."

She fist-bumped him. "Hear, hear."

"So you've got to come back to the dig site for a proper tour. I can show you the rest of the artifacts we've found so far. It's some fascinating stuff."

"I'd love to!"

"I have to go into town tomorrow or the next day to resupply. But how about three days from now? Just stop by anytime."

"That sounds great."

"Can my team and I come out and look at the jaguar you found?"

"Of course!"

They took one last look at the magnificent jaguar and then headed back to the dig site. Alex noticed that Espinoza paused, waiting for his students to all be occupied before he came into view. His secret spot. Didn't want to give it away.

She followed him up the steep embankment, where they entered through the rear of the tent. She bet no one had even noticed they were gone.

SIXTEEN

At the dig site, Alex said her goodbyes and left for the Sweetwater Ranch, looking forward to coming back to the dig site later to check out what they'd found so far.

Alex pulled onto the long drive to the Sweetwater Ranch. She hadn't come this way before, and she drove under a large wooden gateway with several horseshoes nailed on it, all facing up as U's for good luck.

She parked by the house and climbed out. As she headed up the walkway, the front door swung open, framing June. "Alex! Good to see you. Come in, come in." She opened the door wider, ushering her in.

Alex stepped through, emerging into an expansive living room. Intricately woven hangings in vivid southwestern colors decorated the walls. A large weathered cow skull hung above the fireplace, which was a massive affair of river stones that passed through to the neighboring room, as well. From a high ceiling of crossed wooden beams hung several chandeliers made entirely of shed deer antlers.

Alex could smell something delicious and spicy cooking. June waved her through an elaborate dining room with a long wooden table, polished to a shine. An antique wooden hutch stood against one wall, showcasing an array of blue china plates, bowls, teacups, and teapots. "Those were my grandmother's," June told her, noticing her gaze. "Every time I use them, I think of being over at her house. She had this real quiet nature. And never-ending words of wisdom."

Alex smiled in appreciation. "That's lovely."

"Come through to the kitchen." June opened a set of swinging doors and the delicious aroma got stronger. "We've got this huge dining room, but we never seem to use it. The kitchen is so much cozier." They entered. On the far side of a large granite island, George was hard at work, an array of veggies, spices, and other ingredients all laid out before him.

"Just in time!" he said by way of greeting, breaking into a wide smile. "Have a seat while I finish." He gestured toward a set of barstools at the island. Alex chose one and June moved to the fridge. "Beer? Wine? Or I could whip you up something special. A martini?"

"A beer would be perfect," Alex told her.

June turned to peer into the fridge. "Porter? Stout? Lager? IPA?"

Alex couldn't help but smile. "What? You have all of those?"

June smiled sheepishly. "I'm a bit of a microbrew nut," she admitted.

"I'll say," George cut in, finely chopping some green peppers at the island. "They take up most of the fridge. She keeps getting these unpasteurized ones that have to be stored in there or apparently they lose their flavor."

"They *do* lose their flavor," June insisted good-naturedly, and Alex could tell George had been admonished for leaving them out before.

"I'll take a porter, thanks," Alex told her.

June leaned over, rearranging bottles, and Alex heard glass clinking together. "Do you prefer notes of coffee, chocolate, or smoke?"

Alex chuckled. "Chocolate."

"Got just the one, then. You'll like this brewery. They use renewable energy."

She pulled out a Larch Valley Porter by the Grizzly Paw Brewing Company in Canmore, Alberta. Then she drew a frozen pint glass out of the freezer and deftly poured the porter into it.

"Wow! Classy! Frosted glass," Alex said, taking the drink from her. She sipped appreciatively.

June pulled out an IPA for herself and produced another frosted glass. "So how's it going out on the preserve?" June asked, sitting down beside her on one of the barstools. At the stove, George wiped his hands on a towel and then slung it over his shoulder. He started tossing red and green peppers into a sauté pan.

She told them about her run-in with Roger Trager.

June scowled. "That man is downright dangerous."

"You should report him," George added.

"I intend to." Then she added, "But on a positive note, I found some jaguar prints."

June lifted her eyebrows. "Really?"

"Yep." Alex lifted her glass and clinked hers with June's. "Now I just need to see if I can collar it. Get some GPS and video data of which parts of the preserve and neighboring land it's using. I've put out some hair snares, too."

"What will that tell you?" George asked, working a spatula expertly around the pan.

"I can use the DNA from different hairs to see if more than one jaguar is up here. I can also tell things about its diet and health."

June took a sip. "Amazing."

"And if I upload the DNA into a jaguar database, I can see if other jaguars it's related to have their DNA on file. I might be able to tell where the jaguar originated from, if it came up from a population in Sonora, Mexico, or somewhere else."

"Which side of the preserve were the tracks on?" George asked.

"I've spotted them in a couple places. But the tracks on the western side were kind of weird."

June rubbed her thumb through the condensation on her glass. "How so?"

"In one of the places, there were boot prints, too, and these weird little holes that someone had dug."

June immediately put her glass down. "What?"

Alex met her eyes. "Weird holes."

June snapped her gaze up to her husband. "You hear that, George?"

In the midst of adding black beans to his concoction, he merely said, "Hear what?" without looking over.

"Alex found those weird little holes on the preserve, too."

At this, he turned, spatula hovering in midair. "You're kidding me. Where?"

"On the west side," June added.

"That's the side that borders with us," he pointed out.

June rolled her eyes. "I know that, silly."

"Why?" Alex asked. "What's going on?"

George set down the spatula and wiped his hands on the towel again. "We've seen them, too. All over our property. Were yours in a neat little line, dug at different depths?"

Alex started. "Yes. Exactly."

"Boot prints next to them?" George added.

"Sure were."

"Too weird," June breathed, taking another sip of her beer.

Alex pivoted in her stool to face George. "What do you think they are?"

He turned back to the stove, maneuvering the veggies around. "We have no idea."

"How long have you been seeing them?"

He considered this. "What do you think, Juney?"

June frowned. "About two months, I'd say."

He nodded. "Yeah. That sounds about right. We asked our ranch hands about it. They had no idea, either. They've seen 'em all over. Even in some pretty remote reaches of our spread."

"Do your employees have any theories?" Alex asked.

"Do they *ever*," June said. "You name it, they've suggested it. Some prospector digging test holes for gold or platinum or lithium. Someone from the EPA testing the soil for contaminants. Someone obsessed with digging up ground squirrels."

"Personally, I think it's a soil scientist trying to find irradiated soil where aliens landed," George put in.

"George!" June admonished.

"It makes sense!" he insisted. "I know you make fun of me, but I've seen some weird lights out there at night."

June waved him off. "It's just swamp gas or something."

George rolled his eyes. "I don't think we have any swamps out here."

"Well then, it's like those lights in Texas," June insisted. "The Marfa Lights. Some kind of weird atmospheric distortion."

"Or it's aliens," he pressed. "Maybe one day we'll find more than just boot prints out there next to those holes. Maybe we'll find strange three-toed prints."

June shook her head. "So now the aliens have three toes?"

He shrugged, tossing a few flour tortillas into a pan to warm. "Why not? If I were an alien, I'd have three toes."

She waved her hand at him dismissively. "Oh, George." Then to Alex she said, "Just ignore him."

He gave a low chuckle, then turned to mix up some guacamole while the veggies simmered.

"And what do you think, June?" Alex asked.

June furrowed her brow. "It's weird that they're all in a line like that. Precise. Says science to me. But as to what they're looking for, I just don't know. What do *you* think?"

Alex grinned. "I like George's idea."

From across the island, George laughed, then scooped the food onto three plates and sat down across from them. "Dig in!"

The food smelled delicious. Alex tasted her first forkful of flavorful black beans, peppers, and fire-roasted corn. "This is amazing," she told him.

He grinned. "Glad you like it!"

"And I just like watching him cook," June said with a twinkle. Alex could tell she really loved him. It always made her uncomfortable when she was around couples who bickered or sniped at each other with rude little undermining comments. But June and George obviously not only cared deeply for each other but genuinely enjoyed each other's company.

"So tell us about yourself," June said. "How did you come to work for the land trust?"

Alex finished another bite and took a sip of her porter. "My grad school advisor got me the job. I was living in Boston at the time. I'd moved out there to be with my then-boyfriend, but things didn't work out. And Dr. Brightwell, who'd seen me through my dissertation when I was at UC Berkeley, knew Ben Hathaway. They needed someone to see if any wolverines were using a sanctuary they'd recently acquired in Montana. It came at the perfect time."

"Was your boyfriend upset?" June asked.

"We had already broken up by then. So there wasn't anything left for me in Boston. I'm not really a city dweller," she confessed.

"And has there been anyone special since then?"

Alex almost laughed. "Oh no. Not for me. My job makes it . . . difficult."

Alex had gone on a few onetime dates while in L.A.—two men she'd met through Zoe's friends, and one guy she'd met at an art gallery opening. But all three suffered from the same self-centeredness. They'd droned on and on about themselves, expressing little to no reciprocal curiosity about her. Alex had asked thoughtful questions, expressing interest in their answers, yet none of them had expressed much interest in learning anything about her in return.

Zoe suggested magnanimously that perhaps it was because they were nervous and were trying hard to impress her by harping on and on about their accomplishments. That would certainly be better than what Alex had suspected—that they simply didn't care to learn anything about her beyond how she looked.

Alex often struggled with this kind of one-sided exchange, and it seemed to be getting more and more common. She'd been raised to ask questions, to learn about a person, to generate thoughtful two-way conversation. But most of the time now, people simply did these self-focused information dumps. Was that just how most conversation went these days, with people used to talking about themselves through status updates on social media? Was conversation a forgotten art? She was never sure if she should just forge ahead and volunteer information about herself in response even if they hadn't expressed interest, or if the people were simply self-involved and she might as well not say anything.

Needless to say, the dates had been a bust.

And even if she did manage to find someone capable of a conversation, usually when she mentioned to him that she spent months out in the wilds doing work in remote places, he quickly lost interest.

"Being out in the middle of nowhere isn't exactly conducive to meeting people," she added.

June nodded. "Yes, I can see how that would be tough."

"What about your family?" asked George. He heaped a second helping of food onto his plate.

"My dad lives in Berkeley. He's a painter."

George smiled. "Oh, that's cool. Portraits?"

"Landscapes."

"Are you close?" George asked.

"Oh, yes. Definitely."

"And your mom?" June asked. Alex dreaded the question. People grew so uncomfortable when she mentioned that her mother had passed away. They usually didn't know what to say, and hemmed and hawed uncomfortably, which made Alex feel even worse.

"We lost her when I was twelve," Alex said, taking another sip from her porter.

June squeezed her arm. "I'm so sorry. It can be tough to lose a parent when you're so young."

George took a sip of his water and set the glass down. "Hell, it can be tough to lose a parent at any age. I lost my dad when I was fifty-five and I bawled for a year."

"I'm so sorry you lost him." Alex gave him a faint smile. "Yes, it was tough losing a parent. Thank you." She was relieved they didn't get uncomfortable. "My mom was a fighter pilot with the Air Force."

June's mouth fell open. "You're kidding me."

"Nope. She was amazing."

"I'll say," George put in. "I bet she had some fascinating stories."

"She couldn't really talk about most of her work. A lot of it was classified. But we moved around to a lot of exotic places when I was growing up." Alex wasn't even sure of the details around her mother's death. She and her dad had been told that her mother had been shot down while on a mission, that she'd saved her wing mates in doing so and had died with honor and distinction. But they'd never even known where she'd been when it had happened. The Air Force sent home remains in a coffin, but they were so badly burned, they'd been told, that it would be best not to view them. So she'd been buried next to her own parents in Denver, Colorado.

Wanting to lighten the mood, Alex said, "Right now my dad is applying for an artist residency at the Point Reyes National Sea-shore, so he's been spending a lot of time on the rugged California coast, painting cliffs and crashing surf."

"What a job," George said. "Can you imagine, Juney? I'd love to just sit around and paint. My back is killing me from putting up fence posts."

"You should rest up for a few days, George. Give your back a break. I can handle putting them in without you."

He harrumphed at this. "I don't want you to have to do that."

"I don't mind! Gives me a chance to spend some quiet time out on the back range."

"Or you could take a rest with me. We've been meaning to break in this new hot tub we got. And I like seeing June in the altogether."

"Oh, George," she said, her face flushing. "We have company."

Alex chuckled and finished the delicious dinner, and then George brought out flan that had been cooling in the refrigerator. Alex dipped into the tasty cool custard and finished her beer.

George made some hot coffee and they took it into the living room, where he built a roaring fire. June and George told her more about their son and his dream of being a botanist.

Alex really wanted to ask them if they'd had any dealings with the men who had threatened Espinoza. She wasn't sure how to approach it, since she barely knew them, but decided just to dive in. "Have you encountered this white supremacist group that's been active in the area?"

George and June looked at each other, and for a second Alex wondered if she should have brought it up.

June pursed her lips. "We have."

"Gotten some hate mail from them," George added. "Scrawled notes shoved in our mailbox. Our ranch sign was set on fire three weeks ago. We had to replace it. They don't like that we've been improving habitat for the jaguar. They worry that any population that gets established up here will mean laxer border crossing measures."

"Who are these guys?" Alex asked.

"From what we understand," George told her, "they're called the Sons of the White Star. They've been gaining followers over the last few years, becoming more and more vocal and violent."

"Have you gone to the police?"

"Oh sure," June told her. "But we can't prove they're the ones who've been vandalizing us. We just suspect it. None of the notes were signed, and the police don't know who any of the members are. They always hide their faces."

George clenched his jaw. "The worst was that they beat up our horse trainer José pretty good one night. Caught him alone as he was going home."

"That's terrible. Is he okay?"

"Had to go to the hospital with two broken ribs and a cracked collarbone. They did a number on his face, too," June added.

George shook his head. "But nothing came of it. We still don't know who did it."

"José said it was three guys, driving a white pickup."

That was certainly familiar. Alex wondered if it was the same three men who had threatened Espinoza and his team.

"I can't believe nothing has been done," Alex lamented.

George pursed his lips. "These guys are smart. They get in and out fast. They operate in places where it'll take the cops a long time to come out."

"What they need to do is set up some kind of sting operation or get a surveillance team to start shadowing them. But the local police don't exactly have a budget for something like that," June said ruefully.

Alex thought of Pilar and Arturo, of all the townspeople who'd been victimized. "The whole situation is incredibly frustrating." She imagined how easily the situation with Espinoza might have escalated. Predators might not be the only ones who were victims of the "shoot, shovel, and shut up" mentality around here.

When they'd finished their coffee, Alex looked at her watch. It was going on eleven, and she had to make an early start in the morning. She stood up. "I better get going. This has been really lovely," she told them. "I so appreciate your having me over for dinner."

"Our pleasure," June assured her. "And feel free to come down in the next few days if you want to put remote cameras out by our guzzlers. Let me grab that map."

"That would be wonderful," Alex told them.

June returned moments later and showed her a topographic map with all the water sources marked. They walked her to the door, standing framed there as Alex got into her Jeep. She waved good-bye and turned around, bouncing down the dirt road back toward her cabin.

It had been a good night. She wasn't used to having company when she was out on these field assignments. She found it difficult most of the time to make real connections with people. Alex knew that she was a bit of an oddball, one with strong beliefs and ideals. Couple that with her rusty social skills from spending so much time alone in the backcountry, and she always felt a bit awkward. But it had been a pleasant evening, and she was grateful to them for standing up for predators, especially in the face of harassment from this hate group. She wondered how far the men would take it to get their way.

That night Alex got back late. But she wanted to go through the rest of the photos from the memory cards that she'd swapped out that afternoon. She sat down at the small table and fired up her laptop. It had been charging all day, plugged into the Bluetti, which still held an amazing 85 percent charge.

She started flipping through images on the SD cards. The cameras had captured photos of a coyote, more mule deer, and a mountain lion. She wondered if it was the same one that Trager had been pursuing. She moved through more images: a raccoon, another delightful coati, a covey of Gambel's quail.

And then she froze. About a hundred frames in, the camera she'd placed at the top of the plateau had captured a blurry image of something fast. Something with gold and black fur. She held her breath and advanced through the next frames. A short video followed of a jaguar. Alex stared in disbelief. It paused to drink from a seep, then stared right into the camera for several seconds before walking out of frame. Alex replayed the video three more times, a huge grin on her face. Then she punched a victorious fist into the air.

She'd found tracks at this same place, and now a video of the jaguar drinking from a seep. She checked the time stamp. The video had been captured the day after she'd first placed the camera out. That meant that the tracks she'd seen and the video had been recorded on different days, and the jaguar was returning to this area. If she wanted to attach a collar camera to the jaguar, this place would be a good bet.

She glanced over at the tranquilizer gun case. She'd probably have to build a blind and wait there until the jaguar appeared. But this was the most hopeful sign yet, and photographic proof that at least one jaguar was using the sanctuary. She couldn't wait to tell Ben. The next time she was in Azulejo, she'd send him a copy of the video.

Tomorrow she'd set up the blind and await the arrival of the giant cat.

SEVENTEEN

At the top of the plateau, Alex dragged loose, dried bushes and branches over to a small cleft inside a rock outcropping. She pressed into the crevice and then dragged the branches in front of her so she was hidden. Then she rested her back against the cool stone. She'd estimated the jaguar's size and weight from the video and had loaded up a tranquilizer dart with the right dosage. Then she loaded it into the dart gun and propped it up on one knee.

Now all she had to do was wait.

She stared out at the blue sky, listening to the quiet trickle of water from the seep where the jaguar had drunk. She thought about everything the jaguar had survived to reach this remote spot. Poachers, the border wall, housing developments. At least now the jaguar had some federal protection.

She knew that despite a plummeting population, jaguars in the United States weren't listed under the Endangered Species Act until 1997. It then took the U.S. Fish and Wildlife Service seventeen years to designate critical habitat. They made this move after being sued by a number of conservation organizations. And even then the designated area was quite small, even though far more appropriate jaguar habitat was available. It then took them an additional two years to finally draft a recovery plan, nineteen years after the jaguar was listed as endangered. At first this critical habitat spanned parts of Arizona and New Mexico. But after ranchers complained, a U.S.

district judge removed the parcels in New Mexico from protection in 2021. Part of the rationale for the dragging of feet and not putting better jaguar protections in place was that the jaguar was faring a little better in Central and South America. So if it disappeared from the United States altogether, that wouldn't necessarily mean the end of the species. But deforestation was decimating jaguar habitat at a staggering rate all across their range. Two-thirds of the forests were gone in Central America, where jaguars once roamed in far greater numbers. Designating critical habitat in the U.S. would offer the big cats a refuge.

But Alex knew that this decision to designate critical habitat would continue to be met with stern resistance from several livestock associations, just as what happened in New Mexico. They claimed it would put a burden on landowners. When this resulted in removing protections from jaguar habitat in the state, the ranchers' suit was met with a promise by the Center for Biological Diversity to keep fighting to have the critical habitat restored. As usual, the efforts to protect an endangered species were mired in delays and political obstacles.

As she waited, her butt fell asleep and she shifted her weight, kneeling for a time, then sitting cross-legged, then leaning back with her legs straight out. Her back ached from the awkward angle. But the thrill of possibly seeing a jaguar kept her focused and alert. The minutes ticked by slowly. An hour passed. Then two. The sun arced across the sky, shadows shifting. For a few moments, it shone right into the crevice and she had to don her hat to shield her eyes from the glare. But then the sun moved on, returning the crevice to shadow.

She checked her watch. She'd been crammed in there for five and a half hours now and was beginning to worry that she'd picked a spot where the jaguar wouldn't appear that day. If not, she'd just come back tomorrow and hope for the best.

She was just about to climb out of the blind to stretch when a flash of movement on a nearby rock outcropping caught her attention. A long, moving shadow appeared at the bottom of the rocks, cast from an animal standing at the top. Alex leaned out, sunlight hitting her, and blocked the brilliance with one hand. Her breath caught in her throat. The jaguar. It stood at the top of the stones, surveying the ground beneath.

As quietly as possible, she aimed the tranq gun out. The jaguar leapt, landing quietly on the sandy ground beneath. It made its way toward the seep. She watched while it drank, getting its fill.

Then, when it finished and turned to gaze around, she fired. The dart landed in its rump and the jaguar bolted. She climbed out of her position, scrambling over the loose branches and dried bushes at the mouth of the crevice. Then she grabbed her pack and followed the jaguar at a distance, not wanting to scare it even more. It ran swiftly across the plateau, covering hundreds of yards, and for a second Alex thought she would lose it entirely. She hadn't had time to cinch her pack down and it slapped at her back.

But then the jaguar grew sleepy and wobbly, slowing. Finally it slumped over, lying down on its side.

Alex moved to it quickly, kneeling down beside it. It was a male, something she had expected. Male jaguars had larger ranges, striking out on their own to establish new territories. Most of the jaguars spotted in the United States in the twentieth century had been males, though females had been killed in both Arizona and New Mexico in the early to mid-1900s.

She got supplies out of her pack and attached supplemental oxygen to the jaguar's muzzle. She began monitoring its breathing and heart rate. All looked good. She placed an eye mask over the cat's soft face. Gently she affixed the GPS collar camera, making sure it was loose enough to not constrict movement, but not so loose it would slip off.

She'd programmed the camera on the collar to record a ten-second video every hour. It was a special high-tech camera that had been developed specifically for the LTWC. Usually such cameras were designed to fall off at the end of a field season. Researchers would then go to the last known GPS location and retrieve the camera. Only then would they be able to watch the recorded videos. But the LTWC camera was incredibly powerful and was able to send batches of videos and GPS location data daily via satellite, where they were stored on the cloud until downloaded. So Alex could see jaguar videos as soon as tomorrow. All she'd need was an internet connection, which meant going into town.

She pulled out her sample kit and took swabs of the jaguar's saliva and snipped off some of his fur, sealing the samples away in bags.

She looked down at the sleeping animal, amazed at the color and vibrancy of his coat, its jet-black rosettes. Alex knew that sometimes jaguars appeared all black, the rosettes visible only in very bright sunlight. But this was rare, with less than 10 percent having this trait. She snapped a few photos of his rosette patterns to compare with the video she had back at the cabin. She suspected this was the same jaguar, but she wanted to be sure.

She took in the massive jaws, the soft ears, the sensitive nose. Then she swabbed between his toes, marveling at the sheer size and power of the clawed foot. A formidable predator indeed, and such a magnificently beautiful animal. Alex studied the jaguar's vibrissae, sensitive whiskers around his mouth. These allowed him to perceive his position in tight, dark places. They didn't extend beyond the width of his body, allowing him to know, even in pitch-black conditions, if he could fit into a tight space or not.

When she was finished, she administered the sedative counteragent. The jaguar began to stir. She removed the supplemental oxygen and the eye mask, and then withdrew to keep an eye on him.

He rose up groggily to a sitting position, giving his head a vigorous shake. For several long moments, he stared around himself. Then he languidly licked a paw. Alex stayed out of sight. Finally feeling fully awake, he moved off down the plateau.

Alex let out a long exhale. It always made her nervous to sedate an animal. She knew that in the long run, this could help the jaguar population north of the border, and that it was worth collaring him. But if she'd made a wrong move, it could have negatively affected the jaguar. So she was relieved to see him slinking away, back to his regular routine. Elated, she grinned. She'd done it.

She looked forward to learning what path he was taking around the preserve and if he was using the neighboring ranches or national forest. If he was, the LTWC could talk to people about living with predators, disseminate helpful information about coexistence, encourage them to join in like George and June had.

And she could also find out what section of the border with Mexico he was crossing and make the case to the government that such an area should remain accessible to wildlife.

Euphoric, Alex hiked back to the cabin as the sun set. She took a warm shower and then donned her thick fleece clothes. After making a quick meal of nut butter on bread with slices of avocado on the side, she pulled up the photos and video from the remote camera she'd placed on top of the plateau. Then she loaded up photos she'd taken of the sedated jaguar and compared the rosettes. It was definitely the same jaguar.

When she finished, she stepped outside to stare up at the stars. She heard something rustling in the bushes nearby and her head snapped in that direction. She went inside and brought out her headlamp, shining it into the shrubbery. A surprised mule deer lifted its head, eyes glowing in the beam from her light. She immediately lowered the headlamp, the beam shining on the ground. Several small, white objects caught her eye some feet away. She walked over to them and bent down.

Cigarette butts. About ten of them, and from three different brands. Someone had been up here.

Alex shone the light around her, suddenly feeling exposed. She didn't know if the butts had been there before. She would have noticed them, wouldn't she? She couldn't be sure. She made a quick circuit of the cabin, not seeing anything that had been disturbed. Maybe the butts had been there all along. Or maybe a hiker had come through the preserve and waited to see if anyone would return to the cabin. But if that were the case, why three different brands? To her that meant three different people.

She checked over her Jeep, finding it unmolested.

Finally she withdrew into the cabin and engaged the dead bolt. But that night she lay awake, wondering if someone was out there in the darkness, watching.

EIGHTEEN

The next morning Alex awoke with muscles stiff from crouching for so long inside the crevice the day before. But she was full of energy, excited about collaring the jaguar. The next time she had access to Wi-Fi, she could download the videos and GPS locations from the collar.

As she made some hot tea and sat down outside on the bench, she contemplated her day.

She still needed to place some cameras out on the north side of the preserve. It would be a two-day hike if she left from the cabin, so instead she went back inside and consulted her topo map, wondering if she could access the area more easily from the national forest side. She studied the winding Forest Service roads and alighted on a trailhead marked on the map. It was only two miles from the boundary with the preserve and would be an ideal spot to park her Jeep and hike in.

She ate a quick breakfast of dried fruit, nuts, and some instant oatmeal mixed with hot water, and then headed out.

The drive into the national forest was bumpy, along long, rutted dirt roads that she had to take slowly. In a few places, the road to the trailhead had been washed out by flash floods, and these sections she navigated carefully. Finally she pulled into the small parking area, seeing only one other car there: a beat-up Subaru Outback with a host of national park stickers plastered over the bumpers and back hatch. It was empty; whoever owned it must be on the trail. An honest-to-goodness pay phone stood at the mouth of the trail beside an informative placard that displayed a map of the area and hiking safety tips.

She pulled out her pack and cinched it down on her shoulders, then went around to the back of the Jeep to drape a blanket over a small metal box of LTWC supplies that Ben had brought. It was secured with a padlock and didn't contain much—another remote camera that hadn't been working properly, a GPS collar camera, quad topo maps for other sections of the Gila National Forest, some extra batteries, and an SD card.

She set off at a good clip, wanting to make a lot of progress before the heat of the day really kicked in. She half expected to run across the other hiker but didn't see anyone else. She checked the GPS locations that her habitat suitability model had flagged and used her GPS unit to start navigating toward them. She always carried a compass and a paper map as a backup in case something happened to her unit, but for now she just used the little compass on the GPS screen to aim in the right direction.

She crossed a dry creek bed, moving between barren sections of desert and small groupings of pines and rock outcroppings. The sun rose higher and was soon beating down on her head. She donned her trusty wide-brimmed hat.

She crossed onto the preserve and reached the first spot just before noon, finding it to be excellent jaguar habitat. Some piñon pines offered cover, and a spring provided a water source. She selected a tree and attached a remote camera, checking to be sure it was working properly before closing it with a padlock. Then she set up a hair snare.

To the west towered the striking pillars so indicative of the area, fused ash from ancient volcanic eruptions. She imagined how this landscape must have appeared millions of years ago, when so many now-extinct animals roamed the terrain, along with ancient jaguars.

She knew that today's jaguars were remnants from the Pleistocene epoch, or Ice Age, which lasted from 2.6 million to 11,700 years ago. This was the time of the megafauna—huge, lumbering mammoths and mastodons; twelve-foot-tall ground sloths that pulled down leaves from trees. Gigantic short-faced bears roamed the forests and plains, weighing as much as two thousand pounds. And at that time, North America was also home to a variety of big cats, including the American lion, the impressive saber-toothed cat, and the American leopard.

The jaguar's ancestor lived among these fellow felids. Warm tropical forests were replaced by woodlands and plains and desert. Humans arrived in North America, hunting the slow-moving megafauna. At the end of all this tumultuous time of change, only the modern jaguar's ancestor, *Panthera onca augusta,* managed to survive, becoming the only big cat species in North America.

To adapt to changing conditions, species from deer to tapir evolved to be smaller. And so did the jaguar, becoming less massive than its Ice Age ancestor. Other cat species such as the mountain lion, bobcat, and lynx moved into the temperate woodlands, while the jaguar shifted its range farther south and west. Jaguar remains had been found as far north as Washington State and as far east as Florida, Tennessee, and Pennsylvania.

It took Alex most of the rest of the afternoon to reach the second spot she wanted to ground-truth. This one, too, proved quite excellent, and she attached a camera to a tree there and set up a hair snare.

Then she sat in the shade of a rock outcropping and ate an energy bar. She refilled her water bottle at a trickling spring, using the pump handle on her water filter. From a nearby slot canyon, she heard the musical notes of a canyon wren ring out. Above her, three vultures drifted lazily on thermal winds, gliding there effortlessly. A crevice spiny lizard darted by her in the sand, its handsome black-and-white-banded tail flicking. Then it stopped on a flat rock and started to do what one of her zoology professors had called "calisthenics," doing little push-ups on the hot stone to get airflow going.

Feeling rested, she packed up and headed back to the trailhead and her car.

As the afternoon wore on and the sun's heat pressed down on her, she thought about the jaguar she'd collared, wondering how it was faring.

Because the jaguar was an apex predator, its numbers were naturally low already. When additional stressors affected its survival, such as overhunting and habitat loss, the jaguar population was particularly vulnerable to decimation. She hoped they could help this one.

Soon she was back on the main trail to the parking area. She still hadn't seen a single other person, but when she emerged into the parking lot, she saw that the Subaru Outback was gone. Then she frowned, instantly seeing that the driver's side window of her Jeep had been smashed out. She glanced around the parking area. Hers was the only car there, and she didn't see anyone milling around.

Feeling disheartened, she walked to the Jeep and peered inside. The glove compartment hung open, completely empty. She hadn't had anything in there except for the rental car agreement. She moved around to the back of the Jeep where she'd stored her gear. The blanket had been tossed aside.

With a sinking heart, she saw the gear box had been forced open. Someone had cut through the padlock, probably with bolt cutters. She opened the back end of the Jeep, seeing that they'd stolen everything from the box. The GPS collar camera was gone, as well as the faulty remote camera. The maps had been taken, and they'd made off with the backup batteries and new micro SD card.

Alex admonished herself for keeping the items in her car, but at the same time hadn't thought of this remote trailhead as a hotbed for car thieves. But she supposed its remote location made it ideal for such crimes.

Briefly she thought of going into town, but then realized she'd probably have to go a lot farther than Azulejo to get a new window ordered and replaced for the Jeep. Still, it was worth a try. And she could pick up her laptop on the way and download jaguar videos at a hot spot in town.

Feeling disenchanted with humanity, she swung by the cabin, grabbed her computer, and then drove into Azulejo. She pulled her car in front of the town's small one-room library and used their Wi-Fi to look up car repair places. Sure enough, Azulejo offered no such service. She called a glass repair place in a neighboring town. They didn't have that side window in stock but told her they'd order it for her and should have it within the week.

Next she stopped by a small hardware store located on a side street that hadn't been damaged in the attacks. There she picked up some plastic sheeting and duct tape to temporarily seal the window.

Then she drove to the police station. It was a small place. In the main room stood two desks where a couple of deputies worked. A dispatcher sat at the front of the room, and off to the side was a doorway that led to the cells and a private office for the sheriff.

She stepped up to the reception desk and saw Deputy Wentworth working at a computer across the room. He spotted her and came over. "It's Dr. Carter, isn't it?"

She nodded. "Good to see you again."

"How can I help you?"

She gazed up at him. "I'd like to report a theft. My car was broken into."

He nodded. "Sure thing. Come over to my desk."

They sat down and she related what had happened and where, then a list of the stolen items. He typed it all into an ancient whirring and clicking computer that hailed from the 1990s. "I'll also forward this report to the U.S. Forest Service," he told her.

Alex didn't have high hopes that the police would come across her stolen belongings, but it was worth a shot. That collar and remote camera were expensive, and recovering them would save the LTWC some cash.

Then she told him about Trager trespassing on the preserve and his shooting in her direction. "He said it was an accident, that he thought I was a mountain lion. But I don't think it was an accident. I think he was trying to scare me off. But regardless of his motive, he shouldn't be hunting on the sanctuary's land. He shouldn't be there at all. He was trespassing."

Wentworth bit his lip. "We've had complaints about him before, including trespassing onto private property. I'll have another talk with him."

When they were finished, she stood up and shook his hand. "Thank you, Deputy Wentworth."

"Sorry this happened. I'll let you know if we come across any of the items."

"I appreciate it."

She left with a heavy heart, wondering if she'd have more dangerous encounters with Trager.

NINETEEN

Outside, people milled around on the sidewalks, business owners repairing broken windows, hauling destroyed items out of burned-out stores. Alex crossed to Pilar's gallery, wanting to check on her.

Just as she approached, Pilar stepped outside the open door, her grandson Arturo beside her.

"Hi," Alex greeted them. "Thought I'd come check on you."

"That was kind," Pilar said, squeezing her hand in greeting. "Well, as you can see, the police have finally released the scene, and we can start assessing the damage, figure out what's to be done."

"Are they any closer to catching these guys?"

"They say they're working on it," Pilar told her. "But the wheels of justice move a little more slowly when it comes to people like us."

"Let's face it, abuela," Arturo put in. "The wheels of justice are *square* when it comes to people like us."

She patted his arm affectionately. "My boy is less patient. He's a fighter. He fought overseas, you know. In the UN peacekeeping forces. Against evil men just like these."

Alex froze at the mention of the UN peacekeeping forces. Casey had served with them, too, as a combat medic.

Arturo pursed his lips. "Yeah, and I come home to find the same thing happening here. And it isn't the first time. Hate groups are springing up all over the place. It's like they've got carte blanche now to do what they want, and there are seldom any consequences."

Alex eyed all the fire damage inside the gallery. "Is there anything I can do?"

"Well, if you're volunteering," Pilar said with a grin, and Alex knew she was in for it.

For the next couple of hours, she helped Arturo cart out burned tables, easels, canvases, and chairs that were beyond repair. They threw them into an industrial Dumpster that had been parked on the street.

Alex watched as other business owners did the same.

Arturo stood beside her. "It's not just our businesses that were damaged. A lot of people had to go to the hospital for burns. And Román over there?" He pointed to a forty-something man standing in front of his burned-out bakery. "His grandfather didn't make it. Smoke inhalation."

"That's terrible. I'm so sorry this has happened." She told them about the threats at the dig site.

"These guys have got to be stopped," Arturo said, disgust evident on his face.

Alex helped them for a few more minutes, then washed soot off her hands in the gallery's small bathroom. It was toward the back of the building and had survived relatively intact.

"Take care," she told them as she left.

"Gracias," Pilar told her.

"I'm glad I could help."

She took her leave and finished walking down the main street, past other discouraged business owners and their family members.

Wanting to be cheered up, she reached her car and called her dad.

He answered right away. "Pumpkin! I was hoping you'd call."

"Hi, Dad. How are things?"

"Great, great! I've been painting up a storm. Just spent the day at Chimney Rock in Point Reyes, watching for whale spouts. It's such a windy spot that my easel almost blew away at one point. But I think I got some great work out of it."

"That's wonderful!"

"And how about you, sweetheart? How is the preserve?"

"It's so beautiful. And I managed to collar a jaguar! I'm going to look at the first batch of videos today."

"Terrific!"

Alex debated telling him about the car theft and about what had happened in town. She'd already worried him with the attack at the dig site, asking him to get the police for her. But she also wanted to hear his thoughts, so she related what had happened in town.

For a moment, he was just silent. Then he said, "Oh, Alex. That's just awful. I can't even get my head around it."

"I know. Me, either."

"Do you think they'll come back to the dig site? Or come by the preserve?"

"I hope not. I'm definitely keeping an eye out. There's a mountain lion hunter out here, too, and I'm definitely concerned about him. He was on the preserve."

"Isn't it a no-hunting area?"

"It is. But he didn't seem to respect that."

Her dad sighed. "I worry about you, Pumpkin."

"I'll be careful. I promise."

"Okay. I know this work comes with risk. If you need anything, you let me know. And keep that satellite communicator handy!"

"I will, Dad."

She changed the subject then, and they talked about the books they'd been reading. He mentioned an article he'd just read in the *New York Times* about the state of mountain caribou in British Columbia.

Then they hung up, with Alex telling him she'd call again in a few days.

Next she called Zoe, hoping she'd catch her in a free moment. But it went straight to voice mail, so she left a message.

Alex parked in front of the library again and pulled out her laptop. After logging on to the free Wi-Fi, she began downloading the
GPS data and the footage from the collar camera. First she checked
the route the jaguar was taking through the area. Since she had attached the collar, it had spent most of its time on the sanctuary, with
shorter trips onto Milton's property and a foray into the Gila National Forest. Delighted to see that the camera was working properly, she decided not to wait until she was back at the cabin to look
at the footage. She loaded up the first video.

In the frame, she could see the jaguar's chin and the surrounding terrain. It was walking down a slot canyon and paused to drink
at a seep. In the next clip, it was running, the camera bouncing
wildly with the movement. She couldn't make out much from the
blurry video. In the next the jaguar crouched low behind some
Gambel oaks. It crept forward incrementally, likely stalking prey.
In the next it walked, navigating over a wash. In the following clip,
it perched atop a tall rock outcropping. Movement below it on the
desert floor caught her eye. A man, walking around. She paused
the video. Zoomed in on it. Roger Trager, with his rifle out. Quickly
Alex checked the GPS tag for the video and pulled the location up
on her laptop. It was right in the middle of the preserve.

"Goddamnit!" she cursed aloud.

She replayed the video. He was walking away cautiously, alert,
his rifle drawn, not strapped to his back. But he'd already passed the
jaguar's location and was obviously completely unaware of the big
cat's presence above him.

Alex clenched her jaw as she watched the two remaining videos, recorded after the one with Trager. She was relieved to see the
jaguar doing fine, obviously sleeping in one of the videos and walking through a copse of trees in another. She didn't know if Trager
was still hunting the mountain lion and didn't think he'd hesitate to
shoot the jaguar if he saw it.

Immediately she closed her laptop and marched right back to the police station. Deputy Wentworth looked up as she entered. "Did you forget something?"

"No," she told him, walking over to his desk. "It's about Trager again. Proof that he's trespassing onto the Mogollon Wildlife Sanctuary." She sat down and opened her laptop, then played the video for him.

"What am I looking at?" he asked, pointing to the jaguar's gold and black chin.

"It's a collar camera attached to a jaguar."

His mouth fell open and he leaned back in his chair. "Are you serious? On a *jaguar*? How in the hell did you manage that? I didn't even know we had jaguars up here."

"I'm a wildlife biologist. We had all the right permits," she assured him.

He shook his head, his expression incredulous.

Deputy Wentworth filled out another report on the ancient computer. "I'll follow up with this guy," he told her.

She stood up, still feeling rattled and angry. "Thank you."

As she walked back to her car, her cell rang. Zoe.

She answered it as she climbed into the driver's seat. "Zoe! So glad you called back."

"Hey, Alex! How's it going out there?"

"Good in parts, frustrating in others." She told her about being able to collar a jaguar, then about the Sons of the White Star and Trager.

"That's insane," Zoe said. "What the hell is wrong with people?"

"I've been asking that question my whole life."

"I think you should come back to L.A. I don't like this."

"I can't abandon the study. Especially now that I'm getting this great footage."

Zoe sighed. "I know you won't quit. But I worry about you."

"Thanks, Zoe. So tell me about you! How is the shoot going?"

"Ugh. More insanity with filming on a public street!"

"Crazy bicycle guy?"

"This time it was a dog walker. You know those professional dog walkers who walk like fifteen dogs at once?"

"Sure."

"Well, this woman had a whole mess of poodles and dachshunds and German shepherds and golden retrievers. Our pyro guys had just set up this super complicated shot where a series of bombs go off on the street. They had these Roman candle type thingies set up all along the street in these little stands. So fireballs are going to be shooting up all over the place as soon as the director yells action and the pyro guys set them off at the same time as these two big explosions."

"What could go wrong?" Alex asked ruefully.

"So he yells, 'Action!' and the pyro guys light these Roman candle things. And just then this dog walker emerges from around the corner, walks right onto the street, and the dogs see these firework sticks and go lunging forward, breaking away from her. A bunch of them grab the Roman candles and start running around with them, having the best time. Fireballs are shooting everywhere. We go running for cover. It's total insanity. The director leaps up and yells, 'Cut! Cut!' while the AD and script supervisor run for the hills as these balls of fire go sailing overhead. I take cover behind a car, and the fireballs land on the craft services table, setting fire to the paper napkins and tablecloth. The dog walker is screaming for the dogs to behave, but they are just having a ball, running around chasing people, thinking that everyone is playing with them rather than madly trying to escape. It was a total mess."

Alex couldn't stop laughing.

"Finally the dogs ran out of energy just as the Roman candles ran out of fuel. They dropped the sticks and the dog walker managed to grab all their leashes. Needless to say, the pyro guys had to set up the whole thing again, and they'd spent the entire previous day doing it in the first place. So we didn't shoot anything more that day."

"They better have all that on the DVD gag reel."

"Oh, they will. I'm sure."

They talked a little longer about the preserve and a party Zoe had attended, and then hung up. As usual, Alex felt bittersweet, missing her friend and lamenting her own lack of social life, but glad to be out doing the work she felt so passionately about.

As she started up the car, her phone dinged. It was a text message from Enrique Espinoza, asking if she'd like to come out to the dig site tomorrow for an official tour and a beer. She texted back that she'd love to.

As she drove to the cabin, though, her mind turned back to Trager and the Sons of the White Star. By the time she arrived, she was feeling low. But she turned her thoughts to the successful collar camera, and she looked forward to seeing all the artifacts Espinoza and his team had recovered thus far. The thought of having some company cheered her. Between having dinner at the ranch and visiting the archaeology site, she'd been more social than she'd been on previous field studies, to be sure, and it felt good.

TWENTY

Alex awoke in the morning, looking forward to visiting the dig site and examining artifacts. She'd long been fascinated by archaeology and had taken a few classes as an undergrad, along with courses on ancient civilizations, including Mesopotamian, Egyptian, Mayan, and Incan.

To give her body a much-needed rest, she planned to take her Jeep instead of hiking there, and to use the winding dirt road down from the cabin, then drive around onto the main road onto Milton's property and up to the site.

She bounced over the pitted dirt roads, jostling along in her Jeep, all of the windows down except for the taped-up driver's side. A pack of wild peccaries, or javelinas as they were called locally, appeared up ahead and she stopped, letting them pass. A large group with several tusked males, a horde of females, and a whole troupe of prancing babies crossed the road. She delighted at the little piglets and their playful antics as they ran to keep up with their parents. They all paused in a patch of prickly pear on the far side of the road and commenced sampling the juicy leaves and bright red fruit.

When they were clear, she continued on, her bones jarred as she took the well-worn track, the whole car vibrating as she drove over washboard sections. Several dry arroyos crisscrossed the road, and she stared upstream before crossing them. She hadn't seen any storm clouds in the distance in days but knew that flash floods could happen from storms dropping rain many miles away.

Alex felt at peace out here in this remote country, not a house or other structure in sight, just the towers and hanging wire of a distant power line, one that probably led to Milton's property and to other ranches in the area.

She turned onto the drive leading to Milton's spread, seeing immediately that it had been covered recently with fresh gravel. The ride smoothed out considerably and she kicked up less dust as she wound up the road toward the dig site. She wondered how much land Milton owned, and a little spark of hope sprung up in her. Maybe he'd be willing to put a conservation easement on this land so it would never be developed, and it would link up to the existing land of the Mogollon Wildlife Sanctuary.

Considering the fact that he wanted to buy the sanctuary, she doubted he'd do that. But it would be worth asking Ben if Milton had ever been approached about such a thing.

She arrived at the dig site to a bustle of activity. She parked next to the collection of dust-covered trucks and cars and climbed out. The students knelt in their grids, bent over their painstaking work. They turned as she approached and called out greetings. Espinoza emerged from the main tent and waved to her, a big grin on his face. His warmth was contagious, and she broke out in a huge smile herself.

"Alex! Welcome!" he called. She reached him and they shook hands warmly. "Glad you could come out. I've been looking forward to this and have a couple of beers chilling." His nose was looking a lot better, though both of his eyes were still black. One bruise was starting to turn green around the edges, a sign that it was healing.

"Great!"

He leaned close to her and whispered conspiratorially, "Plus it gives me an excuse to take part of the afternoon off and not be stooped over a grid in the hot sun." He hooked his thumb at his students. "But don't tell *them* that."

She took in the whole scene. It reminded her of her graduate school days, research trips with other students, hiking through the backcountry, walking transects, and checking cameras and hair snares. At night they'd gather, telling each other stories, laughing. One guy always had a backpacker's guitar, and he'd strum a few tunes. She missed that camaraderie and wondered where her fellow students were today. She'd lost touch with most of them. They'd all been so close then. Were they out in the field even now, somewhere doing solo work like her, or were they still lucky enough to have the company of like-minded colleagues?

Espinoza waved her toward the work tent. "Come on. Let me show you what we've found. Simón de Aguirre was certainly a looter. Can't believe what all he brought north."

They'd just reached the tent door when a black Range Rover pulled into view, kicking up a small plume of dust along the road. Alex recognized it as belonging to Milton. He drove at a respectful speed, parking with the other vehicles some distance away, where the dust wouldn't settle over the site.

"Here we go," Espinoza muttered. He rolled his eyes.

"What is it?"

"He's just . . . well, you'll see."

Milton got out and strode past the RV and the camper van. But he didn't walk all the way over to where Espinoza and Alex stood. Instead, he stopped at the first grid and leaned over Ming, who was working with a small brush. They exchanged a few words Alex couldn't hear from this distance. Ming nodded and returned to work. He continued to stand there, looming, watching her work for a while. Every now and then he'd point out different areas.

Then he went to where Gordon knelt in his trench. He hovered over the man for a time, then squatted down to talk to him. Gordon nodded, not looking up. Then Milton climbed into the trench and picked up a brush, too. He started working here and there, picking around the area, moving from section to section, doing a little work here, a little work there. He directed Gordon at times, pointing this way and that, clearly criticizing Gordon's work.

Espinoza leaned in conspiratorially toward Alex. "He's something of a micromanager. He's never worked a dig site in his life, though he's funded a lot of them. But he likes to tell perfectly qualified people how to do their jobs and even pick around a bit himself. Not that I'm not grateful for his funding. I am. If it means letting him strut around a bit, give a few unnecessary lectures, and get his hands dirty from time to time, then I'm okay with it." He smiled a little self-consciously. "Sorry. I shouldn't be talking trash about our benefactor!"

"I won't say anything," she assured him. "I've had my own adventures with micromanagers over the years."

"So you get it."

"I do."

He gave her an affectionate squeeze on the elbow. "Cool."

Finally Milton made his way over to the main work tent. "What's on tap for today?" he asked Espinoza, barely acknowledging Alex's presence with a slight glance.

"Still working on the same grids as earlier in the week," Espinoza told him. "Thinking of opening up that flat area to the south of here next week. Now that we know the sort of place Simón liked to stash his stuff, I'm getting a better idea of where to look. And we found a scroll! It's in remarkably good condition."

Milton made impatient *mmm-hmmm* noises the entire time Espinoza talked, clearly not really listening. He motioned toward the tent. "What else have you found so far?"

"Come have a look." Espinoza pulled aside one flap and ushered them in.

Milton hurried inside in front of them, feasting his eyes on the table. Before them lay a number of artifacts: a few more flint steels and horseshoe nails, a handful of links from chain mail. All looked to be sixteenth-century Spanish. And then Alex spotted three small blue stones and three red stones.

"What are these?" she asked.

"*Those*," Espinoza said, clearly excited, "I believe are playing pieces for patolli."

Alex raised her eyebrows. She'd never heard of it. "Patolli?"

"Yes. It was a game, extremely popular with the Aztecs. Commoners and royalty played it. They'd make wagers and call out the name of Macuilxochitl, the Aztec god of games, music, and dance. But when the Spanish conquistadors conquered the Aztec empire, Christian missionaries didn't like the gambling or the religious aspects of the game. They confiscated and destroyed game boards, burned all the records of how the game was played, and ultimately executed anyone found playing the game or even possessing it." He looked down at the colored rocks. "Consequently, we have no idea how the game was played. I don't expect to find a playing board for it, either. Most of them were made of cloth and likely wouldn't have survived."

Milton strutted around, taking in the other artifacts, including the small gold jaguar statue and stone werejaguar baby that Alex had seen on her previous visit.

Milton frowned. "This is it?"

Espinoza gave a little exasperated laugh. "Evander, this is *amazing*. We just unearthed the scroll yesterday and I sent it on to my lab. I haven't examined it yet. You know how much more we could learn? Given how much the conquistadors destroyed of Aztec culture, even just one scroll could be groundbreaking."

Milton waved him off impatiently. "Yes, I know. I was just hoping . . ." Milton's voice trailed off. Then he turned abruptly and lifted the tent flap. "Just keep me posted on what you find."

Espinoza watched him go. "Of course."

"That was a little weird," Alex remarked when he was out of earshot.

"He does that every few days. He's always disappointed. He wants us to find a particular artifact that Simón de Aguirre was rumored to have, that ceremonial jadeite dagger in the shape of a jaguar. So far we've come up empty. But as long as we keep digging, he seems to have high hopes, and I have money to pay my grad students, so I'm happy. C'mon. Let me show you some of the highlights of the site."

They left the work tent, and he walked her over to a small field tent, plastic covering the dig beneath. He lifted the flap and they walked inside. A stone sarcophagus lay before her, intricately carved, the image of a man on the lid. He sported a pointed beard and the helmet of a conquistador. The lid had been partly slid aside by a few inches.

"Just take a peek inside there. Only don't touch it. You'll see why."

She leaned over, finding the stone casket devoid of a body. But a rusty metal blade protruded above the lid. A large spring lay beneath it. She stared closer into the depths of the coffin, seeing that other blades with springs had been distributed all around the edges.

"When the lid comes off, those blades spring up, slicing through anyone trying to rob the grave," Espinoza explained.

"Was his body in there?"

"Nope. It was a total ruse. This was the first trap that got poor Desmond."

She took a step back, looking at the intricately carved coffin lid. "That's some beautiful work, though."

"Definitely worked as a lure. We still haven't found his body. And come check this out." He waved her out of the tent and replaced the plastic sheeting over the opening. They walked a short distance away to where Desmond had been injured when Alex first visited the site. The partially uncovered stone slab was now completely cleared of dirt and had been moved to one side to access the ground beneath it. The long spring-loaded blade that had sprung out of it had been disconnected and removed. "As you know, this is what got Desmond the day you first came here."

"What was beneath it?"

"Nothing except the blade and its spring mechanism."

"Wow. He really didn't want anyone raiding his treasure."

"No, he did not."

Alex blinked in the bright sun, seeing Milton still milling around among the students, giving them orders from the look of things. Ming looked at him impatiently and continued on with her work.

Desmond knelt in his grid, working carefully with a brush. Alex cast her gaze over to Gordon, who was standing at the edge of his grid, holding a small trowel. Suddenly Desmond cried out in surprise and Alex snapped her head back in his direction.

He was gone.

Where he'd been moments before was now just a puff of dust.

TWENTY-ONE

"What the hell?" Espinoza cried and raced over there, Alex right behind him.

When they reached the edge of the grid, Alex stared down into a yawning black hole. From the edges of the opening, she saw ancient splintered timbers sticking out. Desmond had clearly broken through these and fallen.

"Jesus fucking Christ!" they heard Desmond yell from below.

Espinoza knelt at the edge of the hole. "Desmond! You okay?"

"No, I'm not fucking okay," he shouted back. "Something stabbed me right through my arm."

"Hold on," Espinoza told him, then raced toward the work tent. He returned with several powerful flashlights. Ming and Gordon joined them and all shone beams down into the darkness.

As the dirt settled, Alex could make out a deep pit with makeshift stone walls and rusted metal spikes jutting out from the floor. Desmond had landed off to one side, his torso narrowly missing the spikes. But one of the sharp spears on the edge glistened with red. Desmond lay on his side, gripping his arm, blood seeping through his hand.

"How bad are you hurt?" Espinoza asked him.

"Bad!"

Espinoza leaned farther over the opening. "Do you have any broken bones? Trouble breathing? Did you hit your head?"

Desmond shifted on his side, grumbling. "No. I don't think so. Just stabbed through my damn arm."

"Okay. We'll get you out of there." He turned to Ming and Gordon. "Get one of the ladders."

They rushed off to the work tent and came jogging out with an aluminum ladder. Carefully they extended it down into the hole, stationing the ladder's feet between two of the spikes.

"Do you think you can climb up?" Espinoza asked him.

Desmond turned his face upward, staring at them, and wiped dirt out of his eyes. "With this arm? Are you kidding me? Not a chance."

"Okay. I'm coming down then," Ming called. She gripped the ladder and carefully eased herself down into the pit. She had little room to maneuver around the spikes and tentatively crept to the edge. She knelt down by Desmond. "Here. Let me help you up."

"Goddamnit!" Desmond cursed as she got him to his feet. He peered up at the ladder, still gripping his arm tightly. "I can't climb that."

"I'm going to help you," Ming said calmly. She directed him over to the foot of the ladder and urged him to climb up with one hand. "I got you. You're not going to fall."

"I'm not worried about falling," he snapped. "I'm worried about my damn arm falling off."

But he gripped a rung and started moving upward, Ming right beneath him. As he reached the lip of the pit, Espinoza and Gordon got him under his uninjured arm and helped him crawl out. Ming emerged right after, brushing dust off her clothes.

"Let's see how bad it is," Espinoza said, and reached for Desmond's arm. It took some coaxing to get the student to remove his tightly clenched fingers from the wound, but finally he did, sucking in a sharp breath.

The spike had torn through his sleeve there and pierced his skin, yanking away a considerable amount of flesh and even part of his muscle. Alex winced.

Ming stared down at the wound in disgust. "Holy crap. Simón really got you this time."

"Thanks for the sympathy," Desmond complained. "Jesus Christ, this hurts."

Milton remained on the periphery, staring toward them, immobile, his face unreadable.

Espinoza took in the wound, the profuse amount of blood streaming out. "This isn't something I can treat here, but I'll patch you up temporarily." He grinned at his student. "Looks like you earned a trip to an actual hospital."

"Yay me," Desmond mumbled.

"Hold on a sec," Espinoza said, and hurried back to the work tent. He appeared a minute later with the med kit and went to work stabilizing the wound as best as he could. He cleaned it and affixed a bandage. "Okay, I think that's good for now."

"They'll probably have to take a patch of skin from your butt to graft onto that," Ming said, still wincing at the sight of it.

Desmond peered down at the doc's handiwork. "Oh, great. Can't wait."

Just then a wind kicked up, spiraling dust and dirt all around them, and Espinoza wiped at his eyes with his sleeve, trying to concentrate on his injured student. Alex shut her eyes against the torrent of debris, turning her face away.

When the wind finally died down and the air cleared, Espinoza gestured toward the cars. "Okay, let's get you to the ER for some stitches."

Desmond cringed and Ming patted his shoulder. "It won't be so bad. I'll bring a deck of cards for the ten-hour waiting room stretch."

Desmond groaned.

Alex looked over to Milton, who still remained to one side, aloof, an inscrutable expression on his face. Then the briefest of smiles pulled at one corner of his mouth, as if he was musing over something. But then the muscles there twitched and his mouth turned down. She couldn't figure out if he was mad, disappointed, pleased, or something else entirely.

"I'll drive," Espinoza told them, and jogged back to the work tent to get his keys.

As Gordon and Ming helped Desmond to the car, Milton suddenly came to life, a huge grin sprouting on his face. "I think under the circumstances, we should call it a day. Ming, why don't you stay and cover the grids? And everyone, I'd like to invite you to a party at my house tonight. You've all been working hard and deserve a break. I'll have my personal chef whip up something good." He turned to Alex. "You too, Dr. Carter. Please come tonight. I'd like to hear more about your work. You know," he added after a pause, "I've hunted leopards in Africa, so I know what you're facing."

His mood shift had been so abrupt that Alex stood frozen for a minute. She furrowed her brow. She didn't know if he honestly didn't understand she wasn't hunting the jaguars, or if he thought he was offering up some genuine camaraderie.

"Yes, please all come over to my place tonight," Milton insisted. "We'll have drinks and celebrate the fine work you've done so far."

Espinoza, emerging from the tent, caught the last part of this speech. As his students stared awkwardly at Milton, Espinoza said, "Thanks. We'd appreciate that."

Milton slapped his hands together. "Great! I'll see you all around seven." Then he turned to his Range Rover and climbed in. As they watched him drive off, sending up a puff of dust, Ming said, "That was . . . nice?"

Espinoza cracked a smile. "Yes. I think that was him being nice."

Gordon opened the car door for Desmond and helped him in. "Well, I'd never turn down a party," Desmond said, clenching his teeth against the pain. As Gordon fastened his colleague's seat belt for him, Desmond muttered, "I hope he has tequila. I could murder a margarita right now."

Espinoza climbed into the driver's seat and peered up at Alex. "Rain check on the rest of the site tour?"

"Rain check."

"You coming tonight?" he asked.

She couldn't help but be curious about Milton's place. Maybe she could feel him out for his willingness to put a conservation easement on his land. "I guess I am."

"You know where his house is?"

She shook her head.

"Hand me your phone."

She did so, and he made a note of the address.

"Thanks. See you there."

Espinoza flashed those gorgeous white teeth again. "See you there."

They pulled away and Alex helped Ming cover the grids. When they finished, Ming took off to join them at the hospital and Alex drove back to the preserve, intending to spend the rest of her day making some rounds to the remote cameras. A tinge of excitement welled up at the thought of possibly spotting the jaguar again.

TWENTY-TWO

Alex parked her Jeep at the cabin, then grabbed her daypack, loaded it with her water bottle and filter, her rain gear, and a few energy bars and set out. She'd have just enough time to retrieve the memory card from one of her cameras before she had to set out for Milton's place.

As she hiked, she breathed in the scent of juniper and piñon pine. A red-tailed hawk circled in the sky above her, calling out its distinctive cry. She hiked up a steep mountain, following the path of a small creek, and entered a cool area of trees where she'd placed a camera.

She unlocked it and loaded up the first image on the camera's small display. It had recorded over a hundred photos. She flipped through them, finding some videos and images of waving grass and branches as usual. Then she halted on the twenty-sixth image. A jaguar stood there, perfectly framed, staring right into the camera. The next file on the memory card was a video of the jaguar walking out of frame. It wore her collar camera. She estimated how far it had walked from where she had collared it and was overjoyed to see that it was doing well, healthy and active.

She replaced the memory card with a fresh one and locked the camera up again. She examined the hair snare but didn't find any fur caught in it.

Then she hiked back down the steep mountain and returned to

her cabin. She showered and dressed for the party and set off in her Jeep for Milton's place. She enjoyed the drive. The sun was low, the western horizon filled with magnificent pink and gold clouds, and the sky a light robin's-egg blue above her.

She entered Milton's driveway and wound along its freshly graveled twists and turns. She passed a newly paved helipad. And then the house came into view—a sprawling mansion with huge picture windows. She sucked in a breath of disbelief. The place had to be at least 10,000 square feet.

She parked next to Espinoza's car and approached the front of the house. She'd just raised her hand to ring the bell when the door swung open. Milton stood there, a grin on his face. "Welcome, welcome." He waved her inside and she slid past him.

Voices and the clinking of glasses beckoned from another room.

"Everyone's through there," Milton told her, gesturing toward an open set of French doors. "Let me take your coat."

She shucked off her fleece jacket and handed it to him. He hung it up behind him on an elaborate Victorian coat-tree. "What can I get you to drink?"

"A beer would be great," she told him.

He smiled. "Coming right up."

She passed through the open doors, finding Espinoza, Gordon, and Desmond seated around a comfortable living room. Desmond lounged in an overstuffed wingback chair, his arm hung in a sling, his other hand holding what looked like a margarita.

"Hi, Alex!" Espinoza said cheerfully, standing up. He offered her a place next to him on the sofa, and she sat down.

"How are you feeling?" she asked Desmond.

"It's not hurting right now," he told her. "But I'm also high as a kite." He gave her a grin.

"Had to have a bit of surgery, but the ER doc fixed him right up," Espinoza assured her.

Milton reappeared, holding a bottle of Carlsberg and a glass. He set it down on the coffee table in front of Alex. "Can I get anything for anyone else?"

Desmond shook his tumbler. "Another margarita?" His words slurred.

"Should you be mixing pain meds with alcohol?" Gordon asked.

"Oh, don't cluck over me," Desmond admonished him.

Milton took Desmond's glass. "Sure thing." The doorbell rang and he disappeared.

Alex poured her beer into the glass and took the opportunity to gaze around the place. This one room alone was bigger than her apartment had been in Boston. Dark wood beams crisscrossed the ceiling, and a gigantic fireplace stood against the wall.

Espinoza noticed her interest. "If you ask him, he'll give you a tour. He showed us around earlier. Place is gigantic. He's got a home theater and a trophy room."

Alex gritted her teeth at the last mention. "I take it it's not bowling trophies."

Espinoza shook his head.

"Animal heads," Desmond slurred from his chair. "More than you can shake a stick at." He slumped in his seat, looking ready to pass out.

"You should probably avoid that room," Espinoza suggested.

A moment later, Milton showed Ming in. "The gang's all here," he said.

He still held Desmond's empty glass, then noticed the student had fallen asleep in the chair, snoring slightly. Milton placed the glass down on the table. "Guess he won't be needing another refill."

"Probably best," Gordon said.

Ming sat down in an empty chair, and Milton took her drink order, a glass of red wine.

"You want to join me?" he asked Alex. "I want to hear about your jaguar. And I can give you a tour of the place."

"Sure."

She followed him through another set of double doors, down a long hall, past a study, a library, a music room with a piano, and finally through another set of double doors to the kitchen. The room was massive, looking more like a hotel kitchen than a private one.

Something smelled amazing. A man in a chef uniform nodded at her as she entered. He labored over various saucepans and skillets, a bevy of exotic-looking food covering half the island. Copper pots and pans hung from a ceiling rack. Granite countertops lined three walls. Spotless dark wood cabinetry hung above them.

"How long till dinner?" Milton asked him.

"About twenty minutes, sir," the chef told him, then returned to his work.

Milton poured a glass of red wine, presumably for Ming, but just set it down on the island.

"Let me show you my artifact room," he offered. "I think you'd find it very interesting."

At least it wasn't the trophy room. She followed him through a door on the far side of the kitchen and down another long hallway past a small movie theater, where they entered a spacious room.

But it wasn't just artifacts. It doubled as the trophy room. Espinoza wasn't kidding. Alex should have avoided this room. Mounted heads covered nearly every foot of wall space. Gazelles, a tiger, a rhinoceros, a Dall sheep, a mountain lion, a pronghorn, a bison, a black bear, an African lion, a grizzly, a polar bear. The carnage went on and on.

Several framed photographs hung on the walls, and Alex peered at them. Milton with various guides in exotic locales, Milton posing with the carcasses of a tiger, a caribou, a leopard, a cheetah. Her stomach flopped over, a sour taste rising up in her throat.

One framed photo showed him standing over the dead body of an African lion, his foot on its chest as if he were the master of the savannah, hands on his hips, head held high. Two men stood on one side of him, a woman on the other. None looked pleased to be there, and the woman was staring down at the lion, a frown on her face. Alex noticed a striking stone turtle necklace hanging on her chest. One of its feet was chipped, and the pendant looked well-worn and loved.

"Those were my guides in South Africa," he told her. "The men were bloody useless. Total waste of money. But I did bag that lion, no thanks to them."

In the center of the room stood several large glass cases.

He pointed at them. "And these are the artifacts I've collected over the years." Milton waved her over, where she found a variety of historical objects: some Ancestral Puebloan pottery shards with dramatic white and black designs, a bevy of obsidian arrowheads, a clay tablet stamped with cuneiform letters, a Viking valknut necklace with interlaced triangles representing the nine worlds, several ornate Celtic pieces. And then she saw the stone turtle necklace. It had to be the same one. It had the same chipped foot, identical dot and zigzag patterns.

She pointed at it. "Is this the same necklace from that photograph over there?"

He nodded. "It's supposed to grant invulnerability." His eyes grew distant, musing over some private thought. His mouth twitched at the corner. "But it doesn't always work." The skin around his left eye jerked at the corner in some nervous tic. "Come look at this."

He ushered her over to another display case, this one filled entirely with Mayan artifacts. "Many of these are from the classic Mayan period." Alex took in the collection of jadeite statuettes, obsidian knives, elaborate masks with inlaid stone, a small stone carving that depicted a man wearing a jaguar skin. This one she peered at more closely. She remembered reading as an undergrad that more than a few rulers had sacrificed jaguars. Altar Q, which Mayan ruler Yax Pac dedicated in 776 CE, contained the remains of ritually killed jaguars.

"Thought you might like that one," Milton said. "Mayan rulers often wore jaguar skins as a sign of power and divine right to rule. To them, the jaguar symbolized military prowess, strength, and skill." He pointed to one of the stone masks depicting a man's face. "This particular ruler was rumored to possess a ceremonial jadeite dagger, the handle carved in the shape of a jaguar. He used it in ritual sacrifice to become invulnerable. Sacrificed dozens of humans and jaguars. Nothing could touch him. He lived to be well over a hundred years old, surviving every attack on him. That dagger was handed down to his children, who also used it in sacrifice to become invulnerable. Myth has it that eventually the Aztecs ended up with it and reputedly"—here his eyes gleamed—"the very conquistador we're digging up had it in his possession when he fled here." A small smile flickered on his face and he stared off dreamily. "Apparently, during his escape, he killed several Aztec warriors with it. But he was never touched. Not even a scratch. It protected him." Milton went quiet, musing over something. Alex grew uncomfortable in the silence. Then he suddenly snapped out of it. "Anyway," he added, but didn't elaborate.

She took in the rest of the artifacts in the case: several obsidian arrowheads, an elaborately carved Chinese jade dragon, an Egyptian stone cartouche. All the cases were temperature and humidity controlled.

Then Milton reached over and touched her arm. "Should we go upstairs now, or wait until everyone leaves?"

She recoiled. "Excuse me?"

He patted her arm. "You're right. We should wait until everyone leaves. Besides, dinner will be ready soon."

She backed away, looking him fully in the face. "What are you talking about?"

"Oh, come on. Don't be coy. You know what I'm talking about."

"Actually, I don't."

He leered at her, eyes roaming over her body. "Why do you think I invited you here?"

She looked at him, aghast. "I thought you were being polite because I was present when everyone else was invited. And you yourself said you wanted to hear more about my work."

He laughed condescendingly. "I *was* just being polite about that. No, I asked you here because I wanted to get laid."

Alex felt her jaw drop. It took her a moment to find her voice. Then she pulled herself together, suddenly feeling oily and disgusting. "Well, that's not going to happen," she said, her skin crawling.

"Are you sure? I could see my way to investing some money in your work."

Alex shuddered and charged out of the room. She couldn't get back to the living room fast enough, feeling like spiders made of grease were crawling all over her body. She shuddered involuntarily, and the relief of seeing Espinoza and the others was enormous.

Espinoza stood up, immediately sensing something was wrong. "You okay?" he asked her.

Alex tried to laugh it off. "Yeah, I'm fine." But inside she still shuddered in revulsion.

She was about to make her excuses to leave the party when Milton followed her into the room. "Now that everyone's here," he said, as if nothing had just happened, "I'd like to make a toast."

He handed Ming her glass of wine, then raised his own glass, a tumbler with three fingers of whiskey. "To all the amazing work you've done. We've found so many fantastic treasures, and I know that any number of museums will be excited to have them on display."

Everyone lifted their glasses, clinking them together, and took a sip.

"And I just want to thank you all for the time you've spent on my property, attending to this dig."

Espinoza grinned. "You're very welcome. Thank you for funding us." He handed Alex his phone. "Can you take a photo of us?"

She took it from him. "Sure thing."

Ming nudged Desmond awake and pulled him up from the chair. Everyone crowded in, grinning, arms around one another, and Alex snapped several photos.

"It's been money well spent," Milton went on when they were done with the photos. "And I'm sure you'll be very successful in your next venture. I wish you all well."

Desmond was suddenly wide awake and alert. "You make it sound like the dig is over."

Milton lifted his glass again. "It is. Onward and upward to your next project. I'm ending the funding for this dig as of today."

Espinoza set down his glass. "What? Are you serious?"

Milton's smile left his face. "Quite."

"But why?" the archaeologist countered. "There's still so much to be found! We've only found one of the scrolls, and Simón was rumored to have at least a dozen!"

"Can't be helped, I'm afraid," Milton said.

"But do you know how much lost knowledge could be in those scrolls?" Espinoza said, his mouth falling open in disbelief. "You can't end the dig now."

"I can, and I have," Milton told him, no note of empathy in his rigid voice.

Espinoza stared at him in astonishment. "But we haven't even found the jadeite dagger, the one you were so adamant about."

"That doesn't matter now," Milton told him, his lips a pursed, bloodless slash. "He probably didn't even have it. You would have unearthed it by now if he did."

"But the artifacts have been spread over a huge area," Espinoza insisted.

Milton's features suddenly shifted again, a smile parting his mouth. "And you've done an excellent job exploring that area."

Ming stood with her mouth open. "But we haven't even found Simón's body."

Milton lifted his glass again. "That might not be here, either.

Listen. Don't let this spoil our evening! There's plenty more to drink, and my personal chef is preparing quite a meal."

The students looked at each other, shock evident on their faces.

Espinoza stormed into the hallway, grabbed his jacket off the coatrack, and abruptly left.

"Don't take this so hard," Milton told the others. "You'll have plenty of opportunities to participate in other digs. And maybe I can fund something else in your future."

Just then the chef entered the room, carrying trays of hors d'oeuvres.

"Dig in!" Milton invited them.

Hesitantly, they started to pick food from the offered platters, moving like automatons, Ming staring after Espinoza. Alex could tell they were debating if they should stay, that maybe Milton's comment of funding something in the future might be worth sticking around for like good guests.

But Alex was ready to leave.

"I've got to get going, too," she told them all. "I've got an early morning tomorrow." She turned to Milton, biting back what she actually wanted to say. "Thanks for the beer."

She grabbed her fleece jacket from the coatrack and left. Outside, she saw the taillights of Espinoza's car disappearing in the distance. Only then did she remember she still held his phone.

She sighed, feeling sorry for him. She'd go by the dig site tomorrow and return it. He'd probably be there, beginning the monumental task of packing everything up. She could offer her commiseration. For now, she just wanted to go back to her cabin and be alone. She remembered now why she wasn't very social. Too often people simply disappointed you.

TWENTY-THREE

South Africa
Fifteen years ago

Evander Milton had been stalking lions for ten days, and frustration had taken hold. He had hoped to shoot one from a jeep. He and his guides had seen so many while bouncing along in the vehicle in the rugged backcountry. Whole prides of lions just lounging around in the sun. But his guides said that wasn't sporting. So instead they'd been waiting by a damned water hole for two days, endlessly watching for a lion to come down to drink.

He knew he wanted a male. Had to have the mane when he mounted it on his wall.

He sat cramped on a small camp chair inside a makeshift blind that faced the water, rifle growing heavy in his hands, back aching from the hours he'd spent endlessly waiting. Zebras came down. Warthogs. Giraffes. Kudus. But no damn lions. He was beginning to suspect his so-called guides secretly didn't want him to kill a lion and that they were all too happy just to take his money and lead him on a wild-goose chase.

And then he saw one, coming down from a rise, stalking toward the water hole, a breeze lifting its magnificent mane. He clenched his teeth in anticipation and lifted his rifle.

But a guide placed a hand on his shoulder. He turned, seeing the guide shaking his head no.

"Why the hell not?" Milton hissed through bared teeth.

The guide pointed to a herd of Cape buffalo that descended from a rise on the other side. The man gestured that they should move away from the water, give the Cape buffalo space.

Milton shook his head. He wasn't about to lose this chance. The lion came closer, moving languidly, unaware of where he hid in the blind.

The guide pointed more emphatically at the Cape buffalo herd. Milton looked with disinterest in their direction and shook his head with an adamant no. He was not going to move away.

The guide shook his head, tugging at Milton's shirt, and Milton shrugged him off, slapping the man away. Why the hell would he be nervous about a bunch of damn cows? Who cares? He wasn't going to miss this shot.

He raised his rifle to his shoulder and the guide moved away, backing up slowly, joined by the other guide. They withdrew several hundred yards away, the ninnies.

The Cape buffalo herd reached the water and began to drink. The blind opened in their direction, Milton visible from that side, and one huge bull eyed him cautiously, but Milton ignored it.

He put all of his concentration on the scope's view, waiting for the lion to get closer. He didn't want to squeeze off a shot, not with it this far away. He'd miss and it would just make the lion run away. It paused, nose lifted to the air, sniffing. It stopped. Milton grew impatient and his teeth hurt from how hard he clenched them.

With one eye squinted shut and the other peering intently through the rifle scope, Milton felt his face start to ache. His arms trembled slightly from holding them so stiffly for so long. The rifle was only getting heavier, and he'd been sitting cramped up like this for hours. He rested one elbow on his knee to steady his aim. The lion continued to stand still, gazing down at the water hole.

"Move, damn you," Milton hissed.

The lion stared off behind itself, as if waiting for others to catch up, but Milton didn't see any more animals behind the huge feline. Its mane glowed magnificently in the late afternoon sun, its paws massive. It would make an excellent addition to his wall. Or maybe he'd mount the whole body. If it would just get a little damn closer!

His eye began to tear from strain as he stared through the scope. The lion still wasn't moving, still just stood there stupidly, sniffing the air.

And then Milton heard a sudden thundering of hooves to his right and a blinding pain skewered through his body. He felt himself flying through the air, something sliding first in and then out of his side. He crashed to the barren ground, shoulder slamming into a rock. The rifle flew a dozen feet away. Shocked and stunned, Milton had no idea what had happened. Then he heard the thunder of hooves again and looked up to see the huge Cape buffalo bull bearing down on him. Blood stained one of its horns and it came at Milton with terrifying speed. It skewered his leg this time, lifting him bodily up off the ground and flinging him to one side. He landed in the thick mud beside the water hole and screamed with the jarring pain of it.

The buffalo stood still, staring at Milton as if daring him to get up. Milton lay there, feeling the blood leaking out of his side, oozing out of his leg. He tried to suck in a breath and heard liquid rattle inside him. He couldn't breathe. Couldn't get any air.

He realized through the haze of agony that the thing had punctured his right lung. When he struggled to gaze down at his leg, he saw splintered bone sticking out, a ragged, wet, glistening chunk of thigh meat attached only by a thin strip of skin.

He tried to rasp for help but found he didn't have the breath for it. The bull stared down at him, ready to attack again if Milton posed any threat. Damn thing. He wasn't after the bull's stupid herd. It had been the lion. The lion. He'd been so close.

He stared up at the rise to see that the lion had gone.

Then he turned his head to the right, searching the bushes for the guides. He saw both of them, crouching there, unmoving.

"Help me!" he commanded them, but his voice came out in a thin, weedy rasp, barely audible.

The guides didn't move, just stared fixedly at the bull and the rest of the herd.

"Come help me, you damn cowards!" Milton tried to bark at them. But all that came out was a whisper so weak only he could hear it.

Still the bull remained towering over his broken body. The herd moved a little closer to Milton, taking turns to drink, and fear flopped in Milton's belly. What if more of them decided to move in and attack?

Panic took hold as a huge blood bubble rose up and popped on his lips. He was bleeding to death, suffocating, and those useless guides did nothing to help him.

Then he heard a jeep pull up in the distance. The guides slunk off toward it, moving out of sight. Milton didn't dare move to crane his neck to see where they went. He heard the jeep's engine cut out and some distant mumbled voices.

Were they just going to leave him here for dead? Come back and get his body later when the buffalo had left? He'd paid thousands of dollars for this hunt. And not only had they led him on a merry chase, but now they were just going to let him die.

Well, he'd be damned if he'd let that happen. He'd sue the shit out of them. Milton struggled to sit up and the Cape buffalo charged toward him, stopping just short of his gored body. Milton slumped back down immediately, squeezing his eyes shut, waiting for the impact of another sharp horn. But none came. He opened his eyes a crack. The Cape buffalo stood closer now, its head bent, waiting to take out Milton if he dared to get up. So Milton lay there, despair sinking in. But he hadn't heard the jeep drive away. Maybe the guides would come back . . .

Suddenly a woman strode into view, her black hair shorn close to her scalp, her sepia face and dark brown eyes staring down at Milton. She dragged a stretcher behind her. Quietly, she walked right over to Milton and bent down beside him. The bull didn't move. She checked Milton over for injuries.

"I'm going to roll you onto the stretcher," she told him.

Still the bull didn't move, only watching the woman as she worked.

He bit down on a scream as she rolled him onto the stretcher. He reached out, grasping her arm against the agony, and her necklace brushed Milton's shoulder. He recognized the art as Zulu, a stone turtle with painted dots and zigzag lines.

Then he was on the stretcher, the woman dragging him away from the bull, the bull not moving, just staring after them. It made no move to attack.

"How—" he started to ask her, but blood bubbled up in his mouth, cutting off his words.

She didn't answer but closed a delicate hand around her pendant as they reached the jeep. A sharp stab of agony made him see everything so clearly. The bull hadn't made a single move toward her that whole time. The pendant. She wore it, and it had brushed against his shoulder. It had protected them.

Milton stared at the pendant all the way back to the camp as they bounced around in the back of the jeep. He felt something powerful in it.

When they reached camp and the helicopter came to airlift him to the hospital, he begged the woman to go with him. He had to be around the pendant for longer. In fact, he had to have it for himself.

He recovered in a hospital for weeks after that, suffering in agony and cursing that buffalo. Some days he felt like he'd never be healed, that he'd never be able to resume normal activity. Despair gripped him during those long nights when he couldn't find a comfortable position and sleep eluded him. But finally, slowly, his body healed and he was able to move around again.

When he was fully back up to snuff, he flew back to the safari camp where he'd been before. He was not going to go home without a lion. He made them take him out again, and this time he was successful, bagging a magnificent male to take home for his display room.

But all the while he kept thinking of the woman and her pendant. He'd seen her out in the bush again, this time around African wild dogs, and none of them bothered her. That pendant.

He'd watched her arguing with her ex-boyfriend one night, a valet from a nearby hotel. The man had threatened her. Said he'd kill her if she didn't come back to him, and Milton began to get ideas. If he took action, they'd think that boy did it. That he'd lived up to his threats. He'd certainly made them in front of enough people.

Later, on his last night in camp, Milton stole into her tent in the darkness. He slit her throat while she slept and took the pendant, then stood there musing. It must not grant invulnerability every time. Otherwise he wouldn't have been able to kill her. But he knew it had worked at least a few times, and it was worth having.

And there might be other pendants out there, other artifacts and objects that granted invulnerability. If he could find more, if he had a whole collection of them, even if some of them worked only some of the time, he'd be upping his chances. He could live a long life. He could hunt in as many exotic locations as he wanted and be protected. He'd never have to suffer through those kinds of grievous injuries again. He gripped the necklace in his fist and stole out of her tent.

The next day, he acted surprised at the news of her death. He was due to fly out that day, his lion carcass in tow. He kept to his plan and flew back to the States, mounted the lion head on his wall and added her pendant to his collection. He'd find more. He had to.

TWENTY-FOUR

Back at the dig site, Espinoza slumped into his chair inside the work tent and pulled out the bottle of twenty-year-old Scotch he'd been saving to celebrate with his students. He poured a shot of it. Damn it. He couldn't believe Milton had just suddenly pulled his money out like that. The guy had been eccentric from the start, Espinoza couldn't deny that. But to just pull the plug? Without any rhyme or reason? Just end the dig? It wasn't like they weren't finding anything. They'd already found so much! A scroll, the patolli pieces, gold figurines. And that Olmec werejaguar statuette!

Espinoza slipped on a pair of gloves and picked up the statuette. It was so finely crafted. The curves, the details, all so precise. There could be more like this, more scrolls, too. They'd only found one so far, and there could be so many more.

Espinoza took another sip from the shot glass. He'd never been someone who could down a whole shot in one go. He always started to feel sick. So now he just sipped at the glass. Dizziness began to swim a little in his head, the strong drink sweeping away a bit of the bitter disappointment he felt. So he took another sip and another, then refilled the glass.

He stood up, perusing more of the artifacts, gazing over the finds of Spanish origin, like the wall gun, the sword points, and a gold crucifix inlaid with rubies and sapphires. They could have learned a lot here.

He imagined the soil just outside the tent, holding so many se-
crets, so much knowledge just waiting to be unearthed. What was
Milton's deal? It just didn't make sense. Why partly fund something
and then just pull out? They hadn't even found the artifact Milton
was so keen on—the jadeite ceremonial dagger. The guy didn't seem
to be hurting for money or anything. Espinoza thought of how the
guy lived—sheesh, he must be loaded. He had his own freakin' helipad, for chrissakes. He had not just a Range Rover in his driveway,
but a Jaguar in his garage. And this was just *one* of his homes. From
what Espinoza overheard and saw around his house tonight, he had
at least four other houses stashed around the world. One in the
South of France, one in Kenya, one in Australia, and a brownstone
in New York.

Espinoza took another sip, wincing at the burn as it went down.
Maybe it was about debt. Maybe the guy was overextended. He
shook his head in anger and disappointment. Who the hell knew.
Guy was always poking around the dig, acting weird anyway.

And the whole thing had just fallen into Espinoza's lap. Milton
had just strolled into his office one day at the University of New
Mexico and asked Espinoza if he wanted to oversee a dig of the infa-
mous conquistador Simón de Aguirre. At first Espinoza had thought
he was joking. Simón de Aguirre was so steeped in legend that he
almost didn't seem real. Treasure hunters had searched for decades
in New Mexico for Simón's buried treasure, all without result. Tales
of the loot had taken on epic proportions, and searches for it proved
as futile as searches for the Lost Dutchman's Mine or the fabled
city of El Dorado. Most people had begun to think it was all just tall
tales, that no such treasure actually existed.

But then Milton had produced documents dating to Simón's
time. Said he'd bought them off someone who'd had them in his
family. The documents detailed not just Simón's own account of
escaping from the Aztecs, laden with treasure, but even recorded
accounts of workers who'd been hired to bury the loot and build

elaborate booby traps to protect it. The papers included work orders that had been drawn up by Simón himself, outlining exactly how he wanted to be buried, if he ever died.

Espinoza remembered that word *if* in the manuscript. *If* he ever died. As if maybe Simón didn't think he ever would. That he'd live forever.

Well, hell, Espinoza thought. *We all want to live forever. Except on days like this.* He took another swig of whiskey and set down the werejaguar. He'd have to start packing all these artifacts up tomorrow. Carefully cataloging them and crating them for shipment back to the university.

Just then he heard someone stirring outside his tent. One of the grad students, back from the party, he supposed, come to check on him. He had left in rather a huff. But then he paused. He hadn't heard a car pull up. He frowned, listening. Then he heard it again. Very faint footfalls, just outside the tent.

He almost called out, then stopped himself. A bad feeling crept into his gut. Maybe it was one of the white supremacists. Or hell, a load of them, waiting to ambush him.

He paused in the dim light from his work lamp. It was unmistakable now. Footsteps outside. Someone sneaking around.

He picked up a box cutter from the packaging station, fingers tensed around the handle. He extended the sharp blade an inch and stood tensed in silence.

When he heard someone's hand brush the canvas of the tent, he stepped backward toward the rear entrance, but his elbow accidentally knocked over the whiskey bottle. It thumped on the ground, the powerful smell of alcohol filling the confines of the enclosed space.

The front tent flap moved aside, and a figure stepped into view, looming in the doorway. The man wore all black, including a ski mask, so Espinoza couldn't make out any of his features. The figure's hand raised, clutching a silhouetted blade. Espinoza didn't wait to get a better look. He rushed to the rear door, jerked the flap aside and tore off into the night.

He tripped on a rock, almost went down, and caught himself at the last minute. Why the hell hadn't he brought along his headlamp? But if he had that on, then whoever it was would be able to find him in the dark. He raced on, trying to make out rocks and vegetation in the light from the waxing gibbous moon.

He ran down an embankment, then glanced back over his shoulder, seeing the dark figure at the top, hand upraised, the pointed weapon lifted. The man half slid, half ran down the steep incline, racing after Espinoza.

The archaeologist reached the small dry creek bed at the bottom of the slope and jumped over the rounded and jumbled rocks there.

Maybe his pursuer would trip.

But he didn't. Espinoza watched with a pounding heart as the man cleared it in a single bound.

The lightheadedness from the shots was now fully taking over, and Espinoza felt disoriented and weak. His heart was beating too fast and acid rose in his throat. Damn. Why had he been drinking? And on an empty stomach, no less. He hardly ever drank. Usually just when he'd faced a huge disappointment like now. But he couldn't have known this was about to happen.

He dared another look back, saw with horror that the figure was gaining on him, and immediately regretted taking his eyes off the ground in front of him. The toe of his boot struck a massive rock, and he went down, cracking his shin on the sharp edge of it. Pain erupted in his leg and he sprawled on the rocky soil, his head and shoulders landing in a saltbush.

He rolled onto his side, both hands instinctively flying down to his shin, feeling the warmth of blood there.

The man was on him in a matter of seconds. A rough hand grabbed him by the hair and yanked his head back. Espinoza struck out with the box cutter, but the man knocked it aside. Espinoza heard it clatter against some rocks several feet away. Then he saw the man's blade rise in the moonlight and come down with shocking force. The sharp edge bit into the skin of his throat and Espinoza shoved the hand away. He swept his legs out, aiming for the man's groin. His foot struck home and the attacker grunted, doubling over.

Espinoza struggled to his feet, fingers pressing against the wound in his neck. He could feel sticky blood there, but the man hadn't been able to finish the job. The slice hurt like hell but felt shallow. Gripping his throat, Espinoza ran through the brush, heading for the darkness of a copse of juniper ahead.

Behind him the man recovered and took off in pursuit.

Espinoza stumbled, his mind cloudy from the whiskey, feeling awkward and sick. He could feel now that his lower pant leg was soaked through with blood where he'd cut it on the rock. And warm stickiness now soaked the side of his shirt. He kept one hand clamped there and reached the darkness of the trees. A fallen trunk lay in a pool of shadow, and Espinoza headed for it. Glancing back, he saw that the man was not yet at the trees, so Espinoza dove down, pressing his body against the trunk. He shucked off his dress shirt and tied it tightly around his throat, hoping to stanch the bleeding. Then he pulled several fallen branches over his body.

Now he worked on stilling his breath. He was gasping for air. Too loud. He forced his breathing to slow. He heard the man enter the copse, his feet no longer crunching on rock but now on the soft bed of juniper needles. Espinoza heard him run at a jog through the cluster of trees and exit on the far side.

Espinoza allowed himself several luxurious deep breaths. But then the man's progress halted. Espinoza couldn't hear him anymore. He strained to make out anything above the rush of blood in his ears. The wound in his neck pulsed. Then he heard the slow circuit of the man's footsteps around the edge of the trees. Espinoza had lost him, but for how long?

He fought the urge to jump up from his hiding place, to run in the opposite direction of the man's footfalls. But what if his pursuer saw him? Espinoza was in no shape for a prolonged chase.

Where were his students? What time was it? Would they be back soon? Should he wait it out? Or try to circle back and get to his car? He patted his pockets for his phone. Damn. He forgot. He'd asked Alex to take their picture, then left, disgusted, forgetting about it completely. But there was no reception out here, anyway, so it wasn't like it would magically be able to make a call, even if he had it.

He felt the reassuring stab of his car keys in his pocket. Thank goodness he hadn't taken them out and laid them on the worktable. But to reach his car, he'd have to cross the open camp, and his attacker might well expect him to circle back there. Maybe it wasn't such a good idea after all.

He needed a place to hide and bide his time until his students got back from the party. All their lights and engines would surely scare the guy off.

The ruins, Espinoza thought suddenly, the haze of alcohol clearing a little. They were hidden in that crack in the rock. If he could reach them, he could hide in there, all night if he had to.

Now he heard the crunch of the man back on the rocky section again, moving away from the trees. The steps got farther and farther away. Now was his chance.

Espinoza lifted the brush off himself and crept quietly from his hiding space. He stared through the pine trunks, seeing the man now, about a hundred yards away. Espinoza crept to the edge of the trees, angling toward the slot canyon and the ruins.

Using the moonlight, Espinoza stumbled onward, finding the arroyo and cutting across it. His feet slid on the loose soil. He was still wearing his dress shoes, *goddamnit*. He caught himself before he fell, still pressing the shirt against his neck. He made it up the steep opposite bank. His panic grew at the racket he was making.

He tried to pick up his pace, but his legs shook and he felt weakness stealing over him. Loss of blood.

The ruins had never felt this far away before. He didn't think he could make it. He slowed, considering his options. Maybe he *should* angle back toward his car. He paused now, staring back, trying to pinpoint movement in the moonlight. He didn't see any in the direction of the camp. And it was much closer than the ruins.

Rethinking things, he jogged in the direction of the camp, but a sudden rustling in a patch of saltbush startled him. The man jumped out, slashing at him, the blade catching in Espinoza's shirt. Espinoza spun, racing back the way he'd come, heading once again for the slot canyon. He entered a dark pool of shadows in a copse of piñon pine and then a rock outcropping. He crouched down behind it, trying to catch his breath, to quiet the stertorous gasps.

The man ran right by his location, unaware of Espinoza's position. Who the hell was this guy? The man ran to the edge of the copse, stared around, then doubled back, once again heading for the camp. The man had lost him, and likely thought he was still trying to go for the car.

So the ruins it was. When the man disappeared over a rise, Espinoza emerged from the rocks and ran at a sprint toward the slot canyon. But dizziness swept over him and he struggled to focus. His breathing felt ragged, and he longed to stop and rest. But he couldn't afford to.

He pressed on, reaching the second arroyo that he'd crossed earlier with Alex. He stumbled down the bank of it, lost his balance, and went sprawling onto the sharp stones. He felt a rock bite into his knee and winced in pain. The shirt came loose, tearing at the clotted blood of his wound. Espinoza's hand flew up to the cut, finding the blood there thick and goopy. It was coagulating. That was good. But he'd already lost so much blood that the shirt was absolutely soaked. He retied it and managed to stand, his wounded shin and knee crying out in protest.

Another wave of dizziness swept over him and he crashed back down again, sharp stones cutting into the palms of his hands. He thought of the slot canyon, which still lay probably a mile away. The camp was back only half a mile. Maybe his attacker had raced back there, found that Espinoza hadn't gone that way after all, and was now retracing his steps. But moments later, the man leapt out from behind a large rock outcropping and raced toward Espinoza. Espinoza darted to one side, almost fell over, and felt the blade graze his back. He slid down an embankment, the man right behind him. Espinoza whirled, balling up his fist and aiming for the man's throat. He hit home, and the man grabbed at his neck, reeling back.

Espinoza ran across the arroyo and up the other side, adrenaline fueling an extra burst of speed. He glanced back, still seeing the man bent over in the creek bed, gagging and grasping at his throat.

Now Espinoza focused on one thing and one thing only—reaching the safety of the ruins. He ran one step at a time. One foot in front of the other. Rhythmic. Ignore the pain. Press on. He'd make it. He had to.

He staggered into the mouth of the slot canyon and ran along the dry stream bed there. The light of the moon barely penetrated here, a deeper darkness closing in around him. He could barely see the section where the crack lay. He looked back, not seeing the figure in the mouth of the canyon. He had time. He stumbled forward and finally reached the crevice. One more glance told him that the man was nowhere in sight. He'd made it. His fingers grasped at the crevice walls as he heaved himself inside, sliding along the narrow opening.

Then finally he emerged into the large room and collapsed on his side. His breath plumed dirt on the floor and he tasted the grit. He lay there, desperate for a decent breath, his neck, knee, and shin throbbing in pain.

Finally he managed to inhale deeply and roll over on his back. The only light came from wan moonlight filtering in from the crevice.

In the darkness, he couldn't see the ruins, but he felt the huge expanse above him. The houses. The jaguar painting. The refuge.

But then scraping snapped his attention to the crack, and Espinoza swallowed hard when he saw the figure squeezing through, blocking out the diffuse moonlight.

And then he knew. He hadn't tricked the man by hiding here. When Espinoza had changed his mind and headed back toward camp and the man had appeared, striking at him and then miraculously withdrawing as soon as Espinoza changed his course back to the slot canyon—the man had known about this place all along.

He had *herded* Espinoza here.

Espinoza scrambled to his feet, but the man closed in fast. The way he moved let Espinoza know he hadn't really hurt him very much. The man had been buying time, waiting for Espinoza to head back toward the ruins.

Espinoza could barely make out the figure now in the darkness but saw vague movement as the man lunged. He felt gloved hands seizing his throat, then pulling him to the ground. The archaeologist crashed onto the dirt and kicked out, but met only empty air.

The man tightened his grip on Espinoza's throat and the archaeologist's vision began to tunnel, darkness closing in. He pounded at the man's arms, hands grabbing for the man's throat, but the figure twisted out of the way.

Then the figure knelt down on Espinoza's chest, the last of the archaeologist's breath exploding from his lungs.

Espinoza caught the flash of the knife blade in the thin light as the man lifted it. Then the weapon came down, biting into his throat, this time deeply. He felt another slash, then another. The pulsing in his neck grew stronger, and he could feel the blood pumping out of his body.

He grabbed at the man's masked face, at his hands, at his neck, at anything he could seize. But all the while he felt his life slipping away, and his last thought was *Why?*

TWENTY-FIVE

The next day, Alex awoke, her mind still on the party the night before. She felt sorry for Espinoza and his team. The abrupt severing of funds was obviously a huge let down.

She decided she'd drive to the dig site before she started her rounds that day, return Espinoza's phone, and check on them all.

After a quick breakfast, she drove to the dig site, then parked between Espinoza's car and one of the student's trucks.

The scene before her was somber—Gordon was reeling in the awning of his camper and Ming was dismantling her tent. Desmond, his arm in the sling, was gathering up shirts and a pair of jeans that he'd slung over a laundry line and packing them into his camper van.

They turned as she pulled up.

"Hey everyone," she said, climbing out. "So sorry about last night. Can't believe he shut the dig down."

Gordon stepped out of his RV and walked over to her. "And so unexpectedly, too."

She glanced around as the others approached. "Where's Enrique?"

Ming hooked her thumb at the work tent. "When we got back, the light was burning in there. You could smell the whiskey even from outside the tent. We decided not to bother him. He was pretty upset last night."

"I was about to go in there, start packing up the artifacts," Desmond said.

Gordon pursed his lips. "I'll help you. You've got that damaged wing and all."

"Guess that's one good part," Desmond mused. "No more booby traps."

Ming stifled an amused smile. "They did seem to have it in for you."

He widened his eyes. "Oh, that's funny, is it? *You* want to pay my medical bills? Sheesh!"

"You're right. I'm sorry. But you'll have cool stories to impress women with."

Alex immediately realized from Desmond's expression that the only woman he was interested in impressing was Ming, but Ming didn't notice.

Alex pulled Espinoza's phone out of her pocket. "Well, I've got to return this to him."

"You go in!" Desmond said immediately.

"Yeah, you go in there and talk to him," Ming agreed. "Maybe you can cheer him up. You're unrelated to the dig site, and maybe the sight of you will lift his spirits."

Alex almost had to laugh at their eagerness to be let off the hook.

"He's gotten in these dark moods before," Gordon said. "Last semester we lost funding on another dig, and he went on a three-day bender. I made the mistake of going over to his house to check on him and had to listen to a four-hour tirade on academia and how you're expected to publish every year, but how can you publish if your work keeps getting yanked. He was furious. I mean," he added quickly, "not at me or anything. The guy's not a jerk. He just . . ."

". . . can go on for a bit," Desmond finished.

Gordon nodded. "Man's got a gift for tirades."

Alex shook her head, amused. "So you've all been biding your time out here, waiting for one of you to go in and bear the brunt of one of these tirades?"

Desmond nodded. "Yep. That about sums it up."

Alex chuckled. "Okay. I'll take one for the team. 'Once more unto the breach.'"

They watched her go with interest. When Alex approached the door of the work tent, she could smell the stench of whiskey, too. Wow. How much had the guy drunk?

She pulled aside the door to the tent and immediately detected a faint coppery scent hovering above the alcohol. She saw the whiskey bottle toppled over on the ground. Then her eyes went over to the worktable.

Espinoza lay sprawled on it, his undershirt cut open, his intestines spilling out. Her gaze took in the rest of the scene: his face ashen, mouth slack and open, eyes filmed over, arms splayed. Blood soaked through his pants on his knee and shin. Several deep gashes marked his throat, and his dress shirt from the night before lay discarded on the ground, stiff with blood. Flies buzzed around him.

Alex stumbled backward, tripping over the whiskey bottle and colliding with the tent flap. She caught herself before she fell, backing out of the enclosed space.

Her gorge rose, and she swallowed hard. Then she was out of the tent, blinking in the bright sunshine.

His students had gathered around the tent. Gordon immediately rushed to her, placing a steadying hand on her elbow.

"What is it?"

She couldn't find words. She swallowed again. "It's . . ."

Ming rushed forward, flinging the tent flap aside. "Oh my god!" She wheeled backward, crashing into Desmond's injured arm.

"What the hell is going on?" he demanded, wincing and cradling his sling.

He made a move for the tent door and Ming put a hand on his shoulder. "Don't go in there. He's—"

"He's dead," Alex finished. "He's been murdered."

Gordon's mouth fell open. "What?" Before Alex could stop him, Gordon drew back the tent flap and peered inside. "Jesus," he breathed, then stepped back, his face gone blank, the tent flap falling in place. Desmond peeked inside. Then, turning slightly green, he slowly withdrew.

For several long minutes all four just stood there, struggling to process the situation.

Then Ming said: "Who . . . ?"

Desmond balled his fists. "Those damn white supremacists. They said they'd cut him open, disembowel him."

"We have to call the police," Ming said, her voice barely a whisper.

Gordon remained silent. He stared off into space.

"You okay?" Alex asked him.

He didn't answer, just continued to gaze into the distance, his eyes gone glassy. She touched his arm, and he snapped his eyes to her. "What?"

"Are you okay?" she repeated.

He shook his head. "No. No, I'm not." His brow furrowed, then anger flashed in his eyes. "We have to call the cops. Nail those bastards."

Alex still clutched Espinoza's phone. She lifted it now, looking at the bars. None. She thought of using her satellite communicator, getting her dad to call them, but that roundabout method might cause more delays as he tried to explain. "I can go into town," she told them. "You all stay here. I'll get the police."

She turned, the rest of them continuing just to stare at the tent flap.

At her car, she checked the bars on her phone, too. Nothing. So she fired up the engine and began the dusty trek toward Azulejo, hoping she'd get a signal before she got there.

Alex drove, checking the bars on her phone as she went. As soon as she got one, she pulled over and phoned the police to report the murder. Deputy Wentworth answered, and he took down the details and the location. She decided to head back to the dig site, since she was the one who had first seen the body. The police would have more questions.

When she pulled back in by Gordon's RV, she found the group of students much as she had left them, still hovering outside the work tent.

She parked and they all turned to her expectantly. "The police are on their way," she told them.

Ming folded her arms across her chest. "They didn't do anything before."

"When?" Alex asked, reaching their small circle.

"When those bastards came out and threatened us," Desmond told her, "nothing came of it."

"Maybe they still have no idea who these guys are," Gordon muttered quietly.

Ming hugged herself. "That deputy could have examined the scene when he came out. Looked at the tire treads or something."

Gordon nodded. "True."

"And now look what's happened," she added.

Alex looked down then at all their footprints in the dirt. "Maybe we'd better move away from the tent. Preserve the scene."

Gordon nodded. "Good idea. Why don't you all come back to my RV? I've got soda, some beer, whatever you want."

Slowly they made their way over there, then piled into his RV. He invited them to sit at the four-person dinette while he pulled beverages out of the small refrigerator. "Take your pick," he said, lining them up on the table. Alex grabbed a can of papaya juice, Ming a Pepsi, and Desmond reached for a bottle of beer.

"What?" he said defensively when Ming stared at him. "My arm is killing me."

Gordon took a Pepsi for himself and then sat down next to Alex.

They waited then, largely in silence, staring out of the windows and watching for the police.

Deputy Wentworth arrived with another uniformed officer. He greeted Alex and the students, took a brief peek inside the tent, then radioed for a detective.

"It was that white supremacist group," Ming told him. "Those bastards killed him in the same way they threatened to. Said they'd disembowel him, and they did."

Wentworth wrote down their initial statements, and the detective arrived about thirty minutes later, surveyed the scene, and called for the state police crime scene unit. They took even longer to arrive, and Gordon made Alex and the others sandwiches while they waited. But only Desmond was able to tuck into his. Alex decided to save hers for later. The situation was starting to sink in.

She'd liked Espinoza. A lot. She found him affable, easy to get along with. That was rare for her. To think that someone could have murdered him in cold blood, that he was alive and joking around last night and was gone today, just seemed unbelievable.

Then the detective asked them to step out one by one and took more detailed statements from each of them. No one had seen Espinoza since he left the party in disgust. After eating at Milton's, the students had all gone to a bar in Azulejo to talk about Milton cutting the funding. They'd gotten back late and seen the work light on in the main tent. They just assumed he was in there, especially when they smelled the strong scent of whiskey. None of them had peered inside. They'd all just gone to bed, dispirited about the end of the project. Alex related how she'd arrived that morning to return his phone and found the body. No one had touched anything. The detective reproved them for walking on the dirt in front of the tent, as if they should have been psychic and just *known* that Espinoza had been murdered in there and then simply floated above the ground like fairies.

He asked about who owned the land, and they told him how to reach Evander Milton at his house.

The detective took all this down and then informed the students that they'd have to wait until the CSU was finished before they could dismantle the camp. He told them all to get motel rooms in Azulejo while the cops worked the scene. Alex gave him her contact info in case he had further questions, and he let them all leave.

They said their goodbyes at the small group of cars, none of them really knowing what to say, all of them feeling the shock of suddenly losing their friend and mentor.

Alex drove away, sadness sweeping over her, and at an unbidden image of Espinoza's destroyed body, she felt her eyes begin to sting. She stopped at the intersection of the road that led to town. She wiped away sudden tears, but felt more coming, her throat painful and tight. She let the grief come, then finally turned down the bumpy dirt road leading to her cabin.

She wanted nothing more than to get out on the trail, be around wildlife and nature. The day had been staggeringly terrible and she just wanted to be alone.

Back at the cabin, she grabbed her daypack and set off to check on another camera. She didn't have a lot of light left but wanted to check at least one.

She hiked in something of a daze at first, not hearing much around her, not reveling in the solace that nature usually provided. She stopped on the bank of the Mesquite River. Finally she forced herself to be there in the moment, to listen to the lyrical song of a nearby cactus wren, the sigh of wind through the willows, the trickling of the water.

She moved on, reaching her target camera. She checked the images on it, not finding any of a jaguar at first glance. She traded out the card, though, so she could check the photos more carefully back at the cabin.

Then she sat down on a rock and took off her hat, knowing she had to head back to beat the sunset, but just feeling too tired and emotionally exhausted to press on at the moment. Poor Enrique. Then she thought of the jaguar out there, of all the obstacles it had faced to reach this area, and felt hopelessness creep up on her.

She knew that on top of navigating the border barriers and outwitting poachers, jaguars faced the threat of the destruction of their habitat to make way for palm oil plantations. Land was clear-cut to grow this plant, which was found in a vast array of products, including soaps and shampoos and even sweet snacks like pies and cookies. Jungles and forests replaced by palm oil plantations became monocultures, devoid of biodiversity. This trend was sweeping across places like Colombia, Ecuador, and Guatemala, and had already caused devastating loss in Southeast Asia, where nearly 700,000 acres were clear-cut annually, destroying much native wildlife. In Borneo alone, plantation workers had killed nearly 150,000 orangutans since 1999, decimating their population.

But Alex knew that like her, more and more consumers were responding to this destruction, refusing to buy products that utilized unsustainably grown palm oil.

She imagined the jaguar out there right now, perhaps drinking from a seep. She hoped it wouldn't run into Trager.

Then finally she stood up, replaced her hat, and headed back to the cabin.

Once she was back, she took a short but luxurious shower, first in the cold water of the exterior shower to cool off, and then finishing with water from the sun shower she'd hung there. The warmth cascaded over her aching body, sore from covering so much ground over the last few days.

The sun set and she dressed in warmer layers, preparing for the typically cold night ahead of her. She heated up a packet of spicy curry and spinach on the little propane stove and poured it over some rice. Then she ate it outside on the old wooden bench, enjoying the vivid stars above her. She loved the location of this cabin. High enough in elevation to sport trees and shade, it was also far enough away from any big city to offer stunning views of the sweeping Milky Way. She stared up at the Summer Triangle, formed by the stars Deneb in Cygnus, the Swan; Altair in Aquila, the Eagle; and Vega in Lyra, the Lyre. She spotted the bright red gleam of Arcturus in Boötes and scanned her eyes up from there to see one of her favorite constellations, the twinkling C of the Corona Borealis.

A meteor streaked by, and she made a silent wish for the jaguars making their way north to here.

Her mind drifted to Casey, the enigmatic helicopter pilot she'd worked with in the Canadian Arctic, wondering if he was gazing up at these same stars even now, wherever he happened to be. Her heart quickened, her stomach fluttering at the thought of him. That always seemed to happen. She'd never met anyone like him and doubted she ever would again.

A western screech owl sang out a haunting warble, followed a few seconds later by another screech owl somewhere deeper in the forest.

She was just finishing her curry and rice when the sound of a distant car engine interrupted her reverie. She put her fork down, listening. It grew louder and louder, and Alex realized it seemed to be getting closer, heading in her direction. Soon she sniffed the faintest hint of dust on the wind. It grew stronger, and she stood up. She placed her bowl down on the bench.

Now she could see a cloud of debris rising above the trees, dimming the stars there. She heard someone taking the narrow, pitted road up to the cabin way too fast. If it was June or George, she didn't think they'd be racing to get up here. Maybe it was Milton, come back to make another offer.

She swallowed. Maybe some emergency had happened. No one could reach her at her cabin. No landline, no cell signal, and the only one who knew about her satellite communicator was her dad. But he would just text her on it if something was wrong, and he hadn't.

A pit formed in her stomach. Her dad. What if something had happened to *him,* and Ben Hathaway had sent a local up here to get her?

She gazed down the road, seeing headlights now piercing the gloom, flashing on treetops as the car approached.

Then her heart froze and her mouth went dry at the thought of Espinoza. Maybe his killer had targeted her next.

An all-too-familiar white truck spun into view, tearing up the road, a flag streaming behind. All of Alex's fears about her dad vanished, replaced by terrifying new ones.

TWENTY-SIX

Alex stepped back into the cabin and bolted the door. But it wasn't like the cabin was a fortified panic room or anything. It had been built decades ago and was rotting in places. The windows, just thin glass that had become rippled with age over the years, offered little protection with their weather-worn wooden frames. One didn't even shut properly, the lock having fallen off who knew when.

The truck roared up to the cabin, leaving a drifting cloud of dust that slowly carried off on the wind. Three men piled out. All three wore skull masks with guns on their hips, and she suspected they were the same men from the dig site: the driver who had knocked down Espinoza and Gordon, and his two yes-men. They wore gloves, but she could see pale skin peeking out at their wrists and at the base of their masks.

The driver strode up to the door, his leering skull mask illuminated from the light inside the cabin. He pounded on the door with a fist. "We know you're in there!" he shouted.

She didn't respond.

"Just open the door!" he demanded.

Like that's going to happen.

He pounded again and again. "We'll break it down if we have to."

Alex rummaged through her pack and grabbed her bear spray. She still had it from her last assignment in Washington State. Then she loaded a tranquilizer dart into the dart gun with enough seda-tive to knock out a man. She preloaded two more in case his buddies wanted some, too.

"I've called the police on my sat phone," she bluffed, yelling through the closed door.

The driver hesitated. Then he shouted, "Take 'em quite a while to get all the way out here."

She grabbed her sat communicator with one hand and placed it on a windowsill at the back of the cabin, where it would have a view of the sky. She waited anxiously while it fixed its location, then quickly typed out a message to her dad to call 911 and send the po-lice to her location.

"I'm armed," she warned them, facing the door once again. "Just leave."

"We just want to talk to you. Give you something to think about," the driver said, trying to sound calmer.

Alex went quiet.

He waited, then plowed on. "This damn jaguar study of yours has to end. You gotta understand. We need one continuous border wall all the way across Mexico. We don't need places where jag-uars or any other kind of animal can get across, if you know what I mean."

She did. *Any other kind of animal.* Like humans.

"You find jaguars up here, get the government to do some damn fool thing like leave parts of our border unprotected, and we'll get all kinds of murderers and thieves and rapists moving up here."

Alex remained quiet.

"And then what happens to our American way of life?" he went on. "What about us *real* Americans? We get replaced. We lose our jobs. Our kids go to school with drug dealers and thieves. All this 'my land is your land' bullshit has gotta stop," he droned on. "You know what they're teaching our kids in school? That white people are bad. That we've somehow oppressed everyone around us. Our kids are growing up hating themselves, full of guilt."

When she remained quiet, he shouted, "It's our God-given right to protect this country, to live in this country as we see fit."

And no one is stopping you from living in this country, Alex thought with disgust, anger simmering inside her. She just wanted the men to leave.

But the driver was on his soapbox now, reveling in spewing his rhetoric of hate and misinformation.

"Soon all the good jobs are going to be given away to illegal immigrants. There won't be anything left for us. It's bad enough you women think you can steal our jobs, even when you're not qualified to take 'em. They give you our jobs because of affirmative action, and then everything goes to shit. You think trash like them and women can run factories? You think they can join the police force and keep hardworking Americans safe? There's more scum in the goddamn army now than whites. They can't protect our nation."

He was really going at it now, and Alex gritted her teeth.

"I mean, look at you. Don't you have a husband? Shouldn't you be home taking care of him? That's a woman's job. Not out here betraying our country, trying to prevent a needed wall from being built. You should be home taking care of your children and seeing to your husband's needs."

Her mind flashed to Espinoza, wondering if his final minutes had been spent in the heat of a confrontation like this.

She thought about how to play this out. She could remain silent and hope they'd just leave, or she could angrily challenge them, which would probably only escalate the situation. She decided to buy some time by remaining calm but vocal.

"Okay," she called through the door. "You've said your piece and I've heard you."

"So you're going to leave?"

Sometimes Alex could be so stubborn and dedicated to her ideals that she knew when she was about to bite into a whole mess of trouble. "This is my *job*. I was hired to be here."

"Well, then quit," he demanded.

Alex clenched her teeth.

"We don't want to hurt you," he went on. "Not if we don't have to. We just want you to leave." He paused. Alex tensed on the other side of the door. "You hear me?" he shouted, erupting in anger. He turned to one of his cronies. "Get this damn door down."

Peeking through the window, Alex watched his buddy take a few steps back, then hurl himself at the weather-beaten door. She watched in horror as it gave a little. He threw himself forward again, his shoulder colliding with the wood. The frame splintered around the lock.

"I'm armed!" she warned them. "Just leave." Alex gripped the handle of the dart gun, ready to fire it the minute they broke through the door.

But they ignored her. The driver motioned for his crony to try again, and this time, when he flung his weight forward, the door splintered inward, and suddenly the men were inside.

Alex fired the tranquilizer gun at the driver, figuring that the yes-men might leave if their leader was out of commission. The dart hit him in the leg and he looked down, enraged, and yanked it out. "What the fuck!" he cursed.

With a thumping heart she waited for them to draw the handguns from their holsters.

"I warned you!" the driver shouted, his skull mask pulsating as he breathed angrily.

She backed farther into the cabin as he advanced on her. She crammed another dart into the chamber. "It'll take both of you to carry your boss once he passes out," she told the man who had stood by silently while his friend broke down the door. "You really want to do that alone?" She pointed the barrel at the door breaker.

"He's not our *boss*," rebuffed the door breaker, sounding offended that she thought he was a lackey. The third man still stood by the door, shuffling his feet, glancing to the driver for reassurance.

"You fucking bitch!" yelled the driver, his words already slurring. "We're gonna string you up, slice open your guts, and let the vultures do the rest." He started to pull out his gun, lumbering toward her, but already he was unsteady on his feet. He went down on one knee, then the other. The third man, still being quiet, rushed to his side and tried to keep him upright.

Alex kept the barrel trained on the door breaker. "Well?" she asked him. "You going to help your friend get that jerk out of here?" She struggled to keep her voice steady. Her heart hammered and her palms had gone sweaty. What if they all pulled their guns? How committed were they to this attack? What if they *did* string her up and pull all her guts out?

Then the driver fell face-first on the floor, his gun clattering away. The quiet man scooped it up but didn't aim it at her.

"Get out of here!" she shouted at them, feeling a flood of anger sweep over her, wanting to stomp on the driver's prone face.

To her relief, she'd judged right. The yes-men didn't quite know what to do. Finally they bent down, grabbing the driver under his arms, and dragged him outside. With some difficulty they stuffed him inside the extended cab of their truck.

She stayed in the doorway, tranq gun still pointed at them.

The door breaker moved to the driver's seat. "We'll be back. You can count on it!"

She raised the gun, aiming at his neck. In less than a minute they'd pulled away and were heading back down the mountain.

When the dust settled and she couldn't hear their engine anymore, she gave out a shuddering sigh. A few tears of sheer relief streamed down her face, and she suddenly found herself letting out a nervous laugh. Her hands shook now uncontrollably on the dart gun and she slumped down into a chair.

She grabbed her sat communicator and brought up the messages. Her dad had written *Hold tight—police on the way*.

The adrenaline now flooding out of her body, Alex shivered in the chair. She pulled her sleeping bag off the cot and wrapped it around herself. When she heard another car coming up the road, she froze, terrified the men had returned.

TWENTY-SEVEN

Alex gripped the tranq gun and stood in the open doorway beside the fallen door, relieved to see red and blue lights flashing on the trees in the distance. She put down the tranq gun as a police cruiser pulled into view. It parked and Deputy Wentworth stepped out, pulling his hat from the passenger seat and cinching it down on his head.

As he approached, he took in the ruined door. "Holy hell, what happened here?"

"It was those same white supremacists. They broke it down," she told him. "Threatened to kill me if I didn't leave."

"Why would they do that?"

"It's because of the jaguars. They want me to stop."

He frowned. "Why would they care about that?"

"Because jaguars are crossing the border with Mexico, and these guys want a continuous wall that keeps anything from crossing over."

He pursed his lips. "I see."

"They wore skull masks, but I'm pretty sure they were the same men who were up at the dig site."

He lifted his eyebrows. "You mean the guys who had threatened the archaeologist?"

"Yes. Have you made any progress on finding out who they are?"

He rubbed his chin, looking thoughtful. "Not yet. But we're pursuing leads." He studied her face. "You look shaken."

"I am."

"Can you describe anything else about them?"

Alex thought about the pale necks beneath the masks. "They're all white. All around six feet tall, maybe a couple inches shorter. Probably in their thirties or forties."

The deputy jotted these details down in a little notebook, then glanced at the door. "Looks like they did a number on your cabin."

She followed his gaze, wondering how she was going to reattach the door tonight.

"Let me help with this," he said. "I've got some tools in my cruiser."

He walked out to his car and retrieved a box of tools from the back. Together they managed to screw some braces onto the door and get the hinges reattached by drilling new holes in the frame.

When the door was back in place, the deputy eyed it uncertainly. "Maybe you should get a motel room in Azulejo tonight," he suggested.

"I'll do that," Alex fibbed. Already she was planning to retrieve her backcountry tent from the Jeep, hike out a mile or two, and sleep somewhere out in the desert where no one would find her. The close call still had her heart racing, and staying in a motel in a tiny town where word spread quickly did not make her feel safe. They could easily find her there.

The deputy finished taking down her details for his report and then closed his little notebook. "I'm going to do some driving around. See if I can find that truck tonight. You stay safe."

"Thank you."

He returned to his cruiser and pulled around, disappearing down the narrow road.

Alex stood alone in the doorway, then grabbed her backcountry pack with her tent and sleeping bag and started packing. She typed out a message to her father, telling him that she was okay and thanking him for calling the police. She'd call him next time she got service.

But tonight she would sleep in the wild. Tomorrow she'd figure out something else.

Hurriedly, Alex loaded in energy bars, her Sterno stove and fuel, her tiny toiletry kit. There was nowhere she felt safer than out in the wilds. In cities she often felt nervous. She'd had creepy men try to prey on her over the years, following her as she walked down streets or stalking her to her car. She'd been trailed through an underground parking garage once in Boston by a man who'd followed her from a pub. And she had friends who'd been mugged and assaulted over the years.

She thought again of the questions she got when working in remote places: *What about bears or wolves?* people would ask her. *Aren't you afraid they'll attack you?* These questions usually came from people who spent all their time in urban settings, and she found the query ironic. In their entire lives, they'd probably never see a wolf or a grizzly bear outside of a zoo. But they lived, ate, slept, and worked every day with the most dangerous predator on the planet.

Alex found wilderness inviting, not scary. As her heart slowed, she thought over her next move. She wanted to get farther away tonight than she could on foot, so she'd take her Jeep and park it somewhere secluded, where it wouldn't be spotted. Then she'd venture out from there, spend a couple of days camping and hiking around, checking more of the cameras, and then make a decision about her lodgings. Maybe she could book a private vacation rental in a neighboring city, something harder to trace than a motel.

But she knew one thing for certain. She wouldn't quit the project.

After she packed, she hopped in her Jeep and drove in the darkness, on the lookout for hidden cars lying in wait or the flash of headlights from trucks. But the roads were deserted at this hour.

She consulted her topos and took a rugged fire road out through the national forest. It was so disused that bushes grew between the old wheel tracks. They rubbed on the bottom of her car as she passed them. She found another abandoned road branching off from there, something that wasn't even on the map, and took that. It led to a dead end at an ancient rusted water trough. She turned around and pulled her car into the cover of the small grouping of trees. The preserve lay a mile to the east. She grabbed her pack and strapped the tranq gun to the outside of it. Then she donned a warm fleece jacket and climbed out.

She gazed up at the sweep of the Milky Way, feeling reassured. Then she donned her pack and set off toward the preserve, finding the movement of her feet comforting, the familiar feeling of trekking with a backpack on, dipping back into the wilderness.

As she moved through the night, Alex's thoughts drifted to the onza, a folkloric creature whose eyes gleamed like fire in the darkness. Born of a male jaguar and a female mountain lion, the onza was said to have supernatural powers and steal away children who dared to leave their homes at night.

She crossed an old creek bed and made her way around several towering rock formations, steep spires rising up and blocking out the stars. It certainly was beautiful country.

She checked her GPS unit and map a few times, her headlamp flashing over the terrain around her to get a location fix. And she hiked on.

She'd entered the coordinates of the preserve boundary into her GPS unit, and soon it beeped a proximity alert. She passed one of the LTWC's property signs:

MOGOLLON WILDLIFE SANCTUARY

LAND TRUST FOR WILDLIFE CONSERVATION

NO HUNTING

The quiet enveloped her, comforted her. As she hiked deeper into the preserve, she started casting around for a nice sheltered place to pitch her tent. She came to a gigantic rock spire, several smaller ones beside it. She walked to their bases, finding a sheltered, sandy place between them, out of sight from all angles. It was perfect.

She unslung her pack and detached the tent. She rolled it out and went to work putting together its poles and sliding them through the little sleeves in the tent fabric. In moments it was up, and she slid in her sleeping bag and pad. She didn't think it was going to rain, but she put up the rain fly anyway and hauled her pack in under its shelter. Then she unzipped the door and sat just inside it. As she unlaced her boots, a lone coyote barked, then howled. Soon an entire chorus of coyotes joined it, eerie yips and howls filling the night air around her, echoing off the rocks.

The spot was so perfect she felt the sting of tears.

Suddenly the last day and night caught up with her. Espinoza. The men threatening her. Breaking down the door. Bursting inside. She'd been terrified. She felt that now. Here, in this safe place, the fear came rolling out of her body. She shook, a few tears weaving down her face. She wiped them away hastily. She was not going to let these guys get to her.

Out here she felt safe. The solace of nature was strong. She didn't feel alone. Those coyotes were out there, too, playing in the silvery starlight, enjoying life, singing out into the majesty of this enchanted place. And there were also mule deer nearby, and peccaries and gray foxes. She was anything but alone. She was okay. She'd survived the encounter. She'd gotten out of there.

She'd sleep for now, and tomorrow she'd figure out what she was going to do about a new place to stay.

THE NEXT DAY, ALEX PACKED up her tent and stowed everything in her pack. She used her sat communicator to send her father another message, assuring him that she was okay and telling him her plan to spend some days in the backcountry.

She checked her map and headed out toward the nearest remote camera and hair snare. As she hiked, she let the stress of the last few days roll off her. She kept seeing flashes of Espinoza's butchered body. She wondered if the cops had made any progress in the case, what the forensic team had found. Maybe by the time she hiked out in a few days, there would be news.

She thought of Pilar and her ruined gallery, of the men breaking down Alex's door. The place was a hotbed of hostilities, a festering quagmire of people at odds with each other. As if on cue, Alex heard a series of distant rifle shots, and tried to pinpoint their direction. She wondered if hunters, or maybe Trager, were out there, but she couldn't be sure they were on the preserve.

Hiking on, she came to the remote camera and noticed several hairs snagged in the snare wrapped around the tree. She tweezed them out, placing them carefully in a small envelope and labeling it. They were black, and she hoped they might be jaguar.

Then she checked the images on the camera. It hadn't captured any photos of a jaguar, but she spotted the familiar forms of Dave and River, on their way to place out more jugs of water. Their packs were considerably smaller now. They'd been hard at work. She checked the time stamp. They'd passed by just thirty minutes before.

She swapped out the memory card and put in fresh batteries. She had just replaced the padlock on the housing when a gut-wrenching scream shattered the morning quiet.

TWENTY-EIGHT

Alex froze, pinpointing the direction of the screams—cries of terror and pain, long, wailing, and nearby. She spun, the sound echoing off the rocks around her.

At first she thought about ditching her pack. She could run faster without it. But she had her emergency med kit in it. Keeping the pack on, she raced toward the screams, the cries pitched high, pain infusing every note.

Someone was seriously hurt. Alex weaved around bushes and rounded a large outcropping of rocks. The tortured sounds continued to echo off stone, reverberating in the desert air. She sped around the rocks and instantly saw River curled up on the ground in a fetal position. The woman rocked back and forth, blood covering her hands where she clasped one leg. Alex rushed to her side.

"What happened?" Alex asked.

The woman winced, her eyes squeezed shut. In addition to the seeping leg wound, blood pooled on the ground beneath her shoulder, and Alex saw a perfectly round hole in the woman's upper arm. Tears leaked down River's face. She was sweaty and covered in dirt. Alex noticed raw scrapes on both of her knees and elbows, her tank top and shorts torn and dirty. She'd obviously been running, crashing through rough brush and terrain.

"Were you shot?" Alex asked, leaning forward to examine the wound. Instantly her mind flew to Roger Trager, the Wildlife

Services guy, and the shots she'd heard earlier, wondering if he'd fired too close to the activist, trying to scare her off. She glanced around for a shooter, feeling exposed, but didn't see anyone. She wondered what had happened to Dave.

Alex gently pried the woman's fingers away from her leg, seeing another bullet hole in her thigh. A third one had torn through her calf muscle on the same leg. This was no accidental shooting.

"Help me," River cried, trying to roll herself into an even tighter ball.

Alex shrugged off her pack and pulled out the emergency med kit. She retrieved gauze and pressed it to the thigh wound, instructing River to apply pressure while Alex attended to the bullet holes in her calf and arm. The round had passed completely through her arm, likely striking the bone. The one in her calf had also torn all the way through, but Alex found no exit wound in River's thigh.

She pressed gauze down on the other two wounds, applying pressure, trying to stanch the bleeding.

She pulled out her satellite communicator and powered it up, waiting for it to get a signal. She'd paid extra for the option to summon a medevac helicopter in the field if needed. A small switch would toggle it to SOS mode. She just had to wait for it to power on, get a lock on their location, and then send out the request for evacuation.

"How did this happen?" Alex asked her, returning her attention to addressing the woman's wounds. She glanced around again for Dave but didn't see anyone else. "Where's Dave?"

"They ... shot at us ..." River managed to get out, clenching her teeth against the pain.

"Who?"

Just then, twigs snapped to Alex's right. She whirled her head in that direction, seeing Dave streak out from a small copse of trees.

"Oh, Jesus! River!" He raced forward, kneeling down at such a clip that he sprayed them both with sand. "I realized you weren't behind me!"

River gripped his hand tightly. "You came back," she whispered. She tried to struggle up to a sitting position.

Dave cradled her. "I never would have left you. I didn't know they'd hit you."

"Who?" Alex asked.

"We don't know," he gasped, out of breath. "Someone shooting from the rock outcroppings. They chased us. We got separated."

The pool of crimson spread, coagulating in the sand. Alex knew River didn't have much time. She'd already lost too much blood.

"We need to get her to a hospital," she told Dave. "As quickly as possible." She checked the sat communicator. It was powered up now, trying to fix its location.

But before it could finish, the crack of a rifle echoed off the rocks. Alex jumped at the sound. It was close. Loud. Then a second shot rang out and the sat communicator went flying out of her hands, leaving her fingers stinging. She heard men suddenly hoot and whoop in celebration nearby, congratulating the shooter. Then a third shot rent the air, deafeningly close.

She pressed against the rock, gazing out into the blinding afternoon light, trying to pinpoint their location.

A loud, keening wail sprung up from Dave. Alex snapped her head back to him. He cradled River in his arms, but her head now lolled to one side. Alex spotted the perfectly placed bullet hole in the woman's head. It had pierced her skull. She was dead.

Dave screamed in frustration and anger, pressing River closer to his chest. Alex urged him to back farther into the shelter of the rock outcropping.

It was a trap. They'd probably lost track of Dave when the two got separated. So they'd wounded River. Let her scream and call for help. Lured Dave back to her.

It was only a matter of seconds before bullets would tear through him and Alex, too. She gripped his arm. "We've got to move!"

"I can't!" he cried, gripping River's limp body.

"You have to!" Alex shouted at him. She grabbed his arm and forced him to his feet. He stumbled, River rolling out of his arms.

"I can't leave her!"

"She's gone, Dave." She gripped his shoulder. "We'll come back for her. But for now we've got to run!"

She reached for her pack, but a bullet tore through it, a mere inch from her hand, and she yanked her arm back. Another celebratory hoot rang out. She knew they could have made the shot to kill her, but they were toying with her. She'd have to leave it. She grabbed Dave's hand and pulled, moving him to the opposite side of the rock outcropping. From there they took off at a sprint, leaping over bushes and rocks, weaving between trees. Another shot rang out, then another. A plume of dirt sprayed up near Alex's left foot, and another round struck a tree trunk a few inches from her head. They reached a steep embankment and leapt over the brink, stumbling and sliding all the way down into a dry arroyo. She didn't hear any more shots. They were out of the line of fire.

Alex cast around for any kind of shelter, but this section of the preserve was mostly dry, with a few scrubby bushes, clusters of junipers, and shorter piles of stones. She raced for the nearest grouping of rocks, tugging Dave along behind her. He tripped, almost going down, his feet clumsy in his grief.

Then she saw that he gripped his left arm, blood seeping through his fingers. He'd been hit.

"We're almost there," she urged him, and finally they rounded the small rock outcropping. It wasn't tall enough to shield them if they stood, so she crouched down, pulling Dave down beside her.

"They killed her," he cried, too loud. "They killed her!"

"We have to be quiet," she told him. "Let me see your arm."

She tore open the sleeve of his shirt, finding that the bullet had penetrated his upper arm and passed all the way through. She did her best to try to slow the bleeding, tearing the sleeve all the way off and using it as a makeshift bandage. He shook, tears streaming down his face, and Alex hugged him. "I'm so sorry."

"What are we going to do?" he asked between sobs.

Alex listened for any hint of sound—the men approaching the embankment or more shots. But all she could hear was the wind and a red-tailed hawk's cry as it wheeled in the sky.

She glanced ahead. Another small pile of rocks lay about three hundred feet away, and beyond that, another about five hundred feet away. They'd have to keep moving from pile to pile, using ob-structed line of sight if the gunmen came down the embankment. And she had no doubt they would.

"C'mon," she told Dave. "Let's make a dash for that other rock outcropping."

She'd just stood up, Dave rising on shaky legs beside her, when Alex heard the roar of ATVs, tearing down the arroyo in their direc-tion.

In the far distance, Alex knew that the terrain became too steep and rocky for quads to navigate. But out here, where she hid behind the rocks, the ATVs would reach them easily. They had only a mat-ter of minutes.

"Run!" she yelled to Dave, forcing him to move. She took off at a sprint, racing for the large jumble of rocks in the distance. The ATVs swung into view, three of them driving in a line, dust pluming behind them.

One ATV had two riders, and the man in back was leveling a rifle in their direction. Alex weaved, making herself a harder target to hit.

Dave followed close behind, his labored breathing audible even above the din of the roaring engines. A dust cloud pulled her gaze to the distance behind them as she glanced back. She saw three white trucks there, tearing up the terrain, ATVs loaded into their beds. They skidded to a halt when they couldn't follow any farther. All the cabs were crammed with men, and in the bed of one of the trucks, a man sat on one of the quads, pumping a rifle into the air. She could hear them all cheering and shouting as the ATVs took off after Alex and Dave.

The men piled out and rushed to the back of the trucks, readying to offload the quads.

How many of these assholes are there?

Up ahead, a mule deer started out of a copse of juniper and Alex headed for those trees. The deer bounded away, its tail straight up, flagging a warning.

Alex reached the trees just as the lead ATV caught up with them. It spun in a circle, rounding the junipers, trying to block them in. Dave slumped over, one hand on his knee, the other gripping his wounded arm, trying to get a breath. He'd been on the run for much longer than Alex, and it was taking its toll. The bandage was doing little to stop the bleeding, and now his entire arm dripped crimson.

To their right, about fifty feet away, stood another copse. They had only moments before the other ATVs would join the first, trapping them in their current position.

TWENTY-NINE

"C'mon!" Alex urged Dave. Just as the circling ATV passed them, she darted out, aiming for the next cluster of juniper.

The second quad caught up with the first. But it was the third ATV that Alex dreaded, the one with the gunman perched on the back. She could see even from here that they all wore skull masks, but she suspected that the same men who had harassed the dig site and broken into her cabin were among their numbers.

The first two vehicles struck out after them, but she and Dave reached the trees just in time. It was a slightly larger grouping of conifers, and they ran deep inside it. But it was only a temporary hiding place.

She glanced out in the distance. The next bit of cover was a rock outcropping, its base dotted with rabbitbrush. It was tall enough that if they could climb on top of it, the gunman might not be able to get a clear shot.

She lamented the loss of her pack, of her satellite communicator.

With Dave laboring behind her, Alex reached the rock outcropping and leapt up onto the rough stone. Dave struggled, his body exhausted, and she extended a hand down to him. He gripped it tightly and she swung him up onto the rocks. He cried out in pain as his arm moved to grab at a handhold in the rock.

Together they bounded upward. She urged Dave to climb higher, and soon they reached the pinnacle of the rock outcropping, some fifty feet above the ground. The third ATV had caught up with the others, and all three raced to their position. She saw the gunman level his rifle in their direction, and she dropped onto her stomach, pressing flat against the stone. Dave collapsed next to her, spent. She didn't think he had much more in him.

A shot ricocheted off a rock somewhere beneath them. They were out of the man's line of sight.

Alex remained belly down on the rock, scanning the terrain around them. The next patch of cover was another cluster of trees, and it wasn't too far off.

Below them the ATVs circled, the men whooping and shouting at them.

"Bet you wish you'd just left now, huh?" one of them yelled. She recognized his voice. The man she'd shot with the tranq gun. The leader.

"They're crazy," Dave whispered beside her.

"I'm gonna get you back, bitch!" the leader screamed. "You're dead!"

The ATVs gunned their engines, rounding the outcropping. She heard the pop of several handguns and dared a look down below, seeing them with drawn pistols, shooting into the air.

In the distance, the men were still unloading more ATVs.

She watched their circling, careful to keep her head down, and noticed the men were grouped up together, leaving Alex and Dave a small window to bolt when they'd be on the opposite side of the rocks.

She signaled her intention to Dave, and he nodded. Together they crept down the far side of the rocks, keeping low and out of sight. Three large boulders stood at ground level, and when they reached them, they perched behind them, waiting for the ATVs to pass. Alex's heart pounded, and her mouth had gone dry.

She heard the first engine roar by, then the second and third. Then she bolted out, racing for the cover of the trees. Dave lagged behind, clutching his arm, struggling to get a decent breath. She reached the temporary safety of the conifers and glanced back in horror to see Dave collapsing in the dirt. The lead ATV raced into view from around the outcropping, its lone rider bearing down on the activist.

The other two ATVs veered off, circling around the other way to try and flank them.

Alex glanced around on the ground for any kind of weapon, and her gaze lit upon a large broken branch. While the other two quads roared around in a circle, trying to get ahead of her position, Alex raced back to where Dave lay.

As the leader bore down on him, Alex darted out and brought the branch up, connecting with the rider's chest and unseating him. The force of the impact sent her flying backward, where she landed with such violence that her breath burst from her lungs. The empty ATV leapt forward, nearly hitting Alex where she lay, then it came to a halt, idling.

The leader gripped his ribs, rolling in pain on the ground. The other two ATV drivers had seen what happened and flipped around, heading straight in her direction.

Alex had only seconds. She grabbed Dave under the arms and forced him to his feet. "Get on!" she told him as she mounted the ATV. He slid on behind her, gripping her middle, and she gunned the engine, wheeling the quad away from the other two approaching vehicles.

She sped along dangerously, the ATV catching air as she gunned it over ridges and across arroyos. The men followed close behind, and she heard the crack of the rifle.

In her mind, she went over the terrain, trying to place her exact location and recall where help might lie, even just a phone.

She remembered now that they weren't far from an old disused Forest Service fire road. It was more of a rough fire break than a decent dirt road, but it led straight out to the trailhead where her car had been broken into. That trailhead had a pay phone. And maybe hikers would be there.

She veered slightly, aiming for the old road, feeling Dave's arms wrapped tightly around her. He trembled.

She had to get him to a doctor. Wondering how much blood he'd already lost, she felt his grip weaken on her. She lifted her hand off the brake and grabbed his fingers, shaking him. He tightened his hold and they sped on.

Alex raced forward, getting some distance between her and their pursuers, but at a cost. The men obviously knew the terrain a lot better than she; while they drove around difficult obstacles like steep arroyos and trenches that could bottom them out, Alex just made a beeline for the Forest Service road. She jostled and bumped along, almost unseating herself a few times and holding her breath after she topped a few pits and ruts on the ground with axle-breaking potential. She worried Dave would slide off, but so far they were lucky, and she gained enough distance that she couldn't see the men anymore.

With a feeling of immense relief, she spotted the mouth of the old Forest Service fire road and raced onto it. It hadn't been used in years, and vegetation sprouted from the center of it, scraping and slapping at them as they tore by. Branches ripped at her pants, slicing through them, and sharp twigs slashed at her hands.

They hit a washboard section and jarred along it. Dave's grip loosened again and Alex held on to him with her left hand, shaking him awake.

They climbed up a steep grade, the rabbitbrush so thick that it slowed their progress. They crested the rise and came plummeting down the other side, dodging huge rocks that years of rains had exposed in the disused roadbed.

While trying to avoid one giant stone, she hit another and they went up on two wheels for a moment. Her heart juddering, she leaned to the left, bringing the ATV crashing back down on all fours. She gunned the motor, rocketing them over the mess of the road. Somewhere near here, the trail crossed this fire road and Alex scanned the sides of the road for signs of it.

She glanced back, seeing the dirt trail of the pursuing ATVs. They were closer than she thought, probably following her own dust plume.

Dave was in rough shape. There was no way they could ditch the quad and run along the trail to the trailhead. She had to buy him some time.

Up ahead, she saw a break in the vegetation. She slowed, spotting the trail cutting across the fire road.

She stopped, turning around. "Dave. You have to take this trail. There's a pay phone at the trailhead, and it's only a quarter mile away. Maybe there will be people there who will help."

He blinked at her, dazed.

She dismounted, grabbing him and helping him off the ATV. "Run! Now!"

"What about you?"

"I'll draw them away."

Indecision pinched his face. "I don't feel right about this."

"You go get help for us both," she urged him.

At this, he turned reluctantly and started down the trail, gripping his arm.

She got back on the quad and gunned it, taking off at a high clip to stir up that much more dirt. When she glanced back over her shoulder, she saw Dave disappear into the shelter of trees.

Now she just had to outrun the other ATVs.

Alex pushed the engine, the ATV bouncing over potholes and a section of washboard. She spotted a steep arroyo, the old creek bed so low it would shield her from gunfire. They'd still be able to see her dust trail but wouldn't be able to get a clear shot.

She turned the ATV, veering toward it so violently that she almost went up on two wheels again. She could taste grit and dust in her mouth, grains crunching against her teeth. She was grateful for her sunglasses, which offered a little protection from the blasting wind.

She glanced behind, seeing the dust from her pursuers pluming up in the trees where she'd dropped off Dave.

To her immense relief, the dust continued to move instead of settling. They hadn't stopped at the trail. She'd successfully tricked them. Now she just hoped that Dave could get to a phone and get to safety.

But that didn't help her much in the short term. She reached the arroyo before the men emerged from the trees and she banked down the steep sides, bouncing over rocks with such force that she worried her vehicle would get bogged down.

But it didn't. The bed of the arroyo was relatively smooth, and she opened up the throttle, racing forward.

She craned her neck back, seeing the men burst from the trees, heading straight for her. She hoped to gain some ground on them.

Behind her, they entered the arroyo, picking up speed themselves. Alex stared ahead, her heart racing, feeling like she was running out of options.

Ahead, the arroyo twisted away to the left. She banked in that direction just as she heard the crack from a rifle. For at least a few moments more, she'd be out of their line of sight. She stood up in her seat, trying to see above the arroyo's banks, searching for any kind of cover.

She saw an enormous cluster of rocks, giant brown-gray pinnacles of stone at the base of a cliff. If she could reach those, perhaps she could use them for cover somehow. Buy some time. Maybe find a crevice and shinny up the cliff.

Or she could just keep speeding toward town. She looked at the gas tank. A little less than half full. Here the banks of the arroyo grew shallower and shallower. It wouldn't offer any more cover.

Maybe she could find another Forest Service road that led out to

a main road, but she was on national forest land now, and hadn't explored on this side of the Gila. Didn't know where the roads lay. She
heard another crack of a rifle and ducked low. Then another and
another, and saw with horror that they'd swung around the bend,
now with a clear shot of her.

She gunned the engine, veering up the shallow embankment,
exiting the creek bed. The men behind her did the same.

Then she heard another crack and fire erupted in her head. She
slumped forward, a stream of blood slinging out and splashing on
the ATV's speedometer. She felt a heaviness and dizziness, felt herself slipping off the quad. She crashed down on her side in the dirt,
watching the ATV come to a halt a few feet away, its engine idling.

She tried to force herself to stand up, to run, but her body
wouldn't respond. A well of darkness swam around her, swallowing
her. She stared up at the blindingly blue sky, the view narrowing
and narrowing until it was just a pinprick of sapphire, and then the
blackness took her completely.

THIRTY

Alex came to slowly, her eyes crusted shut, a blinding pain throbbing in her head. She tried to open her mouth, finding her tongue coated with dirt. She lifted a hand to wipe at her eyes, but when she tried to turn her head, she found her movement constricted. Something tight squeezed at her neck. Her hands reached up, finding a band of rough, thick material strapped there.

She forced her eyes to open, seeing the dazzling blue of the desert sky above her. Her sunglasses were gone, the searing light making her eyes tear. She struggled to sit up, the thing around her neck almost choking her. Her hands felt along it, fingers finding the familiar shape of the GPS transmitter and camera of one of her collars. She reached to the back of her neck, feeling a wave of nausea and dizziness so intense that for a moment she swam in blackness once more.

When the darkness cleared, she finished feeling along the collar. Behind her head, where the collar fastened, Alex felt a thick padlock.

She tried to focus, to center herself. She managed to sit all the way up, crossing her legs in front of her.

The collar. Someone had put it on her. A tracker. She stared around. She wasn't in the same place where she'd fallen off the ATV. The striking rock pillars were nowhere in sight, nor was the cliff. All around her stretched desert terrain, not a tree in sight, just prickly pear, cholla, and ocotillo.

Her throat burned from thirst. Things came more sharply into focus. She remembered River dying, her race with Dave on the ATV. And she remembered having to abandon her pack. Her supplies. Her water.

She glanced around, not seeing any streams or springs from where she sat.

She reflected back, groggy, her thoughts moving through thick cotton. The person who had broken into her truck. It hadn't just been petty theft. It had been someone far more dangerous. They'd stolen the GPS collar camera, and with it, its GPS log-in instructions, and locked it onto her. And they'd attached it far tighter than she ever would on an animal.

Her head throbbed in pain, and she reached up tentatively to touch her scalp. She felt a bandage there, a large piece of gauze affixed with tape. It sank in. She'd been shot. Grazed probably, but in the skull.

Why hadn't they just killed her? And why treat her wound?

And then her situation came sharply into all-too-terrifying focus. They hadn't killed her because they wanted to *hunt* her.

So they'd left her here to give her a head start? How long had she been out? She lifted her wrist to check her watch, but found it gone.

That's when she saw that they'd taken her boots, too. Her bare feet stuck out from her jeans, the tops pink and sunburned. So she had been lying here for a while. Now she could feel that her face was tender, too, hot to the touch, burned as well.

She tried to stand, to get her bearings, but a wave of dizziness forced her to stay sitting.

She felt as if she were being watched and scanned the terrain for a sign of someone—even the flash of sunlight off a pair of binoculars or a spotting scope. But she didn't see anyone.

But with the collar strapped on her, however, they'd know exactly where she was. She tugged at it, pulling so hard that she nearly choked herself. Then she slid the collar around so the padlock was in front. She pulled on the lock, hard, the pressure at the back of her neck painful, the edges of the collar biting into her skin. But it was fastened tight. She thought about what she had on her. Anything that could pick a lock? She rummaged through her jeans pockets, but found only a small piece of lint. They'd taken everything, including her multitool, the one her father had given her. She had no small piece of wire or sliver of metal. She spotted a piece of ocotillo skeleton beside her and broke it apart so that she had a long thin piece. It was hard. Gently she felt around for the keyhole and tried to insert the piece, but it just splintered off as soon as she tried to work the lock.

She stood up, stumbling to the side as her head swam, and crashed back down to the ground. A wave of nausea surged up and passed. She'd have to find something else to pick the lock. And she probably didn't have much time. They'd know where she was.

A rage built up inside of her. She thought of just staying exactly where she was, daring them to come out and try to kill her. She'd tear them to pieces if it was the last thing she did. But then reason seeped through the red mist of her rage. They could just shoot her. From afar. They might just get bored and kill her on the spot without her ever seeing them again. She scanned the terrain around her, seeing tall cliffs and spires made of volcanic tuff in the distance, a dozen places where someone with a rifle could be hovering, just waiting to take her out.

She picked up a stone and tried to beat the lock open with it. But the angle was just too difficult. She couldn't rain blows down on it with enough force. So she slid the collar around to the side of her neck and craned her head away. Then she brought the rock down again and again, but the lock remained steadfastly shut. After cutting up her shoulder pretty good a couple of times, she realized this method was not going to work. She'd need to find bolt cutters or a piece of metal to jimmy the lock. She tried using the rough edge of the stone to saw through the collar's thick material, but it wasn't sharp enough.

But she might be able to damage the GPS antenna inside the unit now, disabling it. Still clutching the stone, she lay down on the desert floor, placing the part of the collar with the GPS transmitter on a long, flat rock. Swinging hard, she brought the stone down, trying to smash the antenna. But the device was kept in a rugged housing—had to be in order to withstand everything the animal would put it through. She hit it a dozen more times, hoping maybe she'd damaged it. But she had no way of knowing if she was successful.

Her best bet now was to move. To find water. To seek out a tool that would allow her to get the collar off.

Finally she managed to stand, the pebbles sharp beneath her feet. She spotted a large grouping of boulders to her left and started off in that direction, hoping to find a spring she could drink from. That would be her first step.

Her head swam and she almost toppled over, the blood rushing to her brain so powerfully that she could hear its roar in her ears.

She took one step forward, a surge of nausea sweeping up. But she couldn't afford to throw up. She had to hold on to every last bit of moisture in her body. She had to think of a plan.

She trudged toward the outcropping, feeling every slice of sharp ground on the tender soles of her feet. But when she reached the grouping of boulders, she found no spring. So she slogged on, searching for any familiar sight—a rock formation she'd recognize, a stream, anything. But she was somewhere entirely new.

She was lost.

For what felt like an hour, she struggled forward, checking each cliff face or rock outcropping or arroyo for water, but coming up empty at all the locations.

She walked for an indeterminable period of time. She lost all sense of how long she'd been out there, aware only of an unbearable thirst. The bottoms of her feet ached from a dozen oozing cuts. The sun beat down on her mercilessly and she longed for her sunglasses and hat.

A bright spot of red caught her eye and Alex stumbled over to a prickly pear with large red fruit sprouting off the top of its pads. She knew she could get liquid from the fruit. She plucked several off and cast around for a sharp rock to cut them open. Careful not to get pierced by the barbs, she made long slices in the fruit and removed the skins. Then she tore off a section from the bottom of her shirt and wrapped the fruit in it. After finding a larger stone, she pounded the fruit into a pulpy mash, the crimson spilling down like beet juice. Then she lifted the cotton-encased fruit and squeezed it hard, dripping it into her open mouth. Brilliant red liquid spilled over her tongue and she drank every precious drop. It wasn't a lot, but it was something.

Then she forced herself to stand and keep walking. The sun arced through the sky, but she was so exhausted and thirsty she didn't even hazard a guess at the time. Still she stumbled on, checking every little rock face for a seep of water. Why had there seemed to be so many on the preserve, but now that she needed a drink she couldn't find any at all?

Again she spotted a patch of red and staggered over to it, finding a cluster of ripe prickly pear fruit. As before, she plucked several fruits off and pulped them in her T-shirt material, squeezing the juice into her mouth. It did little to assuage her thirst, and she knew that she was dangerously dehydrated.

Her head buzzed with pain as she staggered on. A few times she got turned around, found herself searching for water by a cliff face she'd already visited. To prevent herself from going in circles, she tried to head exclusively east, keeping the afternoon sun at her back, but repeatedly fell down, confused, finding that she'd been walking with it on her left. She suspected she had a severe concussion and found it incredibly difficult to concentrate.

Finally, desperate for a drink, Alex trudged up an embankment and suddenly the sight before her almost made her fall down on her knees in gratitude. Laid out at the base of the hill were two jugs of water. Dave's and River's work.

She slid down to them, her bare feet plowing through sharp stones, slipping in the loose sand near the bottom. She grabbed the first jug, almost tearing off the lid.

She lifted the weight to her mouth and drank a few deep, grateful mouthfuls.

And then the jug exploded in her hands as she heard the distant crack of a rifle. She fell backward, water splashing over her, and went down hard on her butt in the dirt. Dust kicked up around her, showering her with grit, caking the areas where water drenched her. Out of instinct, she scrambled to her feet, panic overtaking her. A bullet hole had pierced the side of the jug.

She stumbled away, staring around her, reaching the shelter of two large boulders a dozen feet away. She couldn't tell where the shot had come from. She was just panicking, not being careful. Exhaustion and thirst had dulled her senses, negatively affecting her thinking. She could be running straight for the gunman for all she knew.

She forced her mind to still, to try to think. She peered out at the remaining jug of water and scanned the terrain behind her, but only flat, level ground with a few dotted ocotillos met her eyes. She didn't think the gunman could be over there. No cover. And he wasn't at the top of the rise she'd just scrambled down.

But on the other side of the rocks where she hid, a tall cliff rose, dotted with juniper and piñon pines, and he could very well be up there. She'd made the right choice in running where she was, but she also knew with a painful thump of fear in her heart that the choice had been random and that she'd simply lucked out.

As she stared out at the ruined jug of water, she watched its twin explode as a round hit it, all the precious water leaking out into the sand.

They'd been waiting for her. Tracking her. The collar was definitely still operational. She had to get it off.

THIRTY-ONE

Alex slumped down against the rocks, giving herself a moment to catch her breath. Where was water? If only she knew her exact location. She'd found so many springs on the preserve, and then of course there'd been the Mesquite River. But she hadn't run across anything like that. Didn't recognize the layout of this land from her time on the preserve or from satellite maps she'd studied of the area.

Given the lack of houses, she guessed she might be in the Gila National Forest somewhere, but she could just as easily be on a more distant Bureau of Land Management property or even on someone's personal spread. Maybe something that belonged to one of the white supremacists. That would certainly ensure privacy. So how far was she then from water? From a phone? From safety?

She continued to rest on the other side of the rock, trying to guess at her pursuers' next move. They probably hadn't split up. They knew exactly where she was, thanks to the collar, so there'd be no reason to split up to find her. But they might split up to flank her.

Suddenly her mouth grew even drier. She hadn't thought of that. They could be looping around even now. Could be getting just the right angle on her to finish the job once and for all.

She looked down at her feet. Myriad cuts oozed blood, while dirt and dust caked in the wounds.

She forced herself to stand, wincing as her weight hit the bottoms of her feet. She eyed a distant grouping of trees at higher elevation than where she was. There could be water there. She steadied herself, one hand on a rock, and then ran out into the open, zigging and zagging.

The crack of a rifle rang out, striking the dirt just to her right. But it was a few feet off. Then another one hit the ground just behind her. The shots were coming up short, and she had the feeling that it might be on purpose, someone toying with her, trying to scare her, letting her know they were out there, that they could kill her at any moment, but wanting to draw out the game. She could imagine them laughing, high-fiving the gunman at how close he got, and a rage welled up in her so powerfully that she found herself running faster and faster, disregarding the sharp pain in her feet.

She tore on, streaking up the rise and reaching the small cluster of juniper. They grew alongside an arroyo, and to her dismay she saw that the creek bed was completely dry. Juniper was skilled at staying alive even during extreme drought.

She tried to swallow and found that she couldn't. Her throat was so parched that her throat just closed up. Her head pounded, both from the bullet graze and from the extreme dehydration.

She knew a human could go without water for three or even four days, but she was also running in the heat, and that would take its toll.

But she couldn't stop. She didn't know what to do.

She braced herself on the trunk of a tree, scanning the horizon. She saw something shimmering in the heat far away, a tall metal structure flashing in the sunlight. It looked like a tower of some kind, maybe a radio antenna. She squinted, wishing for her sunglasses, but with the shimmering heat, she couldn't even be sure it was actually there and wasn't a mirage. She blinked, her eyes tearing in the brilliant light, and stared at it with determination.

Yes, something tall flashed in the light to the south. From here, she could only see the very top of it, a strobe light blinking there. It *was* a tower of some sort. And that meant that maybe there'd be a technician there or a crew, or perhaps even some kind of call box.

She pushed off from the tree and crossed the arroyo, moving as fast as she could on her bleeding feet. She noticed that she left smears of blood in her wake, but it didn't really matter. They weren't tracking her like that. They'd find her no matter where she went until she could get the collar off. Briefly, she wondered how they had Wi-Fi way out here to download her location, but then she realized all they'd need was someone in town with internet, reporting in via a sat phone.

She crossed a section of scrubby bushes, stepping over sharp twigs and thorns, around some of the more jagged sections of rock, taking routes over any smooth sandy sections she could find.

She reached a large, blissfully soft patch of sand and crossed it, but the heat of the sun had penetrated the ground, heat singeing her wounds. She started to limp against her will, and her head swam. A sudden powerful wave of dizziness swept through her, and she went down, falling on her knees and hands into the sand. Her vision tunneled, ears ringing with a high-pitched whining, and she stayed like that, head down, until the wave passed.

Then she continued to kneel in the sand, pushing her hands deep into where it was still cool from the night before. She pressed her feet into it, too, allowing the chilly depths of sand to soothe her cuts.

But she knew she had to press on. Finally she forced herself to her feet and trudged ahead, cursing when the sandy section ended and a field of broken rocks stretched out before her. Now her progress slowed to a painful degree, and she limped across on the sharp stones.

She crested a rise, the stones growing small, turning to just tiny pebbles, and then she could see more of the structure.

It was an orange tower, about thirty-five feet high, standing by itself out in the middle of nowhere. It sported two solar panels and a strobe light blinked at the top. That's what she'd seen flashing. The sun was low now on the horizon, casting a long shadow of the tower across the desert floor.

Hope filled her and she picked up her pace. She closed the distance. When she was within twenty feet of it, she could see a large red button on it, like a panic button. A placard hanging on one side gave instructions in English and Spanish. It was a rescue beacon!

Relief flooded through her system so powerfully that it actually made her even dizzier for a moment.

Two jugs of water stood at its base. She just had to reach that button and then she'd drink. Border patrol would be on their way. She raced forward, hand outstretched, and suddenly one of the jugs erupted in a spray of water. She simultaneously heard the crack of a rifle somewhere in the distance. She reeled back when the next jug of water burst apart as another shot rang out, echoing over the surrounding hills.

But they couldn't shoot the button out. It was facing her, not them. She could still make it.

She squinted, trying to pinpoint their location, desperately glancing around for cover. But only the beacon met her gaze, everything else was just ocotillo and prickly pear that offered no protection.

She had to go for it. It was her one shot.

She stood up and lunged toward the button.

Then she heard an earsplitting noise, the whine of something streaking through the air, and at the last second she saw a speeding object, smoke trailing behind it, heading toward her at a staggering pace. She turned away and ran, stumbling over the desert floor, just as the thing impacted the beacon.

A concussive wave hit her at the same time as a blistering flash of heat. She felt herself lifted up off the ground, thrown half a dozen feet away, where she landed hard amid a cluster of ocotillo. Sharp branches scraped her sides and arms as she crashed into them, landing face-first.

Panicked, she pushed out of them, struggling to sit up, and rolled out onto the desert floor.

Behind her the destroyed beacon lay on its side, twisted and smoking, fire smoldering among the prickly pear. Its solar panels lay a dozen feet away, cells cracked and ruined.

The red button, her salvation, lay on the other side, blown entirely off the panel that had held it. Smoking wires sizzled, their insulation on fire, giving off the acrid smell of burning plastic.

The beacon was gone. Then she heard shouting in the distance, cheering, and pinpointed their location. They were high up on a ridge to the north. She spotted the flash of light off something, probably a rifle scope. They hooted and whistled, celebrating.

And Alex realized this was her chance. They were tracking her, yes, but they were in a high, inaccessible location, and it would take them some time to get down from there. Maybe they were situated in other places around her. She didn't know. But she had to take the chance that they'd stayed together. How else would they have congratulated one another on tracking her and squeezing off those close-call shots? Their egos would demand they stay together so they could show off.

She stood up and ran in the opposite direction, up over a rise and back down it, ignoring the pain in her feet. She ran and ran until she could no longer hear the men. She topped another rise and then another, and now she couldn't see the cliff where they'd been at all, and knew she was well out of their line of sight.

She spotted other cliffs in the distance and trudged toward them, following a wash. As she drew closer, she spied the opening of a narrow slot canyon. Stone walls rose up steeply on both sides. This would make the GPS signal patchy, if it went through at all. She staggered into the mouth of the canyon, the cool shadows enveloping her. Placing one hand against the cold stone, she limped down the sandy wash.

She walked for several long minutes, taking a break now and again to rest her tortured feet. The sand at the bottom of the canyon was tough to navigate. She continually slid in it, but at least it wasn't sharp rocks. She noticed that she no longer left a blood trail. Her cuts had finally clotted as she walked on the soft sand.

She made her way down the narrow, twisting space, staring up a few times to see a sliver of blue sky framed above. This would definitely affect the GPS signal. She didn't know how long this slot canyon ran for, but she wanted to take it to its end, buy herself more time.

Huge logs blocked her way in spots, massive tree trunks that had been washed downstream by flash floods in the past. She was grateful no rain had been in the forecast. If a flash flood hit her in this narrow space, she'd get tangled up in all the sharp debris.

For twenty minutes she wound along the sandy bottom of the canyon, grateful for its long, winding course. Of course, if they tracked her to the mouth of the slot canyon, they could just follow the depressions in the sand she'd left, even if they hadn't gotten a clear GPS reading in a while.

Though she couldn't see it in the narrow canyon, the sun had set by now, she guessed. The light grew dimmer and dimmer, and she trudged on.

And then she hit a wet area, a place where numerous springs trickled down the canyon walls, creating beautiful little green gardens of delicate maidenhair ferns. She rushed to the seeps, pressing her face against the cold stone to drink. But it wasn't more than thin sheen on the stone wall, not enough to quench the unbearable thirst that plagued her body.

She pressed on, wincing with every step.

Then, in a place that had been wet a few days ago, she spotted boot prints. It hadn't rained in a while, and the prints were perfectly preserved in a patch of dried mud. She slowed, staring at them, and then froze.

They were *her* boot prints.

Walking side by side with Espinoza.

THIRTY-TWO

This wasn't just an unknown slot canyon—this was the one Espinoza had taken Alex to, the one with the hidden ruin. Hope sprung up inside her so powerfully that her throat closed.

The slot canyon. She knew where she was. She was near Milton's property, near the dig site. Relief swept over her. She was still miles from a decent water source and help, but just knowing where she actually was made her feel immensely better.

Briefly she thought of trudging on to the dig site, but she'd be out in the open again, and they'd be able to home in on her location. And there was a good likelihood no one would be there to help her. The police had shut the site down. Maybe a cop might be there, securing the scene, but it was a big chance to take. If she was wrong, it could be the end of her.

But if she could find that crack Espinoza had shown her, squeeze into the cliff dwelling hidden inside that vast cave, that would completely block the GPS signal. It could buy her enough time to find something in the cave, something sharp she could use to cut through the collar.

She paused, looking at the direction of the tracks. They pointed toward her. She stared back. That meant she must have walked right by the crack already. Missed it completely. Or maybe she was on the *other* side of it and hadn't reached it yet, and these were their tracks heading *back* to the dig site.

She tried to place herself, tried to remember which side of the wash they'd walked down that day. But her head swam with dizziness, and trying to remember sent a needle spike of pain shooting down from her head wound.

Then it hit her. Those little seeps. She remembered them being near the crack in the canyon wall. So she *had* passed it, too dazed in her dehydrated state to notice it.

She turned back. She didn't see any more boot prints in the loose sand, just myriad depressions left by her just now and probably mule deer and other animals who had used the slot canyon recently.

She continued to backtrack, her feet stinging with every step. She longed for a pair of socks, some moleskin to cover the wounds, and her boots. Seeing the boot tracks she'd left was like an extra stab to her spirit, and she found herself envious of her past self who had those boots on.

She hobbled along, bracing herself against the nausea and dizziness by pressing one hand against the cool stone of the canyon wall.

And about a quarter mile back, she spotted it. The crack. Plants still hung down over the entrance just as before. No wonder she hadn't seen it this time.

Gently she parted the plants and tried to heft herself up into the crack. Her foot slipped on the first attempt, making her slide back down, scraping her shin painfully on a rock. She gripped the sides of the crack again and hoisted herself up, this time getting a solid foothold. Easing her body into the crevice, she squeezed through. It had been easy when she was with Espinoza. But now, her body shook with exhaustion and her feet throbbed in pain as she shimmied her way inside. She glanced back, making sure the hanging vegetation still covered the entrance.

The crack felt far longer than it had before, and in her queasy state she wondered if she was even in that same crevice, even in the right slot canyon. But her boot prints didn't lie.

Then darkness fell over her world. The last slanting rays of daylight had been slim enough, but now, deep inside the crevice, little light penetrated. On her left she felt a gust of wind, sensed the cavernous opening of the vast cave before her.

She pressed all the way through, falling gratefully onto the cavern floor.

She lay there for a few minutes, just letting her body rest, then crawled deeper inside. The people who had built this amazing village wouldn't have left themselves only one way in and out. There had to be another place of egress. If she could get the collar off and find another exit, she might emerge in a place far from where her pursuers had tracked her.

But it was nearly pitch-black inside and she could distinguish only the dim outlines of the stone and the adobe houses above her, perched on the large ledge of the cave wall.

She got to her feet. With hands outstretched in the darkness, she walked forward until she came to one wall. Then she felt her way alongside it. She remembered the rotten ladders lying in pieces on the cave floor and hoped the other exit wasn't high up inside the cave, something she'd need a ladder to reach.

She could smell air moving through the cave, which meant that there was another opening somewhere. She decided to seek it out while at the same time trying to find anything long and slender she could use to pick the lock or anything sharp enough to cut through the collar.

As the last of the light died away, she crouched down on her hands and knees to feel along the floor.

She did a circuit of the entire room this way, finding to her dismay that if another exit did exist, and she was sure it did, it was indeed reachable only with one of the ancient ladders.

Now she focused on groping along in the dirt for something sharp. Maybe Espinoza's team had left something behind all those years ago. An old belt buckle she could take apart to pick the lock.

A bobby pin. A safety pin. Anything. Her hands moved over smooth stones and rotten pieces of wood.

She found a sharp rock and tried once again to saw through the thick material, but after ten solid minutes of effort, she couldn't even feel that she had scuffed up the collar, much less cut through it.

Then she tried again to smash the GPS antenna. She lay down on the cave floor, placing the housing on a large flat rock, and brought another stone down on it hard, again and again. But she still had no way of knowing if she'd damaged it.

Her arm shaking from exhaustion, she let the rock tumble to the cave floor.

In the far distance, she thought she heard the drone of ATV engines. Her heart crawled up into her throat. Damn it. She hadn't been able to get the collar off, and they'd tracked her to the mouth of the slot canyon. Her one hope now was that the signal had been too patchy in the canyon to pinpoint her location, and they wouldn't spot the rock crevice. Hopefully they didn't know about this place. Maybe they'd walk right past it like she had done earlier. Then when they didn't pick up her signal on the other side of the canyon, they'd think that she'd gotten the collar off or destroyed it.

But what if they *did* spot the crack? She gazed around in the darkness hopelessly.

She remembered the placement of the jaguar painting, above a series of wide rock ledges. The first was about six feet up and the next about four feet above that one. If she could climb up there, then even if they did come into the cave, they might not spot her up there.

She knew her footprints must be all over the cave floor. She couldn't see them, but imagined she'd left more than a few impressions of her bare feet on the sandy rock. Quickly she felt along the ground until her hands found a large stick. She placed it on its side and moved it over the dirt floor, masking the obvious signs of her presence.

Then she found a large flat rock, dusted it off, and placed it at the bottom of the ledge. She masked her prints leading up to it. Then standing on the bare rock, she reached up, feeling the lip of the first ledge with her upstretched fingers. She gripped the edge of it and, scrambling, managed to pull herself up onto the ledge. Then, on shaking legs, she stood up on it, feeling a sense of vertigo wash over her. She couldn't remember how wide the ledge was, and it slanted downward dangerously. She faced the wall, pressing her face against the cool stone, and felt upward for the second ledge to her left. Her grasping fingers found it and she jumped up from the bottom ledge, perching her torso on the surface above. Her feet swung free and she slid slightly, desperately clawing at the rock to stay up. But her fingers found a small crack and she managed to heft herself up onto the second ledge.

Now she lay flat on her stomach, nervous because this perch also pitched downward slightly. She didn't want to roll off. She was now about fourteen feet above the cave floor.

The sound of the ATV engines cut out in the distance. They were probably about to make their way down the slot canyon, but they wouldn't be able to take the quads past all the log jams and debris. Even so, their progress would be a hell of a lot faster than hers had been.

She struggled to her feet, feeling along the wall. She remembered another ledge stood above this one, but not how high it had been. Her fingers were rewarded with the sharp edge of a third ledge. She guessed she was probably about level with the houses now but tucked away in a curve, so that if the men swept the area with flashlights, they might not spot her. Especially if she could get high enough and press herself tightly against the cave wall.

She felt along the dimensions of the ledge above and to her left. It seemed at least big enough for her to sit on. But it was more than two feet above her head, and only by standing on her tiptoes could she reach it with her fingertips. She'd have to leap and hope that the rock ledge beneath her wouldn't crumble.

She crouched down and sprang into the air, hands grasping for the cliff. They caught but slipped off. She came down on her cut feet with a thud. Gritting her teeth against the pain, she jumped again and again. On the third attempt, her fingers got a good hold. She swung her legs out, getting some momentum going, and then on the backswing pulled her body up and got her elbows hooked on the ledge. Now she kicked with her feet and pushed off the cave wall, managing to get on the ledge as far as her waist. Her reaching fingers found a crack and she used it to haul herself the rest of the way onto the ledge. She was a good twenty-one feet above the cave floor, she estimated.

The last dim light from the sun had long since faded and her eyes widened in the dark, trying to take in any light, but she could see nothing. She discovered that the old adage *Can't see your hand in front of your face* was actually accurate.

Her mind briefly flashed on a random memory, of being at sixth-grade camp with her schoolmates. They'd gone into a cave and their teacher had passed around wintergreen Life Savers that sparked in the dark when they chewed them. She longed for those sparks now, for any hint of light.

She heard voices, echoing off the slot canyon walls outside. The men were close.

THIRTY-THREE

Alex moved to a sitting position, tucking her feet up under her, her chin resting on her knees. She hugged her legs and shivered in the damp cave. The voices got louder, the men drawing close. She couldn't make out what they were saying to each other, but suddenly one of them called out in a loud, smug way, "Yooo-hooo! We know you're here somewhere!"

She held her breath, her shivering growing more intense.

Now she heard their steps sliding on the sand right outside the cave. She bit her lip.

She couldn't tell how many there were. All of them? Or had they broken into smaller groups? She thought of all the extra men who had shown up in trucks, their additional ATVs. The footsteps grew fainter. They'd passed the crevice.

Alex squeezed her eyes shut and let out a silent exhale.

But then she heard them coming back. "I think it's around here somewhere," she heard one of them say, and her heart sank.

He must know about the cave. About the ruins.

"Yeah, here it is!" the same voice said triumphantly, and suddenly she could hear someone scrabbling inside the crevice.

She tucked herself into a tighter ball.

A flashlight beam pierced the darkness, so bright that it burned her retinas after so long in the pitch-black.

It flashed around the cave.

And then she saw the first man crawl through. He shone his light over the houses, the rotten ladders, but not up to where she hid. "Yep! This is it!" he called to his comrades. He wore a rifle strapped to his back.

Alex pressed against the rock wall with such force that she felt like she would push right through it. Her back braced ramrod straight against the stone, her feet tucked away from the edge, her breath stilled.

Another man crawled through, then another and another. They carried small daypacks, holding them out before them so they could squeeze through the crack. Leaning back on her perch, she could see only their heads, but she spotted the barrel of a rifle sticking up from the back of the second man. They still sported the skull masks, their faces obscured, and Alex wondered why they bothered. She was sure they all actually knew each other. Maybe they didn't want to risk Alex identifying them. The thought gave her some hope. If that was the case, then they still thought she had a chance and could expose them.

"No way she could have found this place," one of the men said. She didn't recognize the voice.

"She mighta known about it from before," the first man insisted.

They shone their lights around and a third man gave a long, low whistle. "Can't believe this has been here this whole time. I never knew about it."

She didn't think any of the men who had spoken were those who had harassed her at her cabin. How many of them were there?

But one of them still hadn't said anything. Maybe she'd recognize his voice. She couldn't make out much and didn't dare peer farther over the edge.

A third shone his light around, a powerful Maglite. Motes of dust drifted in the beam as he flashed it around. Alex spotted a large brown stain on the cave floor by the crevice and wondered what it was. "This place is a tomb. I don't think she's been in here." He shone his light over the cave floor. "See? No footprints." He paused. "I don't hear anything, either. Let's keep going. She probably walked right by this place like we did and is way down canyon. Macon's gonna be pissed if we lose her and he's waiting on the other side for us."

Alex wondered if Macon was the main goon, the one who had confronted her at her cabin.

"All right," said the first man. "Let's go."

Alex held her breath. Relief was so close.

But then the man with the Maglite shone it over the walls once again, stepping back by the crevice to get a full view. His beam spotlighted her on her perch. "There!" he yelled. He fumbled to unsling the rifle strapped to his back and pointed it at her.

But a second man put his hand on the muzzle. "No. That's too quick. We found her. We get to take our time. She's trapped in here with us."

Then the fourth man stepped forward, the one who hadn't spoken yet. He stood in front of them and pulled off his skull mask, slinging it aside. "Wrong," he said. "You're trapped in here with *me*."

Alex's breath caught in her throat. That voice. That Scottish accent. The long wavy black hair that cascaded to his shoulders. She leaned forward to get a better look.

Casey.

"What are you—" one of the men started to say, but Casey struck forward with lightning speed, snaking an arm around the man's neck and bending him over. With a sharp upward jerk of his clenched arm, he snapped the man's neck. The man slumped to the cave floor, lifeless.

The two other men backed away. The first brought up his rifle again, but Casey kicked out just as it went off, driving the barrel toward the ceiling of the cave. A round pinged off the rock there. Then Casey gripped the muzzle and pulled the man to him, kneeing him in the gut. The man doubled over and Casey smashed his knee into his face, the man's nose erupting in a spray of blood.

The third man took a swing at Casey at the same time, but Casey dodged it, bringing an elbow back into the man's throat. The man coughed, sputtering, reeling backward. Still grasping the second man around the neck, Casey kicked out at the third, landing a solid kick to the man's face. He staggered, falling with a thud on his back. Then Casey dragged his struggling prisoner forward and brought his boot down hard on the prone man's throat, crushing it.

The last man struggled in Casey's grip, landed a kick to Casey's knee and managed to break free.

But Casey kicked out, sweeping the man's ankles and tripping him. The man careened face-first onto the ground, and Casey leapt on his back, snaking an arm around his neck and squeezing, keeping the man pinned on his stomach beneath. The man thrashed, trying to break free.

From a sheath on his belt, Casey withdrew a combat knife and drove it into the man's side again and again, rapid strikes at his vital organs. Blood spilled out onto the cave floor, a crimson pool trickling toward the crevice.

The man went limp and Casey stood up, panting. He wiped his blade off on the man's jacket and staggered away from him.

Then he picked up the fallen flashlight and shone it up to where she hid.

"Alex?" he asked.

"Casey," she breathed. "I can't believe it."

He scanned the beam over the series of ledges. "That was quite a feat, getting up there."

She could see now in the light how precarious those ledges actually had been and was glad she hadn't known that before.

"Can you get down?"

She hesitated. "Are they dead?" She swallowed, her voice raspy from dehydration.

He shone the light around at the men, then felt for each's pulse at the neck. "They're dead."

Cautiously Alex edged toward the lip of the ledge and lowered herself onto the one below, then the one below that. At the cave floor, she swung her legs off the bottom ledge and landed with a thump on the cave floor. Then she stood there, teetering, taking him in.

The familiar blue eyes, the way he moved, the wavy shoulder-length black hair.

"Is it really you?" she asked.

He nodded. "Aye."

She reached for him, grabbed him, and his arms snaked around her, pulling her into him. She pressed her face into his hair, breathing him in, that familiar scent, the warmth they'd shared out on the ice during what seemed like a lifetime ago.

"Alex," he breathed into her neck.

After a long moment, she pulled away, fear gripping her. "They'll find me again. I can't get this damn thing off." She tugged at the collar.

"I'm going to cut it off. And then we're going to get out of here."

She almost couldn't think for the intensity of her thirst. Her head pounded and her throat felt like someone had taken sandpaper to it. It hurt to swallow. It hurt to talk.

"Here," he said, producing a canteen that was strapped to his belt. "I don't have much left, I'm afraid, but you're welcome to all of it."

She took the canteen gratefully, drinking the cold water. She left some for him, too. She eyed the other men, seeing if they wore a canteen, but none did. "Do the others have water in their packs?"

Casey moved to the backpacks, rummaging through them, and found another canteen. But it was nearly empty, and she finished it off. He regarded her. "We'll find more. Let's get that thing off."

He handed her the flashlight and produced a multitool. He

pulled out the wire cutters and reached for the collar. She craned her neck away from the rough material as he cut through it. It was tough going, and she was amazed at his careful touch, never nicking her skin as he worked, his combat medic training in play. At last she felt the pressure release and the collar dropped off.

She rubbed her neck. "God, what a relief. I don't think I'll ever collar another animal again."

Casey picked up the device. "Hang tight here for a sec." He grabbed a flashlight off one of the dead men and then ran to the crevice. He disappeared through it, his light going with him.

Alex stood there, blinking, in disbelief. The collar was off. And Casey was here! Her heart thudded, and that nervous flutter in her stomach came back with a vengeance. Just the thought of him elicited a visceral reaction in her. His presence was almost overwhelming.

She waited, the minutes ticking by, and she started to get worried. Where had he gone? What if he'd been captured?

Ten minutes went by, then fifteen. The need to move made her anxious. The men could be closing in even now.

But then she saw flashes of light in the crevice, the slithering of something coming back inside. She switched off her own light. It might not be Casey.

In the pitch-dark, she struck a Jeet Kune Do fighting stance, ready to tear apart whoever it was with her bare hands. She heard her teacher in her mind. *Keep your hands up. Protect the computer.* He'd always referred to one's head as a person's "computer." She held up her hands before her face, bracing for a confrontation, ready to strike out when the person got in range.

The light fell on her, spotlighting her. "It's me," Casey whispered from the crevice.

Alex dropped her hands, exhaling.

He emerged fully into the cave.

"Got rid of it," he told her, his familiar Scottish accent slightly rolling the *r*. "Ran to the edge of the slot canyon and tossed it into a pretty considerable ravine. They'll be climbing around there for hours thinking you're hidden in there somewhere. That'll buy us some time."

He rummaged through his jeans pocket. "And I thought you might be missing this." He held out his hand and she saw her multitool in his palm, the one her father had given her with the engraving "Alex Carter: Adventure Awaits" on it. She was so happy to see it, to see that little bit of her dad, that her throat closed with unshed tears. She took it and gripped it tightly, then stowed it away in her jeans.

Then she stood there, staring at him. Still couldn't come to terms that he was actually there. "How in the world did you find me?"

"I got here a couple days ago," he said, his hands steadying her where she stood. "I've infiltrated this group before. Thought they were done for years ago. But my friend Arturo told me they were back in action."

She lifted her eyebrows. The town was so small. How many Arturos could there be? "Not Arturo, as in Pilar's grandson? You know him?"

He grinned. "Aye, quite well. We served in the UN peacekeeping forces together. I came here to stay with them."

Alex was staggered by the coincidence. "So you didn't . . ."

"Follow you here?" he finished for her.

He'd done so before, showing up at various places where she was conducting studies.

"No, not this time. I rode up on these arseholes just as they killed that activist. Saw you. After they shot you, they were going to kill you. There were fifteen of them there. I couldnae fight them all. So I told them to put the collar on you. That it would be more 'fun' that way. It made me sick to say it, Alex. But I had to buy you some time." He looked down at her ragged, bloody feet. "I'm so sorry about the boots. That was Macon's idea. He's a real piece of work. I heard you had met him, that he threatened you at your cabin. I've been trying to figure out who their leader is, where they're getting all their money."

"You mean the leader isn't Macon?"

He shook his head. "No, I don't think so."

"You said you've had a run-in with these men before?"

"Aye. Not these exact men, but the same organization, the Sons of the White Star. I managed to dismantle them a few years ago."

"Dismantle them? How?"

He winced. "It wasn't exactly legal."

She regarded him. She knew that he'd acted as a vigilante in the past. "Just how not legal was it?"

"Extremely." He seemed to want to leave it at that, so she didn't press him. Now was not the time. "The good news is that now you've got a ride. We can use the ATVs waiting at the mouth of the canyon." He looked down. "Let me see your feet."

She braced herself on his shoulder, then lifted each foot up in turn. He winced when he saw the ragged cuts, sand, grit, and dust coating the wounds. "We'll have to find more water to wash these cuts out. But I've got some alcohol wipes and gauze, and I can fix them up for now. Pick out some of the bigger pebbles." He gestured for her to sit down on a large rock. She did so, and he knelt down before her.

Gently taking one leg, he draped her ankle on his thigh and opened a med kit from his own pack. His touch was quick and efficient, and even when he produced tweezers and picked out the larger pieces of debris, she barely flinched. "Sorry. This is going to sting a wee bit." He wiped her feet down with alcohol. When the alcohol hit the open wounds, she sucked in air through clenched teeth.

He affixed gauze and tape to the bottom of each foot when he was done cleaning it.

Then he eyed the dead men, his gaze pausing on the most diminutive one. "I'll bet that radge there wears a size seven. I reckon that'll do you pretty good." He moved over to the small man and shucked off his boots and socks. He brought them back to her. "Here. Try these on."

Tenderly she slid on the man's socks and then loosened the laces on his boots as much as possible so she could ease her feet inside. Casey was right. The boots were a perfect size for her—a 7 in men's, which meant a 9 in women's.

"Now let me look at your head," he said.

She reached up, touching the bandage there. It had soaked through with blood. "Why do I get the feeling you're responsible for this dressing, too?"

"Aye. It was me. I convinced them that you wouldn't be a very sporting target if you lost a lot of blood. That it would prolong the hunt if I patched you up." He peered up at her, his blue eyes intense and a dark lock of his black hair coming down by his temple. The intensity of his gaze hit her with a visceral strength, and she had to force herself not to look away. Something in those eyes was haunted. Maybe even broken. Not for the first time, she wondered what had led him on this path to being a vigilante. What had he seen in his life? She knew that he'd lost his mom to a bombing when he was twelve, the same age that she'd lost her own mother. But there was something more, she could sense that. A lifetime of deep hurts, of damage.

She waited while he cleaned and redressed her head wound.

Her eyes burned with exhaustion, and she longed to sleep, even for just an hour. But they couldn't afford to stay here, not when the men could track them to the cave.

Casey took one of the rifles from the dead men and slung it over his shoulder. He handed Alex another, then dug through their pockets and packs for extra ammunition. "Are you ready?"

She nodded, draping the weapon across her chest. Feeling much better with a pair of boots on, Alex moved with him to the crevice and they crawled out.

The slot canyon lay in darkness. Faint starlight shone down. She didn't like the thought of using their flashlights. Too easy to spot. So they'd flick them on, shielding the beams with their hands to get a quick picture of the terrain ahead of them, then turn them off and forge on.

They climbed over the logjams Alex had crossed before. Her feet still hurt, but the boots were heavenly.

At one of the larger seeps along the canyon wall, she paused. Her thirst almost made her feel like she was losing her mind. She'd never been so ravenous for water before. Now that she had something to collect water in, she relished the thought of a long drink. She took Casey's canteen and pressed it against the canyon wall beneath a trickle of water, waiting anxiously for it to fill. When a few inches had collected in the bottom, she drank them down, then filled it again. She could feel precious minutes trickling by with the water and knew they couldn't spend much time collecting it. She drank down three more inches, then refilled it, feeling her skin start to prick with nervousness at the time it was taking.

She offered some to Casey, but he gently pushed the canteen back toward her. "I've drunk plenty of water today, Alex. You take it. I'm fine. We'll find more water on our way to get help," he added.

They resumed their trek down the canyon, Alex drinking those remaining few precious drops.

At last she saw two ATVs parked at the mouth of the slot canyon. The men must have doubled up on them, a driver and gunman on each for the chase.

Alex stood in the darkness, listening for other engines, but didn't hear anything.

"I think we can take a route to the dig site," she suggested, "veering around the slot canyon. There might still be police there, finishing with the crime scene."

"Aye, I heard about that poor man. Do they know who did it?"

She looked at him, then gestured at the ATVs. "I assumed one of this group."

He nodded. "Could well be. They certainly talked some seriously nasty shite about him."

"But you don't know?"

"No. It happened before I got here."

She wondered if it was the same men who had broken into her cabin, or maybe this elusive leader that Casey was trying to discover.

Casey stared ahead. "We'll have to avoid the other end of the canyon. Macon is waiting there."

Alex frowned. That was the end of the canyon she'd entered with Espinoza, and it didn't lay that far away from the dig site. So they'd have to flank the site. She thought of a large hill above the dig. Maybe they could drive to the back side, then climb it and peer down, see if any police were still there.

They stashed their rifles on the gun mounts of the ATVs and fired up the vehicles, then took a circuitous route toward the dig site. She didn't worry much about the sound they made; Macon would just think it was the other men, searching for her. She relished the speed after spending so much time limping painfully across sharp rocks and hot sand. Her progress had been agonizingly slow.

But now they motored over the desert floor, weaving around clusters of ocotillo and cholla. The moon rose, casting more light on the surrounding terrain.

As they rode, Alex kept continual watch for the flash of headlights from other ATVs. But so far they were alone. At the base of the hill behind the dig site, they parked their quads and climbed the rise. At the top they lay on their stomachs and Casey pulled a pair of binoculars from his pack. He aimed them down at the dig site. It was completely dark. He handed the binoculars to Alex. She could still see crime scene tape flapping in the wind around the tent. All the vehicles were gone, including the students', but the tarps remained in place over the excavations. She didn't see an officer guarding the site, and figured they'd finished all the forensic work they'd needed to do and had released the area.

"Nobody," she whispered.

She thought about where help lay from there. Milton's place. He wasn't a stellar person, but he had a phone. Then there was the Sweetwater Ranch. Town. But they didn't have a lot of gas. Casey told her that her pursuers had brought extra gas in their trucks to refuel the ATVs. But she and Casey didn't have that option. They had only what was left in the tanks, and she didn't think they could make it all the way to town.

"You know this area far better than I. Where's the nearest phone?" he asked.

"I think we should go for the Sweetwater Ranch. It's the closest as the crow flies."

He nodded.

She didn't like the thought of bringing the men to the doorstep of June and George. She and Casey would have to be careful. Be sure they hadn't been followed there.

They crept back down the rise and climbed onto the ATVs again, heading to the north. Alex rode in front, leading the way to the ranch.

They'd been riding for maybe fifteen minutes when she heard a loud metallic clang of something striking her ATV. She glanced back, seeing a bullet hole in the rear fender. The air started hissing out of the back right tire. The ATV grew sluggish, Casey quickly catching up to her. He stared forward, watching as she struggled to gun it. Then another loud ping rang up from her machine. She startled, glancing down to see a second tire going flat. Her quad slowed even more, then ground to a halt in the loose soil.

Casey brought his ATV to a halt behind hers. "Come over to mine!"

But before she could jump off and run back to his quad, she saw a telltale puff of smoke on a mountain ridge in the distance. She'd seen it before, back by the beacon. Rocket launcher.

THIRTY-FOUR

Alex dismounted, jerking her head toward Casey. "Get off your ATV! Run!" She raced off, heading away from the quads.

He looked shocked and confused but leapt off his ATV and took off at a sprint behind her. A mere second later a deafening explosion threw her off her feet. She landed on her side in the dirt, skidding to a stop. Shaking off the shock, she hoisted herself up on her hands and knees, seeing the smoking wreck of Casey's quad, fire consuming it. He lay a few feet away, lying immobile on the ground. She crawled to him hurriedly.

"Casey!"

He groggily raised his head. Another hiss of the rocket launcher sent a projectile streaking toward her ATV. It impacted it with a fiery boom. Both vehicles lay in a twisted mess, their rifles destroyed along with them.

Alex and Casey ran, quickly reaching a large cluster of rocks, Casey staggering, disoriented. When they reached the safety of the far side, she said, "Are you okay?"

He shook his head and brought a hand up to his forehead. "Aye, I think so. A rock hit me. They really love using that thing, don't they?"

"We've got to get farther away," she urged him.

Together they stole through the night, sprinting from one place of cover to another, then up and over a rise, then another one, until they were well out of the line of sight. With the cover of darkness and the absence of the tracking collar, she hoped they had a chance of losing their pursuers.

They continued toward the ranch, but Alex's legs shook with exhaustion. She didn't know how much she had left in her without a rest. She moved on pure adrenaline now, every part of her hurting. She wasn't sure how long they'd walked since their ATVs were destroyed. She guessed maybe two miles over rough terrain.

They came down on the other side of a rise, finding themselves before a steep mountain. She heard the trickle of water and followed it to a small spring. Gratefully, she refilled Casey's canteen, drank deeply, then refilled it. Then she stared up at the face of the mountain before them. She knew given her state of exhaustion and the condition of her feet that she'd have a hell of a time climbing it.

But then she spotted a yawning black hole about fifty feet away. She moved to it, shining her light inside. An old mine.

Her body ached to rest, and she wondered if they could hide inside there, at least for a little bit.

"Casey, look at this," she said, calling him over.

He knelt down and peered inside the opening, the beam of his light gliding over old timbers shoring up the tunnel.

"Could we hide in here for a bit?" she asked.

"Let's see how deep it goes."

They entered the structure and the temperature went up slightly, still holding some of the day's warmth.

About fifty feet in, they came to an intersection. One tunnel branched off to the right, and the other to the left.

She thought of the "left-hand rule" of navigating mazes. Always stay to the left, and eventually they'd go through the entire tunnel system, provided none of it was caved in or blocked off.

"Shall we go left?" Casey said, echoing her thoughts.

"Sounds good." They ventured down the branching tunnel, cobwebs along the ceiling billowing in the air as they stirred it. A strong musty smell of exposed earth pervaded the space around them.

They came to another intersection and then another, always taking the left branch. Alex limped along, feeling ragged. At another intersection, one tunnel seemed to branch back toward the opening.

"Let me check this out," Casey offered. "If this circles back toward the entrance, this might be a good place to hole up." He jogged down the tunnel and she watched as his light grew fainter and fainter and then disappeared altogether. She extended a hand to lean against the wall, her feet feeling like they were on fire.

She shone the beam around, hoping this place would provide some refuge.

Soon a light appeared in the tunnel and Casey returned. "I think this would work. If we rest here and the men enter the mine, we can listen for which tunnel they take and circle around them. Exit the mine without them knowing."

"If they don't split up and take both routes," she added ruefully.

He nodded. "Aye. If they don't split up."

They journeyed a little farther down the current tunnel. Now they were deep inside. Alex shone her light over the ceiling, illuminating the wires from an ancient lighting system. "Maybe the mine has another exit. It wouldn't be a bad idea at all if we had another way out." She knew that some of these old mines ran for miles beneath the desert floor, twisting in different directions.

So they continued a little farther, Alex sniffing at the air, waiting for a hint of breeze that would mean they were close to a point of egress, straining her ears for the trickle of water from a spring or underground creek that could be further deliverance from her terrible thirst.

But finally they'd gotten so far inside that Casey touched her shoulder. "Let's rest here, Alex."

She sagged her head, grateful. The thought of sleep was so alluring that her whole body ached for it. "Okay."

He took off his jacket and knelt down, then cleared away a few bigger rocks and laid the jacket on the ground. "Here you go."

She sat down, the muscles in her legs almost sighing with relief. Then he sat down beside her. "Do you have anything to eat?" she asked him.

"I've got a few CLIF Bars."

"Sounds great," she said hungrily, her stomach grumbling in anticipation. He handed her one and she tore open the wrapper. She bit into the soft bar. Carrot cake. Her favorite.

"I've got chocolate chip and peanut butter ones, too." He held them out for her.

"No, you take one."

"I had one earlier today. I'm fine."

"No," she said. "I insist. We both need to keep up our strength. And I don't tend to eat a lot, anyway, even when I have the option."

"Another thing we have in common."

She wondered just how much they *did* have in common.

"And for dessert," he said, digging around in his bag.

"You're spoiling me."

He pulled out a small green pack of gum. "Spearmint!" He offered her a piece. She took it gratefully. The burst of flavor in her mouth after so long of being parched and hungry was the best thing she'd ever tasted. He took a piece, too, chewing it thoughtfully. "I guess we should try to get some rest."

She nodded, then stretched out on his jacket. He stripped off his flannel shirt and draped it over her, leaving him in just a short-sleeved shirt. "Won't you be cold?" she asked.

"I like the cold."

She thought of their time out on the Arctic ice together, those nights shivering in a small tent, and felt a laugh rising up to the surface. "Yeah, I remember." She tried to stifle her sudden burst of amusement, but when he started to laugh, she couldn't help it, either. It felt good to laugh, and he had an infectious one.

He lowered himself down beside her. "We'd better switch off the lights," he said. "Conserve the batteries."

"Good idea."

They turned off their flashlights and complete darkness overtook them, so utterly pitch-black that it felt like a physical presence closing in on her. "I'll take the first shift. You sleep," he offered.

She pressed in closer to him, welcoming his warmth, and he lay on his side, one arm wrapped around her. They lay together like that for a few minutes, Alex slowly warming up next to him.

"That *was* a time we had out there on the ice," he said quietly in the darkness. "I think of it often."

Slightly cold in the damp cave, she reveled in the heat from his body. He was like a radiator.

They went quiet for several long minutes and Alex marveled that no matter how much her eyes adjusted to the dark, she still couldn't see anything. She felt like her pupils must be huge, trying to take in the barest hint of light. But there was none.

"Casey," she said.

"Yes?"

"What led you on this path?"

She felt him exhale, long and slow. At first she wasn't sure he was going to answer. But then he said, "Oh, Alex. So very many things."

"Will you tell me?"

Again he was quiet for a long time. Then he said, "Seeing injustice. People not held accountable for atrocities. I think I've always had something in me that couldn't stomach bullies. When I was a kid, I was always standing up for people. I got in more fights than all my friends put together. Somehow I felt it was my duty to protect them. So many kids were scared and it just made me so angry to see. And then after I joined the UN peacekeeping forces, the unbelievable cruelty we saw in Darfur . . ." He shifted next to her, and she could feel him shake slightly. "I don't know. Something just snapped. I couldn't bear to see these terrible things anymore. I felt like my hands were tied by the law, tied by societal norms. Maybe even tied by my own fear at first. I told you about that warlord who had committed so many atrocities in a number of villages."

She remembered him relating the terrible details on a night spent out on the ice, shivering in the tent, hearing the wind howl outside as an Arctic storm raged on. "I remember," she whispered.

"I said that he was killed, that they suspected one of his own men did it."

Alex tensed in the ensuing silence, not wanting to say anything or interrupt. She felt like she was finally going to understand some vital part of him, one of the things that had left him haunted.

"It wasn't one of his men," he whispered. He didn't seem to want to go on, falling into silence. He shifted again, pulling slightly away from her. "I still think about it every day, the feeling of his throat under my blade. The feeling of him going limp, slumping to the ground. The life I'd taken. It damaged some part of me, I think. Deep down, doing that. But I don't regret it. It saved lives. Countless innocent lives." After a few moments, he added, "And he wasn't the only one."

She could feel him pulling away, both mentally and physically. He rolled onto his back, removing his arm from around her. She didn't want him to feel like she was judging him, or even that she didn't entirely understand.

She herself had killed before, though it was in self-defense, and she, too, thought about those people every day. It had left an indelible imprint on her. Even though she knew she'd be dead right now if she hadn't, it had still taken away some vital innocence she'd once possessed. She'd tried to talk to Zoe about it. But Zoe, bless her heart, hadn't had much hardship in her life, and certainly never had to kill someone before. And while she listened to Alex with compassion, Alex knew that deep down Zoe didn't really understand. She kept reassuring Alex that she had to do it. That she wouldn't be here now if she hadn't. But still this dark specter seemed to have been shadowing her life ever since, a manifestation of some damage she'd done to herself in the taking of a life, however despicable the person had been. So part of her got that about Casey. Understood that torn apart feeling.

When she realized he wasn't going to go on, she put her arm around him, pulling him closer and resting her head on his chest. He seemed surprised at this gesture and placed his arm around her.

"Where have you been?" she asked him. "Since we last saw each other?"

"I had to attend to a . . . situation in Syria. I'd barely finished when Arturo contacted me, told me about the problems here. We've dealt with this group once before."

"Were they here in New Mexico that time, too?"

He nodded.

He'd told her once that he'd first seen her here years before, when Alex had been in New Mexico doing an environmental impact study. A land developer wanted to build a golf course and luxury condo project on a piece of land, clear-cutting trees and other habitat to finish the project. But when Alex found imperiled spotted owls there, the developer permits were denied and the project fell through. Casey had told her that it was very important to him that this parcel of land be protected but had never said why.

"What was so important to you about that land not being developed in New Mexico?" she asked him.

He hesitated, then finally said, "I want to tell you, Alex. I really do. But I think the less you know, the better. I'd never want to make you complicit."

She frowned in the darkness, wondering what he'd done.

"And you? How have you been?" he asked her.

She told him about the rest of the mountain caribou study, and then of visiting Zoe in L.A. He listened to her, asking thoughtful questions, expressing compassion about the state of wildlife. He asked after her father and his painting.

This. This was what she missed. This kind of meaningful connection and communication. She didn't need a million friends or a super active social life. That was unrealistic with her job. But if she just had a few connections like this—her dad, Zoe, and maybe now Casey, someone she could talk to so deeply, it would make a powerful difference in her life. But this was what was so hard to find. What she didn't have even with Brad, her last serious relationship. A deep sense of camaraderie. Understanding. Respect. A mutual thirst to know everything about each other.

They both went quiet for a long time. She felt the rise and fall of his chest beneath her head, felt the comforting feel of his arm around her. She didn't know if he was asleep, didn't think so given that his breathing hadn't changed. She could feel the proximity of his face, feel his light breath falling on her. She felt an irresistible pull toward him. Could feel how close their lips were.

He shifted slightly, and she felt his warm breath on the bridge of her nose. He'd moved closer. She lifted her chin, a fire building inside her to feel him. She felt him shift closer, their lips now mere inches apart. She lifted her chin more. She could smell his inviting breath, a slight hint of mint. He lowered his head a little more and she raised hers slightly. Their alluring proximity in the dark quickened her heart.

Then their lips met, and she felt his warmth and breathed in the scent of him, a charge of electricity shooting through her. He kissed her deeply and she met his fire, reaching up to grip his shoulders. His arms snaked around her, and she pressed her body into his, feeling the full, inviting length of him. He smelled so damn good. He kissed her with such passion that she felt intoxicated, her head almost spinning.

She gripped his strong back, their kisses growing wild and abandoned. She hadn't ever felt a fire like this. The attraction was mesmerizing, hypnotic.

"You're incredible, Alex," he whispered. He held her tightly and she pressed her face against the warmth of his neck. "And I'm going to get you out of this mess."

They lay together like that, Alex listening to his soft breathing, feeling the rise and fall of his chest. She wanted to stay awake, to feel him more, but the ordeal had caught up to her. Her eyes closed. She thought she'd just rest for a minute, there in the warmth of Casey's arms. And then sleep took her.

ALEX STIRRED, COMING AWAKE WITH a start in the pitch-black of the mine. She sat bolt upright too fast, momentarily confused about where she was. Blood rushed to her head, making the bullet wound there throb. She lifted her fingers to it, bright green and yellow stars popping in her eyes despite the utter darkness.

"Alex," she heard Casey say, then his gentle hand on her back.

So she hadn't dreamed it. Her hands flew up to her throat. No tracking collar. And it really was Casey next to her.

"Are you all right?" he asked.

She exhaled, closing her eyes, letting her shoulders relax. "Yes. I was just disoriented for a second."

He switched on a flashlight and handed it to her. She shone the beam over the mine, the reinforcing timbers, the stone walls, the ancient decaying electric light system hanging rusted from the ceiling. "How long have I been out?"

"You actually slept through the night."

"And they didn't find us?" She turned to look at him. He stretched. "I thought you were going to wake me for the second shift."

"I didnae have the heart to. Besides, you needed rest more than I. How is your head?"

"I think it's better."

"Let me look." He changed the bandage on it and then those on her feet, cleaning them again. "All the cuts are looking really good," he assured her.

"Thanks to your expertise."

He handed her the canteen and she drank deeply, already looking forward to filling it again when they left the mine. Her thirst felt unquenchable. Her head ached from dehydration and the bullet graze, but she managed to stand.

"I've got one CLIF Bar left," he told her.

"Let's split it."

"Okay."

He tore it in half and she chewed the sweet peanut butter concoction as if it were a meal from a three-star Michelin restaurant.

Then she put the boots back on and stood up, stretching. She'd slept fitfully, part of her worried the men would find them, and part of her restless because of Casey and his proximity. She wasn't sure how she felt about him. He was a conflicted person and she wasn't sure what to expect from him.

Then they left the mine, easing out of the opening after scanning the terrain around them. Alex refilled the canteen at the spring, and they set off in the direction of the Sweetwater Ranch. She felt refreshed after sleep, water, and food, and was relieved to be wearing boots again.

They clambered up a rise, on the lookout for the telltale dust trail from any ATVs. But none were in sight. They climbed up another hill, moving into a higher elevation juniper-piñon pine forest along the crest. As they descended, another flatter section opened up before them. It didn't offer much cover, so they paused to examine the area. Sunlight glinted off the metallic surface of a helicopter in the distance.

She pointed. "Look at that!"

Casey pulled out his binoculars and scanned the horizon.

"Well, what do you know," he breathed, then handed her his binoculars.

She recognized it as Trager's helicopter. It waited on a barren patch of desert floor. The rotors weren't running, and no one was in sight—neither the hunter nor the pilot.

"That's Roger Trager's helo," she told Casey. "He's a Wildlife Services agent who also freelances for ranchers. Hunts mountain lions and pretty much anything they'll pay him to kill, from what I've been told."

"I take it you don't like the fellow."

"Not at all."

He turned, grinning at her. "Then you won't mind if we temporarily relieve him of his helicopter?"

"I certainly wouldn't object." The thought of flying out to civilization rather than walking made her feel twenty pounds lighter. The acute pain in her feet had begun to wear on her, beating her down.

Slowly, keeping behind cover when they could find it, they crept toward the chopper. Casey was an experienced helicopter pilot who'd been flying since he was a teenager and had flown Alex all over the Arctic when she was studying polar bears. She had no doubt he'd be able to fly them to safety.

Alex paused, wondering where Trager was, and listened for rifle shots. She didn't hear anything. Just the wind and two talkative ravens. She wondered what he was hunting.

Focused on the terrain in the distance, Alex tripped on a haphazard pile of dirt. She stumbled but caught herself. Glancing back, she saw a freshly dug mound of earth. As she peered closer, she saw something pale there sticking out of the dirt. She bent down, brushing it off, then yanked her hand away. She'd felt cold, pliant flesh. She sucked in a breath. It was a dead body.

"Casey!" she whispered. He turned, just ahead of her, and doubled back. "What is it?"

"Look." She pointed at a hand sticking out of the dirt. Casey knelt down, traced the body up to the head, and brushed the dirt away, revealing a face. She'd seen that face only once but recognized it. A fresh bullet wound had pierced his skull. "This is Trager's pilot," she told him. "I guess we know why they abandoned the helicopter. No one to fly it."

"Do you think Trager killed him?" Casey pondered.

"I don't know."

Casey glanced around them. "Let's get out of here. We can tell the police about the location of the body when we get to town."

They closed the distance to the chopper, but found the doors locked. Casey produced a lockpicking kit. He inserted tools into the locks, adjusting them, pulling them out, reinserting them, rotating them. Finally the lock sprung on the pilot's side. He opened the door, then unlocked the passenger side, too.

After hopping in, he started a preflight check, going over the instrument panels, familiarizing himself with the helicopter model. Alex climbed in beside him. "Any issues?"

He shook his head. "None."

Alex noticed a tote bag stashed in the back seat. Curious, she thought it might reveal just what Trager was up to on the preserve. She hefted it up and unzipped it. Stacked inside were huge bundles of cash, all hundred-dollar bills. She did a quick calculation. It totaled $355,000.

"Check this out," she said to Casey. She dug through the money, and beneath it found a skull mask.

Casey examined the contents. "It's got to be him. Trager. He must be the leader of the Sons of the White Star. Macon mentioned they were waiting for a big money drop from their heid bummer. I didn't get the full gist of it, but they said they were waiting on some blackmail money from a Texas state senator who had been having an affair."

"Heid bummer?"

Casey turned to her. "Head honcho, as you Americans would say."

Alex thought of the pilot. "I wonder if the pilot found out what he was up to and refused to go along with it."

"Could be he didn't know Trager was part of the white supremacist group." He handed her a headset and she took it, then buckled herself in.

Casey fired up the engine, the rotors beating overhead, slowly at first, then picking up speed. He donned a headset of his own.

Then they lifted off the desert floor, angling the chopper for town. But they'd flown only about half a mile when Alex gasped.

Bursting out from a patch of trees below loped the jaguar with the collar camera. It raced across a barren stretch of desert, then leapt across an arroyo in a single bound. She heard the crack of a rifle, then saw Milton and Trager below in an open-topped Jeep, bouncing haphazardly across the desert floor, in fast pursuit of the big cat.

They were going to kill it.

THIRTY-FIVE

Alex pressed against the window, gazing down. "Casey! We have to stop them!"

He whipped the helo around, shooting off in pursuit of Milton and Trager. Alex could see the jaguar just ahead of the Jeep. Milton drove, careening dangerously over rocky patches and across dry creek beds. She saw two gun cases in the back of the Jeep, one closed and one open and empty.

Trager sat in the passenger seat, aiming a rifle out. But with the jarring motion of the vehicle, he didn't have a hope of hitting the animal as it sped on in front of them. The jaguar veered left, and Milton pulled the wheel too hard, almost flipping them. She could see Trager cursing at him.

Casey lowered the helicopter, coming down almost on top of the men. Milton startled, snapping his neck upward to see the helo descending. He swerved the Jeep to one side, trying to elude them, but refusing to stop. He kept chasing the jaguar. And then Alex watched as a couple of hunting hounds burst from over a rise. They closed in on the jaguar, baying and running, their tongues hanging out in the heat, their feet kicking up huge clouds of dust.

The jaguar kept running, reaching a rock outcropping. In three swift bounds, it leapt up to the top of the rocks then stopped, peering down. In seconds, the hounds reached the same outcropping and moved to run circles around it, lunging and snapping upward toward the jaguar. But it was twenty feet up, well out of their reach. The dogs jumped at the rock, paws scraping the stones, but couldn't get higher than a few feet off the ground.

Casey circled the rock outcropping and Alex could see now that the jaguar was trapped on top of it.

Milton came to a sudden stop, the Jeep spraying up a plume of dirt that caught in the rotor wash from the chopper. For a few minutes, Alex couldn't see anything. Then Casey moved higher and she saw Trager leap from the passenger seat and run toward the jaguar with his rifle.

But Milton didn't go for the second gun case. Instead he ran on Trager's heels, yelling something and shaking his fist, but Alex couldn't hear anything over the thumping of the rotors.

"He's going to kill the jaguar!" Alex cried in despair. Trager leveled his rifle.

Casey careened down, drawing the chopper up beside the man. He rotated the bird, knocking Trager over with one of the landing skids. Milton watched from nearby, an arm thrown up to protect himself from the rotor wash.

Then Casey lifted the chopper again. Trager was nowhere in sight.

"Where is he?" Alex asked.

"Maybe he's under us. I may have just killed him."

He swung the chopper to the right, but still no sign of Trager. He prepared to set the chopper down bedside Milton, but suddenly Alex spotted Trager hanging onto the skid. He started climbing up onto the helicopter. He reached the window, face-to-face with Alex, his expression a twisted mask of rage, his eyes livid, sweat and dirt trickling down his face.

She slammed home the door's lock as he tried to swing open the helo door. He grabbed at the door, then pounded on the glass, perched precariously on the outside of the helicopter. Casey was now almost thirty feet up in the air.

Alex watched in horror as Trager crammed his fingers into the tiny ledge around the door and brought his rifle up. With one hand, he pointed it at Alex through the window, aiming for her head.

Casey rocked the helicopter, then spun it in a violent circle. Trager dropped out of sight. Casey veered upward, ratcheting up the speed. Alex gazed down, barely able to see one edge of the skid, and saw Trager's legs flying out from it. He still clung to the chopper. As Casey stopped spinning the helo, she saw Trager's rifle come up, ready to fire blindly.

Casey rocketed upward, speeding away from the jaguar, now over a hundred feet in the air. He spun the helicopter again, Alex clutching the side of the door, bracing against the centrifugal force. Then she saw Trager go flying off the side of the helo, spiraling out into the air, then plummeting down toward the rocky ground. Seconds later he landed with a puff of dirt, a tiny twisted shape far below.

Alex stared over at Casey, finding his lips pursed, his face grim. Not meeting her eyes, he gripped the cyclic control and turned the helicopter back around, descending. Alex watched the desert floor race up beneath them at a dizzying speed, and then they were rocketing back toward Milton and the Jeep. Alex instantly spotted that the second gun case from the back of the Jeep had been flung open and was now empty. Milton stood next to the dogs, a rifle gripped in his hands. Then she saw with horror that the jaguar no longer stood at the top of the rock outcropping. It lay at Milton's feet.

A sick pit of fear rolled over in Alex's core. Then she got a better look at the rifle as Casey propelled them forward. It was a tranq gun. Confusion washed over her.

Milton set the gun aside and pulled something out of a satchel strapped across his chest.

Casey buzzed him once, twice, rotor wash kicking up huge clouds of debris, but Milton merely stared down at the jaguar, resolute.

"Set it down," she urged him.

Before he'd even touched all the way down, Alex ripped off her headset and swung open the door. She jumped out and raced for Milton. The dogs barked, leaping excitedly around him, running up to her, too, and encircling her. The rotor wash kicked up an enormous cloud of dust and she could barely see. She stumbled forward, eyes tearing, and Casey moved the chopper away to land nearby.

As the air began to clear, she heard Milton coughing and followed the sound. The dust settled and Alex could see now what he held in his hand—a jadeite dagger, the handle in the form of a jaguar. He knelt down by the big cat, bringing the dagger to its throat.

"Milton!" she yelled. But he didn't look up.

She dashed forward, delivering a savage kick to the man's head. His neck snapped back and he lost his balance, falling backward. The dagger flew into a cluster of prickly pear.

She faced off against him, her Jeet Kune Do training flooding into her. *Keep moving. Don't let your feet turn to cement. Protect the computer.*

Milton struggled to his feet. He lifted his fists, coming at her like a brawler, no evident training.

That meant her best bet was to fight him with mid- to long-range moves, deliver a devasting blow, and while he reeled from it, move in and take him to the ground.

He took a swing at her and she ducked, coming up with a punch to his solar plexus. He grunted, doubling over, and she kneed him in the face. His head whipped back, nose bursting with blood. He took another swing at her and she deflected it with her forearm, then moved in close, hitting him in the throat with her elbow. He coughed, clutching at his neck, staggering backward.

Eyes filled with rage, he came at her again, jabbing out quickly for her face. She weaved, grabbing his arm as he missed her, then using his own momentum to propel him past her. He stumbled, landing on the ground. Then she swung in behind him on the desert floor, wrapping one arm tightly around his throat and squeezing. He thrashed, but she pinned both of his legs down with her own, crossing them in front of him. He tried to reach around and grab at her hair, but she pressed her face tightly against his back so that he couldn't get a good hold. He grasped at her, flailing, but she squeezed harder and harder. His lashing grew weaker and then he slumped limply in her arms, unconscious. She stood up, shoving him to one side in the dirt.

Casey ran up, having landed the helicopter and shut it down. "Are you okay?"

She wiped dirt out of her eyes, out of breath from the fight. "Yes." She tugged the satchel off Milton and knelt down by the jaguar. It breathed evenly. But she didn't know how much sedative he'd given the animal. Too much would kill him. She didn't have her supplemental oxygen or a counteragent.

"Keep an eye on Milton," she asked Casey, then ran back to the Jeep and opened a side pocket in the tranq gun case, hoping a counteragent would be stored in there like she did with her own gun. But none was inside. Her heart thumped in alarm. Milton probably had no idea what he was doing. It could have been a lethal dose. And why tranq the cat in the first place? Why not just use Trager's rifle to kill it? Why had he been trying to slit its throat with the jadeite dagger?

And then she remembered the party. The story about the Mayan ruler who had used that very dagger to commit ceremonial jaguar and human sacrifices that granted him invulnerability. He'd lived to be over a hundred, Milton had told her. And the Spanish conquistador Simón de Aguirre supposedly had it among his stolen loot when he'd fled to New Mexico, arriving untouched despite attacks from the Aztecs.

She walked over to where the dagger lay and picked it up. *This. This* was why Milton had funded the dig. To find this specific dagger. She remembered Desmond getting injured that last day of the dig. Everyone focused on him. Everyone except Milton, who had lurked around the periphery. And then that huge dust cloud that had kicked up, making them all turn away. Milton must have found it that day while everyone's attention was elsewhere. That's why he shut the dig down so abruptly that day. He'd found what he was after.

He'd wanted to sacrifice the jaguar with the dagger to grant himself invulnerability, just like the Mayan ruler had. She slid the dagger back into Milton's satchel.

Casey found rope in the back of the helicopter and tied Milton up, then hefted him over one shoulder and carried him to the helicopter. "Don't want him coming to and getting away," he said to Alex. "Let's turn him in to the cops. Meddling with an endangered species—that's got to be worth a hefty fine and a prison sentence, right?"

Alex frowned, thinking of how seldom such cases were prosecuted, and even if they were, what small penalties they carried, even if an endangered species was killed—just fines and little to no prison time. Even if he'd killed the jaguar, the fine in New Mexico for that was a paltry $2,000. She didn't think anything would come of it.

While Casey situated the unconscious Milton in the back of the helicopter, Alex whistled for the dogs, and they came bounding over to her. "I wonder if they're Trager's or Milton's," she said to Casey.

Casey knelt down, holding his hands out. One of the dogs raced over to him, tail wagging, a huge grin on its face. Then the other dog joined him, both of them jumping up and licking Casey's face. He examined their tags. "Trager's," he said. "His name and number are on here."

"What will happen to them?"

Casey gave her a sly smile. "I happen to know that Pilar's been wanting some guard dogs. She just might love these two pups."

They continued to lunge at him happily, tails wagging so hard their entire backs swayed with the movement. It made her feel good to know that animals liked him.

"C'mon!" he said to the dogs, and ushered them over to the helicopter. He held the door open while they bounded inside, sitting down in the back next to Milton. He was still out.

Beside her, the jaguar stirred and Alex backed off. She realized that instead of giving it *too much* sedative, Milton must have erred on the other side, giving it too little. She let out a long, relieved exhale. It sat up, groggy, and stared around. Then its tail started lashing along the ground. Finally it rose on all fours, staring warily in their direction. She climbed inside the helicopter beside Casey and they watched as it bounded off, passing along the back side of the rock outcropping and racing off across the desert floor.

A wave of relief washed over Alex. Her jaw ached and she found she'd been clenching her teeth without realizing it. "Let's go to town."

Then it hit her—despite what he'd said a moment ago about the police, Casey couldn't possibly go with her. There would be too many questions. And he was wanted in some areas. She'd have to go alone, leave him out of it. She'd tell the police what happened to her and that she could now identify Macon. But that was only thanks to Casey's intel. So how would she explain it? And what about the dead men in the cave? She'd just have to say she killed them in self-defense.

Suddenly the radio squawked and her thoughts ended abruptly. "Trager," a man barked. "Where the hell are you? We've been waiting on that money." Alex recognized the voice. It was the man who had threatened her at the cabin and assaulted Espinoza. She felt her fists ball at her sides.

THIRTY-SIX

Casey locked eyes with Alex. "If Trager doesn't answer after too long, he's going to know something's up. And I want to know their position." He grimaced at Alex. "Rocket launcher. If they think it's not Trager in the helo and they're nearby . . ." He picked up the radio, saying one simple word, hoping it would be short enough for them to not notice it wasn't actually Trager. "Macon."

"Where have you been? We lost that damn bitch. Found the collar, but it's been cut off. So we have a special surprise for her. Found one of her friends way out in the back pasture of Sweetwater Ranch. She's one of those damn ranchers who blew off our warnings, so two birds with one stone." He chuckled. "But I need you to fly around, see if you can spot that bitch from the air, tell her we have her friend. We can't let her get to help."

Alex stared at the radio. "Oh no! They must have June!"

She thought over the nearby terrain. The ranch. The dig site. They could risk going for the police, but it would be a long time before they'd get out there, and June could be dead by then.

They had no weapons. Trager's rifle had broken apart in his fall, and no additional vials of sedative were stashed in the tranq gun case. She rummaged around in the back of the helicopter but found no additional guns. Milton groggily came to as she checked under his seat. "What are you doing?" he slurred, still disoriented.

She ignored him and returned to her seat.

Casey winced. "Macon's going to know something's up when he realizes this isn't Trager. And *I* can't say anything because he saw me on the ATVs with you."

Alex considered. "But you were *behind* me on an ATV. Could you convince him you were chasing me?"

He grimaced. "It's worth a shot."

She met Casey's gaze. "I've got an idea. Do you think you can lure them over to the dig site?"

"What are you thinking?"

"I want you to tell them that Trager is dead and that I have the money."

"What?"

"If we can catch them unaware, maybe we can get to June, then get out of there."

"Are you sure about this?"

She nodded.

Casey took a deep breath and then spoke over the radio. "Macon, this is Gator."

Alex raised her eyebrows. *Gator?* she mouthed.

He rolled his eyes, making a *don't ask* face.

"What the hell are you doing with Trager?" Macon demanded.

"I have a better question," Casey fired back, speaking in a perfect American accent. "What the hell were you doing firing that damn missile launcher at me? I almost had her. You could have killed me."

"Looked to us like you were *with* her."

"Well, I wasn't. I was closing in, you idiot. Now I have no idea where she is. But I just came across Trager's helo. He's dead. And the money's gone. I think she might have it."

"What the fuck!" shouted Macon, his voice crackling over the radio. "Where is she?"

"I don't know, but I'm guessing she's headed straight for the cops."

"Goddamn it! Can you take the bird up, see if you can spot her from the air?"

"Will do," he said. "I'll let you know when I find her." He clicked off the radio. "What now?"

"Wait a little bit," Alex said, "then radio them back and say that you spotted me heading toward the dig site."

Milton leaned forward, glaring at Alex, more alert now. "Where is the jaguar dagger?"

Alex didn't bother to turn around. "In your satchel."

"Why didn't you let me finish the sacrifice? It requires a sacrifice!"

Alex turned to face him now, her brow furrowed in rage. "I wasn't going to let you murder that jaguar."

He glared at her. "Do you know how long this has been in motion? What you interrupted? I searched for that dagger for months. Espinoza was completely incompetent. I dug all over the place, making test holes, looking for more of Simón's stash. Even tried to buy neighboring land in case he'd buried it somewhere else. I did more work than he did!"

Alex thought of the strange little holes, the strange boot prints. She looked down at Milton's feet. Sure enough, he wore an expensive pair of North Face boots.

"And when I finally found the dagger, it was right there, right where they'd been digging, the idiot! He knew how much I wanted it. But he worked so damn slow! And even when I got it, it still didn't work." Then he seemed to catch himself and went quiet.

"What do you mean, it still didn't work? How is it *supposed* to work?" She thought of the Mayan ruler. He hadn't just sacrificed jaguars. He'd sacrificed humans, too.

Milton pursed his lips and stared out of the window. "Listen. I've got money. I can pay you both to drop me off. How about fifty thousand each?"

When they didn't answer, he said, "A hundred thousand? For each of you?" Sweat beaded his brow and he shifted in the seat, straining against his bindings. "You name the price. Anything."

Alex frowned. Why was he so nervous? He'd pay far less than that in fines for interfering with the jaguar and he probably knew that. Then a bad thought swept over her. Espinoza. Milton needing to make a sacrifice with the dagger. Had the Sons of the White Star not been the ones to murder him? Had that been Milton's work?

Even though it carried little penalties, meddling with an endangered species was still a crime. He might be processed if they took him into custody. Fingerprints. DNA. Maybe he wasn't in the system yet. He probably wasn't, given his reaction. Maybe he *had* killed Enrique and was worried he hadn't been so careful.

"Did you kill Espinoza?" she asked him, furrowing her brow.

Milton turned away, staring out of the window, his mouth a gray slash. He went silent.

They waited like that for a few more minutes. It was time to radio the men back.

Casey flipped the radio back on. "Macon? This is Gator."

"I hear you."

"I spotted her just east of the dig site. She's definitely carrying the satchel with Trager's money."

"We got her now!" Macon yelled, excitement edging his voice. "Hot damn. That's not far from here. We'll meet you over there. Stupid bitch probably thinks the cops are still there at the crime scene. But them boys packed up yesterday. Ain't nobody out there now."

"See you there," Casey responded and flipped off the radio.

Now that she'd heard more of his voice, she was certain. "That's definitely the man who broke into my cabin. He was with two other men."

"He's always followed around by two little lapdogs, Floyd and Lyle. Floyd does whatever Macon says, and Lyle is just quiet all the time."

Alex met his gaze. "Do you think you can land, continue your cover, and get June away from them?" she asked.

Casey nodded. "Aye. What will you be doing?"

"Hopefully luring them into a trap."

"Wait just a minute," boomed Milton from the back. "Aren't you two damn fools listening to me? I just offered you a hundred thousand each to fly me out of here and drop me off. We don't have time for this nonsense."

They ignored him.

Casey fired up the rotors and they took off, angling for the dig site, hoping they'd be in time to save June.

THIRTY-SEVEN

"Drop me off out of sight, over that ridge," Alex said, pointing to the hill by the dig site where she and Casey had climbed the night before. "Stall them for a few minutes and then say that I'm at the dig site."

Casey lowered the helo and Alex jumped out with the satchel full of money and Casey's daypack. "Wait a sec," he said, leaning over. He grabbed the skull mask out of the bag. "I'll need this."

Alex stepped back and he lifted off. She turned her back to the rotor wash, the dirt spiraling around her, and ran at a crouch to the bottom of the hill.

As he flew toward the men, she skirted around the slope, staying out of sight. She heard the roar of ATVs as she emerged on the far side of the hill. She didn't want to make a move until she saw how things went down for Casey. She pulled the binoculars out of his pack and focused on the scene before her. Three ATVs pulled into view. Alex could see the whole flat expanse before her—where the dig site was, where the men stopped on their ATVs. Tarps still covered the trenches and the plastic tent over the sarcophagus was still in place. Alex guessed they'd be back to finish cleaning up the site later.

The men still wore the skull masks. Evidently they didn't want to take any chances on June getting away and identifying them. June rode on an ATV in front of one of the men, her hands tied together. She looked scared and had a fresh cut on her cheek and a swollen, bloody lip. They'd taken her shoes, too.

The men dismounted, the one with June roughly pulling her off the ATV. June stumbled and went down on her knees. The man hefted her back up and June let out a cry of pain. "Oh, are you hurt?" Macon said, his voice full of contempt. "If you'd been home taking care of your husband like you're supposed to instead of out trying to do a man's job putting up fences, you wouldn't be in this mess. You can thank that bleeding heart bitch when you see her."

Alex gritted her teeth.

And then the chopper came sailing over a rise and slowly lowered, landing some distance away from the men.

Casey shut down the engine and climbed out, approaching them. He had donned Trager's skull mask from the bag. She heard him ask, "It's just the three of you?"

Macon shifted his weight, resting his hand on the butt of his holstered pistol. "I don't know where the hell the others are off to, damn lazy bastards. We got separated."

Alex crept on to the dig site, entering the tent over the booby-trapped coffin that had injured Desmond. She took the money out of the satchel and stuffed the cash inside Casey's pack. Then she carefully slid the sarcophagus lid to the side, not enough to allow the blades to swing out. She stuffed the satchel inside it, leaving part of the strap hanging out, and then slid the coffin lid back in place.

Then she hurried to the pit where Desmond had fallen in.

She tugged on the tarp covering that trench and laid it over the hole's opening, then weighed down the sides with stones. Quickly she scooped up dirt, covering the tarp until it just looked like a patch of soil.

Now she crept toward the men, easing to the edge of the dig site, staying out of view. She crouched down behind three large boulders and took out the binoculars again to check on Casey.

The three men still stood around, the same one clutching June's arm. She looked exhausted and scared, tears staining her face. Macon and Casey still stood there talking, Casey gesturing around. Then he pointed in the general direction where Alex waited.

Her heart thumped, even though that was part of the plan. The men had to be lured out this way.

Two of them had turned to stalk off in Alex's direction when suddenly the helicopter door burst open. The dogs piled out, baying and racing toward the men. The men spun, surprised, and Milton half fell out of the helicopter, his hands still bound. He tripped, then stopped himself from falling at the last second. He stumbled toward the men.

"It's a trap!" he yelled. "They're in on it together!"

Alex gripped the binoculars tighter.

"I'll give you fifty thousand dollars if you get me out of here," Milton told them.

For a minute they just stared at Milton. Then Macon stepped toward him. "I know you. You're the one who let that trash up here to dig around."

"That's not important now," Milton boomed. "Did you hear me? I will give you fifty thousand dollars if you get me out of here." His eyes fell on their ATVs. "Or sell me one of those and I'll just leave now. I don't care what you do to these people."

Macon turned, staring back toward Casey. "What's he talking about, saying 'they're in on it together?'"

Casey shrugged. "Damned if I know."

"Why was he in the back of the helicopter?" Macon asked. Alex bit her lip. Between this and the ATV incident, he was clearly suspicious.

"Caught him trying to steal it," Casey said.

"That's not true!" Milton yelled. "Those two killed Trager. I was just up here hunting a jaguar. I don't have anything to do with"—he waved his hand around dismissively—"whatever the fuck *this* is. I couldn't care less. I just want to leave and you can get back to your little games."

Macon spun on him. "*Little games?*"

"Your little crusade. Whatever you want to call it. It doesn't matter one iota to me."

Casey had taken a few steps back and was now standing beside June and the man holding her.

Milton's brow creased with fury. "Don't you get it, you idiot? He's in on it with her. He knows exactly where she is. He doesn't believe in your ridiculous cause."

Macon's fists balled at his side. "My *ridiculous cause?*" His hand closed on the butt of his holstered pistol. For a second Alex thought he was going to draw it. But instead he spun on Casey. "This true? You *are* in on it with her?"

Casey shook his head, his voice calm. "Of course not. He's just trying to make you doubt yourself."

But Macon didn't look away. He just stared at Casey. Alex could feel the tension in the air, crackling like electricity between the men.

"What should we do?" asked the man holding June. Alex guessed this was Floyd, the more vocal of the yes-men Casey had described. "Fifty thousand dollars would go a long way." Given how quiet the third man was being, she guessed that he was Lyle.

Macon turned to Milton. "You got that kind of money on you right now?"

Milton screwed up his face in irritation. "Well, no, of course not. I don't walk around in the middle of the goddamned desert with fifty grand in my pockets, you idiot. But I can get it for you tomorrow."

"I don't like this," said Floyd. He gripped June's arm tighter. Lyle still hadn't spoken. The more she saw them interact, the more positive she became that these were the same men who had threatened her at her cabin.

"Tomorrow, eh?" Macon barked. "You expect me to believe that crap? You're gonna ride out of here, free as a bird, and then out of the goodness of your heart come find me tomorrow and give me fifty grand? Sounds like *you're* the one who's an idiot." He shook his head. "No, I say better safe than sorry." He pulled his gun out of his holster and aimed it first at Milton and then at Casey. "You wanna tell me where that bitch is?"

Casey waved a placating hand. "Well, hell, I don't know now. This fool has wasted so much of our time that she could be well past here by now. She's probably still not far from the dig site."

Macon gestured to Lyle. "You go check it out." The man nodded and set off, heading straight for her. Alex kept out of sight.

"And what about you?" Macon asked Casey. "Are you loyal to the cause? You came down here, offering your services, saying you were good with tracking, that you could handle a chopper. Was that all just a lie?"

"Of course not. Do you think I would have traveled all the way down here to help you if I wasn't serious about the cause?"

"He's lying!" Milton yelled.

"Shut up!" Macon snapped, spinning in Milton's direction.

And then all chaos erupted. Casey grabbed Floyd, pulling the man's sidearm from the holster. Casey gave him a violent shove and the man staggered to one side, then pulled out a wicked-looking combat knife from a sheath on his thigh.

Casey shot him in the ribs, the bullet passing through his chest and exiting out the back in a red mist. Floyd collapsed, bleeding out on the ground.

Casey pivoted, readying to take a shot at Macon, but Macon ducked and rolled to one side. Milton rushed forward, yanking his hands free of his bonds. He fell on top of Macon, grabbing his gun and trying to disarm him. As they fought on the ground, kicking up dust, Casey and June ran for the chopper.

Seeing the fight break out, Lyle turned and ran back toward Macon. Milton managed to wrestle the gun away and stood up, then aimed down to shoot him. "This is your last chance," Milton said. "Just give me the keys to your ATV."

"Go to hell!" Macon spat. Milton aimed at his head, but Lyle closed in fast, drawing his gun. He took aim at Milton and fired, hitting him in the upper chest. Milton stared down, surprised, then staggered backward, shock on his face. Macon jumped up and raced forward, grabbing the gun out of Milton's hand as the man collapsed to the ground.

"Nice shot," Macon said, turning to Lyle.

Casey was almost to the helicopter when Macon raised the gun and fired. The bullet pinged off the fuselage. Casey darted away, placing June in front of him so she'd be protected from the next round.

Casey turned and fired back as he ran, but the shot went wild, Casey's arm bouncing with the momentum of running. Then he and June dove down an embankment, dipping out of sight.

"Goddamn it!" Macon cursed.

Alex thought fast. Two gunman, Casey with June, who was in no condition for a long chase without any boots on. Alex didn't want to take the chance that the men would close in on their location. She stood up and started running, intentionally making a lot of noise crunching on the rocks to attract attention.

THIRTY-EIGHT

Macon spun, instantly spotting Alex. "There she is!" he yelled. "Go after her!"

"But what about them?" Lyle said, pointing in the direction June and Casey had fled.

"They're on foot. We'll catch up to them. For now let's just get the money."

Milton lay on the ground, writhing, his hands gripping his chest. The dogs ran from person to person, not sure what to do. Finally they took off in the direction that Casey had run.

Alex turned and sprinted toward the coffin.

"There!" she heard Macon yell. "I'll go around!"

She ducked into the coffin's tent, then slipped under the plastic on the far side of it and raced for the cover of a dense section of cholla. The plastic was translucent, and she could see the figure of Lyle slip inside. He almost ran right by the sarcophagus, but then he stopped, staring down. He'd spotted the strap sticking out.

"Over here!" he yelled to Macon.

Macon came springing back and entered the tent.

"That's it," she heard Macon say. "The satchel I gave Trager for the money pickup."

She heard the grating of stone as they slid the coffin lid aside and suddenly a geyser of blood erupted in the tent, red spraying the walls. Lyle screamed, and she saw blood pulsing onto the plastic, strong at first, then growing weaker. One of the blades had evidently struck an artery. She watched his form slump to the ground.

Macon cursed, then came storming out of the tent with the satchel. He unzipped it, finding it empty, and threw it violently into a grouping of ocotillo. "Goddamn it! I'm going to fucking kill you, you bitch!" he shouted, spotting her. "Where is the money?" He drew his handgun, pointing it at her. "Tell me where the goddamn money is!"

She ran for the covered pit.

"Stop!" he yelled.

But she didn't, hoping he wouldn't shoot her if he didn't know where the money was. Movement to Alex's right snapped her attention in that direction. Another man was out there, flanking her. She caught just a glimpse of him as he disappeared behind a grouping of rocks. Her heart gave such a violent thump that it was almost painful. There was another one?

But then the man emerged on the other side of the rocks and she let out an explosive exhale. It was Casey, coming up alongside them at a distance, flanking Macon, not her. He must have stashed June somewhere safe and was coming to help.

But in the next instant, Macon spotted him, too, and slid abruptly to a halt. Macon holstered his handgun in favor of his rifle. He unslung it from his shoulder and took aim just as Casey sped through an open area. He got a bead on Casey and Alex whirled, heading back toward Macon. Macon squeezed off a shot and she saw a puff of dirt plume up just behind Casey's speeding feet.

Her mouth went dry. The next patch of cover, another rock spire rising from the desert floor, was another hundred feet away. Casey wouldn't make it. Macon tracked him, his finger on the trigger, rifle tucked in tightly for another shot, all his concentration on Casey.

Alex collided with Macon with such force that he flew off his feet.

He lost his grip on the rifle, which sailed away into a patch of saltbush. Macon scrambled to his feet and faced off against her. She didn't have time to retrieve the fallen rifle. He pulled his handgun, and as he reached to slide off the safety, she stepped into his space and used a circular sweeping motion to hit his arm. She then held on to it, bending it back painfully behind him and used an upward thrust. His grip loosened on the gun as he fought against the pain, and it dropped into the dirt. She kicked it away.

He twisted in her grasp and struck out, landing a thunderous blow to her rib cage. Pain erupted through her, momentarily robbing her of her breath. But she used the momentum of his punch to pull him forward. He went off-balance, one leg stretching straight out in his effort to stay standing.

She brought her boot down hard on that extended knee, landing home with a sickening pop and crack. He screamed, eyes squeezing shut. As he crumpled forward to clutch at his wounded knee, Alex dove for the discarded pistol. But before she could reach it, she saw that he wasn't reaching down to his ruined knee. His hands kept going down to his ankle. He jerked up his jeans leg there to reveal a second handgun in an ankle holster.

He grabbed it, bringing it up. Alex was too far away from him now, in the midst of reaching for the discarded pistol she'd kicked away. She wouldn't be able to get back into his space quickly enough to disarm him again.

She turned and ran for the dig site, bracing herself as a shot went off. She ran erratically, making herself a difficult target, and dared a glance back. Macon had struck a classic firing stance, legs planted, hands out, aiming the gun.

But he shook, his face a contorted mask of pain. He took a moment to wipe sweat out of his eyes. Alex kept running, darting looks back. When she saw him return both hands to the gun, she dropped to the ground. A shot rang out. Then she got up and scrambled toward the pit she'd covered. She reached a small rise, just high enough to cover her prone body, and flung herself down on the opposite side. She was out of sight now. He'd have to come to her. She crawled in the dirt, scrambling ever closer to the pit until she lay on the opposite side of it.

Macon was furious, his rage getting the better of him. He couldn't kill her, not before he knew where the money was. She heard two more shots go off, but saw no telltale puffs of soil where a bullet had landed. Quickly she darted her head up, seeing Macon firing off to the side, Casey pinned down behind the rock spires.

She stood up. "Hey!"

Macon's gaze snapped to her. He stormed forward, dragging his wounded leg, leveling the gun on her.

"Where is the fucking money?" he demanded again. He was close. Almost on top of the pit. And then he took one more step and landed right on the dirt-covered tarp. He plummeted downward, a shriek of surprise echoing up. And then it was quiet.

Alex waited, listening for the sound of movement. But it was utterly still. Finally she crept to the edge of the pit and peered down. Macon lay skewered below, spikes punched through his stomach, chest, and one leg. Blood covered his torso. He was still alive, his mouth opening and closing silently. He stared up out of the pit, ragged breaths wheezing out of his punctured chest. His eyes fixed on her, high above, and he raised one weak arm. She saw that he still gripped his gun. Alex dove out of the way as a succession of shots rang out, then the sound of him pulling the trigger on an empty chamber.

She crept back and stared down. His eyes had gone glassy now. The gun fell out of his limp hand. His mouth stopped moving and she could no longer hear the tortured breaths. He was dead.

She stood up and slunk back toward the tent, unsure if the other man was already dead or just close to it. But when she drew the plastic sheeting aside, she found him sprawled on the ground in a pool of blood, his sightless eyes blank and staring. He was gone.

"Casey!" she called out. "It's clear over here. Are you okay?"

She heard his voice call back from a distance. "Yes! I'll go get June."

Alex jogged back toward the helicopter, finding Milton gasping in the dirt. Amazingly, he was still alive, barely breathing, but still conscious. Alex bent down beside him. "This is your fault . . ." he whispered, blood bubbling on his lips. "You should have let me do it. If I'd killed that jaguar . . ." But he didn't finish his sentence. His ragged breathing stopped, and his head slumped to one side. He was dead.

Alex stood up just as June and Casey emerged from the bushes. Casey had taken off his skull mask and had cut through June's bonds.

"Alex!" June called when she saw her.

Alex ran forward. "Are you okay?"

June pulled Alex into a bear hug, sobs racking her chest. "Thank you," she said. She pulled away and turned to Casey. "Thank you both so much. I thought I was a goner there for a minute." She looked at them both. "How do you two know each other?"

Casey shrugged. "We don't. I just infiltrated this hate group and knew they were after her."

"Well, I'm grateful you were here," she said.

"Let's get to the cops," Alex suggested.

They rounded up the dogs and loaded them into the helicopter. Casey helped June into the back and shut the sliding door. As he and Alex rounded the helo, Alex pulled him aside. She said in a whisper, "You can't come with us to town. You're a wanted man. And what about June? She's seen you. Won't that present a problem for you?"

Casey placed a hand on her shoulder. "Lots of people have seen me. I know how to disappear. She doesn't know about the men in the cave. All she knows is that I was there and killed a man in self-defense. I don't think it'll be a problem."

"And what about those men in the cave?" Alex asked.

"I'll take care of it. I know how to make bodies disappear,

too. I've done it before. In fact . . ." he started to say, but his voice trailed off.

"Yes?"

"I'll tell you another time."

They climbed inside the helo and Casey started up the rotors. Then he looked down at the fuel gauge. It hovered near empty. "We're low on fuel. Don't think we can make it to town in this. But I've got a truck nearby, and enough fuel to reach it. We'll take that into town instead."

They all donned headsets and he lifted off, June petting the dogs in the back of the helicopter as they wagged their tails and perched their front paws on her lap. Alex turned to watch them. "They like you."

"I like them!" she said.

Casey flew them to where Alex's terrifying ordeal had begun, where River had been killed. Several trucks were still parked there with fuel tanks in the back, the same vehicles the Sons of the White Star had arrived in with their ATVs. The place was deserted.

Casey powered down the chopper and they climbed out. He handed her a set of car keys and shouldered his daypack. "Here. Warm up the car, will you?" Then he moved around to the other trucks, checking something.

Alex helped June into Casey's car, an old 1970s Scout International. Then she came around to the driver's side and climbed in. She looked up, waiting for Casey to finish whatever he was doing. She didn't see him now. She waited, expecting him to pop around the side of one of the trucks, but he didn't. She climbed out and made a circuit of the cluster of cars. He wasn't there.

"Where are you?" she called. But no answer came. She made another round of the trucks.

Casey was simply gone, along with the daypack and all that money.

EPILOGUE

Alex drove June into town, and together they gave a statement to Deputy Wentworth. Alex told them what had happened to River and the bodies at the dig site. She described the death of Trager. Trager's helicopter pilot, she found out, had been about to give evidence against Trager for his poaching activities. She told Wentworth that she'd found the pilot's murdered body.

Dave had made it out safely and called 911. The police had managed to corner the remaining men as they returned to their trucks, where River was killed, forcing them to remove their skull masks. They'd been identified and arrested, the last surviving members of the Sons of the White Star now in custody.

Alex left out much of her story: how Casey had found her, the men in the cave. She merely said she walked until he'd picked her up in the helicopter, just a stranger wanting to help, and they'd come up with their plan after June was taken hostage. June didn't know Casey's name, and Alex played dumb. Neither knew where he'd disappeared to. The police issued a BOLO for him, but Alex didn't worry too much about that. She had the feeling he'd been in tighter spots before.

EMTs came out and patched up both June and Alex. The police had retrieved Alex's backpack, and she used her phone to call her dad, telling him that all was well. Then Deputy Wentworth drove June back to her ranch and took Alex back to her rental Jeep. Alex drove to the cabin, her mind a tangle of thoughts. Now that the Sons of the White Star had been killed or arrested, she felt safe at the cabin again, though she'd have to do a more permanent job to fix the front door. The sun shower awaited her at the cabin, and she reveled in the warm water.

After her shower, she ate a little food and drank so much water that she felt she might burst. Then she lay down on the cot. She slept deeply at first, then more fitfully, her mind playing over the events of the last few days. She wondered where Casey was. Wondered if he was okay. She had the peculiar feeling that he was somewhere close by, that he hadn't left the area yet. On a side street in town, she'd left his keys in the Scout, tucked in the visor, in case he needed it again.

She got up after sleeping for fourteen hours and made a little more food. She spent the next couple of days doing rounds of her cameras. To her joy, she saw that the jaguar was doing fine, traveling safely around the preserve, suffering no ill effects from its ordeal with Milton.

After a few days, she ran low on supplies. She decided to drive into town, to stock up on groceries, and stop by the police station to see if they had any leads on Casey's whereabouts. She hoped they didn't. She wanted to call her dad, and realized she should probably also call Ben, let him know what had happened.

She showered and put on her hiking clothes, then drove into town. The police said they couldn't discuss an open case, but she could tell from Deputy Wentworth's frustrated expression that they had no leads on Casey.

At the grocery store, she bought food and started to leave the store, but a rack holding the latest issue of the local paper caught her eye. She stopped.

Local Landowner Connected with Cold Case Murders

The DNA of local landowner Evander Milton has been connected to several murders, including that of graduate student Dane

Fisher, who was killed on the Berkshire University campus eight years ago.

Alex bought the newspaper and headed out to her car with her groceries. After stowing them inside, she read the full article. They had collected Milton's DNA at his autopsy at the request of Interpol because he had long been suspected in a string of murders across the globe, including the murder of a safari guide in South Africa and a grad student in New Hampshire. While several other men were also suspected in this string of crimes, authorities had not had sufficient evidence to compel a DNA sample from any of them.

The DNA sample taken from Milton matched blood evidence found on rocks near Espinoza's dig site, presumably from Milton's being wounded the night of the murder. His blood had also transferred onto Espinoza's clothing during the attack.

The DNA also matched sweat and saliva samples collected from a ski mask discarded a block from the Berkshire University campus eight years prior. Campus security cameras had captured images of a masked man hurriedly leaving campus that night with a crossbow. He had avoided all other cameras and campus police were not summoned to the location until he had disappeared. But they had found his ski mask in a nearby Dumpster. That night a valuable Celtic torque, valued at more than $500,000, had been stolen from the university. Encrusted with garnets and other semiprecious stones, it had been owned by a mythic king who reportedly lived to be over a hundred years old and was never injured in battle.

The torque, along with a number of other valuable stolen artifacts, were recovered at Milton's home outside Azulejo.

Alex leaned back in her seat. So this had been an obsession with Milton. Trying to steal artifacts to become invulnerable, even if some required a sacrifice. She remembered the woman with the

distinctive turtle necklace in the photo from his South African safari and the presence of that same necklace in Milton's collection.
He'd killed her for it. And then just openly displayed it, thinking
himself above the law. She wondered how many people he'd killed
and how long the authorities had suspected him.

Police had also recovered a ledger book in which he'd detailed
his insane quest for invulnerability, his attempts at different ex-
periments with different artifacts. In the most recent entry, he'd
sacrificed "Experiment 12" in a cave in front of a jaguar painting,
then cut his thumb, finding himself still vulnerable. So he'd posited
that maybe the sacrifice had to be public and hauled the corpse to a
"place where all could see." Espinoza in the work tent. She thought
of the large brown stain on the cavern floor. That had been Espinoza's blood. She shivered.

If only they'd caught him sooner. Alex felt anger well up at the
thought of his disgusting, disrespectful, and entitled behavior toward
everyone around him, his murdering Espinoza. At least now his killing spree was over.

She scanned the paper more, seeing a little item on the bottom
of the front page. Someone had made an anonymous donation to the
recovery fund for the Azulejo business owners. When she saw the
amount—$355,000—a smile crept across her face. Such a specific
and familiar amount—all the cash Trager had stashed in the satchel.
The money Casey had made off with.

Alex called her dad and Zoe, checking in, finding them both
well. Worried, Zoe urged her to quit, but her dad was supportive.
Both knew how important this work was to her. Despite everything
she'd been through, she wouldn't give up. And now that the Sons of
the White Star had been dismantled, she felt safe returning to her
duties on the preserve. She filled Ben in on what had happened. He
was shocked and profusely apologetic, but she had assured him she
was okay now.

She downloaded the latest footage from the collar camera and returned to the cabin, freshly stocked up. She spent the next few days patrolling the sanctuary, finding more jaguar prints. The creature stayed in the area, protected for now.

Alex hoped that if the jaguar journeyed back south, moving between the two countries, that it would be safe, and hopefully soon joined by others.

Her thoughts turned to Casey. She'd half expected to see him again, but he hadn't appeared. She wondered where he was now, thought of the kiss they'd shared, of another adventure they'd survived together. Where was he, and when would their paths cross again?

One afternoon, a week after her ordeal, she sat on the banks of the Mesquite River, listening to the water trickle by. A cactus wren sang its lyrical phrasing from a nearby slot canyon, and a Chihuahuan raven clacked its beak from a juniper tree. She sighed, taking in the gorgeous terrain around her. It was protected. And along with it, the magnificent jaguar.

She hoped that the data she'd gleaned, along with future videos that would come in from the collar, would play an important part in preserving an iconic species of the American Southwest.

She stared into the distance, at a group of towering rock spires and cliffs, and wondered where her next adventure would lead.

AFTERWORD

The jaguar has disappeared from 50 percent of its historical range and has vanished altogether in some countries, such as El Salvador and Uruguay. It is coming close to extinction in the United States, with just a handful of cats remaining.

As recently as the turn of the twentieth century, jaguars were found in California, Colorado, New Mexico, Arizona, and Texas. In the 1700s and earlier, before they began to be systematically wiped out, they were even found in North Carolina, Kentucky, Ohio, and in the Lake Erie region of New York.

If we didn't care, we could just shrug and say, "Well, there are some jaguars south of the United States, so even though they've lost almost all of their historical range here, we're okay with that."

After all, unfortunately that was part of the reasoning to deny protections to the wolverine, a carnivore whose population has been reduced to a mere 300 in the Lower 48. They survive in pockets in the Rockies and Cascades, but they used to range as far south as New Mexico and as far east as the Great Lakes. Thankfully, they were finally listed as threatened under the Endangered Species Act in late 2023, though this decision was decades late in coming and will likely contain loopholes, such as allowing the death of wolverines in traps set for other species. Because there are wolverines in Canada, even though that population is declining as well, some think that is a good enough reason to not protect them here in the U.S.

But is this really the legacy we want to leave behind? To just shrug and leave the survival of our iconic wildlife to other countries while they die off in our own?

Just as with the species in my previous novels—wolverines, polar bears, and the mountain caribou—so far the Endangered Species Act and the U.S. Fish and Wildlife Service has failed the jaguar, in this case by not considering it for listing soon enough, then by missing deadlines once it decided to, and then by delaying the designation of critical habitat and a recovery plan.

We may think of the Endangered Species Act as this infallible piece of legislation that can pull species like the bald eagle and California condor back from the brink of extinction, but those are the exceptions. In most cases, the USFWS waits far too long before even *considering* the possibility of listing, then delays and delays once the decision is made to list, and then further delays developing a plan for the recovery of a species. Lawsuits from nonprofit organizations spur the government on, holding them accountable for missed deadlines. But in some cases, the species goes extinct or is eradicated in the United States before any meaningful recovery plans are enacted.

One thing that must be addressed is establishing and maintaining wildlife corridors in order to preserve not only jaguars but many other species as well. These strips of undeveloped land link islands of suitable habitat and allow species to disperse to new areas and find new food sources. They are also essential to ensuring genetic diversity by allowing different groups to mingle. But human development and land alteration occur too rapidly for species to be able to adjust to the vanishing of their habitat and the disruption of their routines.

Large-scale efforts have been launched toward fixing this and establishing corridors, including the Yellowstone to Yukon Conservation Initiative, which seeks to connect a single corridor from Yellowstone to the Yukon in Canada. The Mesoamerican Biological Corridor will connect habitat for big cats across Mexico and Central America. Another effort led by the nonprofit Panthera, called Panthera's Jaguar Corridor Initiative, seeks to protect a path for jaguars running through eighteen different countries from Argentina to Mexico, linking the habitats of ninety-nine separate jaguar populations.

The lack of such corridors has already led to genetic isolation, taking a toll on many animals that have been cut off from other members of their species through habitat fragmentation. In the southeastern United States, the Florida panther population had been cut off from other pumas, and less than thirty individuals remained in 1994. Inbreeding had made them susceptible to disease, weakened immune systems, and heart defects. So in 1997, biologists translocated eight female mountain lions from Texas to southern Florida, putting fresh genes into the mix. It worked, and the defects were removed from the gene pool after a few generations. The population has started to rise again, albeit modestly. The current estimate of the Florida panther population is a little less than 200.

And it isn't just the development of sprawling housing, industrial, and resort developments that restricts wildlife access. Roads are another big threat. But tree- and grass-covered highway overpasses and underpasses in Canada allow wildlife to cross dangerous roads safely. The U.S. is starting to build such safe passages, although the number of killed wildlife is still staggering, in the neighborhood of one million vertebrates killed each day in the country. Overpasses and underpasses cut down on such fatalities by more than 90 percent, so they are much needed.

The Infrastructure Investment and Jobs Act of 2021 provides $350 million over five years for the construction of infrastructure such as wildlife overpasses and underpasses that will allow animals to safely cross roads.

But so much more needs to be done, not just with corridors, but also with climate change and species protection. Yet what do we do when governments are slow or even refuse to act? Do we just look on hopelessly, watching as species vanish? Or do we speak up? Do we act? Do we fight to restore habitat for these species, to safeguard corridors where they can roam and survive?

There are many ways that you can help in your own personal life. You are a consumer and have the power of your wallet. Check out the kinds of projects your bank is funding. Consult resources that will help you shop sustainably and ethically. Be on the lookout for destructive ingredients such as unsustainable palm oil, grown on clear-cut land and therefore devastating jungles and forests across the globe.

Engage in community science and help researchers determine wildlife populations and trends. Websites such as scistarter.org and zooniverse.org have a wealth of projects you can help with, even from your home computer. Count elephants on remote cameras in Africa. Identify condors landing to feed. Help researchers categorize manatee vocalizations or identify members of beluga pods in the Arctic.

And let's not forget the power of our voices. We can protest, write letters to our representatives, attend local meetings, and make our voices heard. We can't overlook the impact of talking to those closest to us, too. A lot of us feel that if we talk about climate change, habitat destruction, and species extinction with our friends, coworkers, and neighbors, we will be broaching unwanted subjects. But many people are upset by what is happening to our planet and are staying quiet about it, too. Maybe they are worried about the same thing—that they don't want to bring up a gloomy subject and be seen as a downer.

But by talking about it, we can find camaraderie, ideas, and community. If we come together on the local level, we can exact real, meaningful change, even if on a national level, things are progressing too slowly, or even moving backward in some cases.

But we can accomplish this community only if we are vocal.

I truly believe that we can band together and make a real difference. We just have to find the courage and compassion to do so.

TO LEARN MORE ABOUT JAGUARS

Books

Mahler, Richard. *The Jaguar's Shadow: Searching for a Mythic Cat.* New
  Haven: Yale University Press, 2009.

Webb, Elizabeth. *American Jaguar: Big Cats, Biogeography, and Human
  Borders.* Minneapolis: Twenty-First Century Books, 2022.

Documentaries

Endangered Species: The Last Cats - The Wall. Produced by Emmanuel
  Lozano. USA Today Network, 2018. https://www.youtube.com
  /watch?v=c4P7SnW8Y_U.

Jaguar: Year of the Cat. Directed by Carol Farneti Foster, Richard Foster, and
  Fred Kaufman. PBS *Nature*: Season 13, Episode 1, 1995.

Where Jaguars Roam. Directed by Ryan Olinger and Rita Leal Olinger. Fork
  Tailed Media, 2020. https://www.youtube.com/watch?v=6wVyuyoBX40.

Wildlife and the Wall. Produced by Ben Masters. National Geographic, 2018.
  https://www.youtube.com/watch?v=smeoiCqS_YU.

Footage of Jaguars in the Southwestern United States

Jaguar "El Jefe" remote camera footage posted by the Center for Biological
  Diversity: https://www.youtube.com/watch?v=qTC8XdViC5s.

Articles and Academic Papers

Bravo, Juan Carlos, and Katie Davis. "Four Species on the Brink and the Wall That Would Push Them Toward Extinction." Wildlands Network, 2017. https://static1.squarespace.com/static/60b7e4e41506593f7f926fe7/t/60d b8eccbfffec22781f2e66/1625001682073/Four-Species-on-the-Brink.pdf.

Mahler, Richard. "The Tenuous Fate of the Southwest's Last Jaguars." *High Country News,* May 30, 2016. https://www.hcn.org/issues/48-9/the -tenuous-fate-of-the-southwests-last-jaguars/.

Neils, Aletris, and Russ McSpadden. "Viva El Jefe! Arizona's Famous Jaguar Lives, But What's His Future?" Center for Biological Diversity, August 4, 2022. https://biologicaldiversity.org/w/news/press-releases/viva-el -jefe-arizonas-infamous-jaguar-lives-but-whats-his-future-2022-08-04/.

Sanderson, Eric W., Jon P. Beckmann, Paul Beier, et al. "The Case for Reintroduction: The Jaguar (*Panthera onca*) in the United States as a Model." *Conservation Science and Practice* 3, no. 6 (June 2021): e392, doi: 10.1111/csp2.392.

Wildlands Network. "Now Is the Time to Think About Reintroducing Jaguars into the U.S." Wildlands Network, May 11, 2021. https:// wildlandsnetwork.org/news/time-to-think-about-reintroducing -jaguars-to-the-us.

Organizations

Northern Jaguar Project: www.northernjaguarproject.org.

1,000 Cats Project with the Sky Islands Alliance: https:// skyislandalliance.org.

Panthera Foundation: https://panthera.org.

Wildlands Network: https://wildlandsnetwork.org.

How You Can Help the Jaguar

1. Avoid products that contain unsustainable palm oil.
2. Investigate what projects your banks are supporting.
3. Engage in community science projects to help researchers gather

data. Zooniverse.org and scistarter.org are excellent websites for finding projects you can do even from your home computer.
4. Speak up. Talk to your neighbors, your coworkers, your friends about the need to restore habitat and conserve land for wildlife.
5. Write letters to government representatives and corporations, encouraging them to support land conservation, renewable energy, and species protections.
6. Attend local meetings and even organize them to inform others of the plight of wildlife and the need for habitat preservation and wildlife corridors.

Hands-On Volunteer Opportunities to Help Jaguars

1. Sky Island Alliance FotoFauna Project: If you live in the Sky Islands area of the United States and Mexico, you can set up a wildlife camera and submit monthly data on wildlife you've recorded. https://skyislandalliance.org/our-work/science/sky-island-fotofauna/.
2. Sky Island Alliance Wildlife Photo Processing: If you live in the Tucson area, you can help analyze photos from dozens of wildlife cameras and let researchers know what animals, including jaguars, are present. https://skyislandalliance.org/volunteer-help-us-process-wildlife-photos/.

ACKNOWLEDGMENTS

Many thanks to my phenomenal editor, Lyssa Keusch, whose insightful feedback was invaluable. I have loved working with her on the Alex Carter books. Thank you to my new editor, Danielle Dieterich, for so kindly taking on the series with such enthusiasm. Huge thanks to assistant editor Mireya Chiriboga for all her help with this series and for being such a pleasure to work with. And I'm very grateful for Nancy Singer's incredible page design and the keen eagle eye of Jeanie Lee.

Thank you to the best agent ever, Alexander Slater, for his continued belief in me and this series. I mean, seriously, this guy is a rock star.

Many thanks to the readers who have reached out to me to tell me how much they've enjoyed the Alex Carter books, and to my friends Joel, Tina, Kimberly, Jen, Dawn, and Jon, who have been so supportive of my fiction.

Fellow creators Harriet Peck Taylor, Angela M. Sanders, and Sara Varon have been terrific friends, and writer Tara Laskowski regularly buoyed my spirits with wonderful camaraderie, laughter, and commiseration.

I am very grateful to my lifelong friend Becky and all the encouragement and support that has come with that incredible friendship.

And always, thank you to Jason, fellow wildlife activist and creative spirit, for always having my back and being a never-ending source of encouragement, laughter, and camaraderie.

ABOUT THE AUTHOR

In addition to being a writer, Alice Henderson is a dedicated wildlife researcher, geographic information systems specialist, and bioacoustician. She documents wildlife on specialized recording equipment, checks remote cameras, creates maps, and undertakes wildlife surveys to determine what species are present on preserves, while ensuring there are no signs of poaching. She has surveyed for the presence of grizzlies, wolves, wolverines, jaguars, endangered bats, and more. Please visit her at alicehenderson.com, where you can sign up for her author newsletter, which includes publishing news, interesting wildlife facts, green tips, and more.